Mama Couture

A hilarious and inspiring
tale of modern motherhood

Moya Kate

A Stiletto Ink book

First published by Stiletto Ink in 2011
Copyright © 2010 Moya Kate Baldry. All rights reserved.
The moral right of the author has been asserted.

This book is a work of fiction. Names, characters, places, and incidents are products of the author's fertile imagination. Any resemblance to actual events or locales or persons, living or dead, is entirely coincidental or intended to be fabulously complimentary. Please consult your practitioner in relation to your and your baby's health care needs.

The chapter introduction to Six Months (p. 248) is loosely inspired on an email distributed over the internet, author unknown.

National Library of Australia
Cataloguing-in-Publication Entry
Kate, Moya, 1975 -
ISBN: 978 0 646 54241 6
Dewey Number: A823.4

For information about speaking events or to purchase this book, please go to:
www.moyakate.wordpress.com

Cover design by Raoul Teague
Typesetting by David Bradbury

Dedicated to my family

Foreword

Obviously, we are experiencing a seismic shift away from being a GDP-oriented society, one that is still battling the age-old prejudices and malpractice engendered in our traditions and structures, and becoming more aware of our interconnectedness, ecological impact and (lack of) sustainability.

We must change our ways. We must continue to fight inequality and greed in the developed world. As well as improve our fight for people in the developing world. All children deserve love, a safe house, medical care, education, play, healthy food, and a clean environment. The fact that 8.8 million children die around the world before they reach five[1] is unacceptable. And 1000 women are still dying each day due to pregnancy and childbirth complications[2]. When these women die, they often leave babies and small children behind and these children's chance of survival is reduced significantly.

We can do more. We need more women elected to management positions and as company directors, even if we have to force their way to the top. We need more vigorous corporate auditing and accountability mechanisms. We need to educate and facilitate more women into business through various initiatives including microfinancing. We need to donate more of our wealth. You can help achieve these goals. Visit www.tilfisherblog.wordpress.com and join Til Fisher's campaigns.

Nina's Dad is absent in this book. I thought it better to concentrate on Til's journey rather than a relationship or the politics of

---

1   *Global child health campaign strategy*, WORLD VISION, 2010.
2   *Trends in maternal mortality*, released by the World Health Organization (WHO), the United Nations Children's Fund (UNICEF), the United Nations Population Fund (UNFPA) and the World Bank. 2010.

parenting. But all parents need to enjoy work-family balance, to be able to cherish the time they spend with their children, irrespective of their earning capacity, asset value or gender. I hope that point is made clear in the book.

We need to change the way we calculate our success. To count instead the numbers of smiles, hugs, laughs, ideas and lives we share and save everyday. These are the building blocks of any society. And without them, we are worthless.

Moya Kate
Author

Contents

L.M.P.

And you thought you knew it all.

You thought getting your period meant you were safe: safe from getting fat, having to wear jeans with stretchy waists just like your mother, safe from tantrums, teething and homework.

You dope! How could you get it so wrong?

Life was great, you were really growing — as a human being — now, you're going to be lucky to fit into a caftan by Halloween!

Or maybe you desperately want a baby and each month when your period arrives you feel totally depressed that in nine long months there *isn't* going to be a rampaging elephant pushing her way through the delicate habitat of your hoo-haa.

Either way, the truth is this: when your Last Menstrual Period begins you are in fact already pregnant; that is, if you follow the course of your life and two weeks later end up shagging some guy down an alley / behind a club / in a room at what turns out to be his parents' house. Of course if you stayed at home alone, feeling miserable and pathetic, and gorged on chocolates instead, you'd get fat too, but you definitely wouldn't have as much fun as dressing up in a sexy little *Sass & Bide* number and having unprotected sex with a virile bloke who is as drunk and high as you are.

And you're not the only two having fun. In your fallopian tubes another party is gathering force: one little egg, who has stayed at home being the good girl for 30 years, is suddenly released from the convent and like an out-of-control, slippery luge, goes careering headlong into some speeding sperm.

It's just like a car crash, but in this instance it's the emotionless crash test dummy trying to fly *into* the car on impact, not the other way round.

Your egg doesn't stand a chance. She must find somewhere warm and safe to hide and recover from the accident.

"I'm so young, I don't deserve to be born," she screams at your uterus wall (which is looking nice and cosy right now).

Your hormones arrive quickly at the scene and perform CPR. And instead of flat-lining, the oocyte is revived; she takes her first breath, divides, and then multiplies.

Ma Vie en Rouge

My friend Lola is an artist. And French. She has that rare ability to look beautiful, sound seductive, and live a life that is uniquely hers. We met at a cool, beachside Bondi bar when she was travelling around Australia during her gap year.

Having been educated at a British boarding school, Lola had decided she was entitled to a year off. "*Ma mère* thought it would be good for me to see the world and drink like *un feesh*," she told me as we threw back warm beers paid for by God knows whom. Even then, Lola was followed by four lifesavers, two journalists, a Melbourne hip-hop group and half of Bondi's backpackers.

For Lola, her gap year has never ended.

So ten years later, when an invitation to her latest exhibition, *My Birth*, arrives in the mail, I enthusiastically RSVP. To be honest, I'm more interested in fashion than art but since I'm single — and have been for more years than I'd like to admit — I'm hoping the men in attendance will be aesthetically pleasing even if the art isn't.

And I'm allowed to think like that. Not because I'm shallow, but because it's been a long year. I've been working hard in my job as Marketing Manager at an Australian fashion label, *Enegi*, which for the third year in a row, I've grown by another 100 per cent. Five years ago, when I told my boss my target, she drew breath and let out a hysterical laugh that made her look more like a recently facial-peeled hyena than a pint-sized, smooth skinned, one-time Japanese model. I remember being surprised, while standing in our mundane Marrickville warehouse, that anybody that small could sound so sceptical. I set out to prove her wrong.

It took me two years to find our market niche and learn how to communicate effectively with them. But, once I had a nice, sticky relationship developing with our growing customer base, and had paid for Australia's top stylists to take their annual holidays in Paris in exchange for dressing their A-list clients in our samples, we were away. It sounds easy, but it isn't. Maintaining a domestic label and keeping it afloat is an uphill battle, but growing it at scenario one sales figures is almost impossible. At a minimum I work a 60 hour week — tearing my curly hair out trying to come up with new ways to reinforce our brand value — and spend a minimum five nights attending launches, parties and birthdays while attempting to bribe every fashion editor in Sydney to use our samples in their next feature.

It's definitely a lot of fun. I'm not sure if you'd call it a meaningful existence, but we've made it through another year. The girls at the label all still have jobs and small bonuses to throw on well deserved *Burberry* shoes, and the investors, now that we're one of Australia's biggest privately-owned companies, have a few more million dollars worth of shares to leverage — on sports cars, a new yacht, or harbour-side real estate.

I'm not quite sure if this is *right*, but it's the way it *is*. My team of girls dedicate our vast skills and talents to build two collections a year. And because the investors lent their money as start-up capital to the business, they're the ones who reap millions of dollars as their reward. Of course, there would be no profits if the girls got up one Monday and decided they didn't want to go to work and just spent every day at Bondi Beach, but because we live in a post-agricultural, market-dependent society, they have little choice but to show up — either at our label, or somewhere else. It's a little dog-eat-fashionista but that's the way it is.

But my work and its investors' profits are not what I should be thinking about on the Friday night before Christmas! With my bonus burning a hole in my *Balmain* clutch, it's time to celebrate. And with my team of girls all engaged in a diaspora of Christmas-time homeward bound travel, I'll be hitting the town on my own — well, I won't be completely alone, I'll have *Collette* and *Alaïa* with me, and half of Sydney who are already engrossed in the spray-tanned frivolities of the silly season.

I push the gallery door open with more force than I mean to and practically fly into the room. I groan when I see the floor of the gallery is covered in a red goo that sticks to my cream, five-inch gladiator heels (oh, why the hell didn't I just wear my *Louboutins*?). I carefully step through the mess and am greeted by a circle of ten television screens. The people on the screens seem to be writhing.

"Oh, excellent," I tell a fellow exhibition attendee. "Another Sydney sex show".

But when I edge closer to the screens I see legs hoisted into the air or bodies sprawled over large exercise balls. On one screen, I recognise Lola as the woman who is squatting, as if defecating, on her partner's leg. Another woman lies on a hospital bed; her legs spread while a midwife takes a pair of scissors and cuts her fanny in half. As the women's contractions gather force, my terror rises.

I join their screaming.

And then I notice one woman, who remains serene. She looks content, calm, and so I gravitate towards her screen desperately hoping to find relief from the horror around me. But then her face contorts and she looks me directly in the eye and mouths, "Please kill me, just kill me". We both wail for help and as I step back, my five-inch heels slip in the red goo and send me sprawling.

"Excellent work, Matilda," Lola admires, helping me up. "*Tu* look *joost* like one of my women, *maintenant.*"

I stare at the red slime covering my new oyster *Collette Dinnigan* slipdress. Looking like the Bride of Frankenstein was not what I intended when I invested $820 on a half metre of embellished silk finished with a raffia belt, but how can I tell Lola that? Lola only wears overalls, swiped from a local garage sale, and tonight, a white burqa.

"Oh my God, Lola, you can't be serious. It's two days before Christmas! I know you want to remind people that this whole holiday is about Christ's birth, but isn't this a bit much?" I ask her, desperately swiping at the red slime all over my arms and legs.

"You can't be too obvious, *ma cherie, non*?" she quips, relieving a waiter, who is dressed in a red-soaked doctor's gown, of a drink and some canapés.

I can't believe she can eat at a time like this. I take a glass of champagne and throw it back before complaining to Lola, "But it's like a hospital ward with no walls."

"I know. Isn't it great? And this is what *des* midwives and doctors — and mothers! — go through every day. I tried to get real blood-soaked sheets but they wouldn't let me have them — they said something about the smell."

I walk out of the gallery without even stopping to say goodbye. An odour follows me through Bondi as I make my way past the jam-packed cafés and bars lining the beach. It wouldn't have been as bad if it was winter, but this is Sydney — the coolest city in the southern hemisphere — at the peak of summer and it's as hot as hell. The women are sexy and shining, their hair as flat as their stomachs. The only things longer than their legs are the smiles on the faces of the men who are voraciously watching the women dance around in a silly season sex trance.

Except for me. I look like the Grim Reaper.

I traipse around the cliffs from Bondi toward Tamarama and ten minutes later climb the three flights of stairs to my apartment. I push open the door, relieved to finally be in the privacy of my own home, away from the critical, all-seeing eyes of Sydney's glamour-set.

I take the exhibition invitation down off the fridge.

"God, why the hell didn't I read it properly before I went?" I whine to my flatmate, Adam.

"Because you weren't expecting to be educated, you were just looking for some mindless fun and probably a root," Adam says, twisting his gorgeous body around while he finishes his day's Pilates session.

I watch him, transfixed. It really is a crime that a man this gorgeous is not interested in women. Not that he doesn't find us fascinating; he just doesn't want to do us.

He stretches toward the ceiling and 400 muscles ripple visibly.

Feeling my sexual frustration peak, I curb the urge to set fire to my ruined *Dinnigan* and bash my head against the fridge instead.

"Til, what else did you expect? Lola's a serious and confronting artist," Adam says, patting me on the back then retrieving a low-carb beer from the fridge for each of us. "She represents everything that's good about our society: she is our conscience. In fact, I would go as far to say that if *tomorrow* is going to be any better, it will be because of people like Lola. She's so cool."

I can't help wondering when Lola started her *MyFace* fan club. Obviously Adam joined without telling me.

I read from the exhibition essay: "Lola Stephan is a mixed-media artist who makes art as an alternate to the ubiquitous and manipulative power of the mainstream media. 'Art,' Stephan says, 'is the only truly renewable product we can make without depleting our planet of valuable resources or critical skills.' She has exhibited her installation, *I killed the President with my electro ray gun booby* at the Sydney Mardi Gras and the Paris New Artists show. She is currently working on a piece for the Bondi sculpture walk entitled *I defecated on the Heads of State*, which will feature Lola pooing on the Australian Prime Minister and his international counterparts. She has not yet decided what she will do for George W Bush's Sydney attendance at next year's APEC meeting (although we can all probably guess what she's got planned for that one)."

I finish reading.

"It looks great — I'll have to go next week," he says.

"You're sick."

"Of course I feel sick. Have you seen what you look like? Your *Dinnigan* is ruined!"

Before I can feel totally depressed he hands me a glass of champagne. "Now, drink this Til, it'll make you feel better. But only one glass. New Year's is less than two weeks away, I don't want you bloating up."

When I start to pout he tries to relieve my anxiety. "I promise you, you're going to have a great time this year."

As opposed to last New Year's Eve, where I found myself stranded on Kangaroo Island in the middle of the harbour after our party boat left without me. I managed to hail a passing fishing boat sometime after dawn and spent the trip back to Rose Bay being leered at by men who had were covered in fish guts and sprouting way too much facial hair. I shudder at the thought. "You and Dean are really coming out with me? To a straight club?" I still can't believe they're willing to do this for me. If gay men are willing to sacrifice their New Year's to take me out to a bar full of horny, drunk, straight men then I must be getting really desperate or they are the best friends a girl could have.

"Yes, we are. And if we can't get the men of Sydney eating out of your precious little lotus flower handbag then I will no longer be able to call myself a gay man."

He rubs his finger along my face. In a way that's soft and caring, and the only male attention I'm going to get tonight.

"Now, I'm going to have to abandon you but I'm off to see Dean."

And before I can protest, he's gone. Disappearing into a city in the throes of its annual, sexual peak. Leaving me alone with a bottle of champagne and total crap on the television.

I ignore his warnings about bloating (and cellulite) and drink another glass of champagne. Because my life is about to turn around. My social life, that is. I can feel it.

No more sprawling in red goo on gallery floors. No more 12-hour work days. No more stinking up the Bondi boulevard.

I finish the bottle of champagne. And am overwhelmed by a deep sense of peace, accompanied by a sugar high that makes me dance around my bedroom until way past one in the morning.

New Year's Eve

There is something about New Year's Eve that affects our breathing: in-out, in-out, in...

A breathless wonder consumes us as we amass at parties around the world. We can all feel it: a global, conscious awareness that we are participating in something special; that this moment cannot be repeated; that life itself may not be infinite and we must seize every opportunity while we can.

Is it the idea of a fresh beginning, of looking forward with anticipation and wonder that makes us all go a little crazy? Can this epiphany of synchronicity be simply described as hope? Or is something else going on, something hormonal or even — pheromonal?

The crowd shoves and pushes against me, all eyes focused on the clock, as collectively we count backwards from ten. My breathing grows even more rapid with anticipation. After all, this night has been months in planning: deciding where to go, who to go with, what to wear...what to wear! Because to be alone on New Year's is a terrible omen but to be badly dressed is a crime against humanity.

Start the New Year on the wrong foot and my whole year may follow suit. And I would rather be following that *Armani* suit into a dark corner, hiking my ruched, pink and black *Josh Goot* mini-dress even higher, and putting a magenta *Jimmy Choo* slingback in a place it was never designed to go.

The fireworks erupt. The crowd becomes one. The DJ announces: "Happy New Year Sydney!"

Adam and Dean are busy snogging on the other side of the room. I turn my attention back to the *Armani* suit. I take a deep breath. And one step closer toward my future.

"Happy new life to me."

Four weeks

The human female is not the most dangerous predator on earth.

Except at the sales. Then it's every woman for herself. Income, size of handbag and personal asset value have nothing to do with success in this department store. Speed, global fashion sense, and a photographic memory of every *Vogue* ever printed is what really matters.

As the human female has learned to adapt to the lifecycle of trends and discounting whilst continuing to develop sophisticated fashion receptors in her brain, the female shark has evolved at an equally impressive rate. Not only is she speedy, can sail the seven seas and navigate at the same time but she has also developed the ability to procreate without the need of a male mate. That's right! Scientists have discovered a Hammerhead shark reproduced asexually through the process known as parthenogenesis, which they deemed, "An unusual capacity in such an ancient vertebrate species". It also means Miss Hammerhead has none of the usual worries about first dates, hygiene or waxing.

Nor does the female shark go through any of the usual early pregnancy turmoil. No low temperatures, no constipation, nausea or exhaustion. She doesn't even stroll around the ocean looking at a lovely blue space, where human beings would build a shopping centre, and wonder, "Am I really knocked up, and if I am what the hell am I going to do? I think the Dad is George but maybe it was Thomas. I'm not a floozy, but it was dark and I was getting rear-ended after all."

Which makes you wonder, if the female shark doesn't have access to pregnancy tests, ultrasounds and the myriad of other human procedures to confirm her pregnancy, what does she think about? And without these interventions to keep her mind occupied, does she suffer from morning sickness?

None of these empathetic thoughts about the experiences of vertebrates — or insects or mammals for that matter — go through the brain of a newly-pregnant human female. Why? Because she is suffering from the onset of *pregnancy brain*. *Pregnancy brain* is something that all women rely upon at some time in their pregnancy — and after the baby is born, it is referred to as *breastfeeding brain* — because it excuses them of all foolishness, absent-mindedness and curious mistakes. Simply put, women are excepted from logic during this time because their bodies are hard at work.

In a few short weeks, the embryo, which is now the size of an apple pip, is being fed nourishment and oxygen via a rudimentary placenta and umbilical cord. The three layers of the embryo have begun to form: the top layer includes the neural tube from which the brain, backbone, spinal cord and nerves will develop; some cells will begin to specialise to form skin, hair and nails; the heart and the circulatory system appear in the middle layer; and the third layer holds the lungs, intestines, and beginnings of the urinary system.

Maybe this is why a pregnant woman pees a lot? Or maybe she's visiting the toilet a few extra times a day determined that today is the day her period will come. But it isn't.

Finally, she succumbs to the call of the wild, to the inevitable truth, that what was just a hunch is now a concern.

Her hunger to know consumes her, and her hunt for an accurate pregnancy test begins.

Finding out is like coming out

This is not what I meant when I asked for a new life.

The three of us sit huddled together on the couch waiting for the pregnancy test result. Me, who has never even held a baby, and Adam and Dean, the two biggest queens in Sydney, who have gracefully sacrificed their plans for a big night out clubbing to stay home and hold my hand while I pee on a stick.

They didn't think I was being literal.

"What, with your real pee?" Adam asked me abhorred, turning the packet over and over again, desperately hoping the words might change. "Look, Til, I love you more than my own family but there's no way in hell I'm putting my hand anywhere near your hoo-haa."

He looked terrified. So I ended up peeing on the stick on my own while the boys made margaritas and tried very hard to *not* think about what I was doing in there. *Après* pee, I returned to our tiny living room, waving the stick around like a perfume sample. Dean screamed, clutched his eye and squealed that he'd been flicked in the eye with pee. While Adam flushed Dean's eye with water, I laid the stick on top of ten layers of paper towel and took a seat on the couch to wait for the seconds to tick by.

I've been sitting here for an hour.

"It's only been a minute," Adam tells me, taking a seat next to me on the couch.

Dean, who is wearing the gloves I use when I dye my hair, holds up the box. "In less than one minute, your destiny will be revealed…" he says like an evil fortune teller.

I can feel my breathing quicken. In fact, that started when I walked into the chemist and bought the damned thing and brought it home. I should have hidden it. Then Adam wouldn't have found it, he wouldn't have immediately called Dean and told him I might be up the duff, and I wouldn't have had to listen to their hysterical laugher.

But as acerbic and condescending as they can be, Adam and Dean are useful to have around. Because if it does turn out that I have a bun in the oven, I can always tell my mother that one of them is the father.

She wouldn't buy it for a second. She'd take one look at their skinny-boy pants and rock star haircuts and announce that they were as queer as she was.

This is not the time to be thinking about my mother. I'm already under enough stress.

"I never thought I'd be doing *this*," I say to break the silence, waving my hands at the *situation* laid out in front of me on the coffee table.

"Why not? You're female, aren't you? Even the Virgin Mary did this," Dean says while inspecting his perfectly manicured hands. He looks up. "Actually I stand corrected because she is the only smart cookie who can really say 'Holy Fuck'."

"Sweetie, what Dean is trying to say," Adam says leaning in while pouring two more margaritas, "is that he can't believe you were so irresponsible. I mean in this day and age, you should know better."

"I know, I know," I say pulling at my hair. "But I'm 32, I have a career. This is just not supposed to happen to me."

"Well, it's certainly not supposed to happen to me and thank God for that," Adam says and he and Dean chink their glasses in celebration. "I might get AIDS, but at least I don't have to squeeze a baby out of my genitals."

"It's not a disease," I whine, eyeing off a margarita which Adam keeps out of my reach.

"Let's compare," Adam continues. "In pregnancy, the cells divide and multiply (just like a virus), it makes you sick, it can kill you, and if you do survive you have to live with the physical, financial and emotional consequences for the rest of your life. Let me put them in order for you: leprosy, heart disease, and then pregnancy."

I fight back. "I have a feeling you're about to kick me out of my own apartment even though I let you move in after — what was his name — did that thing to you with his family?"

"Bitch, I can't believe you brought that up," Adam pouts and leans back against the couch.

To balance the physicality of the three of us on a two-person couch, Dean leans forward over the pregnancy test while I hover in the middle, not wanting to participate but not wanting to vacate the growing drama either.

"Hmmn," he says.

"What the hell does 'hmmn' mean?" Adam says leaning forward, leaving me alone at the back of the couch.

I watch them jealously. Even in my emotionally fragile state I can admit that they are a beautiful couple: Adam, with his luminous skin, high cheekbones, piercing blue eyes and David Beckham hair; and Dean, a rock-hard Samoan Adonis sent to test the sexuality of even the straightest man.

It's depressing. Seeing them together confirms my fear that my single days are far from over. What man in Sydney would want me — a five-foot-four, red-haired, whining, financially destitute, fashion marketer — when instead, he could live a life enraptured by the charm, intelligence and fornicating beauty of Adam or Dean? Their arm muscles bulge as they hold up the tiny stick and I sit behind them, tortured.

No wonder I have been single for most of my twenties — and my thirties too. I stare at their backs, my eyes narrowed, trying hard to curb an intense stab of jealousy as Adam reaches toward Dean to brush his finger delicately along Dean's straight jaw. Of course this is the only thing about either of them that is straight. It's all disco lights and matching G-strings for their spray-tan dates with these two.

I allow myself to hate them for a second (yes, I am a horribly selfish person) because it's men like Adam and Dean who are responsible for my woeful sex life. Them and the super-sexy, Amazonian women of Sydney who seem to be multiplying at the same rate as gay men. But twenty years ago (oh my Lord, has it been that long?), this city was crawling with straight men. As my friends and I were entering our teenage years, we would daydream about the wonderful years of dating ahead of us. We even marked all the places we would go for dates on the local tourist map: Bondi Beach, the cinemas at Bondi Junction, and of course the blue-light discos held across Sydney's Eastern suburbs and Southern beaches every Saturday night.

After school every afternoon, we would sit at a local cafe and make a list of all the boys we'd eventually date — once they figured out we were alive. And, we agreed, after dating continually throughout high school, we would get married, have a couple of kids and raise them on Sydney's Southern beaches just as our parents had done. By the time we finished school, our dreams had turned to university and careers, but we still met regularly on Saturday nights when that long list of boys had forgotten to ask us out.

One girl did end up getting married straight out of high school — my sister, Jorja. She's the polar opposite of me: six-feet tall, gorgeous and a multi-million dollar success story. We don't speak a lot, probably because I'm slumming it (Jorja's words, not mine. It was even reported in a local gossip magazine, but I just pretended I never saw it so we never had to talk about it) at an Australian fashion label while paying half-rent on a teenie weenie apartment Jorja bought fifteen years ago, before housing prices went the same way as Sydney's gay radar.

So instead of having the time of my life in my twenties, bonking like crazy and having torrid affairs, I ended up slaving away at the office, dreaming about going out on a date while spending my weeknights with drunk, single fashionistas and Friday nights with a few hundred gay men singing *It's Raining Men* at the top of our lungs.

They should change the name of the song to *It's Raining Gay Men* because the women of Sydney are living in a straight-men desert.

I shouldn't complain. My diary is full of fun and my wardrobe teeming with sex. Of course, I'd prefer it to be the other way around but you can't have everything.

How the hell I came to be sitting in my living room — me, a single, sexually redundant female — with two of the most gorgeous gay men in Sydney, while waiting for a pregnancy test result is totally beyond me.

Well, I have a vague memory, and one that fortunately Adam and Dean did not see. Me and the suit! Oh my God, if *he* was a banker, I'd just die of shame. Thank God I was so drunk I gave him the wrong phone number. Not that he was ever going to call me. Men never do. You can always tell they're not going to call: they pretend to punch your number into their phone but they're so drunk they don't even realise their phone is still in their pocket.

Dean breaks my foggy reminiscing with another, "Hmmn."

I whine, "Bloody men, you're all the same." I sit back against the couch while Adam chastises me.

"Ah no, we're not," Adam says. "There is a big difference."

"What, like a straight man knows how to use a penis and a gay man…?" I ask stupidly.

"Knows how to *lurrvve* a penis," Adam says in his best Spanish rent boy accent.

"You're naughty," I tell him, smacking his tight trapezoid, my hand ricocheting forward just as Dean sighs again and leans his muscular back into the soft folds of the couch.

Leaving me sitting out in front, perched on the bow of my shaky life.

And there it is: the telltale line they told me to be scared of on the box.

"Holy shit," we all say together.

"Thank God, it's a boy," Dean says looking at the blue lines and clasping his hands together with glee.

Adam and I stare at each other.

"I'm sorry, Til. He's not stupid, he's just never been through this experience before."

But my heart is pounding so quickly and loudly that I barely register his words.

Seeing my face turn ashen, Adam hauls Dean off the couch to leave me alone with the consequences of my New Year's Eve shag. Eventually my heart slows to a steady, thumping beat, and the space between those beats starts to feel like a scared and empty place.

I spend the next ten minutes listening to the muffled sounds of Adam explaining to Dean that the blue line doesn't mean it's a boy; that it is too early to tell the gender of the baby and certainly not from a $9.95 chemist-bought, pee-on-the-stick pregnancy test.

But their prattle cannot distract me from the reality of my pregnancy: me having a baby! Me, without a husband, ring on the finger, house in the boring, bloody suburbs like my kindred-bitch spirit at high school, Louise Unger, who got fat not because she got pregnant but because she deserved it. I remember seeing her at our ten year high school reunion, all fat and round and glowing, her hideous feet resting on a chair — and the only thing bigger than her ass, which was the size and shape of Queensland, was the smile on her face.

"Holy fuck," I mutter under my breath and hurl the test out the window.

Six weeks

The embryo is not the only one developing dark circles.

But whilst the embryo's facial features are becoming marked with dark spots where its eyes and nostrils will appear, your dark rings are a sign that you've been tossing and turning all night.

As the authors of *What To Expect When You're Expecting* will tell you, you're exhausted because even when you're resting, your body is working harder than a non-pregnant person does when she's mountain climbing (although strangely, you won't need the extra calorie intake of a mountain climber so put that chocolate bar down now), because:

A.   You're manufacturing your baby's whole life support system — the placenta. You're doing the job of a whole hospital full of doctors, nurses, cafeteria staff and the little old ladies with blue hair who volunteer their services by giving hospital visitors weak cups of tea in Styrofoam cups, incorrect directions and those really ugly knitted toys;

B.   You're adjusting — to the idea of being a parent and telling your friends and your boss; or to the financial strain of adding another child to your already packed-to-the-rafters family; or maybe you're just scared because the physical signs are already beginning to show.

C.   You're feeling nauseous all the time and your breasts are beginning to feel slightly swollen and sore. And while you've always hoped for a larger décolletage, and sometimes thought plastic surgery and a quick trip to Thailand might be worthwhile, the idea of stitches and pain is never appealing. At least with cosmetic surgery the side effects wear off!

You reach for your decaf knowing that light coffee drinking is nowadays acceptable (caffeine will cross the placenta but researchers aren't certain to what extent it enters foetal circulation), throw back your prenatal vitamin and try not to throw up. At least being pregnant gives you an excuse not to drink herbal tea (since herbs in pregnancy have not been well researched). You massage your temples trying to alleviate an ever-persistent headache and stand as far from the microwave as possible and try not to think about the millions of other single Sydney-siders, all of whom will be going out tonight — without you.

Your heart beats rapidly but not as fast as the embryo's which hurtles along at 150 beats a minute and has divided into right and left chambers, just like your own heart, which is now considering what it should do.

A friend in Versace...

"I don't think the pattern on your shoes quite fits the description of polka dot, Matilda," my friend, Nadia, tells me when I meet her after work for a drink.

Nadia is a fashion photographer. She eats, breathes, and sleeps fashion. Even though she graduated from the Royal College of Arts in London about 20 years ago, she doesn't look a day over 30. She's gorgeous, super-sleek and wears fantastic pants with lots of zips. Nadia's age is not something we ever discuss; my fashion faux-pas, however, feature regularly on the agenda.

I look down at my ruined gladiators and sigh deeply. They cost five hundred dollars, there's no way I'm throwing them out. I tell her sadly as a matter of explanation, "Lola did it."

Nadia immediately says, "Cool!" And her face lights up.

I hate it when people do that — immediately change their opinion because they can't stand up for their first opinion. Probably because they are used to subverting their opinion to a mixture of media channels that blurt out the latest trends constructed by desperate design gurus whose investors said they'd better make six million dollars that season and not five. This inevitably leads to intelligent people like Nadia making hideous fashion choices while rebuking their own mother, whom at least has the decency to hide at home and not answer the door when her daughter turns up looking like Marie Antoinette crossed with a space invader.

"*Versace*, darling," Nadia tells some wannabe fashionista who has just spent the past hour gathering courage to ask Nadia if she can have a photo taken with her handbag. Nadia runs her hand through her short, brown, $300 per cut hair, and pouts at the camera.

"Children dying of starvation, children dying of starvation," I mutter, shielding my face from the camera's flash in case the photo shows up on *MyFace* or some other ego site.

The girl retreats, satisfied. But instead of criticising Nadia for her excessive lifestyle or questioning the lack of moral fibres in mine, I say, "What do you mean 'cool'? One second ago you were looking at my shoes like I was insane, and now you know that Lola did it, you think they're tripping?"

"Well, Lola's cool."

"And I'm not?"

"I didn't mean it like that," Nadia says without affection.

"Yes, you did. And besides, Lola didn't actually do it."

"Well, why did you say that she did?"

"Because this is what happened to them when I went to her exhibition. But she didn't actually touch them. In fact, if anything it was my feet that walked around in the goo and got this red stuff all over them so you should be heaping praise — onto *moi*," I say laying my hand proudly on my chest.

"But it wasn't your goo, was it sweetie? It was Lola's," she chirps.

"You're killing me," I tell the bottom of my cocktail glass as I slurp the dregs of the margarita through a straw.

"Quite deliberately."

I sigh deeply, replacing the glass with a dull thud on the mahogany bar and beckoning the bartender for five more just like it.

"It shows you know," Nadia says.

"What the hell?" I spit. My anger turns swiftly from Nadia to Adam. "He told you, didn't he?"

"Aha," she admits sucking at the alcohol at the bottom of her glass

"Oh my God, who else did he tell? Did he tell Jorja? Oh my God, he didn't tell my mother, did he?"

"God, Til, take a valium. He told me because I am the only other person you know who's ever held a baby."

I swivel my cocktail stick pondering what she has just said. "I don't even know anybody who's had a baby, do I?"

"I thought you said Lola had a baby?"

"No, she just pretended. *My Birth* is a part of her whole defecating series. She's going to defecate on everybody."

"Excellent," Nadia says. "That girl is so cool."

"I'm cool," I persist.

"No, you're not," Nadia insists. "But you will be soon. Give me those hideous shoes, it's time to go."

"Where are we going?"

"To celebrate your last moments of freedom. After this, your life will go seriously downhill: wailing baby, hysterical, emotional breakdowns at your mothers' group, sitting around hoping you won't die of boredom while random thoughts consume you — for example, why the hell do the suburbs exists? Is it for the betterment of my child or society? Does my husband really need to show up day-in, day-out just so our government can add four million non-essential items to our gross domestic product list? Because surely, my baby would be happy in a caravan travelling around the countryside but instead here I am bored to death in North Ryde while trying to make new shapes out of pumpkin while the baby eats his big sister's poo."

She steals a margarita from the stash in front of me. "So that's why I'm taking you out to buy you your last pair of $1200 *Jimmy Choos*. So, for one more time in your life, you can feel like you're floating on air and not cemented down to earth by the 20 extra kilos you're carrying and that *doesn't* include the weight of the responsibility of bringing another human being into the world."

"I don't need new shoes, Nadia."

"Yes you do, you just don't know it yet. And not ordinary shoes — I mean the type of shoes that will get you in trouble," she says. "But that's probably what got you into this mess hey? A little too much *Jimmy Choo*? Or maybe it was those sexy *Louboutins*? Anyway, we should go now before your gorgeous little feet swell up to the size of balloons or your stomach gets so big you can't see your feet." She pours the drink down her throat. "Oh, Til, what have you done?"

I always wanted one of those alarm clocks that sit by your bed and when it rings you can just smack it off again. There's something so deliberately satisfying about leaning over and punching the source of a racket early in the morning that makes me feel powerful and gives me hope that the day will be a series of successful moments and not a contagious crash of embarrassments.

But my alarm is a stereo which sits on the other side of the room and is automatically programmed to play anything from Paris lounge to Acid Jazz, electronic noise or Kylie Minogue — if I'm lucky.

But today is unlucky.

Today is thrash.

Which always hurts my head and is the reason I stopped going to the *Big Day Out*.

I stumble out of bed, feeling like shit, only to realise my dream of waking up to find I've grown a few more inches overnight has come true. On my feet are the new *YSL* tribute sandals Nadia bought for me last night. Even with the room spinning, I admire the shoes: the lime green and yellow wash of the leather, the inbuilt platform, the six inch heels; they are unnaturally beautiful.

No wonder I feel dizzy.

The sun streaming through my window is giving me an instant blinding headache. My throat is tight and sore too. I smack the input button on my stereo which flicks the brain-killing thrash to a radio station, but the constant laughing, as if the presenters are sitting around a big bag of coke, hurts my head even more.

I hear Adam through the walls complaining about what a hard time the media are giving some wanton celebrity: "She's a new Mum, let her drink and drive with her kid on her lap, c'mon!"

I stumble around my bedroom throwing thousands of dollars of designer clothes out of my wardrobe and onto the floor. The clothes are courtesy of the label I work for, *Enegi,* so I get them for free. You'd think this would give me a big advantage over other Sydney women but it doesn't. The samples I am forced to cohabitate with for an entire season are made for six-foot tall super-waifs. Instead of making me look ultra sexy and rich, I walk around Sydney looking like a pint-sized hooker.

And worst of all, my hair refuses to be straight. I'm living in one of the greatest cities in the world, in the middle of its obsession with straight hair and zero per cent body fat. I fail on both accounts.

It's not all that bad. One day, wholesome and short will be back in vogue and then it'll be my turn to bask in the sun. Under a very large umbrella.

But by that time, I'll be in Paris! My boss, Jaimee, has promised we'll take *Enegi* to Paris Fashion Week as part of our international growth strategy. Staying in Australia is not a viable long-term option; the domestic market will eventually get bored with us and our backers will be forced to invest millions of dollars reinventing the label and refitting all our stores. Better to increase our market-share by going overseas before fickle consumers whittle the investors' capital down to its bare bones.

Right now, we're in the middle of a domestic growth stage. But in two years time, we're going to hit the international market and launch our flagship store in Paris.

And then I'm going to go nuts. I'm going to buy whatever clothes I like straight from the designers at fashion week — and I'm going to wear them too. Because if we show in Paris, then we'll be considered a major success and I will be expected to have a wardrobe full of our international competitors' garments.

And then I'll be happy. It may seem superficial but clothes have always been my axis. Sometimes when I'm bored on a Friday night, while the rest of Sydney is out partying with five thousand of their new best friends, I sit at home with my 500 copies of *Vogue* spread out on the floor around me and rearrange them in order of my most favourite edition to least-most favourite edition.

Adam understands my obsession. After all, he knows that *Vogue* is more than a magazine. To fashionistas like me, it's an institution, an atlas, and a passport.

Because *Vogue* introduced me to the world: to photographers, designers, textures, trends, product, brands, people and cities. I trekked through Cambodia with the models in the *Gentle Gypsies* shoot from June/July 1970; visited truck stops in the middle of Australia while wearing a *Robert Burton* linen dress in January

1988; I even learned to ride a motorbike while smoking a cigarette and dangling my feet over the handlebars at the tender age of ten.

I love the adventure, the spectacle and the ingenuity of every edition. And even though I love the feature stories set in Mauritius, Sardinia or Tokyo, the hot new models, the gossip, the cutting edge designers trailblazing in Miami, Milan or Dubai, it's always the trends adorning the Paris pages that I turn to first.

Paris — the city of lights, love, and really expensive art — is the birthplace of fashion. Cleopatra may have invented false eyelashes but it was the courts of France to which we owe the substantial favour of invigorating every season with a new aesthetic trend.

Paris is my mecca and like all devoted followers I must take a pilgrimage to the holy capital of couture — or, so help me, donate all my *Jimmy Choos* to charity.

A couple of seasons ago, after an excellent end-of-year financial report, I tried to tell Jaimee we had leapfrogged the label's anticipated growth stage and were ready for international penetration. She told me to collect my pie-charts and organised for me to talk to the Board, who listened to what I had to say before taking a few weeks to decide I was immature, inexperienced, and thanked me for my enthusiasm and commitment to the label. I felt annihilated.

By then I'd memorised Qantas' flight schedule from Sydney to Paris and had already started looking for hotels to stay at during Fashion Week.

Jaimee bought me a case of French champagne to help soften the blow. She was nice enough to even sit with me for a few weeks while we emptied each bottle and listen objectively to the daily walking itineraries I had planned. At the end of the case, she told me to pack away my posters of people kissing under the Eiffel Tower (she was right, they are hideously iconic) and to concentrate on my work. She said that the Board was right, our team was too inexperienced to take on the monsters of the euro but in a couple of years she was sure we would be ready to create *fashion terrible* for the European, American and Asian masses. But for the next eight seasons, we would concentrate on destroying the individuality of the Australian population.

I love her sarcasm. She loves fashion as much as I do, but her attitude stops me from developing a serious ego problem.

I also love her sense of style, her penchant for minimalism and ability to construct an outfit that extends her personality into the periphery. She is a third-generation fashionista: her father was a designer in Berlin, her mother a model in Japan, her grandfather made kimonos and her paternal grandmother designed tweed. She has fashion in her blood, whereas today, I just have alcohol.

My clothes look better on the floor than they do on me.

The problem, I decide, is not the alcohol or even that my clothes are wrong; the problem is I just don't know who I want to be today. And if I don't know who I am, then correspondingly, I don't know what to wear.

My head spins with shame.

I decide that my hangover is affecting my ability to construct a temporary identity and one that matches my new shoes. I look down at them lovingly again — and realise I need to vomit.

"I must have had one too many margaritas last night," I tell Adam as I stumble for the toilet. I purge the contents of my stomach into the toilet bowl until I'm empty but I feel no better. Walking back into the living room I realise what the horrible sensation is: it's not the hangover making me feel wretched, it's guilt! Guilt that tells me I if I am so immature to get drunk while pregnant than I am certainly not ready to be a mother!

My head feels so heavy and because I hurl twice more before breakfast, Adam suggests I ring work and tell them I'm working from home today.

He's right. Once the margaritas have worn off I'll go down to the beach and get some sun. Until then, I'm going to put my head in my hands and try very, very hard not to move.

Adam disappears into his room and I hear him giggling. A few minutes later, he returns animated and wearing fresh foundation.

"That was Nadia."

I groan.

"I called to yell at her about the irresponsibility of getting a pregnant woman drunk but she confessed she told the bartender about your condition. The drinks you had were virgins."

"She did what?" I yell. Now I know my life is over. The quickest way to spread a filthy piece of gossip in this town is to tell it to the bartender at *Georgio's*. She may as well have taken out an ad in *Madison, Marie Claire* and *Grazia*.

I picture the gossip trail: me, Adam, Nadia, Nadia's assistant Juan; Antony, the bartender at *Georgio's*; certainly a long list of models, makeup artists, makeup stylists — excuse me, makeup *innovators* — fashion stylists and a long list of their assistants; ad directors and agency staff; shop assistants; and wealthy, lustful bankers who hang out at the bar in a desperate attempt to crack on. In total, 156 text messages would have been sent meaning the news of my pregnancy would have reached Fashion Week Coordinator, Stella, from 44 different sources before eight pm. Stella would have freaked at the calamity heading in her direction and called Jaimee, my boss, and under no uncertain terms, given Jaimee the chance to pull out of Fashion Week early, rather than tempt fate and advertising cancellation fees.

And everyone at the label, from reception to sales, will know. Since I work in marketing, we will be the last to know. Except for HR. HR will have to look up their files to make sure I even work there.

I crumble. "Oh my Lord, I'm going to be out of a job by lunch and it's only six months 'til Fashion Week. I'll never get somebody else's line ready in time."

"So the fact that you're not plastered but suffering from your first case of morning sickness doesn't phase you then?"

"Morning sickness?"

"You have been hanging out with fashion waifs for too long, love," Adam says rolling his eyes. "Not only are they too skinny to ovulate, let alone conceive, but no-one around you has ever been through the process of having a baby, have they?"

I shake my head. "My sister has babies but she doesn't let me near them."

Adam looks sheepish.

I grill him. "You told Jorja, didn't you?"

"Well, I had to tell somebody."

I want to pass out. I want to hit my big-mouthed, physically perfect, and eternally happy gay flatmate in the face and then pass out. All of a sudden this pregnancy doesn't feel like it's happening to me anymore, but the whole of Sydney, and none of it feels right.

"I'm not the first person in Sydney to have a baby you know Adam," I say trying to calm his excitement.

"So you're going to keep it then?"

"I don't really have the time to return it, especially without a receipt."

He looks at me confused.

"Fashion Week is in six months, Adam. Even if Jaimee doesn't fire my ass after she finds out about this, I am going to be hideously busy. In fact I already am. I don't even have time to go to the doctor's to talk about a termination."

"You've got the day off today. You could go today and talk about your options at least."

"Feeling like I do now?"

His hands echo the compassion in his voice. He holds them together, in prayer. "When you're pregnant, or suspect you are, the first thing you do, Til, is go to the doctor's. They always know what to do because that's what they do, they look after people. And you, my pet, need looking after right now."

"I thought it was the baby that needed looking after?"

"No, sweetie, it's you. If you're well the baby will be well, that's how it works." He caresses my cheek in a way that suggests he's sorry for telling me that being pregnant was a disease.

"But it feels wrong, Adam. And not because I'm single — being a single parent doesn't faze me — but having a child just isn't one of my goals. Being a parent isn't a four-week fad or even a trend, it's a lifetime commitment, and if I'm going to enter into something like that, surely it should be something that I've decided I want, not something that happens to me."

Because empathy isn't working, Adam turns to logic instead. "Think of this as an emergent strategy, Til. You work in marketing, and because you have a boss who delegates magnificently, you have become very adept at developing business strategy. Despite being underpaid and undervalued, you wouldn't deny a viable business opportunity just because it wasn't in an earlier strategic plan, would you?"

I pout. Even though I've never pursued an emergent strategy at work, the management textbooks recommend spontaneity especially in a volatile market. And I am feeling quite volatile right now; somewhere between nausea and depression, in fact.

"But it still feels irresponsible when the strategy relates to a human being, not a consumer item that will surely create negative externalities and leave a huge carbon foot imprint," I tell him lifting my head off the kitchen bench.

He rubs my shoulders sympathetically. "I don't see that there's any difference, Til. Look, you can have a baby, it's OK. I know you value your career but the feminist debate never meant to negate the role of the mother, just to destabilise the power of patriarchy. Unfortunately, the extremism that feminism is often portrayed with has undermined its true role. Also, we live in a society where if you believe Kristeva and the other Structuralists, the individual identity can only be formed by rejecting the abject maternal figure."

"Why are you telling me all of this? You're making my head worse," I moan.

"You can't visualise yourself as a mother and that's not your fault. If we pay any attention to the third person effect theory, you'd realise your inability to conceptualise your identity as a mother stems from the fact that mothers are not reflected in the media as an important and worthwhile subject matter. Women as interesting subjects end as soon as they look like they may get hitched: Lucy Honeychurch, Carrie Bradshaw, even Cinder-bloody-rella. As for mothers, the only ones you ever hear about are the Old Woman Who Swallowed a Fly and Erin Brockovich."

He continues and I lay my head in my hands trying to block out his monologue.

"You don't know anything about mothers. Their stories aren't told, you hear general complaints about how stay-at-home Mums aren't paid, while at-work Mums go home to do another 24 hours of parenting and cleaning in 12 hours. But you don't hear about the subtleties, the inner thoughts, the challenges they face as they subvert themselves to everybody else's needs. Our society doesn't consider mothers important. We think drug abuse and globalisation are more important topics and we negate the stories of mothers. But the difficulty of raising a child today and engendering him or her with decent, contemporary values must be worthy of our attention."

"You're really not selling this motherhood act as an attractive opportunity, Adam."

"Think of it this way then. If you were going to buy a pair of shoes, would you pick a high-end designer like the ones you're wearing now, that are orthopedically designed with a built-in platform to help raise you even higher without killing you, or some plastic thing that is only one inch high because any higher and the whole shoe would sag?"

"I don't even have to answer that, Adam. I'm never taking these shoes off."

"Even if they clash?"

"What could clash with lime green?" I say, chastising his narrow-mindedness.

"I'm being serious, Til. I know you, you'd pick the high-end shoe, and in the end it will do less damage to you than chiropractors think because in platform heels you're so high you don't need a bag of coke to make you happy. Nadia did the right thing."

"If I didn't feel so sick, I'd be enjoying these shoes much more," I say, agreeing with him that these are the most delicious shoes in the world.

"Let me get to my point," he says. "The only reason you want the high-end design shoe is because it's marketed more expensively. The shoes are treated like royalty, they're photographed with multiple sources of soft lighting, they're displayed on tiers to the shoe Gods, packaged like jewels, and treated seriously by the media. So, of course you want them. But we don't do that to mothers. They end up in *Target* campaigns looking chirpy but never drop-dead gorgeous, never 'let's run away together and have a mad fling on the Riviera'."

And then he goes in for the kill.

"So, when you think of mothers, you think of yours."

I shudder.

"Exactly. Your disagreements with your own mother, Til, probably stem from the fact that she wants to hold on to you and you know that can't happen if you're to forge your own life. So you reject her, and on a larger scale, this is what society does to mothers too. If you or society were smarter, we would value the people who are largely responsible for the development of the human race."

"This is not the right time to be bringing up my mother, Adam."

"If you keep the baby, you'll be reflecting on more things than your relationship with your mother, Til. But if you want to continue to live your life chained to work, denying yourself an opportunity to raise a thoughtful and generous human being, then go to the doctor today and ask for a termination. It's your decision."

The Hungarian butcher

As I am not enjoying this horrible state called morning sickness, I let Adam make me an appointment, but not with my usual doctor.

My usual doctor looks like George Clooney and wears beautiful cashmere sweaters of varying shades of pastel that he wears in rotation. He has soft feathery hands and a peaceful smile and makes me feel as if I'm standing naked in the midst of a cool waterfall.

Unfortunately, he only sees me at my worst: when my head is stuffy, my nose red, my skin flaky and under-moisturised, and my breath stinking from unabated mucous. Generously, he says that I am beautiful and the common cold I am afflicted with will go away in time if I get some bed rest and eat some real food for once.

So I go home and try to take his advice. Adam makes me chicken soup, we watch DVDs with Dean, and I stay in bed the whole next day and do not think about work.

But because chicken soup isn't going to fix this, I can't go and see him. It will ruin our relationship. He will know I had unprotected, casual sex and I couldn't bear the shame of it. He might not want to touch me with those beautiful hands again.

I sit quivering with fear as the new doctor scrubs her hands with industrial soap and dries them on a rough, beige towel. Instead of welcoming me into her consultation room as Dr Nice Hands does, she glances over her instruments which gleam at her in the morning light.

I decide to think positively, that things can only get better.

But they don't.

My new doctor has the bedside manner of a Hungarian butcher. She wears a polyester jacket and prods my stomach with unnecessary force. Up close, I can tell her hands are calloused and scarred — evidence, I assume, of her previous life spent skinning spring lambs.

I want to run before she gases me and slits me down my middle.

She does nothing of the sort. Instead, she asks me when I had my last period.

"Well, it's a bit sketchy. I've been working hard and my period's been a bit light lately," I tell her.

"So you're anaemic as well then," she tuts, shaking her head at me. "And you probably haven't been taking any folate either, so not a good start for the baby, hey? But never mind, we never knew about these things when I was young, so maybe these warnings are just constructed by vitamin companies to make their shareholders rich, yes?"

I know she thinks that I am ignorant and stupid because she is at least four hundred years old and they didn't even know about brushing teeth back then.

She talks to me from behind her desk but I stay lying on the exam table, too scared to move.

"So, no idea of your last period, hmmn? We'll have to do a scan to work out the approximate due date."

"I know when I last had sex though, does that help?"

"Sure, unless there were many times?"

"No, not many times ... I'm, uh, working pretty hard at the moment," I tell her which is a polite way of saying I'm pretty hard up at the moment. "It was early January, around New Year's."

"Ah, a busy time for babies. Most babies are born in August and September in Australia which is spring — my favourite time of the year, of course," she says, a grimace spreading across her face.

My stomach knots with fear. I look at her medical certificates which are from universities in Eastern Europe and Auckland. Great, I think, so that's how she came to be practising her bad temper in Australia — she had to emigrate to New Zealand before being allowed into Australia.

As if reading my mind she says, "You're having a baby, not heart surgery." Then she tells me I can get off the table, that she's nearly finished with me.

I blush self-consciously and get dressed. When I sit down at the desk opposite her, she starts typing into her computer.

"Well, do you want a scan now or wait until we think the baby is 12 weeks? If you ovulated in early January, by usual calculations your last menstrual period was around mid to late December, so the baby will be due around mid to late September, see? It is easy, hey?"

I tell her I won't need a scan.

"OK, so I will write a letter to the hospital. Do you have private hospital insurance?" she asks, but I shake my head and she tuts again.

"Oh well. The public system is very good here for babies. You will be well looked after but there are many women and you will have to wait for appointments. My suggestion is you book into the hospital and then do shared-care visits with me so you don't have to visit the hospital all the time. Every month with me and then every two weeks after 30 weeks and every week after 36 weeks until baby comes. OK?"

The numbers spin around in my head. I don't say anything so she starts to write them down for me.

"And here is a referral to have a scan performed at 12 weeks to make sure there are no abnormalities and a letter for the hospital. I will write down your details and they will be in touch with you, OK? Now I want to see you in two more weeks. Here is a blood test I want you to get done today so I can check your iron and confirm the pregnancy."

A brief glimmer of hope flashes across my face. To confirm the pregnancy? Maybe I'm not pregnant, maybe the pee-on-the-stick test was wrong?

"But I know you're pregnant, you have that sick colour about you of new mothers."

A wave of nausea hits me. The Hungarian butcher doctor picks up her rubbish bin and holds it up to me. The vomit hits the bin lining and sprays back into my face.

She offers me a tissue. "Ask the nurse to dispose of that on your way out. And I will see you again in two weeks."

And the way she says it, the way she lifts her eyebrows when she shuts the door tells me she means it: be here in two weeks or else.

I am overcome again by the sensation that my pregnancy doesn't belong to me, but to the rest of Sydney. Even this well-educated, vastly experienced doctor with terrible bedside manner has taken charge of my baby on my behalf, as if I am not ready yet to be a mother, as if I don't know what to do.

Fashionista

The funny thing is, I always knew what I wanted to do.

When I was eight, I told people that I wanted to be a gynaecologist but only because saying it in public made my mother curse me under my breath and stand with her eyes crossed until she felt sick.

Around that time, my sister Jorja, who was ten, and I fought about who we were going to be when we grew up.

"I'm going to be Dad," I told her thinking it was a race and I should get in quick otherwise I would end up being Mum.

"You're an idiot," she said, something that I would hear quite a lot growing up. "You can't be Dad, Dad is a boy and you're a girl. Don't you know how it works?"

I didn't. I had no idea what she was talking about. An eight year old has no real idea about sex or gender; she knows that little girls can be cowboys when they are bored with playing princesses but not the other way around — it just wasn't tolerated.

"Who do you want to be then?" Jorja persisted.

"I'm going to be *Chanel*," I told her. The day before I'd overheard my mother talking about her to a friend. They made her sound like the most sophisticated woman in the world.

"You idiot," she said again. "You can't be *Chanel*, that's just a clothing business, that's just *fashion*."

And there it was, the word which would end up directing most of my adult life.

That night, I lay in bed wondering what it meant, this word *fashion*. The way Jorja had said it made it sound terrible, which meant that it must be great since Jorja and I were never in agreement.

But Jorja had said *Chanel* was a clothing business which meant that it must be big because Dad ran the local hardware business and he seemed more important than the Prime Minister. A trip to the shops could take hours because Dad always had to stop to answer questions about building a fence or how to get rid of termites. When the customers left us alone, Dad would keep Jorja and I enraptured, telling us stories about whose house was going to fall down from rot and who hadn't sprayed for redbacks that year. When local kids didn't turn up at school, I sat all day imagining them in hospital with termites crawling out of their ears or their feet swelled up to the size of balloons because of spider bites.

It seemed unfair that I wasn't allowed to be Dad. And since I didn't want to bake cakes and sit around in floral dresses like Mum, then who was I going to be?

Around midnight, when I couldn't sleep from thinking about this new word, *fashion*, I woke Dad up and asked him.

He told me to ask Mum.

Mum rolled over in her sleep and grunted at me, but because I was insistent she threw herself out of bed, and dug out a magazine for me to read.

I'd never seen that type of magazine before, apparently Mum had kept them hidden from us girls, but tonight, if it was going to shut me up, she was going to make an exception.

It was *Vogue*.

My first *Vogue*.

And it was heaven.

The women who stared out at me from the pages were so elegant they scared me and sometimes they were so scary they bewitched me. Who was this *Vivienne Westwood*? She made my stomach flutter just like when you did a tumble turn in the pool. Dressed in the type of clothes I'd never seen before, she looked so dangerous and mysterious (later I would learn that these were models not the actual designer themselves) and the way she looked at me told me she would die if she had to wear one of those horrible, pink ruffle dresses my mother bought for me at *Kmart*. I knew Jorja would hate this woman so I tore her picture out of the magazine and pinned it on my bedroom wall, so when she woke up she would see it immediately and be disgusted.

I was eight and *Vivienne Westwood* was my first pin-up.

The next morning I lay in bed looking adoringly at my future. I knew this was who I wanted to be. I wanted to be like the women in *Vogue*, but I wanted to be like Dad too. I wanted people to look up to me and I wanted to tell them what to do. I wasn't sure how I would fit this into *fashion*, but I knew there had to be a way. This *fashion* world was complicated, even the words in the magazine didn't make sense — later I learned that magazine was a French *Vogue*.

I didn't realise it for years, but by choosing fashion, I did become my Mum. We weren't only in cahoots when we lied to Dad about how much things cost and hid newly acquired purchases in the back of our closets, but we were both obsessed with fashion! And our obsession went further than our purchases and *Vogue* collection. We shared another trait, one that I discovered when I opened my mother's bedside table and found a collection of all the swing tags from all the clothes she'd ever bought.

At first, when I found my mother's stash, I was shocked. Why did she need to keep the proof of her spontaneous, consumer purchasers? Weren't her children enough? Years later, I realised she loved both. She was capable of loving her family and retaining an idea of herself that wasn't related to her marriage status, but to her position in the history of fashion:

"I was there when *Jenny Kee* opened her first store; I remember the time when Twiggy wore a mini skirt to the races; I wore *Tony Bianco* to my daughter's christening, and had to scour all of Sydney to find an appropriately ugly-enough black hat to wear to my father's funeral; God, *Fleming* must have been depressed when she designed it but thank God she was because so was I when I wore it."

Fashion understood her but it also thought about her, in the same way as I now believe it considers me.

After worshipping Kate Moss and trying like hell to look dirty for a few years at uni, I welcomed the arrival of Sophie Dahl and commiserated when she physically diminished in front of our eyes. For years, droll, unimaginative models traipsed the catwalk and I did my best to deconstruct what had happened to fashion.

Where had the female form gone? When had the rule-breaking

role of fashion reverted to a rule-making industry? My clothing designs became uninspired and when the cargo pants craze hit Sydney, I hit rock bottom.

I started looking elsewhere for inspiration, for something to believe in. I joined some student interest groups at uni, Friends of the Earth-type groups, I even went on some protests (and the only thing I achieved was smelling badly); and even though I truly empathised with the causes (trees, rivers, sand dunes, soil quality), I couldn't stand around all day wearing hempy clothes full of holes and leaving my hair unwashed. When one guy started chatting me up and I saw he was wearing stripy socks with the toes cut off (and he had hairy toes), I cut and ran.

With nothing else to do, I started going to all my lectures — even the electives. That was when I found out about marketing. A lecturer started dropping the *M* word, and at first I thought he was saying *Marjorie. Marjorie* did this and *Marjorie* knew all about that. I was jealous and started to listen a little more carefully to what he was saying. After all, *Marjorie* knew about all the people who bought the clothes (today I refer to them as 'customers') and spoke to the Board (no, I'm not going to admit what I call them), who spoke to the bank (ditto).

I knew he was wrong. Women didn't go to the bank with new business plans and get loans. I already knew this because friends had tried and failed. No bank would support a new fashion label when it was led by a woman. But when our male friends tried, as long as they had a lease and some collateral, the bank came on board.

Marjorie slowly gave way to the discipline of marketing and I decided I had found my path. In marketing, I would lead the industry; in design I could only follow trends.

I still had faith in fashion. And people. I truly believed there were people out there who could be inspired to adopt a fashionable life — who could be convinced to construct their identity on a daily basis, and throw off the boredom and disillusionment of a life dictated by pockets on pants. They could stand up to class divisions and synthetic fibres! They would spend $10,000 on a new handbag and not blink. At the time, I had no idea how trivial I sounded, so instead of criticising this type of nihilism and capitalist plundering of resources, I developed my ideas in Segment Analysis Reports where I rejected traditional demographic profiling and completed assignment after assignment using psychographics instead.

I decided that as a fashion marketer, I could give people a choice in directing their identities and their lives. I could be a part of the daily grind, of their dilemma, of their decision about what they needed to wear to be successful that day. I was convinced that fashion was the kindred spirit of health professionals: one heals and saves us from death, but fashion makes our lives worth saving.

I didn't want to draw and construct, or refer and invigorate or even argue with production. I wanted to decide which customer niches our label would pursue; I wanted to manipulate resources instead of fabrics; and to make a label bigger than Ben Hur. I wanted to research diffusion ranges, to organise Fashion Weeks and swindle international exporting rules.

After completing my first degree, I embarked on a degree in marketing which made my mother roll her eyes, mainly because I would not be moving out yet and she would have to put up with me for a few more years. You can imagine her relief.

Who are we wearing/being/projecting today? was the title of my final marketing assignment which was the high point of my six years at university.

When designers threw tantrums, I knew their attention-seeking behaviour, their arrogant belief in an artistic mystique and corresponding *enfant-terrible* behaviour, could never be as productive as a big four page spread in a flashy magazine or catalogue inserted into the Sunday paper. And design knew it too.

"Design is desperate to throw off art's obsession with originality and authenticity while art is today embracing seasonal advances and minor differences between thematic schemes. Fashion has become art in the late 1990s, and art has become…well, so last season," I wrote.

My hypothesis continued. "For even when we ask ourselves, *Who am I today?*, what we really mean is: if the purpose of our existence is the continuation of a functioning society, how do I construct my role in the creation of value and the global exchange of ideas and cash that must occur in a post-industrial economy? Our identities are never singular, and without fashion, our purpose is limited to contributing nothing except the passing of time.

"We can relive the royal courts of France, we can escape our class by having good taste, by dressing successfully, by being people we are not. We can create a new post-modern confidence. And that is the role of the fashion marketer, to convince more people daily that their sense of purpose, their entire value, depends on their wardrobe."

I tested my theories in a marketing plan which included a fashion parade at the Art Gallery of NSW and I proffered to use models who would lay around as if they were dead. Attendees were allowed to undress the models, to steal their clothes.

Even Lola commended me. "*Tu* have turned your audience *ento vulturez*, what fun," she said.

And quite confidently I entered the debate. "But I'm not the first," I told her. "*Margiela* withdraws the model from the product and even *Jourdan* has used themes of death to help separate the product image from the product. How do I connect this parade to other marketing activities, like a catalogue?"

"Do you need to advertise? Perhaps you could rebel and not do it at all?" she asked.

"And open an empty store," I say nodding my head, referring to a *Commes Des Garcons* strategy. "It's all been done. There is no originality in fashion marketing left, and I can't believe it's taken me a whole second degree to figure that out."

"But at least you know *et*."

"All I can do is manipulate public opinion and the media to bring buyers to me."

Which was how, on graduation, I earned an interview at a small, local label.

I sat through the interview desperately hoping they were going to redecorate their offices soon since I only wanted to work somewhere beautiful and fashionable. My soon-to-be-new-boss,

Jaimee, allegedly recognised my talent and determination and decided I could be the person to reenergise the fledgling label after the previous whacked-out CEO got sent to rehab. She told me she wanted to capitalise on my determination before it disintegrated into disillusionment but she didn't want anyone around annoying her with unnecessary enthusiasm. With tongue wedged firmly in cheek, she even renamed the label, *Enegi*.

Jaimee then told me that she didn't want somebody who was going to take the usual paths to building the business into a national brand. She wanted somebody who would take risks, and focus on developing internal resources that were oriented at identifying market trends rather than creating them. This meant we could copy and produce those trends with a quick turnaround, and turn a business that was totally crap into a work of financially successful art.

Jaimee retells the story of our meeting with more embellishment as time moves on; history is reconceptualised by distance from the fact and the number of dirty martinis she has had. The way Jaimee talks about our first meeting, she makes it sound like a *ménage-à-trois*: herself, the label, and wide-eyed, Lolita-esque me. The truth is less risqué. The first thing she did was cut up my credit cards. We agreed that since my first year's salary was going to be directed into paying rent and the large debt I had racked up while at university, and she assured me that no matter how hard I begged and no matter how big a cocaine addict I foolishly became, she would not stand for loans, advances or theft of merchandise.

I gulped a few times wondering if I was being interviewed for a job or parole. But I liked her style. She wasn't the type of boss that interfered with your work, she interfered with your personal life since that was always going to get you into much more trouble.

"But that's what it's like," she explained. "In fashion, your employees are often too consumer-driven to understand that they need to budget, and because they work in fashion are either overpaid (rarely) or working for slave labour (normally). And then you're expected to party with your friends like you're some celebrity but really you're just a hard-working fashionista who must show up at work at eight am. The sweatshops aren't only in China, they're right here too — it'll be 12 hour days and you won't get breaks. But the perks are nice, you get to wear samples, and I'll give you an expense account for taking the fashion editors to lunch — not that they will eat but you'll still manage to spend 100 bucks a pop. And you get to go to Fashion Week. Fashion Week will be key to building our brand and picking up department stores …actually, any stores in fact. Our marketing budget will be small so you will have to do wonders with it. Think outside the box and keep our packaging costs small too — everybody's talking about the environment these days."

And that's what I wanted to hear. Jaimee knew that fashion wasn't just about fashion. She knew that it was about people and that fashion held the pieces of society together just like the seams hold together the pieces of a garment. I hoped that I would look like her someday too. She seemed so self-assured like the well manicured always do, and her style seemed to resonate past the clothes she was wearing. She was shorter than me, obviously of Japanese heritage, sleek, and elegant, with fabulous shiny hair. And I was in awe.

She could have written anything into my position description and I would have done it. The only clause I baulked at was the one that insisted I only wear our label's clothes. I noticed she, however, was wearing *Issey Miyake*. She showed me through the label's last collection and I tried to hide my fear.

On my walk home, carrying a bag of the ugliest clothes I had ever seen, I realised how intelligent her strategy was.

I decided my first task was to talk to HR (who was Jaimee at that early stage) and investigate the fastest, legal method to firing the designer. This turned out to be easy — first, I came up with the idea of asking Jaimee to instigate a new no-drugs-on-work-premises policy and then I planted the designer's handbag with cocaine. Within two weeks of starting at *Enegi*, I'd fired the designer and taken the label in a new niche-driven direction which involved hiring two young and inexperienced designers. They were friends from university, Stella and Sarah — over the top, black-haired Grecian beauties who knew that grunge was on the way out and being wasted in elegant bars was going to be so in.

They crossed *Gucci* with a forethought of *Hussein Chalayan* and *Junya Watanabe* to spawn a look that was more *Commes des Sydney* than the Opera House and even sexier. They stayed with the label for two years before foolishly leaving to set up their own label before going broke a year later from lack of financial backing. They ended up begging Jaimee for their jobs back. By then we had recovered from the hiatus of losing them and had a new design team so she had to say no, we were pursuing a new look and it probably wasn't wise to go backwards thematically and she wished them luck. They had turned the label into a multi-million dollar business and were lucky to earn 60k a year from it, but instead of giving Jaimee the finger, they acted with utmost decorum. They picked up some contract design positions before heading off to New York where they now work for *Vera Wang*. They email us occasionally and we try not to be consumed with stabbing pains of intense jealousy.

After eight years of working in fashion, I am still me: I'm older, 32 now, not so naïve and party with a bunch of friends who number into the thousands (most of them are Adam's, to be honest). Life is fantastically good. I may be a short, average-looking, red-haired Sydney girl, but I wear *Vivienne Westwood* platforms, carry a ten thousand dollar handbag (well, a copy Jaimee bought for me in Hong Kong) and wear an outfit that's to die for on any night of the week. And I love my job. I work with the most talented team of women in Sydney and we have a ball together.

It's only recently I've found myself thinking that maybe there is more to life than this.

Instead of writing killer media releases, I've increasingly found myself stuck in a trance, thumbing fabric and wondering what's missing from my life, what's missing from me.

But today is different. As I look at myself in the mirror, I notice a new angle has appeared and one that can only be explained by the Dadaists as…*MaMa!* It's only a slight protrusion, but that's more than enough to ruin the careers of the top models and, since six became the new four, anyone who works in fashion too. I start to sweat.

I could tell people I'm reinvigorating the *Commes des Garcons* bump collection from 1997, but I don't think I'll get away with that since those bumps protruded from weird bodily locations and not just stomachs and bums. I tell the mirror, "I have become an outdated object of art.

I have become — *a mother!*

Eight weeks

Felicitations — congratulations! The embryo is now officially a foetus which means *little one*. How one little thing can make you feel this sick is beyond you, but gallantly, you get up and go to work before 11am ... most days.

It takes you until 11am because you have to throw up three times whilst trying to eat a nutritious breakfast containing fruit, protein, and carbohydrates, that's low in fat, preservatives, salt and chemicals (let's face it, you're exhausted from just reading all the labels — that's why eating natural or low-processed food is so much better for you, it takes such less effort!). And then you have to find something suitable to wear which is extremely difficult because already your belly is growing. You look up the pregnancy guide book. Ah, that explains why your skirt doesn't fit — the foetus is now around two centimetres long, not much bigger than a grape. You close the book and inspect yourself in the mirror again. Must be a big grape, you tell yourself.

It's not just the size of the foetus that counts. Around the foetus is your expanding uterus, which is growing to accommodate the placenta and amniotic fluids and is about the size of a grapefruit. Be positive, by the end of the pregnancy it's going to feel like the size of the hole in the ozone.

Right now, your foetus is small but incredibly complex: even its organs, muscles, and nerves are beginning to function. Your little grape is beginning to lose its tail and boasts moveable wrists and eyelids. The sexual organs are

46

also beginning to form.

But more importantly, the feet are beginning to lose their webbed appearance and look like real, future shoe-wearing, show-stopping feet!

The beginnings of...

"It's official, you're showing. You'd better take a few days off."

I tell Jaimee that I'm keeping the baby and without looking at me she tells me, "*It* isn't a handbag. You can't return it once it's out of vogue, you know. And it will cry and shit a lot too."

"Actually, I'm used to that, I work with models remember," I rebut. "The fun ones are so wasted they forget to eat and when their sugar levels reach rock bottom they lose it and start blubbering about being ugly and the boring ones, well, they just use diuretics so they're constantly running for the loo."

"But you don't have to wipe their arse."

"Actually, I have," I tell her. Jaimee doesn't know about it because she was in New York at the time, but when a Sydney model called Talia hit supermodel status, the pressure caused her to started doing both diuretics and drugs. It wasn't pretty, especially for me. We never booked her again. Jaimee never found about that calamitous day. I nearly puke just thinking about it.

Jaimee continues looking at my draft marketing plan while talking at me. Sometimes she looks up at me, but instead of looking at my face she stares at my breasts which, I'm proud to say, are growing daily.

"And it will keep you up all night," she says to my chest.

"Kind of like Adam and Dean when they insist on going out for one drink and it turns into a bender."

"And then you'll have to find day care for *It* so you can work and Til, you find it hard to pay your bills now. What do you think you'll do when you're only working part-time because you've just had a baby?"

"Are we going to refer to *It* as *It* for the next seven months? It sounds a little inhuman," I complain.

"I'm trying to be non-gender specific. What should I use then — her, him, them? Oh God, it's not plural is it?" At last she looks me in the face and I see real fear in her eyes for the first time in eight years.

"Oh shit, I hadn't thought of that," I say.

"Do you think it's a boy or a girl?"

"I haven't thought about that either yet. I'm just getting used to the idea of being pregnant, it hasn't really dawned on me yet that I'm having a baby," I say.

Jaimee sighs and rolls her eyes. "Well, it had better dawn on you soon, girly, because you've got a lot of shit to organise."

"Doesn't the body pretty much do it all? The doctors all seem to know what they're doing, they've even got it down to a weekly checklist. All I have to do is show up and whammo, in a few months I'll be sent home with a whole human being to destroy."

Jaimee shakes her head. She knows I'm being precious.

"OK, so you're officially having a baby. Well, good for you," she says and I acknowledge, via a little sigh, that I feel disappointed she's not more enthusiastic about *It*.

"Well, let's write a new parental leave policy," she says. "And one that lets you work more from home, because A (and I'm being selfish here) I still need you to get the marketing for Spring/Summer out and organise Fashion Week; and B, I also know you'll need more rest and time off for appointments, etc."

"And a 20 per cent raise."

"Not on your damn baby's diaper."

And she says it with such conviction that I have to mumble "bitch" under my breath.

"So, how about this," she says, writing in pencil over my marketing plan which means I'm going to have to type up her notes and take them to HR.

"Five months before expected due date, pregnant employee can work from home two days per week if full-time, one day if part-time. Sixteen weeks of paid leave will be awarded to male or female employees commencing immediately after birth of new child (and this includes adoption of children). The employee can elect to reduce working hours (pay will be commensurate with days worked) or work a full-time load made up of equal time in the office and at home. Employees can elect to take their holiday leave and any future leave entitlements that would be due to them for up to one year after the birth. The employer will provide the employee with a laptop and any materials they will need at home to enable them to work productively. And this does not mean champagne."

Jaimee claps her hands satisfied. "There, done. Good. I've been meaning to do that for a while. Of course, if any of the other employees get pregnant because of this new overly-generous policy I will shoot you, Til. God, they'll all be going out and getting pregnant if they find out they can get 16 weeks off paid and then work from home. I betcha as soon as their leave's up, they'll sell the baby on *ebay*."

"Only Didi would do that."

She ignores me. "You forgot to say thank you," she chastises.

"Thanks Jaimee," I say with as much enthusiasm as I dare.

"We'll just have to keep it quiet, announce it on a Monday morning or hide it in an email that says something about tax in the subject line. They'll never read that. Bugger you, Til, this is going to cost the Board a fortune. I don't know how much exactly but this may reduce their return on investment from 1000 per cent to 999.9 this year. They're going to be pissed off and call me all sorts of names."

"Sorry, Jaimee," I say"

"She'd better be bloody beautiful."

And it dawns on me: I'm pregnant with a human being and it could be a girl! It could equally be a boy too which starts me thinking: if I'm physically capable of giving birth to a boy, then there can't be too many differences between the sexes, can there? I realise I have reached a nirvana — a real moment of conceptual liberation — which is followed quickly by an intense bolt of fear.

I could have been born a male and never ever owned a dress. Or heels. I shudder.

I take the rest of the day off to look at baby clothes and wonder which side of the store I belong to.

"Yuck"

"Tacky."

The clothes fly along the rack. Everything is rejected.

"Lolly pink," I grimace.

"*Trajic* pink," my sister Jorja corrects me.

"What?" I ask Jorja who has tracked me down in Sydney's largest department store. I don't know how she found me but I suspect the information probably came from Adam. I thought I'd ducked from view in time but the escalator I was riding led me straight into her evil clutches.

"Us mothers call that *Trajic* pink," she explains. "It's everywhere; the ubiquitous, ugly pink."

Having not spent money on clothes for many years, courtesy of the label and Jaimee who gives me all her last season's favourites, it's been a while since I shopped at a department store. Looking at the prices of these baby clothes, I decide that I probably can't even afford the ugly clothes.

Jorja doesn't shop in department stores; why would she when she practically owns one? Not the business, but the building.

Despite our childhood goals, Jorja didn't grow up to be a nurse. She decided to follow her heart instead of her brains and dropped out of school to stalk some surfer dude at the beach every day. I think she'd read *Puberty Blues* one too many times and fell into the romance of all that STD-attracting behaviour. But all's well that ends well: the guy's parents ran the Bondi real estate agency and she ended up working for them right before the last big boom and made a packet of money. The story gets better. They got married at 22, have two kids, and at last count, own 26 properties around the Bondi and North Shore areas.

Apparently she's worth a fortune. Adam and I rent our apartment from her at a hideously large discount and in return I take her shopping and act as her style guru (her words). She won't wear anything from my label, she says it's too down-market *Versace* for her and she prefers the early *Prada* days or *Donna Karan*, when it was all about function and no ego.

I have to admit she looks pretty good. At a whacking 180cm tall she is often mistaken for one of the models working for the label. Or she was; she's now the wrong side of 30 (or 20 for that matter) to be mistaken for a model despite being as skinny as a wisp after carrying twins and enduring a 60 hour working week. On a bad day — well, let's face it, Jorja doesn't have a bad day. On a good day, Jorja looks like Megan Gale.

It was Jorja who grew up to be like Dad. She's just like him. Everybody knows her and when you walk down the street people stop her and ask her advice on market fluctuations, the latest property she's selling and should they really be offering $4.5 million or $4.9 million because they'd hate to be considered cheap. Everybody takes her seriously and Jorja has reportedly kitted out the Packers, and even Pink, with Bondi apartments.

Jorja rejects more clothes and tells me, "You know, you really should get everything organic and better yet, formaldehyde free. That way the baby won't grow up with two heads or get ADD or autism."

I don't know why I've been avoiding her. Probably because I didn't want her taking over my pregnancy or scaring me with information about all the nasty chemicals in my apartment or how I should really sign the baby up for toddler classes now…

"Because you can't underestimate how much these chemicals impact on the baby's development," she continues.

I turn to another rack.

Other shoppers are looking at us, or to be precise, are staring at Jorja, gobsmacked. They say some women get better with age; Jorja gets better with money.

"But you'll get used to it — if you're having a girl, you'll get given heaps of it."

I realise I haven't got a clue what she's talking about.

"Have you been for any scans yet?"

"No, not for another few weeks."

"Are you booked into an obstetrician?"

"What is this?" I think. "Ask a million questions week?" Instead I tell her confidently, "No. I'm going public," and wait for her response. After all, Jorja didn't even go to a private hospital when she had her babies. Jorja is so rich the paediatrician came to her.

Her hands stop searching through the rack. "You know the public system is so overcrowded, don't you? But you're more egalitarian than I am; I'm just thinking of the baby, Til."

"I know you are," I say. "But the public system is very well-resourced. I'm not turning having a baby into a political statement, but I'm going to be a single parent and have to budget carefully. And besides, I'm having a baby not heart surgery — women used to have babies in the bush and then go straight back to ploughing the fields. At least they ate the placenta first to give them nourishment."

"That's disgusting," she says crinkling her perfect nose. "But I understand why they'd do it. I was ravenous after the girls were born, I just wanted to eat all day and I still couldn't get enough. It must help your milk come in. Now, please promise me one thing," she says, and seeing me roll my eyes, follows quickly with, "and this is the last thing I will say, I promise. But please, after the birth, get some rest. The first six months are really hard, you'll need to get as much sleep as possible. So, no work. Tell Jaimee you can't do anything for six months, or at least lie and get Adam to do it for you."

Jorja must be able to see the fumes rising silently from my head because she immediately backtracks "I know what you do is complex but he could give it a shot. I don't want you getting drained, you'll need all of your energy for looking after the baby."

"You make it sound like a marathon," I complain.

"It's worse, believe me. You'll start feeling human again when the baby's about eight, maybe nine, years old. But when you're tired, it can be really overwhelming. I had Stav to help me though."

"I've got Adam. And Dean."

She nods. "You're lucky to have two Dads to help."

I can tell she means that wholeheartedly. And it's one of the nice things about Jorja.

Despite being incredibly rich, she is completely open to all types of family configurations, sexual preferences, careers, lifestyle choices and bank account balances. Her friends reflect her open-mindedness and dinner parties usually include an assortment of interesting people from the head of new Sydney surf clothing label *Nastee*, a politician, the local postman and her girls' school teacher.

The fact that she is even here today is evidence of how much she cares. I never thought she'd even have time to respond to the text message Adam sent telling half the world I was pregnant, but here she is, looking at hideous clothes with me as a way of celebrating my newly-acquired intra-uterine status. A warm feeling floods over me, like when we used to fight over a jacket or some guy, and occasionally, when she was really angry, she used to wee on me. Of course back then, she had no idea she would grow up to be a multi-millionaire and that certain magazines would pay me thousands of dollars for that type of information. Of course, I would never do it, but when I'm having a bad day, just knowing I could makes me feel better.

Her worried face breaks my concentration.

"But you'll still be the one feeding and that's really tiring on the body, OK? Just take my word for it." She still looks anxious. "Look, I promise I won't interfere, it's your body and your baby. You're going to have to figure these things out for yourself, but do call me if you need anything or just want to talk. I won't judge you or be the condescending older sister."

She hesitates before continuing. "Love may be engendered into us but parenting is not. I'll be here if you want me, OK? And the rest of the time, I'll be trying to keep Mum away."

Which makes me laugh.

Because sometimes, it's easy to forget that we share a communal gene pool. Jorja was dealt all the luck in the world and the looks to take advantage of her fortune. Even her sleek, black hair kills me. It doesn't matter how much product I use in my hair, it will never be like Jorja's. She is the model's model: gorgeous and never has to work at it. On the other hand, I have to spend a fortune on waxing, facials, eyebrow shaping and hair treatments and I still look like a slob.

She starts flicking through the clothes again. "You know, this stuff is just crap. If you like I can give you my girls' baby clothes. They've been washed a million times so all the nasty chemicals should be out of them by now."

"But what if I have a boy?"

"You won't have a boy. What would you do with a boy?"

"Love it, of course," I think. But she's right. I know nothing about football, or how to kick one.

Because the real truth about me is that I can only contribute to discussions that lead back to a visual design brief.

I have never surfed, jogged or even been on a bushwalk. In fact when I was 26, I had to spend a week at a health spa just so I could get some fresh air. Having moved into the city after I started working for *Enegi*, the constant city life and pressures of my first Fashion Week show had turned me into a nervous wreck. I longed for the fresh air of the suburbs but Jaimee booked me into the health spa instead.

Mum refers to it as my time in rehab, but really I was just vitamin D deficient and exhausted.

It's also where I met Adam.

He was there detoxing after a vicious relationship with a passive-aggressive called José. He told me he was in hiding and I looked around the bathroom trying to figure out what he meant. Hiding from what: a facial, a workout session with Dave (as if a gay boy was going to miss out on that) or a hot rock massage?

Adam told me he had fled Sydney, convinced that José's family would hunt him down and break his legs for breaking up with their precious offspring. "Both legs, for the two years we were together," he whispered.

"Gee, they sound like a really supportive Mexican mafia family," I told him. "I thought they would have been ashamed or sent him to the US for a while."

"The US? God, with his looks he'd be Mr Universe by now and totally bulimic," he blubbered into a tissue while we sat hiding in the girls' bathroom which is where everyone went to smoke cigarettes when *being good* got too hard. He offered me a puff but I declined.

I was hiding in the toilets to get my *Vogue* hit. I wasn't supposed to be reading it, Jaimee had banned me from looking, talking or even thinking about fashion, but a fellow health spa inmate who was there for executive stress, had leant it to me on strict instructions I was to have it back before meditation. "Since I will be bored to death otherwise," she had moaned.

I wondered why she was there, since she wasn't really into the beautiful relaxation vibe but explained she'd managed to bribe the masseuse to swap deep tissue for a daily anti-cellulite treatment. She said her boyfriend was losing interest and she was sure she'd found one centimetre of fat on her thigh.

"What is this place" I asked Adam, "LA? Have we turned into superficial, self-obsessed creatures with no sense of our fortune or any sincere concern for the future of the planet?"

He nodded and said one of the reasons he'd broken up with José was the constant body insecurities and purging in the toilet after meals. "It's really stressful being Mexican and having to maintain the perfect gay body," he told me apologetically. "All that sour cream."

I rubbed his back while he continued to blubber into recycled toilet paper that smelled like frangipanis. I looked around the glorious bathroom with its floor-to-ceiling Spanish tiles and Thai statues and wondered — could this be happening to me? How did I end up in this blissful, Byron Bay retreat connecting with a hilarious gay man, eating delicious organic food, delighting in daily massages and listening to the rich and connected bitch and whine about the lack of austerity in their life — and not have to pay for a cent of it?

Jaimee called it *Über Stress Leave*, a new company policy for worthwhile employees.

I decided then and there that I would work myself to the bone if I could spend a week there every year rejuvenating and replenishing my energy sources.

Which is what happened.

Adam wasn't there when I visited the spa every year. He moved into my apartment after our first spa encounter and has been there ever since. We never heard from José, although Adam still wakes up with night sweats after eating Mexican food.

After my return from *rehab*, the label was announced "The next biggest label to come out of Australia since the last one" — how much it cost Jaimee to have them say that I'll never know but I imagine it was a lot of money — I told Jaimee I wanted two weeks every year at the spa and I got the one week I wanted.

I was learning.

Of course, I was too naïve to know about the externalities I was creating in my life. My devotion to fashion meant there were other valuable experiences I was missing out on: I could have been riding camels across the Sahara desert or doing volunteer work in Africa, or working for a marketing consultancy in London and spending all my weekends doing drugs in Soho. Instead, I stayed in Sydney, worked my ass to the bone.

I was work and work was me.

And I was happy.

But one day life stopped me and told me that shagging a guy behind the Bondi Icebergs Swimming Club on New Year's Eve was a good idea. Of course it wasn't, but when you're single, exhausted and drunk sometimes you make really bad decisions. Now I know how George Michael feels. I shake my head. And now I'm even more exhausted and facing the difficulty of bringing up a child as a sole parent and sole income earner. And to help me deal with this new sharp-edged reality, I've taken the rest of the day off to shop for baby clothes that I can't afford.

At least Adam is having fun. On the other side of town he is busily rejecting every baby name from the *World's Greatest Baby Name* book based on the brats who come into his shop.

He texts me the latest: "Lionel — from the sixties, shoplifter, no. Eden — too the Bold and the Beautiful, def no. Delilah — lovely, but will be deflowered at an inappropriate age, no. Any names from you? x A."

I look at the clothing labels on the racks around me. *Peter Rabbit* and *Winnie the Pooh* are out, replaced by clothing brands that all sound like conjoined twins.

I text him back: "Heidi or Hercules — no, the Gods will only get angry with us. Jorja looks incredible, do you think I can ask her what shampoo she uses? I'm def adopted. x T."

He replies. "Aidan — too gay. You're not adopted. Just genetically inferior."

Jorja rings the limo driver and instructs him to pick her up in thirty seconds before snapping her phone shut and acting unusually emotional: she air kisses my cheek and gives my shoulder a half second squeeze. And then she's gone. And although she moves so effortlessly she barely disrupts the air around her, the store suddenly feels as if all the oxygen has been sucked from it.

The store's massive doors slide shut as Jorja glides into the waiting limo.

Disappointment hangs heavily in the sleek interior and highly-glossed aisles and I stand silently with the other awestruck shoppers as if the hundreds of useless, non-essential items around us suddenly don't exist. Until somebody sneezes, the moment is broken, and we return to wandering around the store, absorbed in the promises of marketing gurus and distracted by the hum of the fluorescent lighting.

Except for me. Despite feeling like a complete moron every second I am with her, I love Jorja and can't help feeling disappointed that our lives have become so perpendicular. She is rich in many ways; her beautiful family, her loving husband, her full life. But I'm rich too. I have a boss who appreciates me, great friends, and a family who cares about me. Today has proven just that!

But standing in the middle of the department store, I suddenly feel lonelier than ever.

I already know I won't be buying any clothes. It's ridiculous buying clothes for a baby who won't be born for six months. The season's trends could do a complete turnaround by then and I'll be stuck with the wrong hem length and wardrobe full of the wrong shade of pink. I drop the romper suit.

My purpose, I tell myself with relief as I head out of the store, is to learn how to be a mother, which is no mean feat, considering I only have six months left.

Twelve weeks

You've reached the end of the first trimester. Only two more increasingly uncomfortable trimesters to go. How snappy do you think a pregnant lion gets? Well, it's nothing compared to a pregnant human. No wonder the crash test dummy that got you knocked up is suddenly silent; any time he opens his mouth he says the wrong thing and gets bitch-clawed. The vicious wounds of a pregnant woman's tongue can take months to heal.

But things will get easier soon — for everybody.

By the end of this month, the risks of miscarriage will drop considerably, and with it, the likelihood, frequency and strength of your mood swings and irritability. If you're also one of the 50% of women to suffer from morning sickness, then this should ease this month too.

The third month also marks a fantastic occasion: for many women, this will be the first time they see their baby — via an ultrasound. The first trimester screening (which can be performed between 10 and 14 weeks) is not compulsory but it will indicate whether you are carrying multiple bubs and test for nuchal fold thickness, which can indicate Down syndrome. Thanks to todays technology, you will see how amazingly human-like your baby looks already. The other test performed now is a blood test, which will test for high levels of plasma protein A and HCG.

It's a busy time. For you and bub.

Your baby now measures five centimetres from head to bum and is already busy kicking and stretching although you won't start to feel this until around 20 weeks. You may even look slightly pregnant (especially if you've been tucking into M&M's and stopped doing your sit ups), and you may start glowing. Your features soften and you may appear radiant, healthy, calm and even more beautiful than you usually do. People are starting to look at you and smile. Everybody loves a pregnant woman, except somebody who has a seat on public transport — and midwives.

Losing it

The midwives' clinic is running an hour behind schedule and we are shooting our next season's catalogue today. Like an idiot, I didn't check my schedule, so instead of being at the shoot, I am here at the hospital waiting for my first appointment and scan.

I could cancel my appointment, but the next available appointment is three weeks away and if anything happened to the baby in that time I'd kill myself. Plus, I'm anxious to see what this little baby looks like. If he or she is wearing shoes I will just die of pride.

I pace the waiting room showing off my latest *Jimmy Choos* and text message furiously. The art director informs me, via text message, that she has everything under control and my last minute ideas are not helping anybody. And besides, the talent hasn't even shown up yet.

My heart stops.

I reread the message. At $2000 an hour for the photographer, extra for the assistant, studio fees, makeup and hair designers... and the model isn't even there yet! This is going to cost Jaimee a fortune.

I call the agency and our booker tells me she'll get onto it immediately.

Half an hour later my phone rings just as a midwife calls out my name.

I take a deep breath before I answer the phone and follow the midwife, who weighs me, notices my high heels and then takes my blood pressure. She opens my file, which I've already added my details into. I mouth at her, "I thought it would save time."

She tells me to put the phone down but I have the agency on the end of the line again. She plays with a little circular calendar which I've seen my GP use before to calculate my due date. Another waste of time — I already wrote the due date in my chart too. The only question I wasn't sure about was the one that asked if you smoked, drank, or took recreational drugs? Do they mean all at the same time? So I wrote what all other women would answer, "When I was young and stupid I may have indulged occasionally but I never swallowed."

I hope the baby's health won't be affected by the ecstasy tablet I took the night it was conceived. Just because the pill didn't work doesn't mean the baby's health won't be ruined. Hopefully, it was a dud and contained no illicit materials, or *Ratsak* or drain cleaner, which is what ecstasy's usually mixed with these days. I really hope it didn't have any toxic chemicals in it, because:

1. I don't want the baby's organs to fail and for her/him to die;
2. I don't want the baby to have developmental abnormalities and ruin his or her chances at a healthy, long adult life;
3. It cost me $40 which is a ridiculous waste of money, especially now that I'm looking at bringing a baby into the world and that's going to cost me a cool million.

She keeps flicking through the chart.

"Nicolita," the agency says — I'm sure when I booked the model her name was Nicole — "is on her way, simply held up in traffic."

"My ass," I tell the phone slamming it shut. "She's probably got a head full of blow and they're trying to sober her up as we speak. What do they think I am, a moron? I know how it works."

"Your blood pressure's high," the midwife interrupts.

"No shit. Your blood pressure would be through the roof too if your day had just blown out from $30k to $50k. They'll never get it all done. We'll have to re-shoot which means another $50k tomorrow too." I smash my $1500 PDA on my head.

"Like I said, your blood pressure is too high and if you don't calm down the baby could go into cardiac arrest."

That gets my attention.

"What? My baby's having a heart attack?"

"No, I just said that to shut you up."

She's seen people like me before — and worse. I know there are worse people out there than me. I can only imagine the shit this woman puts up with on a daily basis and whatever she is paid it's simply not enough. I look at her hands and she pulls them back as if reading my mind. It doesn't matter how much she hates me, the fact that my hands are perfectly manicured and look great (my only asset, my mother calls them) and can make even this self-assured, functioning member of society feel awkward, makes me feel ashamed.

I try to distract her by asking if she's going to listen to the baby's heartbeat now and she says, "No, it's time to get the ultrasound done."

She shepherds me back to the waiting room and tells me with no uncertain terms, "Wait here."

I wait. And I wait. I peer over shoulders of other pregnant woman who have hogged all the trashy magazines. I tell them that they're outdated trash not a donut but still they don't let me have one.

I try not to look at my phone. I stalk the halls. "Are you a radiographer?" I ask every passer-by but none of them say yes. I want to throw an outdated magazine across the room. "This is a bloody hospital," I imagine screaming at the wall. "And there's not a bloody radiographer in sight. One of you had better get a bloody radiographer so we can have a look at this baby because that fat midwife over there said my baby is having a heart attack."

The midwife looks up from her desk before biting into a biscuit. She rolls her eyes at me and takes me into the ultrasound room. My wall staring is scaring the other Mums-to-be.

"You have to calm down, the stress hormones you're creating can't be good for the baby. Can't you think about what's best for your baby?"

I feel my blood pressure rise again. My heart palpitates. "That's the problem," I tell her. "It's all I think about. Everyone keeps telling me to do what's best for the baby but as soon as my baby is born, it'll live in a world where *What's best for the baby* doesn't matter anymore. Then in a couple of months the baby will get stuck in day care just so I can pay my rent and then it will go to a school where they still have asbestos in the roof because that's how much our government cares about children meanwhile the politicians' offices are flashy, inner city mansions with views of the harbour. So don't give me that *'What's best for the baby'* talk because we both know that once this baby's out of me there's very little I can do to protect him or her from all the nasty shit," I manage to take breath. "The truth is I don't really give a damn that precious Nicolita is an hour late for a shoot and too high on *China White* to bother coming down to planet Earth. So I'm just as bad as those fat, cigar-smoking politician wannabes who don't want to hear the spiel, they just want the fancy car."

The midwife presses a red button.

"Maybe Nicolita is just going through a hard time, maybe she can't figure out which way to cut her hair or can't keep the weight off any other way except by snorting a thousand dollars worth of coke every day. Or maybe she has a terminally ill boyfriend. The truth is, I don't care. Good on her for floating off into outer space — she should stay there — which is where this baby should stay if it knows what's good for it. But that won't happen. Eventually this little baby is going to come out of me, hopefully with the help of some wicked pain killers, and that's what I'm scared about. In six months I'm having a baby so who the hell are you to tell me to calm down!"

I stand up.

"I haven't even got a cat yet. Isn't that what normal people do? They finish school, they shag their best friend's boyfriend, they feel guilty, they go to uni, they shag their best friend at uni's boyfriend, they swear off men, they get a job, get an apartment, work themselves to a size eight, shag some guy because let's face it, they're so drunk and it's been nearly a year so anyone will do by that stage. Oh and I forgot, somewhere along the line they get a cat. I don't have any maternal instincts. I don't even remember to feed myself let alone another pesky flea-bitten canine and in six months you want me to be the sole carer of a baby? What are you — nuts?"

The midwife sits me down again. "I'm going to call the psych."

"Great. That'll be another two hour wait."

"No, I think I'll get him to come right over."

"I'm not having this baby in a psychiatric ward," I yell at her. "I've seen the garments those crazy people wear and I'm not wearing anything like that ever — even when I'm old and can't shit by myself anymore."

"They might give you something to calm you down, that's what I'm hoping."

"Is that what's best for the baby?"

She rolls her eyes.

Eventually, we are saved by the radiographer. He seems a little surprised to find an over-worked midwife babysitting me. They are, after all, seriously busy people. The midwife gives him the update in gibberish that I can't understand — "Hyper … elevated … blah blah … baby dead."

My heart stops. Is she telling him the baby is dead? Is that why she wouldn't use the Doppler-thingy on me? She didn't want me to know the baby was dead? I've been standing here the whole time rabbiting on and the baby isn't alive anymore? How the hell did she know that and why the hell didn't she do CPR?

The radiographer smiles uncomfortably at me. He asks me to lie down on the bed, pulls up my skirt and puts some jelly on my belly.

I can't believe this is happening to me. My breathing is sharp and rapid. I try to calm it down by doing some deep exhalations and my head crashes back onto the bed. I always thought the baby would be OK, that having accepted I was pregnant, I would behave abominably on occasion but the baby would turn out OK. Then I would lose my baby belly in two weeks just like Heidi Klum.

The head of the ultrasound thing pushes into my belly and is uncomfortable. The radiographer's hands are cold.

We all hold our breath as the radiographer presses into my belly searching for the baby. I expected it to just jump up onto the screen, but it doesn't.

"We have old technology, just be patient."

I try to breathe in but can't.

He notices. He flicks his eyes from my belly to my face and back to my belly.

"Everything's OK. You just have to calm down."

"I've never been very good at hospitals," I tell him. "Not since my Dad died."

And then we see it. The baby, which looks like a grape, has legs and arms — and a tiny little nose. No shoes — but feet!

"See? She's not dead! What would you know?" I tell the midwife, bursting with emotion, feeling the grin spreading across my face! And then the tears.

"I didn't say the baby, I said *you*, if *you* didn't calm down. What's happening to you is really serious," the midwife continues. "This isn't just about what's best for the baby, it's about your health too, you know. But it's normally easier to get people to put the baby first which has the same effect of making their own health a priority."

The radiographer nods in agreement. "You're going to have to take it easy, cut back your hours at work, rest more, eat better. Are you going to antenatal classes?" he asks.

I lie. I nod my head.

The midwife sees right through me. "I want to see you again in a week," she says matter-of-factly.

"Coming back to this hospital and having to wait two hours will kill me," I tell her.

"Too bad. Because you're going to have to see psych now and that's a two hour wait too."

I ignore her and spend the next 20 minutes looking at my baby on the screen while the radiographer checks mine and the baby's organs. Every 30 seconds I ask the radiographer how *she* is.

"It may not be a girl, it's too early to predict the gender of the baby," the midwife says. "We can't be sure until the next scan."

"It's clearly a girl, you can tell by her features," I tell her, even though secretly, I don't have a clue.

The midwife doesn't care if I think it's a tortoise — I'm beginning to bond with my baby. Satisfied, she nods at the radiographer that she's leaving her psycho patient in his capable hands and leaves the room. I take my eyes off the screen just long enough to check out her ass.

Her bottom says it all, "Mother Nature is back on track."
And she waddles happily down the hall.

I always thought psychiatrists wore white coats and carried long, scary needles but when mine arrives he is wearing a bright red nose and a Mickey Mouse shirt.

"Great," I moan facetiously. "They sent me the crazy psych."

"It's animated character day at the children's ward," Dr Naim explains.

He is obviously prepared for an overly-confident and annoying pregnant woman, high on post-ultrasound hormones because when I say, "And you're going as a…?" he cuts me short and simply replies, "A fun, not-scary doctor."

I try to talk but he holds up his hand, silencing me. I am immediately disappointed. They've sent me the one psych in the world who doesn't want to sit and listen to his patients crap on. Smart man.

Instead, he sits down on the couch next to me and says, "I've spoken to your midwife. You see, Ms Fisher, this whole process is intended to teach you patience. Yes, you wait because we are under-resourced but this all contributes to the skills you will need as a mother. Spending half the night consoling your baby because she has wind or is teething takes patience. That's why pregnancy takes nine months. It doesn't take nine months to learn how to be a mother because that takes the rest of your life, but it does take nine months for you to learn to wait."

I sit uncomfortably in my chair. This guy is nuts. He doesn't have a clue what he's talking about. Learning to wait is not going to be a nine month long affair for me. Uh-uh. No way José. Learning to wait is going to take me much longer.

On leaving the hospital with baby pictures in hand, I wait an insufferably long time for the next Bondi-bound train, and try to manage my time like a successful, mature parent. I spend the first minute huffing silently about the impudence of having to wait a whole eight minutes for the next train. The next two minutes trying to engage a complete stranger into a debate about the continuing inefficiency of the Sydney train service, until my new friend closes his book and walks silently to the other end of the platform, and the next five minutes with my head ashamedly stuck in one of the parenting books Adam has given me to read.

It's a little bit heavy on text and there aren't enough fashion analogies to really keep me interested, but I find if I stick to the pictures' captions I can almost absorb the whole gist of the book.

Before long a train idles into the station and I walk on, and joy of joys, find an empty seat. I resume my reading. Under a picture of a deliriously happy adult, regrettably boasting sideburns and cuddling an innocent, easily impressionable child, is a caption: "High authority and high emotion give children a solid framework that teaches them boundaries within an environment of unconditional love and respect."

Which I have to admit sounds pretty cool. I'm not sure about the kid's centre hair part or whether the author intended the parent to look like a paedophile, but I like the positivity of the statement. It's got to be better than living with an insolent child who's been forced to wear a 1970s-style bib-n-brace. I keep reading:

"Standing over a child and complaining to him: 'Now how many times have I told you not to do that' is a waste of time. Because his little brain is too immature to make short-term memories nor understand the inference of an adult's rhetorical question. The child wouldn't have a clue if you've nagged them about it one hundred times, but his brain will remember the interaction with you created huge stress levels for him and that he should avoid you from hereon in as much as possible."

69

I commit the lesson to memory. And write my own caption:

> "Instead of nagging about spillage or inappropriate attention span, reinforce that you are only interested in his development and you love him unconditionally. Ask him to help you clean up the spill, kiss him on his head, and try to ruffle the centre part away making sure he does not notice you can't stand his first attempt at self-grooming."

See, I'm going to be great at this parenting stuff! I'll avoid near-parental disasters by acting indifferently toward broken porcelain in preference to nurturing and protecting our delicate and precious relationship.

The train lurches and so does my heart.

The train and I are one. And so is my heart. It's no longer divided in two!

I want this baby! It's taken me a few weeks to realise it but I do want her (or him). And I want the sleepless nights, the worries and anxiety, the responsibility heavier than the parenting books in my bag pulling at my shoulder. I can't wait to feel a whole hand wrapped around just one of my fingers, to witness the innocence of my child, her trust in me, and feel the joy of us being together. Of watching her grow. Or him.

My finger glides over a picture of a little girl smiling at me and I read the caption under the photo:

> "Toddlers are not yet able to lie or manipulate. Their emotional outbursts are evidence of an immature nervous system, of a little person who doesn't yet know how to control their emotions. Your job is simple: To teach them how."

Dr Naim had said it well. "Don't over-complicate it. Don't worry about tomorrow. All you have to do is direct, guide, and keep them safe. And if you're frustrated, take some time out even if it's just for a breath."

Which is what they say at my Byron Bay health spa too:

> " Oxygen will fill your lungs, fill your stomach. Breathe in the life-giving energy of fresh air and when you can't breathe in anymore, slowly let out the stale, old air from your body, expel all the toxins, until you start to breathe in again, feel the life-giving energy fill your stomach, keep breathing in ...

I walk to the bus stop which will take me home to Tamarama.

The Chinese say the 1000 mile march begins with one step, but perhaps learning to be a mother starts with one breath too, in then out, giving calming, life-giving, energy. I meditate on this as I wait for the bus and I make an affirmation:

> " This breath will give me time to think, to balance logic and emotion, to Google my question, to call my mother, to learn not to yell at the baby whom I will love with all my heart; and then on the out breath I can let go of all the anxiety and fear. Let go the old stale air and my expectations and be ready for the next challenge, whatever that may be."

And immediately, my bus home arrives.

Nicolita

My next challenge is to try to keep Nicolita on planet Earth.

Yesterday's shoot had been a disaster. When she'd finally shown up, she was so high they couldn't get her to stand, let alone wear clothes. Which is OK if you're a prostitute, but not if you're a fashion model.

The stylist had given up trying to contact me on my phone. So the shoot has rolled over to today and I am back on deck and in charge.

Today, Nicolita is sullen because I won't let her snort anything until her makeup is finished.

"Treat them with respect," Jaimee has always told me about working with models. "And if that doesn't work, treat them like children. In fact, that goes for everybody not just models. You'll get your primadonnas, and your sweet Miss Innocents — 'I want to do it my way because I know my nose looks too big if I let you photograph me from my left side' — to the 'I'm just happy to be working' girls. They're a treat, but they don't go very far."

Nicolita does not belong to the latter category. She is blonde and six-foot-three. She looks like the German supermodel Gisele Meichen on a good day and today, Frau Dracula.

She pouts at me.

"Five more minutes, Nicolita," I tell her while staring intently at her reflection in the mirror. The makeup has taken nearly an hour. Hair is done. Photographer is ready.

When the makeup artist finishes, Nicolita jumps up, clapping her hands like the spoiled birthday girl who has just been given a pony.

But this skinny, gorgeous girl does not want a pony.

"Blow, blow, blow," she cries bouncing up and down.

Her minder pulls a bag of coke out of her handbag and the hairdresser, a consummate professional, tells her, "God, *Nicole*. Can't you do that somewhere else?"

I know it's illegal and highly unprofessional to snort blow on set, but if we're going to get one shot of this girl without her pouting, I'm going to have to let her have it.

Nicolita follows me to the toilets while I, a woman with child, hold her hair back so she can snort cocaine off the makeup artist's mirror.

"I swear if I ever have a child that turns out like you, I will be pretty pissed off," I tell Nicolita wondering what the hell I can do to make sure that doesn't happen. Lock her in her bedroom until she's 40?

She throws her head back as the rush hits her.

"You know that shit is bad for you don't you, Nicolita?"

"Get out of my way, fat bitch," she says and pushes her six-foot-plus towering strength past me.

I hesitate. Because I don't know which of her insults I find more inappropriate. My anger quickly subsides and is replaced by pity. I step into the photographer's shot. "You know, *Nicole*, if you have to get high to feel confident enough to hit a pose, then you're pathetic." I walk out of the shot. I can tell my years at the Byron Bay health spa have taught me a lot about self-worth and confidence. I may not be a gorgeous six-foot model but I'm good at my job and I don't need cocaine to do it.

Then I stand back and watch.

For 15 minutes, Nicolita is fantastic. Watching the photographer direct her is a beautiful experience. I can tell the shots are going to be perfect. But fifteen minutes later, the high has passed, and Nicolita starts to pout again and loses her confidence. She even falls over when posing. She storms off the set.

I follow her to the toilet and tell her, "No more coke, *Nicole*" but she ignores me.

She cuts it up again, takes out her purpose-built cocaine pipe and snorts another hit. And then another.

I yell at her. I grab the rest of the coke and throw it into the toilet. The Bride of Frankenstein turns on me. And she's very, very scary.

"What the hell did you do that for, bitch?"

"You're such a cliché, *Nicole*. Just because you're a model doesn't mean you have to fall for this shit. You're throwing your talent away and you can't afford to do that because there are a million girls right behind you. You should be saving your money and starting a line of merchandise and capitalising on your good luck; but the way you're going, you won't even have enough money to pay for a stripper at your twenty-first birthday. You're pathetic."

Which is also what you don't tell a model whose cocaine you've just tossed into the toilet bowl.

She lunges for me but misses by miles (how the hell she missed my bulging body, I don't know) and grabs at my hair, attempting to pull me across the room.

The photographer who's been watching closely steps in and drags Nicolita off me before pinning her arms back behind her head.

Like the adult I now realise I am, I spit at her.

Then I turn around, pull out my phone and calmly call the agency requesting they send another model. I give their director a run-down of what has happened and she offers to cover all the shoot's costs. She tells me she'll have a look at the books, see who's available, and call me back.

I tell her, "I want the hottest, most expensive model you've got and I will wait a week for her if I have to. Any later and we'll miss the whole season. So I don't care, Abigail, if you have to double-book someone and fly her in from Timbuktu, she will work it and you will pay for it. And remember, I want the best or I'll spread this story all over town."

Abigail assures me she'll do what she can.

"I'll wait to hear from you," I tell her calmly before snapping my phone shut.

It's a victory. I mark the air with my finger. One for me, and one for baby.

Maybe this waiting business isn't so bad after all.

"I liked you better the other day," I tell the psych who's wearing his ordinary doctor clothes at our second appointment.

"Sorry to disappoint you," Dr Naim says. "But you seem calmer today, what's been going on?" he asks in a voice that seems to me to be bordering on the chagrin.

I shake it off. I've already decided that if the hospital's going to give me free psych sessions during this pregnancy, I may as well make the most of it. Even if I have to invent a few little friends just to keep the scam going. I like talking and I particularly like talking about what's happening to me.

I tell him that I have experienced a nirvana. And explain the whole Nicolita episode.

But instead of worshipping my growing maturity, he frowns at me. Which I hadn't expected and my heart plummets. I think I expected he would ask me intently for more details while hanging off every word I said, then deliver a series of high fives and back slaps before asking if I wanted to join his super-mature, grown-up, Sydney mothers' club.

I keep talking. "Because if she had shown up and was straight, I would have got great shots for the catalogue, but because she fucked up, I've now got Agnàs Dussau in the catalogue and all of the costs have been covered by the agency. My boss thinks I'm fantastic and I just got another month of paid parental leave out of her. And even though we're a week behind schedule, which is a lot when you're trying to get Summer ready by March, we're in a fantastic position. And so is my baby. I brought a photo, would you like to see?"

I thrust the baby's ultrasound picture at him. I've been carrying it with me and looking at it nonstop for the last week.

But he's still frowning at me and I haven't a clue why. I try to convince him. "So, my lesson is that I can't control everything, I just have to know when to intervene and be confident enough in my abilities to pick up the pieces."

"Hopefully, it won't be the baby in pieces," he says quietly.

"Of course," I tell him still feeling confused. "But I can't hover over my baby and not let her try to take her first step in case she falls. Because if I do that she will never walk, let alone run or climb Mt Everest."

"And what about Nicolita?" he asks. "What happens to her?"

"Are you saying we should have re-booked her? After we gave her two chances?"

"All I'm saying is that you work in a high-pressure industry. Perhaps Nicolita thinks that her behaviour is warranted; maybe she thinks that's how a supermodel is expected to behave?"

I'm bewildered. I honestly thought he'd be on my side about this. I cross my legs, and then decide he must be analysing my non-verbal actions too, so I uncross them. Then I cross them again, scared that I'm being too obvious about hiding my defensiveness. He stares at my legs, waiting to see what I'll do next.

"I'm not operating a supermodel development agency, Dr Naim. I'm trying to promote a clothing label in an already overcrowded market. I don't have time or money to waste on her illegal and immature behaviour," I tell him emphatically.

"Some might say your industry preys on the young."

I'm ready for this remark. I've heard it all before but it still shocks me that talented, educated people can treat you like a worthless dog just because you work in fashion and they save lives for a living.

"The fashion industry employs millions of people," I tell him. "Some of them have moved to the city to work in sweatshops because their land has been flooded for dams or repossessed for industrial expansion. They could be begging on the streets if it weren't for our little superfluous industry," I keep blasting him. "This way, instead of starving, they can save money which more often than not, they send home to their families. A lot of young people are in fact educated and fed by fashion."

He nods his head.

"I've got twenty women working at our label, and they all have mortgages or massive rents to pay, and they will be unromantically thrown out on the streets if they can't pay. Little Nicolita is paid very well to wear fashions designed by other people, to be shot by highly experienced photographers, and for her photos to be expertly positioned in the marketplace by people like me. She's just the plastic doll on top of this season's fruit cake. She needs to understand that."

Dr Naim says nothing.

"Little Nicolita has probably had it too easy. Her career is not my responsibility."

"No?"

"It's her agency's responsibility. We pay good money, the agency should be teaching her how to behave."

"They've taught her to behave the way the client wants her to. Some people may find her irresponsible behaviour exciting," he suggests.

"Her behaviour is annoying, frustrating, risky, and could have cost me a lot of money. Why the hell would anyone think that's exciting?"

"You helped her snort cocaine, an illegal substance, on set, off the makeup artist's mirror. You even held her hair back."

The muscles in my knees go weak. "Oh, yeah, right. I did do that, didn't I?"

"Would you do that for your daughter?" he says motioning toward my legs.

I re-cross them. "No way."

"Well, why would you do that for somebody else's?"

My answer is honest but stupid. "I thought she'd behave if I let her have it. I thought I'd get what I needed from her." I listen to myself and change my tact. "I thought I'd get what I'd paid her for."

Dr Naim plays with his tie. "Excuse me for repeating myself but I feel I must for clarity: you let an employee snort cocaine at work so that she wouldn't throw a tantrum."

"Basically."

"And again, would you treat your daughter that way?"

My eyes narrow. We both know he's backed me into a corner here. "Are we talking about a massive tantrum, Doc, like the one kids throw at the shops in front of a million people? Because if we're talking about one of those, I'd let my child snort cocaine off the toilet seat to stop her embarrassing me in the middle of *Coles*."

"No, you wouldn't."

"Yes, I would."

He sits silently, punishing me, until I relent.

"OK. I understand what you're saying," I concede.

But he doesn't start talking about me again — or my baby. He keeps talking about Nicolita. I feel betrayed. After all, this is supposed to be about me, and all we're doing is talking about some over-paid, stick creature who's probably out there right now, having a fabulously irresponsible time, not thinking about the sweatshops that sustain her, and coked out of her brain.

He continues. "It sounds like Nicolita wanted you to behave that way. She wanted you to chastise her and throw her stimulant in the toilet. She's out of control and she knows it."

"By showing up three sheets to the wind and calling me a fat bitch? Are you sure, Doc?"

He ignores my sarcasm. "She's desperate for somebody to give her boundaries. To tell her how to behave. By calling you a fat bitch, she was just testing you. She wants to know if you're in control, if you believe in your authority. You did the right thing dumping her coke in the toilet, but you should have asked for it the second you walked onto the set that morning. You should have told her friend to leave — since Nicolita is over the age of 18 she doesn't require a chaperone at work — and told Nicolita how you wanted the shoot to work. And then when she verballed you, you could have run through the consequences for her. She would have toed the line."

"I think she's beyond controlling her behaviour, Doc."

"Then if she hadn't agreed to your conditions, you should have called the agency immediately, and fired her from the set."

"I gave her a chance."

"You gave her permission to snort an illegal substance at work and you helped her to do it. You see, Matilda, fashion is entirely an experience of the eroticism of the voyeur. And even more so today, with fashion reproduced copiously on television and in print media. Mulvey first theorised about the role of men and women in fashion as the passive side of scopophilia, or voyeurism and exhibitionism.

Have you heard of her?"

I nod. Another lie. Of course I hadn't.

"I'm telling you this because it relates to children. Babies do not have consciousness, the ego still has to be constructed. Jacques Lacan calls the formation of ego the mirror phase. Then we get the Oedipus complex in which language plays a major role. Between six and eighteen months, when you hold your baby in your arms in front of a mirror, your baby will begin to see that you are separate beings. This is vital to the baby's own identity. Mirrors are not to be repelled as if they encourage vanity. They are crucial to our development."

He continues his diatribe. "But Nicolita acts like Narcissus looking at himself in the mirror. When she looks at herself in the mirror she identifies with the image of herself as the Other. She sees herself through Other's eyes. She is critical and overly critical because she is female and works in fashion. She is the model, and that's why they are called that; they are a symbol of perfection. It is an enormous responsibility."

My head falls into my hands. I'm starting to think I want a big bag of coke too.

He continues. "And you behaved just as she wanted. You were critical, which she was expecting. Although I know little of her, I'd assume she has critical parents. She believes she can never meet your approval or be good enough, hence her reliance on cocaine. For those few moments, she feels fantastic, she feels as if she is fulfilling her role and meeting your expectations."

"And when I criticised her, I fulfilled her expectations that she deserves to be criticised."

"And then she needs another hit. She's desperate for your approval. When she did well, did you tell her that?"

"No. The photographer usually directs the model."

"And was the photographer male?"

"Yes."

"The male voice is not the only important one. You have an opinion and you have power, she needs to hear it from you. In much the same way your baby will need to hear you tell it when it's doing the right thing. Don't criticise the bad all the time, sometimes ignoring bad behaviour is best and instead praise her for doing well."

"So I should have just let her keep snorting herself into oblivion?"

"No. You also did the right thing. Eventually the message will get through to her but she's an addict and that message could take months of rehab. What's her agency planning on doing about it?"

"Nothing, I guess. They'll just void her contract, there's always another wave of gorgeous, skinny young things just around the corner."

"That's right, the older, damaged ones, get cast aside."

I can't believe he's describing Nicolita, who is only 18, as damaged goods.

Our time is up.

"And what role should her parents play in this?" I ask him standing up.

"Why don't you read some books and get back to me with an answer. I'll see you in two weeks. And make sure you sign up for an antenatal class, keep focused on what's happening to you now."

I promise to heed his advice and book in to a class as soon as I get back to work.

Four Months

The fantastic news about reaching the four month mark is that your morning sickness should subside now and you may even start feeling more energetic. If you suffer with acute morning sickness, Hyperemesis Gravidarum, you may not be so lucky. You need to watch out for dehydration, malnutrition, and later, severe abdominal pain and confusion. If you fall into this category, you'll just have to tell your husband / partner / de facto / boyfriend / girlfriend that his (or her) blow jobs are going to have to wait. Yours, on the other hand, should continue frequently since this may help with your feeling of malaise.

Even if you're feeling fantastic, you should be conserving your energy and watching what you eat. If your partner has a problem with this, you can refer them to alternate, albeit professional, services. Really, that's no different to you going and getting your waxing done, is it?

If your partner still isn't convinced, you can tell him (or her) this old wives' tale: giving blow jobs can cause the umbilical cord to become knotted or wrapped around the foetus' neck; receiving them, causes the foetus to develop a high IQ, a love of classical music and high resistance to chemical substance abuse.

So, kick back, relax and enjoy your fourth month of pregnancy!

You owe me one (a favour, I mean).

You've got the glow

The news around town is that the girls at *Enegi* are all on *something*. Then people wriggle their bums and make a face like they're sucking on a really long tube.

Yes, the rest of Sydney thinks we're all doing Colonic Irrigation. If you haven't heard of CI (it's also called Colonic Hydrotherapy), it's a natural detox method that cleanses and hydrates your insides. Basically, they use a long hose to shoot water up your bum and flush you out. It's the botox of the 21st century, except it doesn't have nasty side effects or make you look like a Hollywood actress.

But not everybody's done it yet.

Which is why the hottest fashion editors in town have collectively asked me to lunch.

"You're all looking so fucking fantastic, you walk around like you're on cloud nine, your skin's luminous, your nails are long and natural, your hair's never looked better. C'mon Til, tell us where you go."

I look into one of the most elegant faces in Australian fashion and tell her, honestly — "Marrickville."

She mouths it back to me, winks, and jots it down in her Blackberry using a skinny pointer and some kind of code.

But they don't all buy it.

"Marrickville? Isn't that where your offices are? I didn't know anyone that great was operating out there. What's her name?" asks Madeline.

I try not to feel hurt. "I don't think you can pin it down to just one thing."

"I knew it," Marie-Cate, who sports ravishing black hair, tells me. "I told them it wasn't just the hose. You all look like you've had six months at a Tahitian spa. You're drinking Noni juice, aren't you?"

She's talking about the juice from the Noni tree which some supermodels swear by. But I shake my head.

"So, it's not the hose," says Cleopatra. "I knew it wasn't — I told them you were pregnant so you couldn't have it done."

"Yeah, but it's not just Til who looks great, all the *Enegi* girls look fantastic," MC (as she insists on being called) says emphatically.

"Well, Jaimee has put us all on a high-nutrient diet and we're exercising five times a week — I'm doing two sessions of Pilates, pre-natal yoga, and a couple of five-kilometre walks on sand each week," I say, very impressed with myself.

"Exercise? Is that it?" asks Elegance.

"Not quite," I tell them, before blushing, which I try to cover up by asking the waiter for more tofu sticks.

"Damn it, Til, stop beating around the bush and tell us. If you do, I'll spot you a piece of cake," Cleopatra bribes me.

I bite my lip. Cake doesn't fit into my high-nutrient diet, but I guess if I picked a low-fat cheesecake at least I could fill my protein and dairy quota for the day without filling the baby's tiny body with trans-fats. I'd have to go easy tomorrow though. "Alright," I tell them. "And while I feel totally comfortable telling you," I say to Cleopatra, "after all, you're so young and out there, I feel a little embarrassed telling her." I nod my head in the direction of Elegance. "She never talks about it in public."

MC and Madeline wave me down. "Don't be ridiculous, it's the 21st century, you can tell us anything."

"OK, well here goes," I start. "Well, you know when we were growing up and all the magazines talked about sex and how to give a really good blow job…?"

Three nod but Elegance shakes her head innocently.

"And I grew up thinking I had to be really good in the sack to land a guy. Well, it turns out I'm complete crap, which is probably why I'm having this baby on my own, but the girls at work, it seems, are really good at it. Not only are they all hooked up, but since Jaimee read that giving blow jobs can be a risk to the baby, and receiving them is good for him or her, well, she's insisted that we all…get them, on a regular basis."

They stare at me.

So I mouth it. "Blow jobs."

The waiter at *Georgio's* drops the tofu sticks. I look up at him, feeling a familiar sensation of dread. This is going to be all around Fashion Week by the time I get back to work.

At least the disgusting sucking motions will stop. And the tongue flicking can begin.

"You bitches!"

I turn to Cleopatra who's staring at me gobsmacked. "You're mad?" I ask her.

"God, no. I'm jealous as hell. It's hard enough finding a man in this town, but a man who'll go down on his chick six times a week? That's unheard of."

"Why six times?" Elegance asks quietly.

We all say it in unison, "Because Wednesday's wax night."

"Ouch," she says.

"But you're single. Are you getting it too?" Madeline asks me.

"I'm afraid not," I say. "This is just the pregnancy glow. Now that I'm four months, I feel really fantastic and for the first time in my life I can honestly say, I don't want a guy or need a guy, and as a result, I don't look desperate."

"I'm going to do something on this," MC says and the others shout her down.

"No way, I'm doing it, it's so much more my readership," Cleopatra says confidently, putting in the first call to her features editor.

Gracie, another editor who is impeccably styled and fashionably late to the industry, arrives at our table and takes a seat. She doesn't even notice me (although everybody in the bar turns to look at her, she's so ravishing). While the other editors fill her in on the goss, her sunglasses widen with surprise and she licks her lips.

With the other editors are engrossed in their chatter, Elegance and I share a tofu stick and I can't help but notice she has a faraway look in her eye.

I apologise and she brushes me off.

"Does this mean my ad discount still stands?" I ask her.

And she says, "Not bloody wrong, you girls rock. I don't suppose you've got any jobs going at *Enegi*?"

The other four editors laugh hysterically, falling over each other, slapping Elegance on the back.

I relinquish my seat and scuttle from the bar.

I guess I can't really tell these editors the truth, can I? These women are surrounded by products that claim all sorts of miracles, it must be hard for them to remember that sometimes the cheapest, safest and most natural glow, truly does comes from the inside.

And it's called happiness.

Five months

By now, every woman you meet is sure she knows the sex of your baby. Perfect strangers stop you on the street to comment on your spreading midsection. If they also feel a need to share their own birthing horror stories with you, simply silence them by telling them you're a Scientologist. Because the only thing worse than listening to the intricate details of other woman's labour stories is the various gender-prediction methods that other well-intentioned women will subject you to. In fact, you will feel more objectified than a size 14GGG model on the cover of *Playboy*. Your well-intentioned but malicious maternal friend achieves this by:

A. making you turn around and looking at your ass. This type of scrutiny is enough to make you scatty even after finishing an eight week watermelon diet, let alone when you're pregnant and stuffing your face 16 times a day;

B. looking at (and even fondling) your breasts to test for heaviness (a boy) or roundness (a girl);

C. touching your stomach which can be very confronting when all you're trying to do is pay for your groceries and suddenly you're set on from behind by a bunch of geriatrics hyped up from a morning at bingo, rubbing their germs all over you;

D. suspending a wedding ring (this is usually performed by married women to non-married women) on a string over your hand. If the ring swings in an oval or circular motion the baby will be a girl. If the ring swings from side to side it will be a boy. If the ring swings in a dollar-sign motion, the woman has perfected the art of showing off her $20,000 Tiffany's platinum wedding ring, and you can rest assured the activity is about her, not you.

E.   asking to look at your ultrasound pictures and trying to determine the baby's gender from the images. At least this method has scientific backing, but the idea of showing your baby's first photos to a practical stranger, who will then scrutinise the foetus' genitalia, just seems a little wrong.

And who cares? After all, the baby will be what it is — a screaming, sucking, bag of wind. You'll love your baby, no matter which gender it is. Which is why you want to wait until the baby's born to find out. Right?

Let me ruin it for you. By the time you give birth you will be so tired the doctor or midwife could tell you your baby was a leprechaun and you wouldn't care. Boy or girl? "Just take it away!" you'll scream at her.

But if you do want the baby's gender to remain a mystery until you are too comatose with exhaustion to care, then please, don't let me stop you.

Because by the fifth month, there are plenty of other things to focus on. Like what's happening to your baby.

By five months, your gorgeous little baby will measure between 18 and 23 centimetres and weigh nearly 500 grams. Those fabulous little ears that started to take shape just a few weeks after fertilisation are capable of hearing and recognising sounds now. Other exciting developments include eyebrows and head hair, and its skin, which is wrinkled, pinkish and translucent, is covered with a greasy white substance called vernix which helps make the baby more slippery and move through the birth canal (see, Mother Nature has done a lot to make the birthing process easier on you).

If you're having a boy, then his testicles will start to descend from the abdomen into the scrotum. And this is visible when you go for your second trimester ultrasound. So if you don't want to know, make sure you tell the radiographer so they can avoid that area.

You can talk about other things; like your baby's movements. If you're a first time Mum, then you will generally sense the baby's movements around the start of your fifth month, a whole month later than second and third-time Mums.

At first, it feels like a slight tickle, like a butterfly is caught inside of you. You may even think you've just got wind again, but soon enough those tickles will turn into noticeable nudges and then, when you feel a *My Little Pony*-type prod, you know it's not lunch, but your baby's way of saying hello. At first the baby will rejoice in flipping around the amniotic sac, performing somersaults and kicking you at all hours of the night, but by the eighth and ninth month, as its movement is restricted, you'll see a whole foot trying to push out of your belly. It's exciting at first — until your internal organs are pushed up into your ribs and the baby still wants more room and starts kicking on your bladder. You can prepare for this by starting to make detailed maps of your city and the location of every public toilet now!

But the baby's not the only thing on the move at this stage — so is your placenta. If the placenta is still low in your uterus, there is a good chance it will move up before you give birth. But if it does cover the mouth of the cervix, this is called placenta praevia and it makes vaginal delivery impossible; you'll be booked in for a Caesarean.

Maybe you're jumping for joy about this, or maybe you're not so thrilled about being denied the 'right to push'. Either way, I'm not going to be righteous about the benefits of vaginal deliveries (a faster recovery time is usually considered its biggest advantage) or say you're *too posh to push* if you chose a Caesarean (which involves major abdominal surgery). After all it's your body. And I'm not going to judge you.

Because seriously, there are more important things to be worried about.

Like, what you will wear tomorrow? By now, there is no hiding from anybody that you're pregnant. You can't even fit into your regular clothes anymore — and worse, your shoes may not fit you either. Some pregnant women's feet swell a little due to pregnancy fluids and even a loosening of the joints which make your feet spread out more than usual, and that's all. But after you've reached the fifth month and you present with swelling and your blood pressure rises to more than 140/90 or more, you may be diagnosed with preeclampsia.

Which is pretty serious. And worthy of discussion.

Mild preeclampsia shows with swelling of the face and hands with sudden excessive weight gain and protein in the urine. Left alone, this can develop into severe preeclampsia, which is accompanied by a further increase in blood pressure, blurred vision, fever, headaches, low urine output and severe pain in the upper abdomen. Preeclampsia is usually treated by delivering the foetus. There are medications you can take, but the ultimate cure is delivery. If you're not ready to deliver the baby, it's very likely that you'll be hospitalised for the rest of the pregnancy.

It's not the only serious condition that can develop during pregnancy, but it does show you that eating a proper diet, getting plenty of rest, keeping your stress levels low, and attending all of your medical appointments are incredibly important.

Hopefully, mild swelling of the feet is the only nasty side effect you will experience throughout your pregnancy.

Tell your feet that.

If you can still see them, that is.

If you suspect that you still have feet, please book in for a pedicure now and buy some better-fitting, flat shoes now. I'm sorry to say this *Jimmy*, but you will have to go back into the closet for a few more months. But when we can wear you again, rest assured, our love for you will have manifested ten times because of time spent apart.

What (not) to wear

Just when I think I'm really growing (cognitively), I fall apart.

Out of sheer desperation, I call Lola and tell her about my plight.

"Hmmmn," she says and starts muttering in French. "No, I am not talking to you," is all I can translate.

"Do you want me to call back later?"

"*Non*, not you *cherie*, I was talking to my husband. *Maintenant*, about you, I don't know what you should wear, isn't that what you do, tell people what to wear? Am I your parent, no?"

I wonder at how she manages to derail both John and me in a couple of sentences. I remind myself that Lola really is very smart, and that I shouldn't call her about these things in future.

I retaliate. "No, I don't tell people, I persuade people. There is a difference because they have a choice."

"Then choose, *ma cherie*, get out your little black book of capitalistic neuroses, throw it up in the air, and see which mainstream cliché it lands open at. Maybe you will get lucky and you can dress up like a *Playboy Bunny*. Or you could shock everybody and go naked."

"No, it's OK, I think that might be going a little too far for Fashion Week."

"Til, pregnant women are so in right now."

"Yes, if you're a movie star and can afford *Armani* to make your couture gowns for you."

"Now, you are thinking like a victim. You are beautiful, even if you are a little bit bigger than you used to be, it's because you're having a baby, Matilda. Women do it all the time and they look lovely. It's a perfectly natural function and you cannot preserve a whole species of animal without one of the sexes putting on a few pounds around the middle. It is not, how we say, the ends of the earth." Lola wraps up our conversation by wishing me luck and telling me, in French, to keep her up to date. She has a show in Paris to organise so will be gone for a few months, but will hopefully be back in time for the birth.

But our conversation does little to assuage my growing anxiety about my physical proportions. I have never weighed this much in my life!

When my anxiety escalates to a full-on public panic attack, a security guard babysits me while I breathe into a brown paper bag — mind you, the brown paper bag he offers me is rumpled, stained and judging by the stench coming off him I can only assume he's used the bag to carry the day's liquor supply. Nor has he washed in a really long time.

He rifles through my bag and finds my phone. Soon, Adam is rushing across town from Chatswood to Wynyard station.

I've never been very good in underground places. I've never even liked underground clubs and have avoided them at all costs, even back in uni when grunge was *de rigueur*. It was the lowest point in my life. Almost as bad as this.

"Because when Jaimee called and said all of the shoes for our Fashion Week parade had fallen into Sydney Harbour and I had to replace 30 pairs in 30 minutes and get them to the Opera House — I panicked," I tell Adam who arrives sweating and dishevelled at the platform, relieving the security guard of his babysitting duties.

"Why didn't she get someone in design to do it?" Adam asks me.

"You know me, I panic the most, I get things done."

"But you're not getting it done, you're here having a panic attack."

I breathe into the brown paper bag and shake my head. "No, I got it done, I'm on my way to my ultrasound."

"And you didn't call me? God, I could have raced around getting the shoes for you, you shouldn't be getting this stressed out."

Disapprovingly, Adam picks up my handbag and thanks the security guard for watching over me. We traipse out of the station and find a bus that will take us to the hospital.

A half hour later we're walk along John Hopkins Drive to the

Royal Prince Alfred Hospital ultrasound clinic.

"You really should be wearing flat shoes by now, Til. The stress on your back from those heels must be terrible."

"The one thing I don't like about being pregnant is how everyone keeps telling me what I should or shouldn't be doing. The only person who doesn't is Lola. She told me I should go naked to Fashion Week."

"You asked Lola what to wear?"

"I did. Why? Is that bad?" I ask him confused. Usually he's such a fan of Lola's.

"Lola is not the person to go to for fashion advice. My God, didn't you hear about what happened on the flight to Paris?"

I shake my head and slow our walk down so I can breathe without huffing like a galloping horse.

"She wore a shirt onto the plane which had 'terrorist' written across it in bright red paint. She wore a jacket so nobody saw it until they were a couple of hours into the flight. It caused quite a stir apparently. Singapore wouldn't let the plane land and some of the passengers tied Lola and John to their chairs until they landed. They even had their luggage confiscated and were interrogated at Singapore airport. Considering the history of Singapore, that is not the place to piss off the customs officials."

"Why the hell would you wear a terrorist t-shirt on a plane?" I ask incredulously.

"I don't know, I guess to cause a ruckus. You know what Lola's like — I bet she secretly videoed the whole thing."

"But how does that fit into the defecating theme?"

He shakes his head and pushes the door of the ultrasound clinic open. I check in at the desk and we claim the last two available seats.

"So are you going to find out?"

I ignore the question.

But he persists.

And even though I love Adam, I selfishly want to be the only person to see the baby before it's born. Don't get me wrong, I love showing a picture of the baby to everybody I meet, but to see the baby on the screen, breathing and bumping around inside of me, is so intimate that I don't know what I'm going to say to Adam.

Because today is the day I'm going to find out if I'm having a boy or girl. I need a few months with my baby where I'm the only person in the world who knows his or her gender. It'll be our little secret. Something just between me and her/him.

But Adam has already guessed I would prefer to do this on my own and leans over me, pushing into my bladder, to tell me that he won't be going inside with me…unless of course I really, really want him there.

I squirm uncomfortably, holding on to my full bladder.

The radiographer calls my name.

Hoping to assuage Adam's curiosity and my guilt, I ask him to wait for me so I can show him the photos.

He watches me pick myself out of the chair, my legs wide apart already, which is not flattering considering I'm wearing three inch heels and a dress cut up to my thigh. And he waits until everyone is watching me waddle over to the midwife before he calls out, "Subway slut — I know you did it with that security guard today!"

The crowd of mothers-to-be, in their gentle pullovers with pink ribbons tied over their bellies, stare at me.

The radiographer, who's seen and heard a lot in her time, ignores him.

Instead she looks at my exposed thigh.

Suddenly, I realise the dangerous territory *Enegi's* designers have taken us into this year. While the burlesque theme looks amazing on the hyper-skinny, perfectly made-up models, it makes me look like a Kings Cross callgirl. And I won't be the only one.

I fume. I turn around and give Adam the forks.

"You can't stay mad at me for long!" he calls as I follow the radiographer into the ultrasound room.

And he's right. Five minutes later, I'm beaming.

Six months

By six months, the foetus is a whopping 30 centimetres long and weighs approximately a kilo. Which means congratulations are in order. If your baby is born now, with the intervention of intensive care, he or she will have a slight chance of survival. The odds aren't great, but it is possible. Of course, the longer your baby stays in the womb, the better it is for him or her, but the relief some women feel at getting to this stage is enormous.

Because the weight of the responsibility of becoming a mother (for the first time or sixth) can weigh very heavily on some women. And some women feel like an emotional wreck one minute, joyful and tearful the next. Some read every book they can lay their hands on, others talk to their friends, mothers and sisters about their experiences, and others just walk around town like they're on valium.

Suddenly, you see Mums everywhere. In fact, you may realise that half the women you work with are Mums. Those dark circles under their eyes aren't from partying but from being up half the night with their children. And those pictures on their desks aren't their favourite features by *Shop 4 Kids*, those models aren't even models at all — but their families.

And that's what you're going to have soon too — a family.

And a pram.

The ugliest device ever invented, the pram is a requisite feature of every family. The pram has recently been discovered by urban design gurus and has been redesigned for the 21st century. They fold, the wheels come off, some have even been named after 4WDs, but one thing's for certain: no matter how much your pram costs, it doesn't know how to change a nappy.

A curious feature of the modern pram is that everywhere the family goes, the pram goes too. It's like an uncle or second aunt on your mother's cousin's side, but this pram won't fiddle with the kids.

You stop looking at pregnant women walking past you and start looking at every mother pushing a pram. And you think one of two things:

A.   I can't wait to be a Mum and push my little baby around like that, oh how cute; or,

B.   my God, how ugly. I'll never push a pram. The bloody baby can walk.

You picked A. right? Liar.

While your baby's eyes are capable of opening and closing now, it's about time you kept yours open. Instead of burying your head in a pregnancy book, take a look around you: watch how pregnant women walk around the park while doing their lunch hour exercise program, how they sway when nobody offers them a seat on a train home, at the hormonal pigmentation appearing across their faces. Then let your imagination loose, because in a few months these women will become mothers.

Which category of mother will they fit into? And more importantly, which one are you?

The harassed, anxious mother:

This mother tries to finish every task as if:

A.   she's getting paid for it (which she isn't. In fact, she's not even getting any superannuation contributions, which in part is another reason why most women end up retiring with much less money than most men);

B.   everyone is watching and judging her (which they probably are);

C.   her children are her life and their development and happiness is paramount; she runs a tight ship and everybody on board plays a part — sometimes as Cinderella, a fairy, a pirate, a ballerina, a truck driver. She cleans the house and fits in a myriad of age-appropriate activities such as learning to swim, to read, to eat, how to be a good friend, put his/her dishes in the sink, and make a bed all while smiling but feeling inwardly exhausted yet incredibly satisfied.

The calm, happy mother:

This is the mother we all want to be, she:

A.   lets the kid mash Play-Doh into the carpet and bed linen;

B.   lets the kids put themselves to bed for their morning nap (and they actually go to sleep while singing how much they love her);

C.   has a cup of tea, ignores the housework and the dirt on the kids' clothes;

D.   is happy, energised and her chakras balance;

E.   knows all the words to every nursery rhyme ever written because she understands how the human brain works and the link between music, rhythm and language development;

F.   is a human myth, a fairytale, an enigma.

The energetic, frantic mother:

On a good day she reminds you of Superwoman, on a bad day, the Joker; this mother:

A.   organises all the playgroups and selects the children alphabetically so as to not exclude any child;

B.   bakes wonderfully organic food but likes a Scotch or two before lunch;
C.   walks the kids to school and then goes to the gym where she spends her entire workout flirting with Jean-Paul, her personal trainer;
D.   works from home, orders everything over the internet, including the Daddy.

The ignorant mother:
Can be any age, and belong to any religion or socio-economic group. She:

A.   yells at the midwives and paces the hospital yelling for the doctor;
B.   works flat-out as if she is not pregnant despite all the warnings, kind of like a truck-driver who insists of driving a dangerous load of toxic chemicals while on acid himself;
C.   acts as if she is the first woman who has ever been pregnant;
D.   thinks that after the birth of the baby, she will never get anything done again, that this is the end of the road for her career rather than accepting that motherhood is just another life experience more similar to a winding path through a daisy-filled park than an empty car park.

The psychotic:
Most mothers behave like this on occasion, out of sheer desperation and lack of sleep. Normally about five times a week. She thinks about these things often:

A.   I could poison a child's lunch with mild diuretics so he will have to stay home and then my child can take his place at Kindy tomorrow;
B.   I can spend $100 on a child's haircut;

C.   I will have the child christened when the circus comes to town, and I'll bribe the trainer to instruct the elephants to spurt water instead;

D.   I'll do it all just to piss off my own mother.

The organic, earth mother:

Can't understand why most mothers hate her. After all, this is what she thinks about:

A.   I could become a teacher, but perhaps I should be focusing on the environment?

B.   don't these people realise they could be walking their kids to school, surely they can't all be in a rush?

C.   damn, this sling is really digging into my shoulder. I know it looks great, but I wish I had a fucking pram.

My other pram's a *Porsche*

"Just when did prams become an accessory?" I ask Nadia who has kindly joined the search for my latest status symbol. Now that I've started working part-time from home, in accordance with *Enegi's* new parental leave policy, my shopping days have increased exponentially.

"About the same time as Posh got her implants," she answers.

"Really? The pram obsession must be older than that."

"Why do you think woman invented the wheel, Til? They were sick of pushing the pram around on square blocks. After the wheel, prams were *de rigueur.*"

"Does *Armani* do prams?"

"I don't think so. *Armani* Mums have nannies for that. They wouldn't be seen dead pushing a pram."

"True," I say realising I am starting to take this seriously. "I did some research. At the top of any good contemporary, Sydney Mum-to-be list is the *Bugaroo*, but I don't really want to spend $1500 on a pram. I didn't even spend that much on my first leather jacket." I finger the pram fabric in my hand. "It's a nice design, but I'm not sure about the green."

"The green's awful. OK, *Bugaroo* is rejected on account of the designers including green in the swatch. Maybe they were going for the Greenies."

"Oh no," interrupts the sales assistant who is standing behind the counter. "Greenies carry their children in slings, they wouldn't push their babies in such a passive and disconnected device as a pram."

We turn and thank her.

"So, we won't be getting a sling then," Nadia says.

"She's kidding," I tell the sales assistant, whose name is Julia and looks very helpful.

"Yes, I am kidding," Nadia adds. "I do love the Greens, about as much as I love not wearing my fur coat when it's fucking freezing in Milan."

"You don't even have a fur coat, Nadia, so you can stop behaving like a child, please," I tell her.

The sales assistant ignores me. She's already figured out that Nadia makes all my purchasing decisions. "There's the *Jeep* and the *Phil & Ted* is popular although we don't stock it," Julia helps. "The *Mountain Buggy* comes from New Zealand and is used by urban professionals, but if you work in fashion, which it looks like you do, then you'll have to get the *Bugaroo*. It really is an excellent pram, and only useful for walking around on city streets. I take it you don't hike or connect with the natural environment in any way?"

"Of course not," Nadia confirms and I see her shudder at the thought.

This type of hilarity reminds me to put Nadia at the top of my Christmas card list.

She continues. "It'll have to be the *Bugaroo* then."

I turn to Julia. "OK, I'll take one," I tell her. "But not in green. Pick something else."

"Excellent. Would you like a foot warmer?"

"No."

"A rain shield?"

"No."

"An authentic *Bugaroo* comforter?"

"No, just a pram with round wheels please."

"Ok. That'll be $1899 and are you happy to accept delivery in three months?"

"I thought it was $1500?"

"That's the sale price on the green."

I groan.

"She'll take the green," Nadia decides.

"Excellent," Julia says. "Well, there's no wait on those, you can have one today."

I tell Nadia that I'm not sure but she cuts me off. "$1500 is a good price and besides, Adam wants to practice."

It occurs to me as we push the green pram from the store that Adam and Nadia talk more to each other these days than I talk to everybody else around me. I think they have mine and the baby's whole lives planned out. Nadia even signed up for life insurance on my behalf. "In case you cark it during labour," she told me later when the documents arrived.

"So how does it feel?" she asks me gesturing toward the pram.

"It's kind of weird pushing a pram without a baby in it, like I'm some kind of baby-obsessed freak," I tell her as we stroll out of the store.

"There's one more thing we need to do," Nadia tells me.

"I hope it has something to do with food, I'm starving."

"And that's — take you to the Parent Room."

"What's that?"

"Lordy, lord," Nadia exclaims summoning for help.

She leads me towards the public toilets but instead of entering the women's we sail right past and walk through an automatic door with a picture of a baby on it. "I always wondered what that sign meant," I tell her referring to the baby blob image as the inner workings of the Parent Room unfold before my eyes.

Mothers are rushing around looking absolutely exhausted, trying to carry masses of ugly bags and children. Some Mums are seated because they have — yes, that is a baby, attached to their breast. My nipples shudder. Others are changing babies' nappies on tables. Some women are hiding behind curtains and I only know they're there because I can see their feet. No *Jimmy Choos* anywhere, I note disappointed.

I ask Nadia, "What can they possibly be doing in there that requires a curtain — it's not like they're doing cocaine, is it?"

She shakes her head.

A couple of men are sitting in the Parent Room domain too but they're trying to do anything but look at the women breastfeeding which means they spend all their time looking at who's coming through the sliding doors.

Time stands still. Even the sliding doors have stopped to gawk at me — no, not at me, at my pram! Some smile politely, some snicker, one mother even snaps a curtain closed after complaining that she's going to puke at the green.

Nadia walks me through the Parent Room. "When you need to change the baby's nappy or feed, you come here."

"Why can't I just do that outside?"

"No one quite knows the answer to that," she tells me bemused. "It's kind of like an unwritten social law although I guess there is some logic to it. They don't want you feeding a baby in the toilets because that would be unhygienic."

"But there're toilets in those cubicles over there."

"I know, but they don't count. They're germ free although you should wash your hands after using them."

"Why can't I just breastfeed on the run, while I'm shopping or getting lunch?"

"And push a pram at the same time? Only if you're a supermum."

"I see."

"So this is where society wants you to go. You come here and do your business and make sure you only go *out there* to get from home to the shops — and vice versa. If you do that, everything will be OK. So, in summary: don't take the baby to work, people will hate you mainly because they're not allowed to; don't take the baby to restaurants, bars, or Fashion Week because Jaimee will certainly kill you; and whatever you do, do not take the baby anywhere near your mother because she will certainly kill you with stories of what a bad mother you are."

"So I just stay here?"

"Precisely. Until the child can shit on its own and then you're allowed back out there."

She points towards the sliding doors again.

"Thanks Nadia. I don't know what I'd do without you."

"That's alright."

We leave through the effortlessly quiet sliding doors again but this time we have to press a buzzer to get out.

"That's to make sure you haven't left the baby behind," she says.

We push the empty pram back into the busy traffic of the shopping centre and as the brands and logos wash past me in a blur, I contemplate how Nadia knows all of this stuff — about babies and prams and social order. And why am I so clueless?

Finally, I ask her, "Nadia, do you have a baby?"

And she says, "Don't be stupid, Til, I have two."

At home I ask Adam about Nadia's babies.

Adam sits me down. He can see that I am not only confused but scared.

"Til, Nadia is 45 although she doesn't look it. She has two children, although they're quite grown up now. Bethany and Tom, ring any bells now?"

I nod.

"Bethany is 21 and works at Nadia's studio as an assistant, she has a lot of piercings and tattoos and kind of scares you. You went to Bethany's 21st birthday party last year. It was at some pub near Sydney Uni. You had to drink yourself into a stupor to deal with the décor. And Tom, he's your typical 16 year old, cramming all the time for exams and bonking his brains out every weekend. You don't see him much because he's either at school, the beach, hanging out with his friends, or at his Dad's. He has a life."

"But they don't call her Mum."

"No, they call her Nadia because that's her name and you too can elect for your child to call you by your first name and not *Mum* if you so wish."

"Nadia is so cool."

"Yes she is, and a rather good Mum too. You should listen to her."

"I can't believe I had no idea," I tell him still feeling like an idiot. "I've seen her with them, with Bethany and Tom, but they seemed more like friends, I never realised they were her children. She doesn't even talk to them as if they're kids; she treats them with respect — as if they're human beings."

"Well, they are human beings, Til."

He watches me carefully, in case my brain implodes. And then he reiterates for me, "Babies are human beings, Til. You don't have to treat your child like an idiot. You can follow Nadia's example and help your child develop into an individual with their own thoughts and ideas."

"Why didn't Nadia tell me? I've never even asked her how her kids are. Doesn't that seem wrong to you?"

"You're self-absorbed, Nadia knows that."

"I'm an idiot," I tell him self-deprecatingly, but feeling sure I deserve it.

"Yes," he responds. "And hopefully Nadia will give you a lot of advice along the way because she has raised her children particularly well. They're individuals, they're empathetic and they have direction."

"God, I can never see her again, Adam. I'm so embarrassed. I had to ask her today if she had kids."

"It's OK, Til, because you're not a parent. You live on a different planet to people with kids."

"But I am a parent, Adam. I have a baby inside me and I'm an absolute idiot. For Christ's sake, I bought a green pram today."

"I can see that," he says looking at the hideous monster taking up most of our lounge room. "Nadia thought that was quite funny too by the way. She said she's going to take it back for you. She even took a photo on her phone, for posterity."

But I'm not feeling very hopeful. I'm feeling rather stupid. I can't even remember how to fold the bloody thing.

Which is when it hits me.

I'm never going to be ready to be an adult before my baby comes out — let alone a parent.

Seven months

Welcome to the third trimester. What started as a car crash now looks more like an asteroid hurtling through space. And while the asteroid tail illuminates the sky at night, keeping you up until all hours with its fantastic show, we all know this comet's bound for planet Earth and its impact zone is going to be a lot bigger than your fanny.

Because your baby's head is getting bigger...and bigger. And while the prolactin keeps pumping through your body, preparing you for the task of stretching to make way for your baby through the birth canal, you worry about how well your fanny will cope with the baby's rapid brain growth.

As you walk through the fruit and veggie aisle at your local grocery store, you pick out fruits that look about the same size as your baby's head: a peach, you could manage, but a rockmelon? What the hell! But don't worry, your cervix will dilate to ten centimetres, approximately the width of a small grapefruit. You handle the ridiculously large rockmelon in one hand and the grapefruit in the other...even to your untrained eye, it still doesn't look probable.

You end up buying one of each, determined to do the experiment at home, where nobody can see you.

You start obsessing about the labour. When will it start? How will it progress? Maybe you'll get lucky and it'll all be over in an hour, or maybe you'll go to the toilet one day and find the baby sitting magically on the floor. Everyone will applaud your bravery and swift birthing skills and from here on in, you'll be known as the Baby Fairy.

In your deluded hormonal state, you start telling yourself

you don't need a stork, or Mother Nature, or a hospital full of trained midwives. You're going to be one of the lucky ones; the ones who give birth without even breaking a sweat.

Of course, to have a baby your waters (membranes) have to break. Sometimes they break early, sometimes they break as late as delivery. But at least this gives you something new to obsess about. You start writing a new list:

The worst places in the world where my waters could break:

A. at my boyfriend's parents' house on their really expensive sofa that they shipped in from Milan;
B. at work, in front of my boss;
C. they won't break and the midwife will have to pull out a really long crochet hook and stick it up my hoo-haa.

In your dreams, you're followed by little old women who crochet booties constantly. And they tell you that they're not old, they're only 24 but have had two kids, that's why they look about 104 years old.

You start feeling breathless. Not only because blue-haired women are haunting you but because the baby is restricting your lungs and pushing your vital internal organs up into your chest. You feel every gram of the 1.3 kilograms of the baby's weight. And then there's the placenta, which will be relinquished by your body after the baby is born (during the third stage of labour) and weighs around 750 grams. Plus, the amniotic fluids and extra breast tissue. All up, an extra five kilos is hanging off your stomach, but it feels like five hundred.

Relax.

You're not alone. Billions of women have been through pregnancy and childbirth before. And most of those didn't have access to excellent medical care and pain relief.

So take it easy. Two months may seem like a short amount of time, but when you're carrying a watermelon around, two months may seem...indeterminately long. Some days will be very difficult — you may get haemorrhoids and won't be able to use any creams (but a high fibre diet and plenty of fluids will help). You may get varicose veins, headaches, feel faint and exhausted — but remember, being pregnant is a temporary state: this will end, and then no matter how much you want to, you'll never be able to fit the little critter back in there.

Rub your belly as much as you can. Put your feet up. Feel pregnant, look pregnant, get people to fetch things for you and buy things for you. Get the nursery ready, start planning disciplinary strategies and where you will hide the broccoli.

And start thinking about whether you want to eat the placenta. It's highly nutritional and a lot cheaper than multivitamins. In some cultures, it's even considered a delicacy.

See, I've taken your mind off the size of the baby's head!

Enter Louise

Looking in the mirror, I realise I have reached a new level of swelling.

Nadia agrees.

"My God," she says when she arrives to take me nursery furniture shopping. "I think they'll admit you into the *Guinness Book of World Records* for swollen feet."

I pull up my skirt to show her the rest of my legs and she backs away in shock giving her best trannie-like impersonation. She grabs at Adam for safety. "They say you will live if you stay close to the ground," she shrieks dropping to the floor where Adam joins her to yell, "That only works in a fire, not when you are running from a hormonal yak!"

They attempt to run from the monster, bouncing off the horrible monster's enormous belly, and hiding in cupboards until they realise *It* can still see their feet.

I make them margaritas and start to guzzle one.

Adam leaps to the baby's defence and drags it from my hand. "I think you should just stay home and get some rest, Til," he says with real sympathy at last.

"Yeah, put those horrendous feet up, puh-lease" Nadia interjects.

Adam tut-tuts at her as if she has finally gone too far.

"I could just order over the net," I suggest.

"Yes, lets," Nadia agrees clapping.

The three of us take pride of place in front of Adam's laptop and Nadia and I admire the photos of Dean which flash up but cringe at the lovey-dovey message which bursts across the screen like fireworks.

"Very nice, but how about we go straight to those baby sites, hey?" Nadia suggests taking over the mouse but not before I start thinking that Adam should really be this baby's mother.

And because Nadia says, "Here we go, some horrible blue and pink baby sites at last," I'm pretty confident she knows what I'm thinking, "At least Dean loves Adam and the baby should have two loving parents who can take care of it."

In my head, she tells me to shut up and start looking at cots.

We spend the next hour bumbling through thousands of consumable goods I'm quite sure the baby will never need while Adam writes a wish list, leaving me with nothing else to do but choose between a handcrafted $4000 highchair and the ever-growing desperate need to get high.

And then we see it. We lean closer to the laptop screen.

"A two day sale at Bondi's only baby shop."

"I didn't think people in Bondi had babies," Adam utters what we are all thinking. "I know people bring babies to Bondi but somehow they never quite belong — they think they're being cool but really their super-cool days left them far behind when they decided to copulate and produce something you can't legally take into a bar."

Nadia reminds him that I am having a baby.

"Oh yeah, shit, sorry, Til," he says.

I retaliate by mentioning the little stash he nearly got caught with when entering a bar the other week.

"That doesn't count," he says. "That was Paddington and besides, I was still high when the police frisked me and Dean got some really good photos of it. I'm quite a legend around town, you know."

I hate him sometimes. He is the Australian male version of Lola which means everything he touches turns to gay gold. I return to my thoughts about making him the baby's mother.

"OK, let's go," Nadia says shutting the laptop screen without logging off, sparing us another view of Dean's white smile and gorgeous ass.

Adam drops Nadia and me off in front of *Bondi Babies* and waves cheerily at us while the pregnant women queuing outside the store check me out.

I know they're doing it because I do it too. *The Pregnant Woman's Comparative Test* is something new to me but it can keep me amused for hours. See that pregnant woman standing over there with that blissful, serene look on her face? This is what's really going through her head, "Is her bump bigger than mine? Gee, I wish I could have a donut. Why the hell does she look like she's still glowing, while I just look red-faced and retarded? Where did I leave my feet? Damn, she got a *Bugaroo*, I'd better get one too."

Nadia bribes the door bitch (since when did small stores hire security?) with a pair of her latest *Jimmy Choos*, and the queue of women burn holes in my back as we walk into the shop ahead of them.

"My God, did you see her ass? What about her feet? Have you ever seen such a bump? I reckon she's three months overdue already," I hear them bitch about me before they turn their attention to the next poor woman, a startled gazelle who looks so frightened by the queue of rampaging hormonal woman that she doesn't get out of the car without her husband's urging — or prodding, to be more precise.

Nadia drags me over to the furniture section. "Now, please tell this lady what the baby will need," she tells the sales assistant. "And can you give her another 50 percent off?"

The woman gives us her "I'd love to help you but I'm with a really nice customer now and I'll get to you in about, ooh, a hundred years" smile.

I consult Adam's list and tally it up. Even on sale, the list amounts to $14,000. I tell Nadia that I'm giving up. "Jesus, whoever said that all babies need is love just hasn't heard of 21st century consumerism. I mean, really, do I need those things that wipe the poo off the baby's ass or can I just wash it off in the tub like my mother did? But wait, the new fangled baby bath, which is really just a bucket, costs $100 too. Do these baby wankers think I'm nuts or what?"

A few pregnant women edge closer to me so they can hear me flip out. Their bellies touch and embarrassed they scatter. Except for one who emerges from the cantankerous mix of hormonal blobs like a skinny, smiling angel. I'm just about to tell her to fuck off when I realise this is my worst nightmare come true.

"Matilda?" she asks.

"Til, yes."

"I thought it was you, oh my God, you're huge!"

Louise Unger, whose date I stole for the high school formal, is staring at my feet in a way that makes me feel more like a freak than when I turned up to school with a new punk hairstyle gone wrong.

Nadia looks on amused.

She's right though. I am huge. "Well, it was nice to see you," I say and try to move out of Louise's path.

"No, wait, when are you due?"

"Anytime now," I lie, hating it when people ask me this. I make a mental note to never ask anyone this question again. As well as an assortment of other queries that translate as a personal attack, including:

Q.   So, do you know what you're having?

A.   Oh, I'm not having a baby; I'm doing a survey on how stupid the rest of the population is.

Or,

Q.   How are you feeling?

A.   Like ten margaritas wouldn't even come close to making me feel better.

And my favourite:

Q.   Gee, I bet you can't wait for this whole hideous experience to be over right? Well, just wait til childbirth…

A.   To which I respond with high-pitched laughter, backslapping and nervous stomach rubbing.

Nadia prods me. "In two months — she's due in two months."

Louise turns to Nadia and introduces herself as Louise De Menton. "And, you're…?" Louise asks her trailing off.

"Nadia Malcovich, Til's lesbian lover, yes," Nadia switches into her best Russian accent and Louise drops her hand which she's been shaking for too long now to be considered sincere.

I grimace.

"Well, the baby will have two mothers, that's great," Louise says trying to be nice. "I'm a step-Mum too so I know what you'll be going through — except that one of you isn't the hideous ex whose head you want to tear off with a blunt, infected knife on most days."

I can tell Nadia is immediately interested. "Oh, what do you mean?"

"I shouldn't moan, I love being a step-Mum and I'm a Mum too, but my husband's ex just has the total opposite parenting ethos to us and it creates problems. But enough of me, I can't believe you're going to be a parent, Til, you just never seemed the type!"

"Well we just accidentally walked into a sperm bank and what do you know, here we are," Nadia teases.

"And you didn't want to carry the baby?" she asks Nadia.

"What and look like that? I don't think so."

They both laugh.

"Look, it was really nice to see you again, Louise," I say butting in, "but Nadia is my friend. She's just trying to ridicule me by telling you all this. The truth is, I got knocked up by some guy I'd just met and my birth partner is going to be my gay flatmate while his boyfriend looks on via a wirelessly connected webcam. We hope. Is that enough, or would you like my parenting plan too?"

Louise's face drops.

"Oh, Til, I'm sorry I didn't mean to intrude, it's just really nice to see you. I always liked you and admired you and was quite jealous of you to be honest. I knew you'd have a great career, but you always thought I was stupid and pointless and would end up getting married and pregnant at 25 which is pretty much what I did. But I'm happy, even though we have our challenges."

And like Mother Theresa, she walks off.

"Which happens when you marry someone three times your age," I mutter at Nadia, suddenly feeling ashamed of myself.

"She's really nice, I can't believe you made her feel so bad about herself," Nadia whips at me.

I silently punish Nadia by sending an eagle to claw out her eyes.

Louise comes back, which even I have to admit is pretty brave of her.

"Look Til, this is my store and I'd be happy to give you another

25% discount on anything you want, and I'll get it delivered too, but don't go overboard hey? Most of this shit you don't really need. Or you can come over to my place and pick out what you want from my garage. My babies are all big now and I've packed up all their things, but I'd rather give it all to someone I know than sell them second hand. So it's up to you, here's my address and phone number, just give me a call before you come, OK?" She walks off and a million pregnant women swarm around her.

I read her note. "And that's how Louise and I became friends," I tell Nadia as we leave the store.

Eight months

By now, you're ready to give birth. Because if you don't, you're going to explode, you tell everybody around you. Luckily the baby's lungs are reaching maturity now too, meaning she or he can be born safely. Excellent, you think, the baby can come anytime now and I'll be ready.

But your baby may have a different idea. Lulling deliciously in amniotic fluid, your baby thinks, why rush things? Why go through all that when I can hang out here, being fed nourishment and oxygen from my mother via an umbilical cord which will reach a massive 60 centimetres long at birth, and put on approximately 15 grams a day without anyone calling me fat?

Before you start hyperventilating and prodding your stomach, trying to bring on labour, remember: eventually, all babies must come out, to have their time in the sun and to bask in your love.

If you're still worried about the birth, please put your fears aside and start thinking of others. In developed countries, we have excellent healthcare services and the infant mortality rate is very low, but in other parts of the world women and babies are still at risk. Globally, 529,000 women die as a result of pregnancy and childbirth complications of which 99% of these occurred in the developing world.[1] "Direct causes of maternal mortality include haemorrhage, infection, eclampsia, obstructed labour and unsafe abortion. Childbirth

---

1   *Make every mother and child count* (Overview). World Health Organisation. Switzerland. 2005. p. 10

is a moment of great risks, but in many situations over half of maternal deaths occur during the postpartum period. Effective interventions exist to avoid most of the deaths and long-term disabilities attributable to childbirth.'"

The reality for babies, sadly, is even worse. Each year 3.3 million babies – or maybe even more – are stillborn, more than 4 million die within 28 days of coming into the world, and a further 6.6 million young children die before their fifth birthday.[2]

Some women who do survive a long labour then develop Obstetric fistula, a condition where a hole develops between either the rectum and vagina or between the bladder and vagina after severe or failed childbirth. These women then suffer lifelong incontinence and can be shunned by their husbands and families, living in poverty and isolation. The condition is treatable through reconstructive surgery, and of course, preventable through access to medical care during labour.

Many of these women give birth without the assistance of trained medical attendants or pain relief. So while you're skimming over the following birthing aids available to you (and it is not an exhaustive list, other techniques are out there), please think of the women in the world who still give birth at home or by the side of the road; alone, scared, and possibly dying.

Acupuncture

Some hospitals and birthing centres will allow acupuncture on labouring woman. It involves the use of needles inserted into the skin by a trained practitioner for relieving pain and even inducing labour once you have reached full term.

---

1   *Make every mother and child count* (Overview). World Health Organisation. Switzerland. 2005. p. 11.
2   *Make every mother and child count* (Overview). World Health Organisation. Switzerland. 2005. p. 4.

Birthing ball

If you want a natural labour, you'd better start doing 1000 squats a day now. Because you will not want to sit on a chair while in labour, especially one with a hole cut out of the seat. That is insane! If the first thing your baby sees is you sitting down on the job, he or she will never let you sit down again. You will be destined to spend all night, every night, until the child is aged 39, pacing the floor waiting for the little shit to burp or finish his homework.

Best bet is a birthing ball. You can lay over it if you're having a posterior labour and the glorious ball of air will embrace you and absorb your pain. It will even nurture, protect and support you more than a pillow or new diamond earrings. You can even use it in the shower and the ball will hum with life underneath you (especially if you're using a combination of techniques, particularly gas).

Doula

If a hospital or birthing centre full of doctors, nurses and midwives isn't enough company for you, then you can seek the assistance of a Doula, a trained labour companion. The Doula will not leave you to attend to other patients or to go watch the footy. Research shows women who use Doulas generally have shorter labours and less intervention with drugs, induction or forceps deliveries. She (or he) can give advice on relaxation techniques, breathing, massage, and provide verbal encouragement and hand-holding when your husband or partner faints or says his hand hurts too much. She (or he) can also call an ambulance when you punch your partner in the gob for complaining that things are taking "soooo long".

Drugs

This is one instance when it is legal to inhale. Gas. Other drugs, like pethidine or even an epidural block, must be injected into the body. Talk to your practitioner about risks and advantages.

Fireman's Lift

In some countries, like the Netherlands, women routinely give birth at home. Going to a hospital to give birth is — to the Dutch — all Double Dutch to them. But if things go haywire and a woman does need to go to hospital in a rush, then it's not the ambulance whom the Dutch midwife calls, it's the fire brigade. Because in the Netherlands, most houses are built with such steep steps that it's too dangerous for a contracting woman to climb down them while in labour. When the fire brigade comes, the woman is winched through the window to the street below, where she must then bicycle herself to hospital.

This story doesn't really make giving birth easier but it does give you something to visualise while we talk about our next technique.

Om's

This is a very distant cousin of the TENS machine (see below). In fact, these two are so distantly related that they could interbreed and never throw out a wranger (a redhead). An Om is a vocal sound used in yoga. Try squatting on all fours and making a very loud Om sound. Lengthen it: Oooommmmmmmmm. You can even change it up a bit: OoOooMmmm-fucking hell-mmmm.

You can even try to send the sound down into your vagina, making it resonate and vibrate all the way through your uterus. Some yogis say this is a very effective pain relief and your baby will love it. Your baby will love hearing this story too, especially at his 18th birthday party when all his mates are drunk.

Squeezing your partner's genitals

Although little research has been conducted, most women

agree that this technique really helps them bond with their partner during labour. Other women have requested their partner undergo a vasectomy on discovery that not only is the obstetrician qualified to stitch them both back up but s/he may even give a group discount. Other women have even offered to perform the vasectomy themselves — especially if their partner has elected to cut the umbilical cord — with the same pair of scissors. After all, fair's fair.

TENs

A transutaneous electrical nerve stimulation uses electronodes to stimulate nerve pathways to the uterus and cervix, jamming these pathways so that the pain messages can't get through to the brain. Think of it as gridlock for the 21st century labouring woman. Do not use in water.

Visualisation

Picture something, anything, absolutely anything but the image of your vagina ripping and tearing to make way for the baby's head. Think instead, flowers opening in bloom, of a hippopotamus' mouth (which looks enormous and capable of lots of things), of your baby experiencing a peaceful and calm labour, while you breathe him or her out of a hole the size of the universe.

What babies really need

In the middle of my baby shower, I stop eating for five seconds to reflect on what a great time I'm having:

1. Louise De Menton (née Unger), whose boyfriend I stole at our high school formal, is hosting the shower for me and it is the most elegant affair I could have imagined — a waiter serves us cupcakes weighed down with enough pink and blue icing to paint the Opera House, and tiny, cucumber sandwiches. We chink our silver spoons and swirl rose tea in antique bone china cups while being serenaded by a string quartet.

2. Jaimee has given me the most beautiful maternity dress that she had made for Sarah Murdoch, which according to women's tradition should be handed on to the next lucky Mum-to-be, in this instance, *moi* (no, of course I didn't wash it, are you mad?).

3. The presents are excellent except for Jorja's — my sister, who last year was listed in the *Financial Times* with an estimated personal worth of $30M, gave me a scrubbing brush with an accompanying note that says, "Breastfeeding's going to hurt like hell (someone should tell you now rather than let you find out later when you're hormonal and exhausted). The brush will help you start preparing your breasts for feeding. Use harsh movements toward the nipple. X Jorja."

4. I've been allowed one glass of fake Moet.

5. We've raised $2256 in donations for a maternal health charity by auctioning three things:

A.   the right to give my baby his or her first bath (I won that one, I can't believe it cost me $256! They're right, parenting is really expensive);

B.   the status of Godparent (Jorja bid $1000, bless her);

C.   inclusion on the MMS message list bearing news of baby's birth and first picture (we raised another $1000 for that one).

I sigh blissfully, astonished by my fortune. Here I am, kicking back while a beautician gives me a pedicure, imagining that I'm Sarah Murdoch and my baby will inherit millions from her gorgeous father. How perfect! Adam and Dean squeal with delight as yet another gorgeous baby outfit is laid across my tummy and everyone goes, "Oooooh".

I pop another chocolate into my mouth.

Of course my baby will be penniless and not have a father but it will have the best two gay Dads Sydney could offer and a wardrobe to die for. I congratulate myself with another sip from my imaginary glass of champagne.

Louise pours me more sparkling apple juice and I smile up at her out of bliss. In fact, I'm so happy that I don't even mind when Ursula, from design, asks for more string because she thinks my belly is much bigger than the length provided for the game, *Guess how big the pregnant lady's belly is.*

Jaimee sits next to me on the couch. She gives me an update of the list of names, gender, birth weight and labour times which is currently doing the rounds.

A rupture goes through the gaggle of women at Cairine's contribution: Cladianus, boy, 12kg and 46 hours.

Jaimee mutters, "Clueless, totally clueless," to me under her breath.

"What the hell kind of name is Cladianus?" asks Didi from design.

"That was my father's name," Cairine says acting shocked when everyone groans.

"Listen to some of the others," Nadia says grabbing the list. "Now, I won't identify which woman is responsible for each hideous suggestion, but here we go: Basha, a boy — excellent idea Kelly, when he grows up he'll be a hit at the juvenile detention centre."

The crowd laughs.

"Hermaphrodite — fantastic, just what this city needs, Jane, another teenager confused about her sexuality and hoping to blame it on her mother. Oh, and this one's brilliant — Co-Chita — otherwise known as Cock-eater by the boys at school."

The crowd groans.

Jaimee grins. "That was mine," she whispers to me. "Do you like it?"

"Remind me not to let you near the hospital. Knowing you, you'll steal the birth certificate form, give the child the name of Cladianus Cocketa and forge my signature," I tell her.

Jaimee laughs and helps me up so I can go pee for the 100th time that day. On the way to the bathroom, I stumble across Louise talking to her step-daughter, and because I'm in such a good mood, I decide I must be a welcome addition to their little heart to heart.

But they both turn around and glare at me. The step-daughter, Gretel, storms off, knocking over Andrea, Louise's youngest daughter, as she flies past.

I try to apologise and make a run for the toilet but Louise cuts me off.

"It's not you, I'm sorry Til, it's Gretel, she's a complete bitch," Louise covers Andrea's ears so she can't hear her swearing. "Takes after her mother, I'm sorry to say."

Andrea sheds her mother's hands and claims her prize, a promised empty plastic teapot. She runs off happily to the lounge room to ask the besotted ladies if they'd like some tea. When she leaves, Louise runs her fingers through her hair. "I just don't know what to do with her," she vents.

I gather she doesn't mean Andrea. I try to tell Louise that I'm just on my way to the toilet but she keeps talking. I have no choice but to sit down so my bladder doesn't burst.

"Do you remember how I was telling you I want to write some children's books?" Louise asks me and I nervously look toward the toilet door.

"Sure," I nod. "That's a really nice idea, Louise. I'll buy one."

"Except that I'm thinking of calling mine, *Cinderella's a Slut.*"

I take a deep breath. "As refreshing and contemporary as that sounds, I don't know if people will buy something like that. Especially for their children."

"But it's true. I want to write the true story, where the step-mother is busting her ass trying to include her step-children in her family's life, to provide for all of them and teach them that money doesn't grow on trees, and all Gretel does is sit around filing her bloody nails."

"How old is she?"

"16."

"How are things with you and Tony?" I ask. Having recently met Louise's husband, I can tell they totally adore each other. Tony is not three times older than her, as I previously conjectured to Nadia, but 40, tired and hard-working like most other ordinary Dads.

"Good, things are great, but his kids just cause us so much stress. And they don't even live with us. Imagine what it would be like if I had to deal with that every day? Oh, and you haven't met the worse one yet, Christine, she's an absolute bitch. She's got her Daddy wrapped around her little finger. He's so guilty about her mother being such a totally inadequate role model that he just gives in to her."

I look around. I always thought Louise was rich but I can tell from her modest house that she's more house-proud than house show-off.

"I know you think the baby shop is just my little side thing, something to keep the rich bitch occupied, but the truth is we really rely on that income now. Tony's ex-wife got the house in Rose Bay so we're here at Bondi Junction trying to sustain two mortgages because we bought after the property boom so it cost us a fortune."

I tut-tut and watch Jaimee slip into the toilet ahead of me. "Damn," I mutter.

Louise thinks I'm acknowledging her plight.

"But, do you know what's worse? His ex got some other man to marry her and she's sitting at home complaining about raising her two kids and I've got three kids, a business and a husband who's away trying to make money so we can keep this house, and I have to ask why, why bloody bother? All we're doing is paying tax, child care and child support. We hardly see each other, the kids hardly see Tony and then those little bitches show up with their attitude, they treat everybody around them like shit, they're totally materialistic, and are seriously a bad influence on my girls. God, some days I just want to drown them in the bath," Louise says banging the kitchen table with both her fists.

The pots and pans rattle.

"The step-kids you mean?"

"Of course."

"Good."

"What do you mean good? I'm horrible, you should be calling me the worst names under the sun because I just threatened to drown two children in the bath. And they can't help it; they're just learning this behaviour from the TV."

"Bullshit, Louise. Those girls know exactly what they're doing; they're taking advantage of you. They have a choice. They see how you behave and they could model your behaviour but they're too lazy to bother. So tell them what they are, and if they don't like it, tell them to get lost."

"But they're kids, Til, they have a right to know their Dad and until they're 18, I can't really shut them out."

"Yes, you can."

"How do you know?"

"I work in fashion, I've met heaps of little up-starts before, Louise."

I don't tell her about Nicolita in case she starts worrying that Gretel will end up like her too. Some people take on too much responsibility, while others do nothing. And even though I don't know Louise that well (in fact, all I really know about her is that her boyfriend in high school was a good kisser), I can tell she falls into the latter category. I hammer the point home, "You need to communicate to Gretel that her behaviour will not be tolerated. There are children out there dying of starvation and disease and you intend to spend all your time and money helping them, instead of funding Gretel's shopping sprees."

"What money? Why do you think I had the sale on at the shop last month?"

I remember how Louise walked up to me that day, smiling and happy, as if she didn't have a care in the world. And now she's telling me she didn't do it to clear excess stock, but to raise some desperately needed cash for her own family's needs. "I really have to give you some money for all the baby stuff you gave me," I say not knowing what else to say.

"No, Til, it's fine really, you're an old friend and it's karma. Your baby doesn't have a Dad and I'm happy to help you. See, I am a nice person, I wouldn't resent the girls if their mother hadn't ripped their Dad off like some hooker at a flea market."

I laugh because I just can't help myself. "Louise," I say through my giggles, "you're hilarious. At school you were always so nice I just couldn't believe it was true, but you've got this real nasty streak and I just love it. I love this new Louise. You should definitely do it," I say and when I see the shocked look on her face, reassure her that I mean she should write the modern fairytale, and not that she should drown her step-children in the bath. Then I grab her arm and, laughing, drag her upstairs after me. "Now where is the bitch?" I call out.

"In her room," Louise says pointing to a door at the end of the hall.

After banging on the door a few times and hearing a sullen teenager yell "Fuck off" at me, I barge through the door pulling Louise into the room after me.

The teenager shies away, clutching her mobile phone, looking at me with sheer terror. "Now listen here, you little piece of morose consumption. I know you're a spoiled brat, but these people in this house deserve your respect because without them you'd be scabbing cigarettes from the kids you call *cock-eaters* on your way to school now." (Thank God Jaimee sat next to me at the baby shower, I think.) "Do you understand me?"

The teenage bitch says nothing but I can tell she's shocked. Some colour has drained up to her face from her expensive trainers. I keep going:

"You're nothing but a boil on the ass of these decent people and if you don't start pulling your weight, get a part-time job and good grades in school, you're going to end up scabbing your way through life. You probably don't even care whether I'm a feminist or not, but I am, so I want you to pull up your socks or get used to people around here calling you a scab. OK, Gretel?"

She tells me to fuck off again.

So that's when I let her have it.

Louise rushes downstairs while I pull myself together in the upstairs bathroom. I can hear her babbling about our adventures to the rest of the baby shower's delight and, faintly, through the walls, the feeble complaints of a teenager still tied to an *Ikea* chair, desperately trying to shake the mad pregnant woman's pee off her leg.

I remind myself to thank Ursula. She was right, my belly was bigger than the piece of string but it was long enough to tie up Cinderella's foul-mouthed, lazy, cousin next door.

Nine months

Besides the insidious discomfort of being nine months pregnant and feeling like you weigh 100 kilograms, people keep asking you, "Have you lightened yet?" You look at your stomach, which is now the size of a football field, and resist asking them if they are on drugs. Lightened? Isn't that what happens when they get the baby out of me?

You try to get off the couch to make it to your weekly prenatal appointment just so you can grill your practitioner for answers to the following:

A.   when is this baby coming out of me? What the hell do you mean we'll let nature take its course? That's what got me into this mess, now you take it the hell out.

B.   what the hell is "lightening" and why hasn't it happened to me yet? What's wrong with me?

C.   even the clothes at the maternity shop don't fit me anymore, do you have a tent you can lend me?

D.   do you have to keep sticking your hand up there?

E.   when do you want me to call you? When the contractions start, the chocolate runs out, or when my membranes break?

These answers may vary depending on how much you are paying the obstetrician (at $400 per hour why not let you just sit there and babble?) or if the midwife is having a good day or not.

If you're in a low-risk category, it's been some time since you saw your baby at your last ultrasound, so you're probably feeling either immense relief that it's all nearly over (and you can start a lifetime of parenting the little biter), while some women still feel anxious or impatient. If you're in a high-risk category, then you probably feel exactly the same as those mentioned prior. You'll be fine and so will your baby.

Your baby's movements in your uterus are restrained now, meaning you will be feeling less movement but you should still keep track of them. Now that the baby is bigger and you're busy with last minute preparations, you may not notice movements. You can set aside time each day to count ten movements. It may take ten minutes or longer. Sometimes baby may be asleep, but if two hours go past and you can't prompt your baby to move (and move ten times) then you should consult your practitioner.

If you haven't finished up at work yet, then you must be getting close. Don't forget to send an email around advising everyone that you'll be on maternity leave so all good office gossip should be forwarded to your personal account. Of course, some of you are already at home with other children. If that's the case, make sure you spend some special time with your big babies and organise a babysitter so you can get your waxing done. Seven out of ten babies come after their due date, but if little bub does come early, this is one occasion when a grazed field is better than an old-growth forest (especially if you need stitches).

Which brings us to our last point. We all know when labour ends, but when does it begin?

Most women associate labour commencing with burst membranes (waters) or contractions.

So let's start with the membranes. Membranes usually smell more like semen, while urine smells like urine (so you can't tell people your waters just broke, if really, all you had was a little accident). If your membranes are stained greenish-brown in colour, this means that meconium may be present and the foetus may be in distress. You need to go to a hospital immediately. Your waters may also just trickle, and many women have their membranes artificially broken by their practitioner (we discussed this earlier, remember the long crochet hook?).

Contractions are another good indicator that labour has begun. But how do you know whether you're having a real contraction or just ate too much lunch?

This might help: there are three types of labour: pre-labour, false labour and real labour.

Pre-labour can begin up to a month before real labour begins. Pre-labour is usually accompanied by lightening and engagement: the baby moves down lower into the pelvis, although this may not occur until later if you've had a baby before. Pre-labour may also see the start of cervical effacement and dilation. You may get intensified Braxton Hicks contractions (a tightening of the belly), or cramps, groin pain or backache. You may even lose some weight, your vaginal discharge may change and you may even lose your mucous plug.

False labour usually involves contractions that do not progress in frequency or severity. These contractions should subside if you walk around or take a bath. The pregnancy books won't tell you this but I will: sometimes these contractions can go for three to twelve hours without any lightening, cervical effacement or dilation. After a month of it, occurring irregularly, you'll be feeling pretty exhausted and will be screaming to be induced.

Real labour: ahhh, the holy grail for pregnant women. But every woman is different. Here are some key indicators that you're in real labour:

A.   you're cleaning like a woman possessed and re-arranging the furniture (especially if it's the middle of the night);

B.   you have called ten people in ten minutes to ask

them if they think you're in labour;
C.   you huff and puff and scream when the contractions start because the pain is growing in intensity;
D.   you're experiencing contractions that increase in frequency and severity and last between thirty seconds and a minute until they are regular and approximately three minutes apart;
E.   you have a show that is pinkish or bloodstained;
F.   you can feel the baby's head in your butt; or,
G.   you have a baby sitting on your chest.

Once the baby is out, you still have to deliver the placenta, this is called the after-birth or the third stage of labour.

There really isn't much else I can tell you, except take it easy and don't be surprised when you're in active labour, if you hear a strange noise, something like a cow mooing and you wonder where it came from...

Birthing pool

The next 86 million light years, 64 months and 2030 hours pass by really slowly while I sit on the couch and watch my feet swell. The only thing that cheers me up is a phone call from Lola congratulating me for peeing on a wayward teenager: "Because *en* most other *culturez, zat* would be considered wrong", she said. And a weekly visit from Frederick, the masseur Adam has hired to get me physically prepared for the birth.

But today, Frederick has called ahead and suggested we meet at the Bondi Icebergs Swimming Club, a refuge for the truly cool and beautiful people of Sydney.

Since I would never swim at the Bondi sea pool even when not pregnant (they don't call it Icebergs for nothing), I can only gather Frederick means we are there to have a healthy lunch and look at the beautiful people around us. I arrive *sans* togs, and with an appetite that only four bowls of spaghetti will curb.

But Frederick does mean swimming.

I look at the icy cold September sea water and tell him, "Not on your bloody life, Fred," at which he grins, and produces a red bikini and an old ladies' bathing cap and tells me to get changed. And then he starts to undress.

The one good thing about living with a gay flatmate is that he has impeccably good taste in men. I try not to lick my lips as Frederick undoes his pants. I feel a swarm of female eyes turn as a ripple of bronzed stomach muscles are exposed. Suddenly, I know I am the luckiest girl in Sydney, so cheerfully pluck the red bikini from him and go to change.

There is no denying it: if I was to allow myself to objectify a fellow human being as nothing more than sexual prey, I would have to conclude that Frederick is a to-die-for specimen of the male gender. And a shining beacon of hope for the women of Sydney — for according to Adam's sources, Frederick is a rare specimen: a totally gorgeous, highly evolved, yoga-loving, *straight* Sydney man. Not only has he perfected a courteous demeanour but he delivers his calm, eloquent sentences from lips surrounded by a two-day growth. His eyes are warm, brown and brooding and protected by perfectly arched eyebrows; he looks like he belongs to a highly endangered species of deer. But it's the way he looks at you, as if you are the only woman in the world who matters, and how he listens to every word you say and every breath you take, that really makes me swoon. I'd follow him to the ends of the earth. Or today, into a freezing cold sea water pool.

He smiles at me, takes my hand and helps me into the pool.

Everything is different in the water when you are nine months pregnant. The weight, which feels like you are carrying a wounded beast on dry land, suddenly becomes buoyant, and your skin delightfully slippery. Frederick puts his arms around me and carefully places a floating device under my arms. For the next hour, he gently pulls and pushes my body into all sorts of positions and tells me when to breathe.

Now I understand why he brings a bikini and not a shameful, one-piece scuba diving outfit to disguise the bump. Why cover it? The bump, whose prisoner has been kicking me for months and giving me hideous indigestion, now feels like the most natural, extra appendage in the universe; so beautiful in fact, that I feel like a dolphin sliding through the waves, gliding next to her newborn pup and gorgeous, faithful husband.

I feel so sexy I could just die or give birth right there.

At the end of our half hour, Frederick helps me out of the pool and as he pulls me up, gravity returns my pregnant body to its hideous land-born reality, and I feel a downward pressure so strong that I double over in pain.

He supports me as I cling to his shoulders desperately. "It's nearly over, Til," he whispers into my hair. "This will be over soon — what you are doing is beautiful and natural and you look gorgeous.

You've never looked so beautiful and you will be a superb mother, kind and patient and creative."

Even though I'm experiencing excruciating pain, caused by the physical exertion and anxiety of returning to a world where my weight is not supported, I try to listen to his words and believe him. I grab at him, digging my finger nails into his back and let out a hideous wail for help — just as my waters break.

Black hole

The universe is this big. That is also the size of the hole the baby is trying to come out.

The midwife confirms, "You're one centimetre dilated," she says snapping off her gloves. I can hear she's disappointed.

I lie on the birthing ball, exhausted. "But I've been in labour for hours," I moan.

"Are you sure you're in labour, maybe it's just indigestion again?" Adam offers.

I shoot him one of my looks that says, "Even a jury of mostly gay men would acquit me right now". I start to inhale the gas as if my life depends on it as another contraction hits.

The midwife butts in. "No, she's still in early labour but she's not progressing. This isn't going to be *peasant*."

"Peasant? Who the hell said I looked like a peasant?" I yell at her.

Adam mouths words at me but they disappear into the bubbles of gas sliding down my throat. The bubbles turn into a knocking sensation — "Rat a tat tatt, rat a tat tatt, get me the bloody hell out!"

Another contraction starts. "Kill me, just kill me," I yell through the pain.

The midwife waits until the contraction is over and says something to Adam about going to get a *foctor*.

I collapse over the birthing ball letting the shower water fall onto my back. The gas falls from my mouth. I don't know what the hell a *foctor* is but I hope it's some kind of strange device that's going to pull the baby painlessly and quickly out of me. Seeing the desperate look on my face, Adam turns the gas up while the midwife is out of the room.

I start singing a little song about this thing called the *foctor* until another endless contraction starts. I suck on gas, and suck on gas, as if my life depends on it.

"Here he is," Adam says and moves away.

The *foctor* leans over me. "Hello," he says from a stainless steel head. "I'm the *foctor* and I'm going to make all of this pain go away." But he doesn't. Instead, he tightens the CGT around my belly and the baby goes "Beep, beep, beep, beep", and the pain responds, "Stab, stab, stab, stab."

I projectile vomit all over the poor *foctor's* sterile head.

He wipes the vomit from his face and tells the midwife to turn the gas down.

"Turn it down? What the hell?" I scream at his disappearing back. "Turn it the bloody hell up!"

I sniff the air, noticing the sickly, sweet smell of my innards.

The midwife takes the gas from my mouth. My bed is wheeled out and wheeled in to the operating surgery. The colours around me change, the lights begin to flicker.

"They're not going to try and operate in the dark are they?" I try to ask Adam but he just wipes my brow with a beige, wet cloth.

I plead with my eyes about the cloth but he doesn't pay any attention, putting the horrible thing back onto my forehead.

"What the hell type of hospital is this?" I scream at him silently. "A training hospital? I knew I should have paid my medical insurance and then I wouldn't be stuck here with doctors who are more interested in playing a new game called *Blind-folded Operation*. What are they laughing about? Are they really going to slice me open and stitch me back together with only one eye open?"

But Adam's not listening to me.

I hear a voice over the loud speaker and look around for the source of the noise but all I see is a television screen with my stomach on it.

"Just count back from 10," the voice cuts through the pain.

I can't see Adam.

"Just count back from 10," the voice says again from the tower.

"10, 9, 6, 3, 4, blast off," I say.

She is this big.

Bigger even than the universe.

When they hold her up to the sun she is so big she blocks out the light.

And she is beautiful. Feet, head, legs, toes, fingers and a long umbilical cord which hangs between us, keeping the mothership connected to her adventurous and brave spacewalking astronaut.

"It's time to repair the shield, save the planet from imminent death," the *foctor* says.

They're talking about me.

The stars flicker again as they finish my repairs.

"Prepare for re-entry," the voiceover says.

I tell the spacewalking astronaut to take cover in the clear plastic crib. Adam watches over her waving a camera in the air to document the landing.

"Journey complete" the voice says through the microphone when the sutures are done.

"We're home," I say to the voice: "Tell everybody who's out there, there's new life in tow."

Nouveau Née

The asteroid that exploded into a million pieces on impact has strangely left only one little fragment behind.

Me!

I'm the scary, red, swollen little alien screaming from the clear plastic crib.

And I'm not the only one who's angry.

Your fanny, which took the brunt of the force, kind of like Poland or Afghanistan for that matter, may not feel the same again for a couple of weeks, months or even years, but you should be up and about within a few hours of giving birth. Which is great because the maternity wards are filled to the brim and nobody's going to bring me to you just because you're exhausted after 24 hours of agonising labour.

If you had an episiotomy (that's when they use the scissors and cut you front to back to make way for the baby's head) or were torn badly, you may not walk well for two weeks. It basically feels like you've got 100 haemorrhoids down there, right? Ice packs for the first day or two and then salt water baths can help. Keep the area clean and sit on cushions if you can. Try not to look at your mate with hatred.

If you paid good money for the assisted-landing method, otherwise referred to as the sports car, C-section or the Californian (that's when they do the tummy tuck at the same time), your recovery may take a little longer. Some women swear by a Caesarean birth and don't mind the recovery at all. But Caesareans are abdominal surgery; you will need to respect the healing process. No heavy lifting.

Either way (vaginal or sports car), for the next six weeks, you're in the post-partum period. In some cultures, the new mother isn't even supposed to leave the house during that time: it's all bed rest and settling baby into a feeding and sleeping routine. No housework, no cooking, and no shopping (and that includes online). You'll be hormonal and tired which means you could make rash decisions you will regret instantly ("Oh yes, the baby really does need a six foot purple pony that does everything except clean up its own poop!").

The post-partum period is supposed to give you all the time in the world to enjoy — *moi*!

Watch me carefully. I'm pretty amazing and have been born with an amazing set of reflexes to help keep me alive. So even if you're not real bright, a slow learner, or have no one to teach you what to do, just relax — I'll teach you what you need to know — and thanks to the wonders of genetic programming, your body will do the rest. And even if you've had kids before, undoubtedly you will have forgotten half of it and I'll have different needs to the last baby.

I'm not worried, I hear you say, I've read all the books by experts with five PhD's and who collectively can boast four thousand years of parenting experience between them.

Well, good for you.

Don't listen to them — especially, the *baby whisperers*. You know, they tell you how to listen to a baby's cries and what to do. Well, it's all crap. And this is why: I will not follow the rules, and if I do, you will have stupidly followed my advice and won't have read the books.

But the reason I'm telling you this is to make it very clear to you that THERE IS NOTHING QUIET ABOUT A BABY!

Especially me. The noise I make is not meant to drive you insane, it's designed to get your attention and to stop you from what you're doing. I don't mean to be a pain in the ass, but you're my lifeline and it's really important that I train you to respond to my every need, at every second of the day. Without you, I'm toast.

I'll need to be fed every two hours at first, stretching to three and then four hours by the time I'm two months old. When I get a white line around my mouth, you need to burp me. In fact you should burp me after every meal (even interrupting the feed to burp me regularly) by holding me upright and patting me on the back gently. If it's stubborn wind, you can try laying me on your lap and lifting me up again into a sitting position to compress the air in my lungs and force the wind up.

If I go all grey around the mouth, I probably have bottom wind and need to do a poo or fart. You can help this along by gently bicycling my legs — remember my hips are delicate, you don't want to pop one out. While speaking of the bottom end, newborn babies make explosive sounds when they poo. This should settle down within a few weeks and is nothing to be ashamed of. If the idea of smelling and checking a baby's poo grosses you out, then get used to it because it's part of the job. The poo will start off black because of the amniotic fluid in my system, and then turn a mustard colour and then may even turn green for a while. If I'm straining to poo, you may need to investigate constipation. Breastfed babies rarely develop constipation, but bottle-fed babies can. Talk to your healthcare practitioner if you're at all worried and baby isn't sleeping.

You're not getting much, are you? Sleep that is. Babies need sleep, just as much as new parents. Swaddling helps some babies to sleep, but when they're a few days old, some babies like to sleep with their arms out of the swaddle. In many non-Western cultures, babies sleep with their parents for weeks or even months or years (this is called co-sleeping). Why the hell would people do that to themselves? I hear you ask. Well, can you imagine a cot in an igloo? Of course not, Eskimos don't even let their babies touch the ground for the first year. But Western cultures like to segregate and privatise, and baulk at sharing bodily noises at all times of the day and night. It's your choice.

Sleeping position. Which must also be discussed in reference to SIDS, Sudden Infant Death Syndrome, and is the term used to explain infant deaths that have no other identifiable causes. In recent years, the SIDS rate has fallen. Research indicates that the best sleeping position for me is on my back at the bottom of the cot. Tuck the sheets in under the cot so the sheet can't reach over my head. And do not use cot bumpers or heavy blankets or quilts. Keep me in a cool room with good air filtration and don't smoke near me, in the house or even outside (I will know).

The best thing you can do for me, to stimulate my aural development and to get me to go to sleep, is to sing to me. It doesn't have to be a complex nursery rhyme, just you humming or making "shhhh" or "shush" sounds can be enough to send me off to la-la land. Especially if you coordinate your singing/shushing with wrapping me lightly, and gently rocking and bobbing me in your deliciously warm arms.

See, this baby stuff is easy — and fabulously relaxing too.

Meeting Nina

The room is abuzz with so many visitors that the midwife has to come in and tell us to keep it down.

Nadia kisses her and offers her a glass of champagne.

"And don't stay too long either. Til's had a hard labour she needs to rest," she says. Sadly, she refuses to add the champagne to my drip.

But she's right. I am exhausted and can only put up with these crazy people for a few more minutes before the pain medication sends me into a proper sleep.

"What went wrong?" I ask Adam who is hovering near the baby.

"Sweetheart, you didn't dilate and then she went breach. The doctor decided to do a Caesarean, he thought the baby was in distress. But you'll be OK, a little more recovery time than usual because you had the exhaustion of going through twenty hours of labour as well as getting cut. The midwife said it's going to take a good month or two before you feel right."

"But we're here to help," Dean says stepping forward. "And Til, she's so beautiful I can't believe it, she's even got my nose."

Adam and I smile as his excitement spills over and fills the room.

Nadia steps forward holding a little bundle. "Do you want to hold her, Til?"

The midwife nods that it's OK and helps me hold the baby high on my chest away from the sutures. The baby seems to be struggling.

"She's hungry that's all, so I'm going to have to milk you for colostrum and give it to the baby. You're not up to feeding her by yourself right now," the midwife says.

Adam, Dean and Nadia look on while the nurse does just that: milks my breast by squeezing my nipple. A thick yellow liquid oozes out and she collects it in a tiny cup.

"Liquid gold," she says as the colostrum drips into the cup. After collecting a teaspoon, she sucks it up into a syringe and slowly squirts the liquid into the baby's mouth.

"Wow," says Nadia. "It's just like feeding a baby lamb."

"The baby's a bit tired too from the drugs that passed into her system," the midwife says before gently resting her hand on my arm. "And that's OK, you were in so much pain, don't beat yourself up about needing pain relief or having an emergency Caesarean."

Her words take away some of the freakiness of having my best friends watch my boobs being milked.

She rewraps the baby and puts her back in her plastic cot. I fight the conflicting feelings of being disappointed that I can't hold the baby for longer and relief that if she's in the cot, I can get some desperately needed sleep.

"You won't be out of bed much for a few days so make sure you always wheel her around in her cot, don't carry her. And when she's hungry or needs to be changed, buzz a nurse and they'll help you, OK? I don't want you doing any of this on your own just yet. If you feed incorrectly you'll get nipple damage or you could drop her because you're still on pain medication." The midwife looks at me closely and then tells the others that I'm exhausted and they're going to have to leave.

I've never been so well treated in my life. I'm thinking of never going home.

"Sweetie," Adam says as he hovers over my bed, trying to delay his departure. "Can we ask you what her name is?"

I tell him the secret I've been keeping to myself for the last four months. "It's Nina."

Nadia starts to cry. "After me? Nina Cockeater? Oh Til, how cool is that?"

Nadia has taken up the role of security guard at my door, only letting visitors in to see me and Nina for five minutes, and only while I'm awake.

When my mother comes to visit, Nadia slips into the room first and asks me if I'd prefer to pretend to be asleep. I tell her she's terrible and she raises her eyebrows at me like I'm an idiot.

I try to sit up in bed but fall back against the pillows in pain.

Nadia returns with my mother who fusses around the baby and tells me she looks nothing like me. Then she tells me I look a sorry sight and should pull myself together; that she was out of hospital in two days, before they'd even had a chance to stitch her fanny back together.

Behind her, Nadia is doubled over, and I'm not sure if she's trying hard not to laugh — or vomit.

That night, I dream about the midwives trying to sew a zipper into my fanny while my mother tut-tuts in the corner. I wake up with a fever and in hideous pain. The *foctor* is again called and he prescribes antibiotics and more pain relief.

I make the mistake of telling Nadia about my dream, and kindly, she goes easy on my mother. "See, I knew I should have taken your mother out shopping for synthetics and shot her the day I found out you were pregnant," is all she says.

Jorja arrives and is the first visitor allowed to hold the baby.

Nadia concedes that as Aunts they must look out for each other. She lets Jorja stay for ten minutes, before whisking her away so I can rest.

Little Nina has a feed and drifts off into a heavy sleep.

She's so breathtakingly beautiful, even with her ruddy complexion and scaly, newborn skin, that I start crying.

I could watch her all day, her tiny chest breathing in and out, her little fingers still curled up tightly in a ball. Her size is unfathomable and I still can't quite believe this amazing experience is happening to me. Somewhere in our vicinity, I'm quite sure Dean Martin is practising his favourite songs of love. He's as in love with my daughter as I am, I'm sure of it.

More visitors come and go all day, and although they bring me flowers and chocolates, no Dad arrives, and I start to wonder if I have done the wrong thing.

Adam and Dean visit again but as they are not the biological father, I wonder if the baby has noticed and if this is what she's crying about, "W-h-e-r-e's d-a-d, waaaah?"

And I start to obsess over whether the nurses know I'm a single Mum. Do I look like one? I never thought I'd be one; actually, I never thought I'd even be a Mum, but I'm starting to suspect the nurses know there's no Dad on board. Maybe that's why they're being so nice to me?

Finally, the march of visitors slows and I fall into a deep sleep. I dream that a nurse is milking my boob and when she turns around she has 400 sheep to feed by hand and there's no Dad to help her. But then I remember we are in the middle of a drought, a Dad-drought, and what she is doing is probably right.

When Nina is four days old, he turns up.

But when he walks through the door, the moment I have been imagining for the last few months…feels different.

He even looks different. Maybe it's his incredible tan, his lean biceps, his inner core strength.

He smiles at me and I say, "Gee, you look wonderful, not at all like I remember."

And then I realise that's because it's not him. It's not Nina's Dad.

It's Frederick, my masseur.

"Hi, beautiful," he says to Nina bending over her cot and gently stroking her little hand. "Welcome to our profound world."

Then he turns to me, and the power of his full attention on me makes me feel dizzy. I remember the smell of his neck and the feel of his skin under my hands as I clung to him while we waited for the ambulance to arrive.

"She's sweet Til, congratulations."

I wait for him to kiss my cheek but he doesn't. He stands at the end of the bed still clutching a bouquet of fragrant lilies.

The distance between us brings back a sudden longing in me to be pregnant again, when I was as huge as a house and this delicious man put his hands all over me on a regular basis.

"Thanks," I manage to tell him.

"I heard you had a rough time. I wanted to swing by and see how you both were."

"We're fine. Well, we will be," I say even though I'm still not quite sure if that's true.

"God, Til," he says and his face crumples with emotion. "I hope I didn't have anything to do with it. I've done that with heaps of other woman who were close to term but none of them ever had a labour like yours."

His words, which tell me I'm not the only woman he's cajoled into active labour at the Bondi pool, make me feel instantly sad — and stupid. So it was just his job! God, what have I been daydreaming about these last few days?

"And I didn't make any of them wear such a sexy little swimsuit either," he adds as if reading my mind.

I groan. "God Fred, I must have looked hideous."

"Not at all," he says and finally bends down to kiss my cheek. "You are the most beautiful pregnant women I have ever seen."

His words are still ringing in my head when the baby wakes up and starts screaming.

Fred comments on what a good set of lungs she has and I realise that Lola has walked in and is watching us.

She kisses me first, flirts with Fred, and picks up the baby as if she is the most experienced mother in the world. She coos at the baby, giggles, and then sniffs her. She looks like the original baby whisperer.

523s

"Babies smell divine, *oui*?" she tells us and holds the baby under my nose so I can take a whiff too. She is not impressed by my insipid effort. "*Non*, a big smell, Til, drink her *en* like she is *da* most delicious burgundy."

I try to do as she says and notice a faint aroma, but Lola tut-tuts, retrieves the baby and asks if she's been bathed.

"God, I hope so," I tell her.

"Damn, they smell even better before they are bathed. All that Mama juice, *oui*?" she says to Fred who grins and agrees.

"My sisters all smelled like that when they were born. I still remember it, the whole hospital ward seemed to be filled with that smell," he tells Lola, who is looking at him as if she totally approves of him. But I know that underneath that look, some really dirty things are going through her mind.

Fred adds, as if explaining to me, "I'm from a big family: two boys four girls. I'm the eldest."

"You never told me that," I say, suddenly amazed by how little I know about this gorgeous man. I tell Lola, "I've been seeing Fred — no, I mean, Fred's been massaging me throughout my pregnancy — and I never knew that about him."

"Well, we were focused on you the whole time, Til."

I'm not sure if that is an insult or another act of generosity. I also can't figure out why I didn't take any interest in finding out more about him. Normally I'm full of curiosity about new people, but with Fred, I purposefully steered clear of asking him anything personal. Probably because I didn't want to hear about the gorgeous Scandinavian model I was sure he was married to and the two gorgeous kids they have together.

No wonder I resigned to enjoying his massages and moaning to the kindest person on earth about how uncomfortable I was. Learning anything more about this man — while the reality that he was totally out of my league stared me harshly in the face — would have been emotional suicide.

"I'm going to have a baby."

"Lola?"

"*Oui*, John and I are having a bub. Oh, it is going to be such fun, she is going to be naughty, yes?"

Fred kisses Lola on the cheek and congratulates her. I motion to Lola to come closer and give her the biggest hug my perforated stomach will allow. I try to hide the humongous tears streaming down my face but Lola catches me wiping them on her shirt.

Lola asks me what's wrong and Fred moves in closer. He sits carefully on the bed and cradles my face in his hands. I breathe deeply. It's been four days since this man touched me but it feels like months. I try to gather myself together but that only makes me cry harder.

"Today's day four, your milk's coming in, Til. Mothers always get emotional when their milk comes in, and you're probably on medication as well to help with the pain. There's an incredible amount of hormones going through your body, it will take some adjusting to but you'll feel normal again, soon."

I hope he is referring to the enormous jugs on my chest. Having always been flat-chested, I enjoyed my enlarged bosoms during pregnancy, but my milk boobs are enormous. I feel as if the baby has crawled out the wrong hole and is now sitting in each breast.

"You're right," I tell him. "I do feel really heavy."

He picks up Nina expertly and hands her to me. "You should probably give her a feed, it will help," he says and holds Nina up to my chest and over my sutures. "There, make sure her mouth is wide before you attach her, yes, perfect," he says guiding the baby onto my nipple.

For a second, I wonder how my masseur knows how to attach a baby to a woman's breast, and decide that he doesn't have two kids at all — he must have six hundred.

Lola interrupts my thinking. "Do you remember my exhibition, Til?"

"Of course Lola, how could I forget it," I reply while half-smiling, half-freaking out at Nina suckling at my breast.

"What do you think now?"

"I had a Caesarean so I didn't get to push."

"And Adam videoed it?"

"Of course. Dean said he fainted three times."

I explain to them the wireless webcam hook-up to Dean's house.

Fred is openly watching Nina feed from my breast, gurgle, suck, suck, gurgle.

"You're doing really well," he tells me which takes any weird sensations away.

"Were you trained as a midwife in another life?" Lola asks him.

"Probably, although I think it's just because I was the eldest" he says. "I saw my Mum go through this five times and she was sick with a few of us so I used to bring the baby into her. Kids from big families have seen everything. That's probably what made me want to do massage — I've seen what the human body is capable of. When a mother touches her child on her head, the child just feels so loved. I wanted to be able to make people feel like that too."

Lola's face has returned to worshipping Fred but my head has started to wonder if this guy is too good to be true. I believe the story about the five brothers and sisters (although it is a little hard to swallow), but I'm pretty sure, judging by the expert way he holds a baby, that he's got a wife and dozen children of his own waiting at home. Which means, if he's flirting with me, it's a horrible trick to play on any new Mum, especially me. Because there's no way this gorgeous, straight, flirty but emotionally stable, in-touch with women, financially secure man (apparently he charges $200 per hour for a massage which even in Sydney is pretty good money) is single. It's much more likely that he's a pretend-man: he looks like a man, acts like a man, but really, is a total freak.

I tell myself that *Fred* can't be real and that as soon as he walks out the door, I'll never see him again.

Which is what he does next. He kisses me on each cheek, congratulates us both again and says goodbye.

His visit lasted five minutes.

I tell Lola when she asks, "Who the hell was that?" that Fred was simply completing a post-partum visit to a client who will be so busy with feeding, crying and turning into someone who doesn't get dressed until three in the afternoon, that he'll never have to see me again.

She says, "Til, you haven't been dressed before three for months, all you do is eat, and besides, the sexual tension between you two was incredible."

I tell her to shut up. A. I've never believed in sexual tension, it's all just tension; and B. I will never see him again. Nina is my priority now. And C. the last thing I want right now is sex, especially with staples holding my stomach together and my fanny feeling bruised from the baby's head knocking up against it for hours.

She picks up Nina carefully and whispers to her in French.

Watching her, I can't help but feel a pang of jealousy thinking of the wonderful times she has ahead of her while the excitement of bringing a little baby into the world builds: of watching her belly grow and going for scans, of talking with people about the little baby and sharing your joy (but not your fears) with them. I start to prattle off a list of questions at her about the baby's due date, where's she having it, has she been sick, names, and how's John coping?

She answers each with such positivity that as her mouth chatters, I realise how much more I know about this whole pregnancy experience now. I finally feel confident enough to be pregnant! I know nothing about looking after a baby, which is the stage I'm at now, but that's life — you're always one step ahead of yourself, and it's not until you look back that the bad stuff melts away and you realise that the last stage was fun — even easy.

Six Weeks

The parenting books will tell you everything you need to know about a baby's development milestones. It sounds silly, thinking of a tiny little baby experiencing a *milestone*, but that's exactly what's happening.

I may still look like a screaming, eating, pooing blob but significant changes are occurring. I was born with a sucking reflex and an enormous capacity to love and learn, but in just six weeks I've come a long way toward adapting to life outside of the womb: I can now breastfeed easily or take a bottle, I've got better head control, and can find my thumb.

You can help me reach my next milestones by tickling me and playing with my arms and legs and torso. This will help me to learn that I can grab at things and kick too.

I'm ready for stage two: fun!

So here's the most important titbit you can ever know about babies. When a baby is born, her brain has a million little wires sitting in her head, waiting to link up. Playing games of activity, discovery, and visual and aural fun will help the process. These games include: singing, stroking, tickling, rolling, clapping, walking, bouncing, wiping, fidgeting, holding, moving, reading, sharing, caring, and smiling.

Right now, you don't need to worry about paying out a hideous amount of money to an expensive private school or fund a trillion piano lessons, you just need your hands, a few nursery rhymes (you can sing them or buy/rent a CD), and some time together, preferably every day.

Some books refer to this as *the Golden hour*. Of course,

an hour is a bit optimistic at this stage — ten to twenty minutes will probably suffice — but as I get older and my attention span lengthens, I'll really enjoy spending time with you doing different things.

The first game we should play is *tummy time*. *Tummy time* teaches me to lift my head and build up my stomach, back and arm muscles. By putting me on my tummy (but only when awake and never on anything soft or near stairs), I'll also learn to dig my toes into the ground and push off, practising my first steps toward crawling. And never leave me alone — even if you're dying to do a pee — something will surely happen to me if you do.

See, I got you, didn't I? It is OK to leave me on my own for short periods of time. Seriously, it is. I won't starve or die of loneliness if you leave the room for two minutes. I will know that you've gone because I can't see, hear or smell you, and I'll let you know you're horrible for leaving me, but I will be OK. So, make yourself something to eat, go to the toilet and have a shower. I will be OK.

And yes, I can see you. When I'm holding onto your little finger and looking up at you, it's your face I can see. Everything else is a blur, except you. I'll learn to recognise your voice first, so talk to me as much as possible. Soon I'll be turning my head when I hear your voice, and you'll love that!

And no matter how many times you try to excite me into my first smile (not a reflex smile but a genuine smile), you should know that it will have no effect — blind babies smile at the same time as sighted babies.

But it is a sight to see. So is the next game.

Twinkle, Twinkle Little Star may not be exciting to an adult, but to a baby it's the greatest game on earth. Not only are you singing to me but you're waving your magnificent hands above my face. You may be tempted to go and spend money on an all-singing and all-dancing mobile to put above my bed. Save you cash for a rainy day because my eyesight is still terrible. The best thing you can do for me is to make one: the first colours babies can see are black and white, so cut shapes out of coloured cardboard or material and hang those no more than 30 centimetres above me head. Any higher and I won't be able to see it at all. Then swap those shapes for primary colours (red, blue and yellow), then secondary colours (which are made by mixing primary colours, but again you can use cardboard or material), then pastels, and metallics. Keep rotating the mobiles until I'm around six months old, then you can add a pull down toy.

By the time you've finished doing this, you will be prepared for any primary school art homework project. But be very careful that I can't choke on any of the objects hanging from the mobile. This is very important.

Choking. Every mother's worst nightmare. Soon you will be convinced that everything is a choking hazard. Air, breastmilk, bubbles, clothing, sheets, toys...the list goes on. But while you're panic-stricken about objects in my proximity, I need to be close to objects to stimulate my brain development. That's why you should never leave me alone (see point above).

But even though I'm developing, it doesn't mean the rest of the world is. Be careful out there. You're a new Mum (even if it's your second-time or more, I am new to you!). You're hormonal and tired and you may be starting to feel like the world is out to get you. If you are feeling down, crying a lot, or even sensing that you may want to harm yourself or your baby, then talk to your health practitioner and seek help. Being a Mum is the hardest job on Earth, Mars, or even Taurus' brightest star — Aldebaran — or any other star recognised by the International Astronomical Union for that matter.

Suffice to say, you are not alone.

The screaming banshee

Being a mother is the most difficult thing I have ever done. High school, degrees in marketing and fashion, making outfits to wear to Mardi Gras ten years in a row, surviving eight Fashion Weeks, and finding a car park in Bondi on a Saturday, all pale in comparison to the screaming banshee that now haunts every hour of my day.

She screams at me for feeds, she screams when I don't put the booby in her mouth fast enough, she screams when she's full, when she poos, and even when she's screaming — she's screams on top of that too.

Adam says she has a higher pitch than the annoying North Shore brats who bully him at his store, bitching at him about not having the dress Paris Hilton wore when she was in Sydney, all while sending videos of themselves to their friends, not for feedback, but so they can show off about how much money they're spending.

I tell him to sell the shop and stay home with Nina and I'll work but he says, "Darling I don't think that will ever happen," in a way that is final and somehow demoralising.

Is my little screaming banshee that bad even a godless, gorgeous gay man wouldn't want to swap ripping off soulless, tweenage consumer junkies to spend more time with her?

Adam assures me that he loves her but that only a mother can put up with that screaming all day.

My doctor says it is nothing to worry about, that babies cry and it's totally normal.

"Yeah, but all the time? I was at *Georgio's* the other day and they asked us to leave."

"You took a baby to a bar? Serves you right then."

Although half of my brain wonders how my 400 year old

Hungarian butcher doctor knows what *Georgio's* is, the other half is smart enough to not tell her that I was meeting Jaimee because I'm behind on writing next year's marketing plan. I thought I'd get heaps of work done while the baby slept, she was a goddamn angel at the hospital, but since getting home she's turned into a little hell-cat.

What's worse, the midwife Jorja hired to help me through the first few weeks has disappeared, saying I had it all under control. I look at the screaming ball of baby in front of me. Under control? Is she nuts?

She's not the only one. Jorja, who has two full-time cleaners, three gardeners, a chauffeur, and a nanny, has visited us every couple of days — to clean my apartment. She even brings her own gloves. You'd think if the apartment was such a pig sty that someone with her personal wealth would just lend me one of her cleaners, but she doesn't. My sister will always regard me as her little sister, the kid who used to hide her clothes under her bed instead of putting them away, and who used to put the dishes back in the cupboard still dirty when it was her turn to do the washing up.

I know, I'm a slob, but that was when I was really, really young.

Jorja, however, still remembers. So, instead of sitting on the couch commenting on how tired I look and how beautiful Nina is, like our other visitors do, Jorja simply walks in, says hello, makes me a cup of tea, and then starts scrubbing my little two bedroom castle like she's Cinderella on speed.

I don't have a problem with it but I really wish she wouldn't wear her *Prada* pants while she cleans. Not only did they cost $1800, but they have a really slim cut so when she's down on all fours scrubbing baby vomit out of the carpet, her G-string rides up above her pants and then she looks like any regular tart who's had a few too many drinks and has fallen out of her wedges while stumbling for a cab.

As her skinny butt waves in the air, I can't help but giggle about it to Nina. "Now there's a sister," I tell my delicious baby. "Even though Jorja turns up looking like a supermodel, she leaves hot and bothered with a giant dirt streak across her face just like any normal person. Remember this moment, Nina. Jorja may be a filthy rich snob most days of the week but she has a generosity of spirit that is sadly all too lacking in this world."

I don't know what I'd do without her. The stitches have healed (even that nasty little infection I developed has cleared) but because I lost a lot of blood, I still feel exhausted and can't lift anything heavier than Nina. I definitely can't stand long enough to wash up, or carry a basket of washing down three flights of stairs to the laundry. No, without her, I'd be cactus right now.

Jorja's visits last about an hour, but with all the cleaning to do, that doesn't leave her much time to spend with Nina. But Nadia says, as First Aunt, that's her job. Jorja's job, as Second Aunt, is to keep the pig sty gleaming. I thought that was Adam's job but he said (tongue-in-cheek of course) that as the only male of the household, it's his job to pay the bills and then go out and get smashed and root his boyfriend.

Not having any chores to do gives me a lot of time to think about Nina's birth. I can't help but feel disappointed in myself — after all, I took care of myself, I exercised, I even massaged my perineum. How could it have gone so wrong?

To make me feel better, Nadia visits every couple of days and does nothing except keep me up to date with all the good Sydney gossip and play with Nina.

I look forward to her visits as much as Nina looks forward to finally releasing some wind that's been bothering her all day.

Nadia calls Nina her *Little Viper*. Sometimes, Nadia bathes her for me, cuts her nails (which seem to grow a centimetre a day), gives her a little baby massage, dresses her and takes her for a little walk to Tamarama beach.

It all sounds deliriously helpful, but the entire time Nadia is bathing her and walking her, Nina is screaming. Understandably, Nadia's little trips last about ten minutes. She walks into the apartment defeated, saying she can't stand it anymore and can I please shut her up.

I attach Nina to my breast and she sucks quietly for a while and then starts screaming again. I hand Nadia some ear plugs and we argue at the top of our lungs about whether there's something wrong with Nina.

"The doctor says it's normal."

"Like bloody hell! The thing's possessed," Nadia yells back.

Nadia kindly never relates any stories about when she was a mother and how she did things. Adam says it's probably because she's forgotten.

"Because of all the ecstasy she's taken?"

"No, Til, real Mums forget. They're so sleep deprived they just can't remember any of it."

"She's not always like this," I tell Nadia in a desperate attempt to keep her visit from ending soon.

But Nadia leaves — only to return with Louise, armed with an exercise ball.

Louise shushes the baby and starts bouncing up and down like she's at some guerrilla gym class. Nina keeps screaming.

I watch her — up and down up and down — until I nearly pass out.

Nadia and I flake out on the couch discussing that this must be how Louise got her figure back.

Nadia shouts, "She has got a nice ass."

"I heard that," Louise yells back.

And then something magical happens. Nina goes to sleep.

Louise whispers to me over Nina's head, "It's just wind pain. What are you eating?"

Because breastfeeding is making me ravenous, my diet consists of ten times the amount of food I ate while I was pregnant. When Adam comes home from work to cook me dinner, he goes to the fridge, announces that it's empty again and goes out to get more supplies.

I tell him it's his fault, he insists on spoiling me with home-made muesli and fragrant stir-fries full of every vegetable that can be found at the Sydney markets. When he's not around I subsist on delicious leftovers, fruit salad, and enough yoghurt, lentils, sprouts and sesame seeds to sink Fashion Week. Of course I'd like to be eating chocolate but Adam scared me to death with his warning of,

"A second on the lips, a lifetime on the liver."

So I've been eating deliciously healthy food and only occasionally gobbling up all the chocolate in the house.

I'm quite proud of my discipline but Louise, who is looking at me like I'm a demented fool, is frowning.

"Nina could be reacting to the food coming through the breastmilk. So you'll need to go on an elimination diet. No wheat, no lactose, no eggs, no nuts, no seafood and no warming foods — ginger, capsicum, onion, oranges, broccoli, cauliflower and garlic are bad for some babies. Do that for two weeks and see if her system settles down. Then you can try introducing foods slowly and see if she reacts."

"How will I know if she reacts?"

"The screaming, Til."

"But I thought she did that because of her immature digestive system?"

"It could be, but Andrea was the same and I had a lactation consultant who specialised in allergies come in and that's what she did with me. It turned out Andrea was lactose intolerant. Some babies are born with the enzyme to break down lactose and others aren't, they can never have lactose, while some develop it when they're older and you can gradually introduce dairy with those."

"God, what do I eat then?"

"Salad, lots of rice, meat, some babies react to soy so don't replace dairy with soy milk just yet, and all the other veges I didn't say before."

"I'm going to starve."

"I'll get you some rice cakes," Nadia tells me, and I can tell by the way she says it, that she knows my new eating regime will probably kill me.

"Just eliminate and then introduce, Til. Keep a diary. That will help you remember. It's not forever, Nina should improve immediately if it's food that's causing a reaction. If it's not food, then what harm have you done? On the other hand, if you don't eliminate, it could be years before you realise there's an allergy and by then her digestive system will be a mess."

157

Nina's only six weeks old and according to Louise I've already scarred her for life.

The guilt forces me to stay comatosed on the couch.

I don't know how Nina can sleep through all the bouncing; just watching Louise bounce up and down is making me feel sick. It's one thing to bounce on your own but to watch someone bounce on an exercise ball is another matter entirely. And with my stomach still store from the Caesarean, I don't think I can bounce on that thing for a minute. Following Louise's elimination diet sounds like hell but it's got to be better than the bouncing.

"This is forever, Til," she iterates, still bouncing. "Being a parent will last for the rest of your life and if it's not wind, it's the flu or teething or the horrors of getting her into kindy, and soon it'll be boyfriends and high school, then getting her into university or rehab."

"Spot on with the rehab bit," Nadia chips in.

Now it's my turn to return the death stare. Nadia shrinks away.

I beg Louise to stay while I have a sleep *sans* earplugs and like an angel she does.

As my head hits the pillow, I fall into a deep sleep. I even let go of all my guilt. I'm going to need my sleep, especially if I'm going to deal with the rest of my life.

My mother watches me bounce up and down.

I can tell what she's thinking, "If my daughter had married years ago I'd have four grandkids by now and I wouldn't be sitting here watching her bounce up and down like a fool. But, if she hadn't done some bouncing up and down like that ten months ago I wouldn't be sitting here with this grandchild, so I should be grateful for small mercies."

She motions to me to give her a turn at quieting the baby, and relieved, I hand her over. Mum stands perfectly still and holds

Nina like she has a contagious disease. Within seconds, Nina is screaming again.

"I've just never heard a baby cry so much, there must be something wrong with her," she says handing Nina back to me. "You never cried like that and your sister certainly never behaved that way."

I wonder how she thinks a six week old baby is capable of *behaving*?

We're only one week into my elimination diet. Nina keeps screaming after some feeds, but more often than not, she feeds, burps and goes to sleep for four hours. Louise says her digestive system might still be calming down, the Hungarian doctor says that she's growing out of it. Either way, I'm starting to feel more normal. I tell Mum, "She'll be fine, I'm sure."

"I don't know. Margaret was telling me they think babies who cry a lot grow up to have that Attention Deficit Disorder."

"Margaret is vicious old tart and knows nothing about children's health or development, Mum, so just don't listen to her," I tell her.

"Maybe it wasn't ADD, maybe it was a crack addiction or something horrendous like that."

"I think you're confused, Mother."

"No, I'm sure that's what she said."

Margaret's far-fetched and factually incorrect stories, evidence of early dementia or a lifetime committed to meanness, have been scaring me for years, ever since Margaret's husband cashed in his inheritance by selling the family farm and moving his young family to Sydney where he ran the local post office. Sometimes he worked at the shop's counter, the rest of time he flirted with his friends' wives, offering them "special Royal mail deliveries". On Saturdays he drank.

Surprisingly, Margaret's husband made it to a ripe age of 60 before dying, leaving her with a fantastic house on the North Shore and no other income.

My Mum's second husband left her for a 40 year old veterinarian.

Mum doesn't talk about it much but I guess she's as scared at her age at the prospect of being alone as I am of being left alone with

Nina, the screaming banshee.

Mum and Margaret have been friends for years; when they're not fighting with each other or trying to outdo each other with their overseas trips. They don't go to Alaska or New Zealand like normal old women, they go to places like the Melbourne Casino and islands off the coast of Scotland. Not for the fun of it or to *grow*, but because both of them are shopping for new husbands and those are the places they believe they'll find lonely, rich, old men. Mum thinks she's going to rescue some old crony before he jumps off a cliff like some endangered species she saw on the Discovery Channel.

Whereas Margaret is just looking for anything with a pulse.

After talking to herself for a while, Mum decides it's time for lunch. She potters around the kitchen before remarking that there is nothing substantial to eat and the apartment is a pig sty.

I turn away from her.

The good thing about having a screaming baby in the house is that I can pretend I can't hear Mum speak. My mother has the power to even turn me against my sister. I make a mental note not to let her in the house again.

Nina purses her lips together and tells me she's got wind.

I'd like to have a conversation with my mother about how excited I am that Nina is already communicating with me. I'd like to boast about how clever she is for a six week old and how much I love her. I'd like to explain what a great mother I'm becoming and all the things I've learned about my daughter. Like when she has a trapped burp and her little lips get a distinctive white line around them. Or when she has a fart and she goes grey from her nose to her jaw.

Louise told me that. In fact she has taught me most things I know about my daughter. I kind of expected to learn these things from my mother or sister but all my mother keeps talking about is what a crap mother I am and all my sister does is complain that that's exactly what Mum did to her too.

I stop rocking for a while and take Nina down onto the floor and start bicycling her legs to move the wind through her intestines. We do this for a while and then I push her legs up into her stomach and she lets out a big fart. She looks shocked. But not as shocked as Mum.

"My God, was that baby? My dear, she'll never get a boyfriend like that."

When I was a teenager I never understood her. My Dad used to try and pacify me, after witnessing another screaming match between myself and Mum (mostly about how much we hated each other), by telling me that my mother didn't have the privilege of a good education but I could learn tolerance and respect by being nice to her in spite of her many challenges. I told him that if I didn't stand up to her now she would push me around for the rest of my life. He nodded and said, "Quite right, quite right."

When Dad died of a heart attack at 45, I wasn't surprised. No one knew he had a heart problem but I told the doctor it was worn out from Mum nagging him about all the things she wanted, and how unlucky she was to have married him. Now I know it wasn't that she hated him, she was just bored, and totally unfulfilled by her role as a housewife.

But as a kid, I didn't understand that.

My most vivid memory of Dad before he died wasn't at the hospital, but at home. We were watching TV and the news reporter was talking about a man who had killed his wife with the toaster. Naturally, I asked Dad if he'd ever thought about doing that to Mum for us.

I remember he'd laughed so hard he spilled his beer all over the couch and that got him into more trouble with Mum. But when he said goodnight to me that night, he told me he didn't care, it was worth getting into trouble with Mum to have such a good laugh.

He even told his friends about it and after that they treated me with a new level of respect. I wasn't a kid anymore; I was one of them, one of the blokes.

Since Dad died, I still catch up with his friends the Saturday before Christmas at their local surf club. I can tell they appreciate my visits but I like seeing them even more; they are my last link to Dad.

Mum sees me looking at the calendar and I can tell she knows what I'm thinking, but instead she says, "Now I've bought Nina some clothes for her Christmas present so you don't have to worry about that expense."

I shudder. I don't believe they still make baby clothes that my mother would want to buy. I bet they're all pink. As a baby shower present she bought me six breastfeeding bras, all in the same horrible shade of tent-brown. In fact, they are so big and rough, I could stitch them together into a tent — except that my sewing machine might reject the fabric.

I try to be nice. "Mum, you shouldn't have, really. Nina's been given plenty of clothes already. You should save your money for one of your trips."

"And not get my granddaughter anything for Christmas? Don't be a fool, Til."

"Well, you could get her something she needs, I'll tell her about it when she's older, how you got her something that she really needed for her first Christmas present."

"And what does a baby need except her mother and something to keep her warm, Til?"

I think about her logic and silently question, "In this day and age — gee, an understanding, sympathetic grandmother who shuts up occasionally and doesn't compare grandchildren? Or how about a trust fund for those kindy fees which are surely going to break me?"

But I don't say that. Instead I tell her, "Well, a few hundred bucks for the rent wouldn't be too bad as a present, especially since it's now November and we're living in Sydney not some fucking freezing cave 600 years before the concept of private property was invented."

She gives me one of her looks that says, "Sorry, love but I didn't hear a word you just said."

So I give her my look which says, "I just saw my daughter smile at me and it was beautiful, so beautiful in fact that I'm not going to tell you."

My mother's visits teach me one thing that the books never talk about: being a daughter is a hard job and now that I'm a mother, I'm going to have to respect that.

Three Months

Most of your day now revolves around somebody else's demands, which sounds a lot like your old life when you were working, and even though you still feel underpaid, your exhaustion has risen to an all-time high.

So here's the truth of the matter: most babies sleep really well for the first month. And then we wake up. This is a long enough period, decided by Mother Nature, for most Mums to recover from the birth. Then the really hard work begins. By the time I'm three months old, you'll feel like you're 300 years old.

It's certainly not marathon training — you're just watching TV, feeding, burping, filling in your baby diary (which is strangely fulfilling if you add photos, you should try it), sleeping for one to two hours at a stretch, and trying to feed yourself. Has it really been a week since you washed your hair? Why didn't you notice that foul smell before? What the hell have you been doing?

You feel like you've been out on the piss for a week and the strange little friend who followed you home still hasn't left. Or bought any food.

But I'm kind of amusing and starting to make sounds that indicate I come from planet Earth. I'm even starting to look around, as if the contents of your apartment are somewhat interesting: couch, carpet, feet. Let's do it again. Yes, there's the couch, that's carpet even though the pattern's too 1970s for my taste — maybe they switched parents on me at the hospital, I'm sure I asked for an art deco apartment — and there, those feet again. Gee I'm tired. Just looking at those feet

163

and hoping they will have a pedicure soon is making me tired. But even if they're not particularly beautiful, they'd better be exactly where I left them when I wake up because if they aren't, I'm going to start screaming again.

Dadda

I have a pile of magazines to read and sometimes, when I'm not too exhausted and my eyes can actually focus, I try to read one. Sometimes my right eye wigs out and I have to abandon the literary sagas of my heroine so I can *rest*. Apparently this is what I'm supposed to be doing — sleeping, when Nina sleeps. Having always been a night owl, it's working OK for me. And Nina loves having me at her constant disposal, to fetch toys, makes sounds, give her booby, call the ambulance when the wind gets really bad and I scream at her about not knowing what to do.

That's when I feel really alone. When she's screaming and no matter what I do, I can't help her. And there's no partner or father there to swap the "I don't know what to do for her" looks with. No partner or father to tell me that I'm doing my best. And no partner or father to hand the baby to when it all gets too much.

Of course there's Adam, but three nights a week he's at Dean's and on other nights they go out, so he's more like a drop-in visitor these days. "Now that you're through the worst of it," he says before going out again.

I look at tiny Nina on the floor, still twenty years away from being able to make herself a sandwich, and wonder how he can think for one second that I'm through the worst of it?

(Ten o'clock. She's awake. Food time.)

I'm getting used to being on my own without any adult company during the day. I think I'm even starting to need less external validation. Yesterday, when I asked the fridge if I'd changed Nina's nappy already and it didn't answer me, I didn't get upset. I've learned to accept the fridge will only emit a nice quiet hum which is strangely reassuring.

("Burp.")

But it's weird not having to get up and go to work. Somehow I feel like I'm on a permanent sickie, or a student playing truant on exam day, but I know this delightful dream will be over soon and I'll be battling the rush hour across town again. What I've also realised is that the Sydney fashion world will keep turning whether I show up to work for a few months or not.

(Nina smells like vomit. Time for a bath. She's so slippery, I worry I'm going to drop her every time.)

But even though I'm dreading going back to work, I can see its positives. For example, I now understand why they invented the concept of work — not to chain us to the system or enslave us or to even ridicule us — but to keep us out of mischief. The weekend consists of three nights for a reason, two to get smashed up and one to recover.

(Bath over. Now I get Nina dressed and put her down for kicking practice. I watch the morning TV programs.)

Of course I still see the point that disadvantage is constructed and that racism and bigotry stem from our obsession with duality, and we really need to convince the major religions of the world to look forwards and not backwards — heck, I've even read Polanyi and am opposed to traditional economic thought as much as he was — and even though I tell the TV all this, it just doesn't care. All it wants to know is whether I'm going to buy a bagless vacuum cleaner or not.

"If you throw in some steak knives, I'll think about it," I bargain.

And the TV replies, "You're pushing your luck, fatty, but I'll give you a free workout DVD if you buy an Abs machine."

"No thanks," I reply. "I already have two under the bed."

Nina slept for six hours straight last night.

And I feel amazing.

I still look like a train wreck but I feel like I could conquer Mt Everest. Strangely, I don't have the energy to conquer the Mt Everest of laundry that is sitting in our bathroom.

I tell myself to take it one step at a time. If Nina sleeps through tonight then I'll consider doing the washing tomorrow. Having felt catatonic for the past few months, I don't want to waste any of this energy on meaningless activity — I'm going to save it up for something truly worthwhile, like sitting on the couch and watching Nina play on the floor.

Nina's on the floor a lot. In some cultures that would make me a bad mother. Hell, in some neighbourhoods, especially those where a $2000 pram is *de rigeur*, they would call Child Protection Services. Even in Africa, babies are carried all day, but I imagine that's because most African women are working — they simply don't have the luxury of sitting on the couch all day while the last of their parental leave entitlements dries up faster than baby vomit on polyester carpet.

It was Louise who told me to put Nina on the floor: "Definitely on the floor, not the couch, because she will inevitably roll off just when you've drifted off and are enjoying an erotic dream featuring a stunning man called Horatio," she told me ignoring the shocked face I made. My brain cart-wheeled. Louise daydreams about a hot guy called Horatio, that's how she gets through dealing with the public 12 hours a day at the store. On really stressful days, I'm sure Horatio does rather naughty things to Louise on the shop counter. I tried to shake it off by putting Nina on the floor and never thinking about it again.

Of course, the irony is that I rented a beautiful bassinet for Nina to sleep in (at $60 per month why can't she spend every second of every day playing in it?) but apparently she needs to be on the floor, stretching and kicking, pushing off and letting her head bob up and down.

No wonder I feel so bored some days I can barely stand. I've been sitting on the same couch every day, waiting for my stomach muscles to repair and looking after a tiny human being and while her needs are demanding, they're repetitive which is strangely reassuring and exhausting. All she wants is booby, a clean nappy, sleep, and for someone to get the wind out. If she started demanding I do her homework, her hair or gave her $50 for mobile phone credit then I'd be totally out of my depth.

So, the floor it is. And I move her mat around the apartment so she's got something different to look at every time.

Now that Nina a lot bigger, and is enjoying kicking her legs and throwing her arms all about, she's enjoying the space the floor offers her. She still wants booby on a regular basis and then we go through our burping-screaming ritual for a half hour, but then she's happy to have a nap before we start all over again.

I try to spend as much time as possible thinking about how beautiful she is, and not counting the number of hours I spend sitting around watching TV. When Adam leaves in the morning, I'm sitting on the couch feeding Nina and watching TV, and I am usually in the same position when he comes home.

But we do get out. Sometimes I put the Nina in a sling and manage to get both of us and a bag of clothes downstairs to do the laundry. Then we sit outside, under a tall gum tree, Nina cooes and gurgles at me from the shade and I relish the small amount of vitamin D oozing into my body. I look out for wildlife to show her but considering we're living in Sydney's eastern suburbs in the 21st century, wildlife is about as rare as a straight man. Sometimes I imagine that I can see a koala nibbling leaves high up in the tree, but it's just a hallucination stimulated by the breastfeeding hormones. Most of the time, all we see are a few crows and millions of ants.

When the washing machine's finished and I've hung the washing, delicately reaching above my head to hang out Nina's tiny little outfits, we tromp up the stairs again, sad to leave the bare, dry backyard behind but happy to not have to listen to the drone of Sydney's endless traffic anymore.

Then I make something to eat and drink another litre of water (I've never been so thirsty in my life from all this breastfeeding) and we sit down for the afternoon feeding-napping session which is commentated by Ellen DeGeneris. After Ellen dances around (which I find even more cathartic now that I'm recovering from abdominal surgery), she introduces the day's program.

"As part of our Spotlight on Worldwide Mums series, our guest today is Matilda Fisher," Ellen says. "Til is 33 and has just had her first baby, a little girl called Nina. Til is a single Mum living in Tamarama, near Sydney's famous Bondi Beach. So what does a single Mum in a big, fast-paced city go through these days? Is it easier today for women to have children out of wedlock or do the financial pressures scare the freaking hell out of them?"

Ellen continues. "You'll like this, ladies. We've put a secret video camera in Til's apartment and we're going to follow her every move, just to see just how stressful life as a single parent gets."

"Gee, this is going to be great," I tell Nina. "I betcha I really flip out. Doesn't Ellen's hair look good?"

Ellen cuts me off. "Well, Til's had a rough time since her baby girl was born but she's still looking pretty good, and I like the *Prada* dress the baby's wearing."

"Oh it's not *Prada*, it's mine," I tell Ellen. "I made it. Do you really like it Ellen? Did you really think it was *Prada*?"

But Ellen ignores me. "Oh look," she says to her audience. "She got really excited that time and nearly dropped the baby. Hasn't anyone shown this woman how to burp a baby?"

The audience moans and shake their heads.

"God, this is bad," I tell Nina. "Even the Americans have turned on me."

But Nina gurgles again that I'm doing a fabulous job and gives me one of her *You're the funniest, craziest, best Mum in the world* smiles. I turn the TV off.

My daughter rocks!

She is the coolest thing in Sydney. She is the only baby I know in Sydney.

And this is what Adam wants to talk to me about.

After making me dinner and tidying the apartment he sits me down for a little chat. Dean pretends to wash the dishes.

"We're a little concerned about how little you're getting out, Til," Adam says. And then he leans closer and whispers to me, "Dean thinks you may have… *IT*!"

"AIDS? Dean thinks I have AIDS?" I say shocked.

Dean appears. "No, God no, Til, I didn't say that! Adam, what the hell did you tell her that for?"

"I didn't say that at all. I meant, do you think you may be a little depressed?"

Dean is shocked. "I'm not depressed, why the hell did you ask me that, I thought we were here to ask Til if she was depressed."

Ah, so that's *IT*. I smile at my two caring boyfriends. "No, I'm not depressed," I tell them. "But considering I haven't had a full night's sleep in three months and I'm a new parent, I think I'm doing really well. And that's mainly because you guys give me so much support," I add — because it's true, but it's statements like these which will get me out of cleaning the apartment for the next month.

"You just don't go out with Nina — other Mums are out there shopping and cruising around and seeing people, we're just a little worried that's all. But if you change your mind and want to speak to somebody, I could give you some numbers."

"Are you reading from a brochure?"

Adam crumples something in his lap. "No."

"Give it to me," I demand and like a good boy, he does.

The brochure shows a woman sitting on the floor next to her dishwasher while her baby screams in the corner. She looks like she's been crying for days.

"Ah, come on boys, does that look like me? When do I do that?"

"It's not about what she's doing, it's about how she's feeling, Til…alone, isolated, dirty," Dean says and shudders while looking at me.

"If you want me to clean the apartment more just tell me but the midwives at the hospital said not to, 'just let the place fall apart around you and spend as much time with your baby and resting as possible'," I quote. "They also said an Ayurvedic massage every day would be good," I hint.

We all think back to when I was pregnant and Fred used to come by every week for my massage. We all sigh.

"So go out and get one."

"Damn," I mutter, disappointed that they didn't take the bait. "Well, it's not that easy, Adam. Firstly I'd have to take Nina with me and she'll scream and interrupt the massage and I'll be so tense it'll hardly be worth it. And I do go out, I did the laundry today and showed Nina all the trees in the garden. Oh, and we saw a dead lizard too."

"But out, out, Til — like, further than our street."

"OK. I'll try. But I just haven't needed to Adam. I really feel like I'm just taking this step by step and I haven't wanted to get out; I've just wanted to spend time with Nina. I don't want to wheel her around the shops because that's just a waste of time and I'm only feeling physically recovered from the birth now. Do you know how hard it is getting a pram onto a bus? And I'd have to walk it back up the hill which I just haven't been up to. I've been doing my exercises quietly, when you're out, but I am probably ready to go a bit further now, you're right."

They both look relieved.

"I forgot about the Caesarean bit," Dean says.

"Well, I haven't," I tell them. "Look, tomorrow I'm going out to the doctors for her four month check-up so that's an outing, isn't it? And if you really want me to I'll sign up for some mother-baby hook-up thing. Apparently the hospital organises them too."

They both decide that will be very good for me.

Now that they're happier I ask Dean for a shoulder massage, since all the feeding is killing my back, and over my head I see him and Adam swap weird looks.

"What?" I ask suspiciously. They look sheepish and say it's nothing, but I can tell it's something important, something they'd rather hide from me.

Adam breaks my concentration by offering to massage my feet and I forget about them and their little look.

Instead of booking an appointment with the Hungarian butcher doctor, I book Nina in to see my old doctor, the one with the nice hands.

As the smell of my unwashed hair has started to permeate the apartment, I devote all morning to washing and scrubbing myself clean while Nina plays on a rug. When she's not sleeping or screaming, I fetch toys for her and play peekaboo, popping my head out of the bathroom every ten seconds so she doesn't start screaming again. Because we haven't left the house much, packing the bag with enough nappies and incidentals takes me over an hour. We end up rushing to the doctor's, and when he calls us in to his consultation room, I can feel my heart beat faster.

This is the first time I've seen a male member of the species, who isn't Adam or Dean, in months.

Even though Doctor Nice Hands is over 50, he is sun-tanned and wearing a new camel-coloured cashmere sweater. His hands are also freshly manicured, and his nose a little smaller than I remembered.

"Til, it's so good to see you," he says and kisses me on the cheek. "And congratulations, I heard your wonderful news from Adam."

"Probably. He told half of Sydney," I say, noticing my left cheek flush.

"And this is your little bundle of joy."

Nina is kicking her feet in her pram, making little gurgling noises.

"This is Nina," I tell him, feeling the usual tug at my heartstrings whenever I think or talk about Nina. "Isn't she just the most gorgeous baby you've ever seen?" I ask him while picking her up carefully out of the pram.

"She's definitely in the top ten."

I realise I'm grinning at him like I'm an idiot. But I'm sure he's used to new mothers standing in front of him like stupid, stoned mullets, while they boast about their beautiful babies and feel the sun's rays radiating on them.

He allows me my moment in the sun. Then he motions to me to put Nina down on the examination table.

Dr Nice Hands leans over Nina and inspects her ears and eyes, and listens to her chest. He takes her head and length measurements, and checks her hips. He asks me all the right questions: date of birth, which percentile she's following, how many times a day she's feeding, how many wet nappies she has, how she's sleeping etcetera, etcetera.

Nina lays perfectly still for him, doing her perfect baby routine (which she only does for strangers). He handles her carefully, his gentle hands showing her she is the most important baby in the world.

But he asks nothing about me, so I try to make it about me. I skip over the answers to his questions and change the subject of our conversation to the birth.

"Ick. Well, maybe next time it will go better," he says and takes Nina's medical book from me.

Obviously, I feel deflated. I'm still getting used to my new reality, where the centre of my world is no longer me, it's Nina.

"So, you've been seeing Dr Scary. Excellent, she is a great physician, a total God in the world of Paediatrics, you couldn't have picked a better doctor for Nina. Couldn't you get in to see her today?"

I start to panic. Why the hell would he ask me that? Shouldn't he be happy I've come back into the fold? After all, he's got all those cashmere sweaters and a new cosmetic surgery habit to finance. Shouldn't he be relieved I'm bringing him a new patient?

"Til?"

"Ah, I wanted to get the go ahead to start a Pilates class," I lie. "And since you're my usual doctor I thought I should come here."

"Well, I'm honoured to meet your little girl but do you mind if I recommend you see Doctor Scary from now on, she is a very experienced Paediatrician even though she doesn't like word to get around."

I'm confused. "Why wouldn't she want them to know?" People would pay the receptionist hundreds of dollars to get a bulk-billed appointment with a real Paediatrician, this woman must be crazy.

"She'd have them queuing up for days, if she did. The only

patients who know are the ones who bother to ask their doctor for a recommendation to a GP with Paediatrics experience. I told Adam about her when he called for you. He didn't tell you?"

I try to blame my ignorance on my post-partum brain.

Dr Nice Hands gives Nina the all clear for her four month immunizations.

I tell him I have already wiped her legs with an anaesthetic to numb the pain.

"Good, good," he says with more relief than I thought appropriate.

I raise an eyebrow, but luckily, he doesn't notice my instant loss of confidence.

His hands shake as he tears the tiny baby needle packet open. He syringes the immunisation liquid into the needle, taps it and squirts it, a little too vigorously and it hits his medical certifications hanging from the wall.

Suddenly, I want to be back in the Hungarian butcher doctor's consultation room. Even if her certificates are so old they're greying around the edges, even if she smells of fish stew, even if she holds Nina by the scruff of her neck like she's a sack of potatoes.

He rubs the skin on Nina's legs with a cleansing wipe, and then rubs it over his forehead to catch stray beads of sweat which are swiftly appearing across an increasingly worried brow.

"Well, here goes," he mutters.

As soon as he punches her skin with the first needle, Nina starts screaming which makes his hands shake more.

Dr Nice Hands prepares the second needle and I hold Nina tightly, trying to steady her leg and say, "hush-hush" sounds into her ear. "Be brave, little one, it's nearly over," I tell her but she can't hear me over her screaming. Dr Nice Hands tries to tip her head back to administer the rotovirus immunization, but most of it dribbles down her chin.

"Is that enough?" I yell at him over Nina's screaming.

"It only takes a drop, hey Til?" he yells back.

And I know he's not referring to Nina's vaccination.

I leave in a filthy mood — angry at him for turning out to be a condescending asshole, and especially angry at myself for exposing Nina to a fraud. Well, not a fraud entirely, he is a registered GP, but not the undercover Paediatric specialist who has been caring for me and Nina for the previous year.

Even though Dr Scary treated me like I am the stupidest Mum-to-be in the world, she was right to treat me with such disdain. Not only was her approach a refreshing change from the world of fashion, where everyone is at least nice to your face before they stab you in the back, but she got my attention and made me read five parenting books a month.

She was right to be bossy and confronting; just like my High School History teacher who signed me up for detention when I told her I found the necessity of learning history demeaning.

I head to a Bondi café to calm down and order a decaf soy latte and salad piled high with prawns. I feed and burp Nina for nearly an hour. Dr Scary has told me previously that this is quite common; babies usually find immunisations traumatic and want to spend more time than usual at the breast. She's always encouraged to wait an hour in her surgery if required, to make sure Nina hasn't reacted to the needles and so I can nurse her in peace — as opposed to Dr Nice Hands who nearly pushed us from his consultation room while reaching for the bottle of vodka he must keep in his bottom drawer.

I banish thoughts about the morning from my head. "No point dwelling on it now, Til," I tell myself.

I dive into reading the café's pile of trashy magazines, while gently rocking the pram backwards and forwards while Nina sleeps. While I catch up on Lindsay, Miranda, Gwyneth, and Megan, I hum about what a beautiful baby Nina is as waves roll onto Bondi Beach, emitting a soft shhh, shhh sound.

It's a perfect hour.

But short lived. All too soon, Nina is crying again and looking for booby. As soon as she's attached and happily sucking away, I motion to the waiter for another coffee which arrives promptly, overflowing with silky-smooth, soybean froth.

Life in the cafe returns to a blissful, breastfeeding peace and when I look up to take in the beautiful view of Bondi — I see *Him*, walking right past the café.

And he looks different.

Not like I remember at all.

Because it's not Fred — it's *Him* — Nina's Dad!

And I nearly drop my coffee on Nina out of sheer panic.

My first instinct is to hide her, to shove her and the pram under the table (it will never fold down in time — I can't believe I stopped to consider this!) — and then they walk into the café.

They!

He's with someone.

A woman. Not a bad sort really, kind of frumpy but cute looking in her day, which was about ooh, five minutes ago.

When I notice the pram.

They slide past me pushing a brown *Bugaroo* which looks new while mine has that second-hand, non-consumer junkie, non-needlessly-creating-massive-carbon-footprint tinge about it! Who am I kidding, really? Mine looks like it's been run over by a truck, and probably was, I bought it on *ebay* for $20. The baby in it can only be a couple of weeks older than Nina at most.

"Holy fuck," I mutter over and over. Because this is the worst of all scenarios! Even I couldn't have imagined anything this bad. I bounce up and down in my seat and murmur through gritted teeth, "I don't know what to do! What the hell am I going to do?"

Nadia would know what to do.

Nadia would put her tit back into her bra, pull down her shirt, put the baby in the pram, pick up the magazine, put her sunglasses on and wait until they leave. Nadia wouldn't give a toss. "There was nothing between us, it was just a quickie and although Nina has a right to know her Dad and half-brother/sister, this is certainly not the time to introduce them. It would be an urban faux-pas to ruin this woman's day."

That's what Nadia would say. And also:

"Maybe this guy isn't the father of the woman's baby. Or maybe he is, and the baby has some genetic illness and someday will need to borrow some of Nina's DNA? Fuck. What the hell if Nina needs to borrow his?"

Damn. This is *soooo* not the time to be listening to Nadia.

They sit at the table next to me and I can't help myself: I stare at Nina's half-sibling. God, they're so close in age they could be twins — except that they don't have the same mother. I jiggle my feet under the table to hide my anxiety. What if he shagged us both the same night? No, that's disgusting.

I start an imaginary conversation with Adam instead. He suggests a more positive mindset:

"Maybe it's not his baby, maybe he's just a friend, Til. Maybe the woman's his sister and he's the baby's Uncle or godfather."

The baby has thick black hair. Just like his Dad. I even remember running my hands through it while we were screwing and thinking, "This guy will never go bald, lucky bastard — I really should remember to ask him his name after we've finished shagging because he's not that bad at it."

Fuck the positive mindset. That's what got me into this mess!

The woman smiles at me and wonders why I don't smile back.

Because this is what the sisterhood of mothers do: we look at each other and each other's babies and we smile. It means, "Hi, you look well, oh what a cute baby, she has your nose." The sisterhood of mothers is not supposed to say, "By the way did you know I shagged your baby's Daddy on New Year's Eve?"

The woman gives Nina's Dad a look that says, "Look sweetie, another one of those lonely, isolated, dirty Mums who talks to the dishwasher."

When I notice the rings. Oh my God, they're married!

I panic. I give Nina one of my biggest smiles, because I'm determined to not let this woman think I'm depressed, and quickly throw my purse and Nina's toys into my bag. I'm putting Nina into the pram when I realise my breast is swinging — I haven't put it back in my bra — shit! I haven't even put my boob back in my shirt! Bugger, I look like a freak! A millions times over.

I know they're watching me, their eyes are wide open.

I want to tell him, "Yeah go on mate, have another look at my boobs, not bad hey?" but my mouth doesn't work. It's firmly clamped shut with fear.

I pull my shirt over my breast and put on my sunglasses and hat all while holding the magazine as close to my face as possible, and muttering, "Shit, shit, shit."

When I get home, I realise that I forgot to pay the bill.

That's why someone was running after me from the café. I thought it was *Him*, I thought he was calling, "Hey I saw you, I remember you, do you want to meet my wife and kid?"

But it wasn't. It was just my waiter, who ashamedly had to go back to work, sweating and panting, to admit he couldn't catch the crazy lady, even though she was carrying an extra ten kilos, seriously out of shape, and pushing a pram.

When Adam comes home he finds me sitting on the kitchen floor, crying next to the dishwasher. Nina's screaming has reached fever pitch.

"God, Til, that's it, we're going straight to the doctor now."

"No, no, it's not that, Adam," I sob, my bloodshot eyes appealing for understanding. "Listen to me, I saw *Him*!"

"Fred?"

"No. *Him*, Nina's Dad. And he's married — and Adam they have a baby."

"Holy shit."

He sits down next to me on the floor and holds me while I blubber about how I am the worst person in the world. Then he tells me to calm down, that I'm scaring Nina.

"This isn't the worst thing in the world, Til. At least you know he's probably not the scumbag he could have been. If he got some other woman to marry him, he can't be that bad."

"Except that he screwed me when he was married to her."

"You don't know that. Maybe they got married recently because they were having a baby, maybe it's not even his, maybe she was out shagging some other guy and that's why they weren't together on New Year's. Maybe it was his sister."

"It wasn't his sister."

"Well, it was New Year's, Til. If she wasn't out partying with her husband then it's her fault really. No woman lets a straight man out in Sydney alone at New Year's without expecting something like this to happen."

Strangely he is making sense. Everybody knows it's true. That's why Sydney woman spend up to $500 just getting their hair cut and their legs and other bits waxed for New Year's. Getting laid on New Year's is a major achievement for every Sydney woman — gay or straight, rich or poor — that is, after putting a deposit on a flat in Bondi.

"Now, let's go get you a facial," he says. "Your eyes are all puffy and hideous."

Underneath a mass of hydrating cream I start to feel myself escape my state of delirium. I try to think — not about how much this is costing Adam — but about what happened in the café. I replay every second.

Were they holding hands? Were they obviously in love? Does she love him while he loves her like a straight flatmate would? Maybe he feels trapped in the marriage? Maybe he's a Mormon and is merely trying to follow the original Mormon teachings that a man should have more than one wife? Except that we weren't married.

Did he look at me? Did he recognise me? Did he see Nina?
Did he see Nina?!

And it hits me. All this time I've been fretting over whether he remembered me and Nina was within a metre of her Dad and he didn't have a clue. This could have been her one chance to meet him!

And I missed it. I missed giving Nina the chance to meet her Dad.

I feel like the worst mother in the world.

I could have said to him, "Look, would you mind holding my baby while I just pop off to the loo, I'd give her to your blissfully happy wife who is totally clueless you're an unfaithful prick, but she's got her hands full already. 'Why not leave her in the pram?' you say…why didn't I think of that… oh because she'll start screaming that's why, so just bloody hold her."

That's what I could have done.

Then when Nina turned 18, I could have told her that she

met her Daddy, that he looked down at her and thought she was beautiful, and yes, he had knowledge of her — not that she was his — but that she existed.

Lola, who has been bedridden for the last two weeks and is now 32 weeks, has heroically made it to my apartment to cheer me up after my disastrous encounter with Nina's Dad.

She sits on the couch with a tight, soccer-ball belly sticking out of her at right angles, and her swollen feet up on a cushion, while we watch Nina play with her first doll. Lola has kindly amputated the doll's head and legs to ensure Nina is introduced early to the concepts of diversity and respect for all human beings.

Nina, with full enthusiasm for the idea, tries to gnaw the doll's arms off with very sore gums.

She gives Lola a look of pure gratitude. And so do I.

I express my guilt at not being the one to visit Lola.

"*Non*, forget *et*, you have a baby on the outside, *c'est plus difficile* when you can't take it everywhere like a doggy in your purse."

She's got a point. Getting a pram onto a packed Bondi bus is a nightmare.

She continues. "I heard about your little adventures, I have come to ask you something."

I feel the shock of slipping over in red goo at her last exhibition sweep over me again. "Uh-ho," I say, although I try hard to contain the sound.

Nina looks at me like she's in heaven as dribble runs over her happy chin.

"*Non*, it will be fine, once this little rascal's out of me we are going to shoot the day you had yesterday."

"You want me to re-live yesterday — which was the worst day of my life, worse even than the day I went through 20 hours of excruciating labour and then had to be cut open and have Nina wrenched out of me? You want to video my humiliation?"

"*Non*, not humiliation."

"Mortification, degradation…what else would you call it?"

"Tell me, Til, you feel mortified because you saw the father of your child with his baby?"

"And his wife!" I complain.

"And you see that as your fault? Well it isn't. This whole situation shows us that our society has complex systems that are far from organic. Take marriage, you don't need it to have sex and have babies but you do need it in a society that has litigated control of humans' lives through *deux* of the most oppressive concepts ever created: patriarchy and private property."

"And this mumbo-jumbo about pricks and rent rises has something to do with me…how?"

"Because your guilt is depressing," Lola says pulling at her hair. "You're screaming, 'Ah, he has a wife, a baby, I'm a total slut,' when you should be screaming, 'I have the most beautiful baby in the world and who cares whether her parents know each other or not'."

"Well, Nina might care. What about when she's older? Will she suffer from not having her father around?"

"Except Nina has *deux* doting Dads, Adam and Dean."

"Yes, you're right. Jesus, am I being that self-obsessed; counting my shortcomings instead of my fortunes?" I whine.

"You can't help it. It's how we're reared: to always want more, to acquire more, be more. You should be less capitalist. We're human beings; we're meant to be ruled by chaos, our resources and our knowledge are supposed to be shared. But instead we live in a society bound by rules and that commodifies our resources — except women's resources, these we don't even count. The ones we count, we use to pollute the earth and fill it with junk."

Lola fills her mouth with pie. "Then we take parents away from the children they love, we send them off to work just so some people can make a profit and control more of the world's resources. Which leads me to question, if all cultures ignore women's contributions — except matriarchal cultures like the Australian Aborigines — then why do other cultures control women so extensively? Is it because women are an under-valued resource and therefore should be guarded — by ignorance, from ignorance, I'm not sure which? But I know I'm not valueless, I'm just undervalued by the market pricing mechanism."

"Nobody said the market was smart."

"Exactly. It is a very big assumption by government that the market will correct itself and find equilibrium. It's not how human beings work; everything we do is swayed by bigotry, including the market which we manipulate every day. But the people who suffer are the disadvantaged and women."

"So whose responsibility is it to fix it? Is it mine?"

"The irony is that the patriarchal system is supported by women. Without us, without us bearing children it would collapse, because future growth would diminish and die out. With an ageing population consumption would wane and industry would have no long-term return on investment. If women even went on strike from child-bearing for just a year or two, it would throw the world into chaos. Women are more powerful than they can ever know. But instead of thinking like that, you're here moping because you have relegated all your power to a nameless guy."

I sigh because I know she's right.

"But it's not your fault you have this mindset. Mothers' work is not even included in our gross domestic product calculations: they count cow's milk because it is farmed by a man, we count feed that's given to other animals, but not women's milk which is fed to a human baby. Without babies, there is no future — no future customers, no future employees and no-one to look after us in our old age. Women hold the very fabric of society together and yet we do not count. Instead, it's all about polluting the earth and threatening the future of life on this planet. We don't even tax businesses enough to pay for the damage they cause; most of the time we don't even bother to measure it. And we're so busy working and paying our mortgage, trying to stay solvent in a process that's destined to destroy our planet, that we are compliant, evil collaborators."

I look down at Nina who is still gnawing on the legless doll.

"What have I done, bringing Nina into the world when it's like this?"

"You can start by not giving a damn about this silly man."

"What am I going to tell Nina when she asks about him?"

"That he *waz* mugged and died."

"I can't tell her that."

"The truth then?" Lola suggests.

A memory flashes before my eyes. "Maybe when she's older."

"The censored version then. That you bumped into him in the corridor one day and you never saw him again."

"But I did see him again. Oh Lola, this isn't about me, I missed giving Nina a chance to know her real father. I'll never forgive myself."

"And ruin the other woman's happiness in the process," Lola says matter-of-factly. "You had a choice between two awful crimes: to ruin Nina's chance at knowing her father, or ruin the other woman's family. And even if you had told him, there's no guarantee he would have wanted to be a part of Nina's life. He obviously wants to be a part of his other baby's life. Do you have a right to spoil that, just for Nina?"

This is why I love Lola, she is able to consider the Greater Good. When society is telling me to think about my daughter, Lola thinks, "No, think about the other woman's child first. And if you still feel like shit, give something to charity, that'll make you feel better." Lola tries to reach for the last piece of spinach pie which is sitting on top the coffee table and she nearly rolls off the couch in the process. I jump up and pass it to her.

"So you realise you are not a total slut?" Lola asks.

"Yes, I'm feeling better now, thanks."

"Good for you, no more melancholy, no more throwing yourself headfirst into a garbage bin just because you ran through Bondi with your titty hanging out?"

"No."

"Because it's Bondi — lots of women out there with nicer titties than yours. I'm sure he never even looked."

Lola tries to perform a pelvic tilt exercise but can't lift her stomach off the couch. "What is happening to you represents a normal, contemporary dilemma. And that's why I want to document your experience."

"I don't think so Lola, I don't want to be in a documentary."

"*Non*. It will not be you. I will put a bag on your head. Our society doesn't care what your face looks like, you are just tits and ass to us. So will you let me video you naked, you did after all show half of Bondi your boobs?"

"I'd be degrading myself."

"But you wouldn't, Til, think of it as a step forward for Nina's generation. She will be able to watch this when she is bigger and see how hard it is to be a mother even in the 21st century."

Nina has fallen asleep on the floor with the doll hanging out of her mouth. I'm too scared to move her: you know what they say, "Never, ever, ever wake (or move) a sleeping baby."

"What will she see exactly?" I ask fearfully.

"The minute-by-minute experiences of a mother. The dramas and frustrations of getting baby ready to go out, of baby shitting just as you get to the door and you have all these bags over your arms," Lola gesticulates widely. "Of carrying baby and baby bags down the steps, only to find the pram has flat tyres; how hard it is to push the pram over irregular gutters while shopping falls off the pram only to get stuck in the middle of the street as a truck bears down on you; you nearly having a nervous breakdown in a café because you are so tired and confronted by your daughter's father's promiscuity that you leave a café with your tittie hanging out of your shirt. It's so real, it's great."

I am so horrified by the picture she is presenting that I cannot speak.

"Just think of how many people this video will speak to," she finishes.

"It'll end up on YouTube or on some porn site. No way. I am not appearing in your documentary or reality Mum show or whatever you want to call it, Lola. And that's final."

She blows air out of her lips. "But I call it a reflective video. It's my job as an artist to open people's minds. To encourage them to recognise their own mindsets and support that intuitive voice which says, 'Hmmn maybe there is another side to this story that I haven't heard in mainstream media'."

"No they won't. They'll say, 'Now look at that poor schmuck, she must have a really low level of self-esteem to let that prick phase her'."

"See? It's working already."

"I see what you're doing, Lola."

"See what?" she says innocently while stuffing the last mouthful of pie into her gob.

"And thank you," I tell her as she rubs her belly blissfully.

"It's alright."

New parent group

Due to Adam's constant pestering, I resign to his demands to rejoin the real world and commit to finding *friends* for Nina to play with. It seems weird that she need friends; she can't even sit up and spends her whole days slobbering on any object she can fit into her mouth, but apparently she has complex social needs that I don't understand yet.

Friends. Other little babies. And since babies don't usually wander around Sydney on their own, I am also resigned to finding other adults with their own little babies.

Adults. Real ones. Not like the usual crowd I hang out with.

Even though I have a baby, I still don't consider myself an adult. I'm sure there are other people out there like me but I don't want Nina hanging out with their kids. I want Nina to meet babies whose parents have a stronger moral compass than me, who live in a house with security windows, keep lots of parenting books on their shelves, and who are so patient even Gandhi would rip out their hair and call them self-righteous fucks.

And I don't know anybody like that.

I know approximately 9345 people (to be honest, Adam knows about 8000 of them and they're kind enough to wave at me, the others I know through work). The idea of having to meet new people with high ideals and much better awareness of global events scares me to my inner, unwilling to grow, please-just-let-me-obsess-about-fashion-all-day core.

Unfortunately, Adam is not going to *enable* me to remain the same emotional age as Nina for my entire life.

He brings home a flyer from a Bondi community noticeboard:

"New parents' group welcomes all parents with new babies.

Bondi Surf Life Saving Club Café. 10am. Thursdays".

"See? That simple," he says plonking the flyer onto the fridge under a magnet bearing Nina's first photo.

I complain to him in a last ditch attempt to avoid going.

"They're probably axe murders or paedophiles and are only pretending to be parents so they can chop Nina up into a million pieces," I wail.

"They're neither, Til. They're normal people with normal social needs whose children have normal developmental needs and don't want to feel like clumsy, undersized, undeveloped freaks living in a world of giants."

Which pretty much sums up how I feel most of the time.

But I keep trying to dissuade him. I moan, "If I don't know these people already that means I have nothing in common with them. They obviously don't work in fashion because we're all too poor or skinny to have children, they don't work in media because they're all gorgeous and rich and have nannies, and they don't know you — so they must be straight and therefore, dull. So that's it, I'm not going."

He tucks my hand through his arm and makes me sit on the couch with him. I notice his legs look defined and skinny next to mine.

He makes me look him in the eye. "Til, you're straight and you're going. And besides, you do have something in common with them — you have a baby! You're a human being with a biological capacity or desire to reproduce. What you haven't accepted yet is that being a parent normalises you, it takes fashion and work out of your identity and leaves you feeling exposed to the one thing that really matters."

"Nina?"

"A personality." He rubs my shoulders now like I'm warming up for a fight. "You can't hide behind hem lengths and the irony of trends that are, let's face it, lost on the masses forever. You are going to go to this new parents' group and you are going to be nice. You are going to show Nina that you have social skills and know how to use them; you are going to show her how to greet people appropriately; you're going to shake hands and introduce yourself and Nina; you're going to make eye contact and illustrate to Nina successful verbal and non-verbal communication skills; and you're going to listen to what other people say without shouting them down or rolling your eyes."

Which just about takes all the fun out of it.

Despite my reticence, I wake up on the morning of my new parent group debut feeling Adam's enthusiasm for me to rejoin the real world taking seed in my stomach.

The morning progresses perfectly: Nina feeds, burps and lets me dress her without screaming or vomiting and soon we're venturing out into a gorgeous summer day of blue sky and radiant sunshine. Pushing Nina down the Tamarama hill toward the beach, and around the cliffs to Bondi, a magnificent feeling spreads through the rest of my body as the sun and wind combine to create an intoxicating effect of carefree bliss.

"Weird, isn't it?"

I turn toward the voice. Its owner motions to the bodies on the beach and makes a funny face as if they're all aliens from another planet: women in string bikinis showing off their perfect bodies with not one stretch mark in sight; women who have all the time in the world to read magazines while watching the eye candy roaming the beach from behind their humungous sunglasses; bronzed bodies surfing on perfectly formed blue waves; men hanging out near the toilets, flicking their wet hair back and forth; and the lifeguards with their stripy zinc noses whose job it is to watch everybody (just in case they didn't feel watched enough).

What I find the most confronting is that just over a year ago I was one of them. I had a little yellow *Zimmerman* one-piece that looked like it had been slashed and showed off lots of skin. I was newly spray-tanned and the healthiest I'd ever been thanks to a combination of gluten-free food, plenty of fruit and lentils, vegetable soup and ten spoonfuls of spirulina, taken daily. I felt fantastic.

Now, I'm sweating under the umbrellas at the back of the beach looking like a gothic frump.

"I used to be one of them, now look at me," the woman says to me self-deprecatingly.

I turn toward her again. She is wearing cut-off shorts and a singlet that is pulled down to expose both breasts to the world. While I consider the irony of her statement, I remain tight-lipped: at least the women on the beach appear to be wearing all of their bikinis.

She attaches a tiny baby to her breast before flopping the non-feeding boob back into her singlet and taking a seat.

I suddenly feel even more conscious of the black maternity dress I am wearing on an extraordinarily hot summer day. In fact, I haven't felt this uncomfortable since I found out I was pregnant and spent every morning throwing up sixty times into the toilet.

But I'm not sick now — or even pregnant. So why am I suffering a torturous black maxi dress when I could be sitting, like this other women does, as comfortably in her body and her role as *The Breastfeeding Mother* as the painter Margarite Gerard intended?

My breasts start to leak in shame.

No, not shame, Nina is crying.

Instinctively, I start rocking the pram and shushing her and she settles again.

The bare-breasted woman is staring blissfully at her child and I notice for the first time that she's not alone. Five other women are seated around the table in equally semi-nude states all nursing or rocking small babies.

And they make such a beautiful sight, my breath catches in my throat.

Individually, each woman looks like a Botticelli angel but collectively, they appear as a contemporary sitting of Gauguin's masterpiece *Maternité*!

I want to scream at the thousands of people on Bondi Beach

to turn around; to ignore the cavorting of the salted exhibitionists pitching their self-absorption all over the beach and instead embrace the true beauty gracing their presence: these six women and their gaggle of babies all suckling at the breast! But no-one on the beach hears me; they carry on adjusting bikini straps and puffing their chests out, ignorant and self-absorbed.

Collectively, the women look up and smile at me and one of them says, "New parents' group," and just like that I am ushered into the fold.

I belong.

I have a baby.

And I'm welcome. Despite my inappropriate attire and attitude.

Judging by the size of their babies the title of the group is apt. These women's babies are all a few weeks old. And they've managed to make it out of the house already! In comparison, Nina should be pushing her own pram or at least graduating from baby school.

I collect Nina from the pram and the Mums coo over her.

"Oh, she's gorgeous! How old is she?" one asks.

"Four months," I tell her and all the women nod as if expecting more — because although they're sleep deprived, they're new Mums; they'll tell you anything about their baby if you let them.

"Her name's Nina, I had a Caesarean and am only just getting out and about."

Again they nod reassuring me that I am not a social outcast. I have a baby, a pram, a scar across my once-perfect abdomen, and it's OK.

"And I'm Til."

Nothing more, nothing less.

"Hi, Til," the Mum closest to me says. "I'm Nathalie and this is Jeremy."

"He's beautiful," I say to her and can't help but lean closer and stroke her tiny baby's hand.

The other Mums in the circle take turns at introductions.

"I'm Loni and this is Rylah."

"Sam, and this is Amelia and Isabella," the third says referring to her adorable twins.

"I'm Emily," the woman who first spoke to me says. "And this is Lilja."

"I'm Kylie," another says. "And this is Koby."

"And I'm lucky last, Donna, with the littlest, Elli," says the woman who finishes the circle to my left while flicking her bra open and letting her baby chomp down on her boob.

I follow suit, flicking my bra open with a cavalier nonchalance and Nina, happy to not have to struggle with the usual privacy screen I try to erect each time I feed in public, snatches at my breast like a ravenous crocodile.

The other Mums go crazy.

"God, what a hungry little monster," says Sam laughing.

"I wish mine did that — he just plays with it most of the time," Kylie says. "I'm having so much trouble getting him to attach properly."

The other Mums join in with gusto asking for a demonstration and subsequently offering advice and support.

Sitting there, baking in the sun in my black dress, I'm amazed by how nice everyone is and why I haven't tried this before. I'm starting to feel more normal by the second, even if I am perspiring like a 16-year-old on her first date.

"I'm just going to the café. Would you like a frappé or iced tea or water?" Loni asks, carefully placing her little baby over her shoulder.

I shake my head. "I emptied the Sydney dams of water before I came," I say pulling out a one litre drink bottle. "Don't go anywhere without it. But thank you."

The Mums switch from talking about breastfeeding attachment to funny experiences they've had while trying to hunt down water.

Emily admits to a drinking-from-plastic-bottle paranoia and worrying about ingesting carcinogens and passing them to the baby through her breastmilk if she leaves the bottle of water in the sun. "And it doesn't even have to be left directly in the sun. I worry if it's a hot day and I've left the bottle on bench in the kitchen instead of putting it in the fridge," she explains.

Which is followed by laughter, not of mockery, but agreement. It seems these Mums all have their own unique paranoia. If it's not carcinogens, it's rodent poo or leaving the baby with a babysitter.

I nod in agreement. "Between rodent poo and an evil grandmother, I know which one I'd rather leave my baby alone with. My Mum would throw out all of Nina's clothes and paint my whole apartment pink if I let her in the door. The only reason she lets my gay flatmate stay is that she's hoping people will think he's the real father."

Which leads to more laughter and I feel my serotonin levels skyrocket. As Nina slips into a deep sleep I acknowledge the pure joy of feeling her sleeping head resting on my shoulder. Looking down on her, at the millia spreading across her nose, and her soft, feathery skin, she is perfect, She's lost her little feeding flap — the gorgeous little bit of skin at the top of her lip that emerged a couple of weeks after she was born — so now her lips rest in a perfect pout.

In her sleep, Nina catches her fingers in my hair and gently tugs at it.

New parents' group chitchat carries on for another hour and is interspersed with blissful breastfeeding silence.

Loni, who seems the social organiser of the group, takes down my phone number and gives me a copy of everyone else's. "Just in case you need to talk to someone if you're having a bad day or need some advice. Although we'll probably be calling you, since Nina's so much older and you have more parenting experience than us."

"Nina's not much older," I say deflecting her compliment.

"No, but when you've only been a parent for three weeks and you suddenly meet someone with a four month old, well you become like a God to us newer Mums. And look at you, you're so sophisticated, so together."

"Me? God no. I feel like a goth next to all of you. You've brought me back to life. It's been fantastic meeting you, I'm going straight out now to buy some summer clothes that a new Mum should be wearing, not this over-priced tent I had to buy to try to disguise my pregnancy. As soon as I get home I'm going to burn this thing."

She laughs at me and her baby Rylah stirs in her arms. "No, don't do that, pack it away for your next pregnancy," Loni says. "Or some other pregnant Mum would love it, I'm sure."

"You're right," I tell her. "I don't think I'm having any more babies so I'll donate it. Not as much fun as a sacrificial burning, but more certainly more productive and less likely to produce greenhouse gases."

She doesn't pry for any more personal info from me or make a comment about environmental politics which was all the rage last year. Instead she says, "Oh I want more…in a year or two. We'll see how we go with this one first."

The group starts packing up their multitude of bags, tucking their babies into prams and slowly dissipates.

I leave on a high, feeling like I have thirteen new best friends whom I know nothing about and whom know nothing about me. It's a fantastic situation. Just a group of woman sitting around feeding their babies and swapping stories about how to best look after their little bundle of joy — and themselves.

Another rush of serotonin hits me, a high I haven't felt since the last time I bought a pair of *Jimmy Choos*.

Which starts me thinking. And puts a glimmer in my eye.

"Who says you can't push a pram wearing five inch heels and a pair of boardies?"

"I do," says a voice behind me, resolutely.

I turn to the voice.

Louise is standing in front of me with her hands on her hips. "You were talking out loud, you know."

"I've just been to meet my new parents' group," I tell her proudly. "And you know what Louise? I fit. I'm just like them. I feel … sun-kissed. I know who I am now: I'm a Mum and that's all that matters. And you know what else? There's others just like me out there."

"And they don't have a thousand dollars to spend on a new pair of shoes and neither do you, so get walking, chick," she says while bending over and playing with Nina's feet.

"I know, I know. I'm off to buy some summer clothes and some really cheap singlets so I can just hang a boob out whenever I want and feed Nina. And you know what, I don't care where I do it — on the bus, at a café, on a park bench, heck if she wants I'll even stop in the street and feed her right there."

"If you're going shopping, Miss Breastfeeding Queen, I'm coming with you. With the high you're on, you're likely to put stripes with paisley."

Louise, Nina and I spend the next hour acting like kids, raiding the cheapest surf shop we can find, putting together a wardrobe any carefree, new mama would die for. And all for under $100.

At home, I parade around the apartment and Adam, overjoyed at seeing me this happy, does his best to approve of my assortment of colours and fabrics, even though he is horrified that I am considering wearing mass market consumer apparel. Sometimes, he can be such a fashion snob.

"So, what did you think of the parents?" he asks me.

"Well, they're all Mums and they're all lovely. There are no Dads even though I'm sure they'd be welcome. You should come one day."

"And what do they all do?"

"Haven't a clue. We didn't talk about personal stuff at all. Although you came up of course — I can never have a conversation without mentioning you. But it was fantastic. To these women, I'm just Til, Nina's Mum, who's doing her best and is happy to be as supportive of the other Mums as I can be. Look, we even swapped numbers."

He nods happily at the list of numbers taking pride of place on the fridge right next to Nina's photo. He even agrees to watch Nina so I can take an absolute aeon to shower and wash my hair. And while I skip off to the bathroom, I'm sure I hear him crumple the postnatal depression flyer and throw it into the recycling bin.

Five Months

Just when you thought it was about to get easier.

Trouble is brewing.

Underneath the gums of some young babies, the first signs of tiny little white teeth can be seen. But the trouble they cause can be monumental. For some parents, the sign of the first teeth is not something to be rejoiced; instead it signifies the end of the baby stage and the relentless march of infancy and then toddlerhood.

Of course, every stage of a human life is exciting and beautiful, but it can be difficult for some parents to let go of their dependent, gorgeous baby. Which is why Mother Nature invented teething. A teething baby insists on being held 24/7, and while this is OK when I was all new and wrinkly and only weighed three kilos, a screaming, wriggling heifer is another story.

There is something else driving my development forward at a frightening pace.

I've started to move.

Not just tummy-time wriggles where I lift my head and look at you adoringly for a second before my head goes crashing back to the ground, but real, guerrilla-style push-ups!

At first you'll think that it's just sleep deprivation causing you to hallucinate, but then it happens again and you can no longer deny it.

"She moved!"

Some babies will spin around on the spot and others will reach an arm out toward a toy and make a grunting noise as they shove themselves dismally at it. Some babies will just scream and refuse to do anything. And others will roll over and then wonder how the hell they're going to get back onto their stomachs (all the time while screaming or giggling).

But when your baby pushes herself up from the floor and puts one hand forward and then another, before crashing and rolling onto her back, you'll stand there frozen to the spot before rushing around the apartment looking for the video camera.

"My baby moved!"

You call your mother, who comes around, and watches the baby, as engrossed in her achievement as you are — which is strangely irritating, you were hoping she might tidy up a bit.

Your friends are more useful: they tell you to start *babyproofing*.

Babyproofing means getting your house ready for a crawling infant who will explore every nook and cranny and try to suck on any electrical outlet that you have neglected to install a safety plug in. You will also have to pack away all chemicals, medicines and detergents by putting them up high in locked cupboards. You'll also need to put locks on all doors that the baby shouldn't explore (remembering to leave some open to her, like the plastics and cooking utensils drawers) and putting away any breakables and furniture with sharp corners.

Babyproofing can take months. As your baby develops and can get higher and higher, more and more things will have to be removed from danger. Because after crawling comes climbing. And advanced technical skills. There is nothing more annoying to a sleep-deprived parent than watching a small baby, who is just out of reach, change the channel while slobbering all over the remote.

The sound of trouble

Just when I think life couldn't get any better, or my bank account lower, Jaimee calls to tell me her life is over.

As somebody who doesn't have children, she doesn't think to ask if this is a good time.

It isn't. It's not Nina giving me trouble, it's me. I'm going through a stage.

Nina is starting to make backward rowing motions across the floor and I am so charmed by it that I forget about all earthly matters and watch her for hours. Until I get hungry and decide to put something in the microwave and then go back to watching her. In fact I never take my eyes off her which is how little mishaps keep happening.

When the phone interrupts my daily session of obsessing over Nina, I get up to answer it, and that's when I see the microwave is smouldering.

"Oh shit, fuck, help me, ADAM!" I scream before throwing the fire blanket over it as the smoke alarm starts ringing and electric circuit breaker shuts off all power to our apartment block with a major thud.

And then it's quiet. Even the refrigerator has stopped humming.

"Oh shit," I say again and madly start waving at the smoke which is lingering in the kitchen.

Adam swoops into the room, surveys the damage (which is very little, surprisingly), swears about this being the last time, grabs Nina and tromps out of the apartment to switch the electrical-thingy back on.

I stand next to the microwave waving the smoke away with a tea towel.

When the refrigerator starts humming again, I know everything's OK.

The microwave goes *bing*.

And stupidly, I open the door.

A wall of carcinogenic, black smoke hits my face and sends me backwards.

The phone, which I'd dropped next to the microwave, rings again.

"What the hell just happened," Jaimee screams down the phone at me. "I called, you answered, then you started yelling, "Holy fuck, holy fuck call the fire brigade I've just killed Adam.""

"No, I didn't, Jaimee," I tell her, amazed at how calm I feel. "I would never swear in front of Nina."

Of course Jaimee doesn't believe me and insists on a full run-down and a scowling Adam reappears with Nina, who is now screaming for her lunch. And I feel exactly the same way. And there's no way in hell I'm eating the carcinogens of a burnt organic chicken pie.

I tell Jaimee to meet me at the local surf life saving club for lunch.

The Tamarama Surf Life Saving Club has the most beautiful view on earth. It's not elegant or cool like Bondi, but understated and intimate, just like Tamarama beach.

When you ask tourists to describe a typical Australian beach, they'll tell you that it's big, has lots of white sand, and is riddled with British backpackers learning to surf.

Which is the exact opposite of Tamarama beach. The beach at Tamarama is more like a cove, protected by small cliffs on either side, and tiny. The beach is only 100 metres long. Definitely too short to jog across, and yet long enough to attract those bearing beach umbrellas and a gaggle of kids. It's perfect for families and people like me who are terrified of the open ocean and the massive sharks that swim in it.

And Tamarama has very little surf so it's peculiar someone even bothered to build a surf club here at all. But they did. A surf club for people who don't like to surf.

Just like me.

Because I arrive before Jaimee, who has to hike it from the city, I sit in a lounge overlooking the crystal clear Tamarama waves and watch the midday heat settle on the sand like a haze of pot smoke; thoughts which only intensify my hunger so I order some pizza bread (since when did carbs come back on the menu at a Sydney eatery?) while waiting for Jaimee to arrive, and I breastfeed Nina.

And I watch a lifeguard with rockhard glutes stroll up the beach carrying a longboard over his head.

"Ah," I tell myself. "Life has really gotten better since I started leaving the house."

Jaimee arrives looking fabulous, wearing skinny jeans and a sequined *Sass & Bide* top.

"New?"

"No, last week," she says taking off her humungous *Versace* sunglasses and sitting down.

I giggle. "Of course, it's not new then."

Having been out of the fashion industry for five months, I am enjoying some new-found objectivity and an ability to laugh at it all. Even the words *Fashion Week* don't seem to send major thrills through me anymore — OK, little thrills, yes, but not major tidal wave spasms.

I wait for her to comment on my outfit but of course she doesn't. Either she is too polite or too self-obsessed to notice I am wearing a bright pink singlet, blue board shorts, white *Volleys* and massive pink sunglasses which are shaped like hearts. I bought them because Nina thought they were hilarious, and even if my ensemble makes people think I'm insane, I don't care. *As long as my daughter is amused*, is my new motto.

Nina giggles at me. Apparently I am still the most hilarious mother in the world. The sunglasses are definitely worth the ten dollars I paid for them.

"Ah, she is just gorgeous Til. She's really starting to look like you."

So far most people have stayed away from that topic, the *Who does Nina look like* discussion. Because if it's not me, it must be *Him* and they don't know *Him,* so they can't really say if it's my nose or his so they just shut up and try to avoid any awkwardness.

"So, the thing I wanted to tell you, Til, is that my life is over," she dumps, and then orders the waiter to bring her a very expensive bottle of champagne. Jaimee belongs to a group of people who think that no matter how awful the catastrophe — be it bankruptcy or a bad hair cut — champagne is the only proper accompanying beverage. Your ex-husband died? Drink champagne and use his *Visa* card one last time before the bank cancels it. Your shares trebled overnight but your business partner sold them right from under your nose? Drink very expensive champagne and charge it to someone else's *Visa* card.

But really bad things never happen to Jaimee, so when Jaimee tells me that her life is over, I'm assuming she means she wasn't allocated one of 50-only celebrity handbags made by *Gucci.*

It's a game, and it's one that amuses me immensely. "So, how come so glum, Jaimee? Did *Georgio's* close down?"

"No," she says taking off her sunglasses and exposing truly black circles underneath her eyes.

I'm shocked, but I continue the game, "Fashion Week's been cancelled?"

She shakes her head. "God no, they can cancel Christmas if they like but never Fashion Week. Don't say such things, Til."

"Next season's designs have been lost in some terminal computer failure and it's all Didi's fault?"

"No. Look, stop guessing. I'm just going to come out and tell you," she says taking a deep breath.

I start feeling genuinely worried. Deep breathing in others is never a good sign — it means they're overly anxious or have just entered therapy and are ready to tell you *ALL* about it.

Jaimee sighs, "Because even though it's my life that's over, it's yours too."

My heart sinks.

"You know how I told you we have this great parental leave policy and you can have your 16 weeks paid leave on top of your annual leave and then work from home three days per week and come back full-time — when you're ready?"

"Vividly."

"Well, it's true, except there will be no office."

"Don't tell me they've gone virtual?" I ask her.

"They've gone bust."

The words sink in slowly. They've gone bust. Not like me, who is *busty*, but like dead bust as in not having a dime, cent or even a euro.

"Shit, shit, holy fuck, bugger Jaimee this is worse than setting the microwave on fire."

"I know, I'm really sorry, Til, but if it's any consolation we're all out of work, it's not just you."

"And this month's pay?"

"We've got lawyers onto that."

I don't breathe for ten whole seconds. How could I when I've just been told I've lost my job? But it's more than that: I've lost the girls at work whom I love as much as I do Adam; I've lost Fashion Week which usually means the absolute world to me; and I won't be able to pay any of next month's rent. Dean will have to move in and I'll have to move to Jorja's or Mum's, which gives me about as much pleasure as the strap-on dildo some guy gave me for Christmas once.

I can hear Margaret, my mother's bitch-friend, in my head, "I told you it was happening Jean, she's one of these boomerang kids, she's coming back to bleed you dry and stab you in the back with one of those carving knives you picked up in Nova Scotia while you were bird watching."

"His name was Ted Goodwin," Mum would reply. "And if my daughter needs me, she needs me and that's what I'm here for."

Which is true.

Jaimee is fanning me and saying something about my lips going blue.

She throws a glass of cold water over me and I gasp, shake it off like a wet dog and thank God we are at Tamarama where that kind of behaviour is tolerated — and not at Bondi where the same gets you sent to rehab.

"I'm thinking about Nina," I say and start to cry. "The poor girl, she's going to have to go through life wearing Jorja's girls' hand-me-downs and I'm going to look even worse — I'll have no sample clothing to wear, no hair and makeup account or Fashion Week shoes left behind by some vague, hungry gazelle."

Jaimee rubs me on the back and tries to soothe me. "I don't like to say it at a time like this, but nothing could be worse than what you're wearing now. Luckily Nina's young, she won't remember it. Promise me you won't take any photos in this stuff, Til. I'd better ring Nadia and send her to Mauritius on a fake shoot so she can't see you in this. She'd be devastated."

But I'm not listening to her. I'm as angry as hell. Jaimee talks to the Board all the time, how could she not know this was coming?

So I ask her directly and she holds her hands up like I've tried to shoot her.

"I'm an idiot, Til, I didn't see it coming. The Board didn't renew its store leases last year, they told me they had some estate agents looking for better commercial space, and I believed them. Stupid me, hey? It looks like they've been planning this for a while."

"So they haven't gone bust?"

"Not exactly. No, the directors pulled the money out and ran."

And even though I should be as angry as hell at her, I know she's not to blame. Jaimee's a great boss, not a conniving thief; if she says she didn't know, then she's telling the truth.

We both look at poor, defenceless little Nina sitting on my lap.

"What will you do?"

"How am I going to get a job with a new baby, Jaimee? I've got her booked into day care but not for another two months and that's only two days a week. How am I going to find something else that will pay me for doing nothing for the next two months, and then let me work from home part-time?"

"You could always do phone sex."

"Get real, Jaimee. I'm not doing that while my daughter is around."

"Well, the good news is that you've got the rest of the week off," she says somehow managing to sound chirpy about it.

"And what about all the work we've done on the label?" I moan at her. "Look how much we've put into building it, we were two years off showing at Paris. I was going to go to Paris. We were going to be the next *Dinnigan*."

"No, we weren't, Til."

And she says it so defiantly that I whisper under my breath, "What do you mean, Jaimee?"

"We weren't ever going to Paris." She sighs and refuses to look me in the eye. "The owners never wanted to go overseas; unlike you they thought OS was just too big a sea for them. They were only amusing you by listening to your international penetration strategies. Of course, I always believed the label could do it. I hoped that you'd change their minds."

But I'm not listening to her anymore. All I can hear is Jaimee telling me that we were never going to Paris.

I'd staked my whole career on it! I'd stayed at that blood-sucking company even though they under-paid me by about 25% because they said I'd be the one to take the label into the international market.

I wail at her, "But it was in the business plan! You promised me!"

Jaimee goes a vivid shade of red. "No. The Board promised you. I just agreed with them so you wouldn't leave."

"You what?" I cry out and someone at the back of the restaurant calls out "Lesbian spat" and stands up to watch.

I keep yelling at Jaimee, with tears streaming down my face. "You told me you would take me to Paris. You said that it was because of me that *Enegi* is now one of the most recognisable brands in this damn country and that we could crack Europe or at least China. And so I worked my butt off for eight years and now you tell me there was never going to be Paris?"

"You would have done the same thing in my position. Now calm down, you're scaring Nina."

I look at Nina, who does seem a little scared of me. Her little face scrunches up, her lip starts quivering and then she lets out an almighty scream as if her little world has just crumbled.

Because it has. I leave Jaimee sitting by the big windows staring out at little Tamarama cove. As I buckle Nina into the pram, I decide I'm glad we didn't go to Bondi today. The sight of the wild, ravenous sea would have reminded me how vulnerable Nina and I are now without the protection of the label and its meagre but reliable income. And to rub salt into the wounds — I was never going to Paris!

I start the uphill walk home to the apartment.

Paris was just a fake employee incentive, probably thought up by the bastards who just sponged every last cent out of the company before paying its employee entitlements!

This train of thought leads me to a crashing halt. HR knew about it! And Accounts. That's why they didn't want me to take all of my holiday pay up-front. Bastards. Luckily I made them pay me all of my entitlements before I went on maternity leave.

"See, your Mum's not totally clueless," I tell Nina proudly, but the words sound empty.

After leaving the pram in the downstairs garage and heaving Nina and all our gear up three flights of steps, I open the door to the apartment and am greeted by the lingering cent of burnt carcinogens.

Which I gather is an analogy for my life.

I make a decision. If those bastards won't take me to Paris then I'll take Nina.

And I won't back out of it or use it to lure her to pee on the potty. I'll make it happen. I'm not sure how yet, but if I can take *Enegi* from the scummy little whacked-out label it was before I came along and turn it into a Fashion Week icon, then I can do absolutely, bloody anything.

"Mum, I'm stuffed. There's nothing I can do."

My mother, who hasn't seen me come within a hair's-breadth of crying since my Dad died is now sitting on the couch next to me rubbing my back while I wail into a box of tissues. We are both in a state of shock.

Nina is asleep, thankfully Mum managed to get her to go down. I was too upset to even hold her, every time I looked at her innocent, wide blue eyes I broke down.

"How could they do that to me? How could Jaimee do that to me?"

"Well, it's probably not her fault, she wouldn't let this happen to you, to any of her staff, if she had any control over it."

"But she lied to me about Paris."

"When you were ten I told you you'd get pregnant just from kissing a boy. We do what we have to do. You don't hold it against me, do you?"

I take that as a rhetorical question.

"Besides, there's plenty of things you can do," she continues. "You did two degrees and excelled at them both."

"But that was years ago, that doesn't matter."

"It still shows that you're a hard worker. And really, that label was nothing before they hired you, and now look at it; what's their turnover now?"

"Over $20 million."

"And how much were you getting paid?"

"Not enough."

"Well, you've learned a lesson then."

"Yeah, I want a big, fat bonus next time and share options and a car and…."

Mum interrupts, "Do you really think that will make you happy?"

"No, but it's what I'm worth."

Her head bobs from side to side. "I get paid $38,000 a year and I do my best too. Do you think I'm worth that?"

"That's not what I meant, Mum, you know it. You're priceless. You drive me insane, but I love you, you know I do."

"Well, of course I do. I don't think I'm worth any less than you, not half, nor any more, not one time or 100 times. I may be older than you but I have needs the same as everybody else. The fact that some people are paid one million dollars a year while others subsist on thirty thousand seems a little opportunistic and disrespectful if you ask me. So, I don't know if you should ask more or less in your next job, but it should take you where you want to go. If Paris is what you really want, then you should go work for someone who will take you there. I may not be as smart as you, but that's what I think."

"Oh Mum, you're so right," I say hugging her fiercely. "I have been an idiot."

"Well now you're a broke idiot, but at least you're learning."

She pulls free and takes the few short steps to the kitchen to make tea. While the kettle boils I wail at her some more.

"I'm just not ready to go back to work. I'm loving being home with Nina and now I'm broke, I'm going to have to sign on for social security."

"Well, there's no shame in that. It's not your fault this has happened. That's what it's there for."

While I blubber into a tissue, I make a mental note that Mum doesn't offer me a loan. She's worked a full-time job since Dad died unexpectedly at 45, leaving her with two teenage daughters and no life insurance. Mum sold the hardware business to pay off the house, but she's had to work since to support us and then herself. Even though Jorja's rich, Mum won't take money from her; she's insistent that she's not going to be a burden to us and I know her retirement nest egg means the world to her. She wouldn't touch it for anything. Not even her grandchild.

Which makes me feel even worse. My mother is super-independent, planning and scrimping and saving for her retirement, and here I am blubbering because I've put myself into a situation where I can't feed myself and Nina. Because I've lost my job, which can only be considered my fault since I made Jaimee write that new parental leave policy. And it is equally my fault that I don't have any savings.

I moan and drop my head into my hands.

"I've been such an idiot. One minute I didn't have a care in the world and now I've got a baby and no job. I should have planned for this years ago."

"Well, you didn't know you were going to have a baby," she says and looks over her glasses at me. "God, none of us did. It came from out of the blue. One minute you're single and everyone was calling you my spinster daughter, the next you've met a guy and are having a baby. It's a shame it didn't work out. I didn't even meet him, did I?"

Mum knows all too well that she didn't meet him. But she's avoiding the reality, which is another sign that she's conveniently delusional — a survival skill developed by anybody over the age of 50, when all your friends' kids are living in the suburbs, married and totally fucking boring, except yours.

"You could always ask Jorja for a loan, until you find something."

"No. No way. I'd rather die."

"Your sister loves you and she's rich. She wouldn't mind."

"I'd feel like a complete moron if I had to borrow money from her."

"I thought you said already you feel like that."

"That's a whole new level of moronic. I can't go there."

She's judging me. I know she is. "Not even for Nina?"

I bury my head in my hands. "I can't do it, Mum. It's bad enough that Jorja's this super-success story; she's got more money than God. I went to Byron last year for my yearly retreat, she went to the Himalayas then on to New York and met Tom Ford. The only thing I've ever done is slum it at *Enegi*."

"When your sister said you were 'slumming it', she didn't mean it badly."

I look up at Mum incredulously. "How could 'slumming it' ever be construed positively?"

"She meant you were undervalued, that your job was beneath your talent, but she thought you were intensely loyal to stay at a little Australian label when you could have easily sold out and gone on to bigger things. She thinks you should be the Editor-in-Chief at US *Vogue* or running *Gucci*. She thinks your business acumen is second to none."

I sit, gobsmacked. "How do you know this?"

"Well, I asked her didn't I? After that silly article on her came out, I read it and because I thought her comments were unfair I told her so. She explained to me that her comments were taken out of context, as they often are. She wanted to talk to you about it, but you hadn't read it apparently. You weren't interested in her success."

I can't believe she's managed to turn this around so that now I'm the bad sister. She places a cup of tea in front of me which I burn my mouth on, rather than risk talking to her.

"Your sister, if you sat long enough to listen to her, is guilt-ridden by her fortune and spends a great deal of it funding community work in third world countries. That's why she was in Nepal and Tibet last year, she wants her girls to understand their fortune — and by that I mean their fortunate lives — and she wants them to realise what life is like for most of the people on this planet: poverty, war, famine, no sanitation, no health care, no opportunities or education, and slave labour. Next year they're off to Jordan…" she mumbles, "or is it Iran?"

I want to cover my ears and not listen to her anymore. Life was fine when I thought my sister was just an über-God; gorgeous but absolutely talentless. Now it turns out she has a thyroid in over-drive and it's focussed on fixing the planet. Meanwhile, I've had my head buried in fashion for so long that I barely know the rest of the world exists — beyond the fashion pages of Milan, Paris, Tokyo and New York.

Mum sips her tea thoughtfully. "Most rich people think their wealth separates them from everybody else but Jorja doesn't think that way. She thinks her wealth gives her greater responsibility.

"Why does she keep making millions out of her property investments then?"

"Your sister doesn't believe in the privatisation of resources, but I guess she doesn't know any other way of making money. She can't do what you do, so she keeps doing what she does and invests her profits back into communities that need it."

"Which makes me feel even worse. All I do is make clothes."

"Well you don't even do that, do you? Other people at your work do that. You sell them. But you do it rather well."

"But that's not much is it?"

"Well, no, it's not saving lives. Jorja says it much more eloquently than I do. She says things like, 'That Til, she's got her finger on the pulse, she thinks things a good season before people know they want it, and then she's ready for them'. That what you have is a gift, the team you've built around you at *Enegi* is another sign of your brilliance, apparently. She has complete faith in you, that's why when you said you were having a baby, Jorja was absolutely thrilled. I never heard any of that, 'Oh but she's going to be a single Mum, she'll have a tough time'-talk from her. It was all about what an amazing parent you'll be, how the baby will grow up with the most open-minded parent in the country, what beautiful clothes she'll have, what an interesting personality. Her fashion friends all want to poach you too apparently, but she's always said you're too loyal to leave *Enegi*."

I'm not quite sure if I believe what Mum's telling me but I like the last thing she said. "So maybe one of her friends could offer me a job?"

"It's Jorja. She knows everybody."

My heart soars. "Who do I want to work for then? That's the question. And will they let me work from home two or three days a week so I can be with Nina? And I want to go to the Paris fashion shows, it doesn't have to be every year, but even just once. I'd be happy with that. What I don't want is to have to work full-time."

"Well, that won't do Nina any harm."

"So what would do Nina harm?" I ask, amazed that she hasn't off-loaded any criticisms of my parenting yet — and she's been here a whole hour!

She takes a sip of tea and rests her feet on the *Eames* chair I bought Adam for his last birthday. "I'm sure you've read all the books, what do they say?"

"That some kids can overcome any so-called disadvantage. Unless of course they're already dead from malnutrition or completely inadequate health care."

"Well, you don't have to be concerned about that happening to Nina. And you're in a much better position than other mothers. You won't have to work two jobs to make ends meet, and you've only got one child to worry incessantly about."

She rubs her eyes and I feel her life's toil emanating from her.

Of course she's right. Now I feel guilt ridden, as well as moronic and broke. Mum looked after both Jorja and me with little help from Dad; even before he died, he was always at work or doing paperwork at night. Then when he died, she was our only source of income. I forget too easily that I spent most of my childhood being raised by a single mum.

Mum yawns again and I know it's time to send her home to bed.

"So, I'll get another job. Paris would be nice but what's important is Nina," I decide out loud and even though I can feel a deep pressure of disappointment fill my chest, I know that's what I must do.

"That's my girl," Mum says. "I know what you're going through, you feel catatonic with worry that you won't be able to give the best of everything to Nina. And you're numb, isolated, and exhausted. I'm happy to help you with Nina when I can, if you want me to. You know I work five days a week, but I can come by at night or the weekend if you need me. And I promise I won't interfere in your decisions — Nina's your child, not mine."

"Thanks, Mum."

And then she goes in for the kill. "And I won't buy her any more clothes."

Which makes me tumble against her chest and cry even more.

Around dawn, I wake up to hear Nina crying in her cot. I shake a blanket loose off my shoulders and sit up on the couch. I must have fallen asleep after Mum left.

I walk into my bedroom and Nina immediately switches from crying to giggling.

"Oh, my little angel," I tell her picking her up and cuddling her close. And she smells so divine that I never want to have to put her down. But if I'm going to be able to afford to feed her next week, I'm going to have to find a job.

Preferably one that lets me take Nina with me everyday.

But since that's not going to happen in this town, not for a very, very long time, then that leaves me with only one option.

The woman at the childcare centre laughs out loud hysterically. "You want a place for your child — here — immediately?" And then she starts laughing again.

I ignore her sarcasm. "Yes, please, that would be nice." And I nod vigorously. "I know it's short notice but I've had my name down on the waiting list since I was three months pregnant, so if you've got a place I'd like to take it."

"We don't have a place for you. Not now, not ever." She closes the book with a thump and such conviction that the hairs stand up on the back of my neck.

"But I asked for a place starting in May. How can you not have a place for me?" I ask incredulously.

"Our mothers have had their names on the waiting list for years. They all need a nursery place."

I know I shouldn't challenge her but I can't help myself. "That means they've had their names on the waiting list since before they were pregnant, that's ridiculous, not to mention totally unfair."

"Well, some people are very good planners," she says churlishly. "This is a very well-regarded nursery. The very smart women plan their babies around *our* vacancies."

Which means she's seen my child care benefit percentage. And obviously to her, I was not smart enough to marry a billionaire. I stop myself from bashing her in the face.

"You could try some other day care centres."

But the other 15 day care centres tell me the same thing. Some are nicer about their delivery, but the message is the same.

We traipse home defeated and wait impatiently for Adam.

All of this stress is making me exhausted. I should be trawling the internet looking for a job, but I sink into the couch instead.

The only thing I have the energy to do is pick up the phone and call Jorja. She excuses herself from another celebrity-prone dinner to take my call.

"Mum told me," is the first thing she says.

Even though I can feel a swarm of tears erupting again, I say, "It's not that big a deal."

"Mum said you were catatonic," she says and her calm voice steamrolls any attempt I can now make at nonchalance.

I blubber into the phone. "It's a shock, that's all it's not my fault."

"Well, of course it isn't. You weren't on the Board. You weren't part of the decision to fold the company. They must have been planning this for months. It's a pity they didn't leave any money to pay the employee entitlements, but I hear Jaimee's got the solicitors onto it."

"How do you know?"

"I looked into it. I may not have a double degree, Til, but I've done a few corporate governance courses. I know the directors haven't met their legal responsibilities but it will take time…"

The sound of cheering crackles down the phone and Jorja's voice is obliterated.

"Where are you?" I ask her when it dies down.

"A fundraiser at the girls' school. I'll just go outside for a bit so you can hear me. We just hit the $100k mark."

"Your school raises more in a year than I earn?" I ask her incredulously.

"Not a year, this is just one night. There'll be more fundraisers throughout the year."

"What are you fundraising for? A Justin Bieber concert?" And for the first time in two days, can't help but laugh.

"Farming equipment and wells for a women's co-op in Malawi. Women in Africa usually aren't allowed to handle the cash crops, but because these women are doing it so successfully, their village allows them to grow and manufacture their crop and sell the by-products. The co-op runs the bank accounts too so the women's husbands can't rip them off and use the money to buy alcohol. It's really unusual, but we're hoping they'll become a role model for other villages."

"Right." Now I really feel redundant. "Your kids are more successful and intelligent than I am. Not to mention better humanitarians."

"You're humanitarian, Til."

I sniff back tears. "I'm not. I've done nothing to help my fellow woman."

"You and the girls at *Enegi* donated $50,000 tonight. Didn't Jaimee tell you?"

For the hundredth time this week, I feel speechless. "We did what?"

"Your donation's been organised for some time. I was thinking about donating the money back to you girls, but Jaimee said not to, that you all have savings plans."

I look at the phone I'm holding, wondering if I'm talking to my real sister or an alien. Or maybe the phone is altering her words? Perhaps she intends to donate $50,000 to me? Her words ring in my head, *savings plan*, but my mind is blank.

"Jaimee was insistent. She said it's company policy that 15 per cent of your salary goes to a savings account, and five per cent to a pooled charity account. It was the first policy she instigated when she took over the business. She's knows exactly how uncertain the rag trade can be. She wanted you all to have a nest egg, and to give other people sanitation."

"Which probably explains why I have no money every month," I tell her. "By the time I have 20 per cent taken out of my take-home, plus rent, it's no wonder I scrape by every month."

"Jaimee said you were told about it when you started working for her, she set up two accounts, one for your salary and the other for your savings. The donated money is salary-sacrificed so you wouldn't even see it, unless you checked your pay slip."

"I've never checked my pay slip."

"Last year you, and I mean you and the *Enegi* girls, collectively gave $50,000 to the women of Uzbekistan and $50,000 to Afghani refugees to start a market and rebuild their local schools."

"I should know more about this," I tell her, flabbergasted.

"Jaimee says you're always so busy marketing *Enegi*, and keeping it afloat, that she doesn't bother you with it."

"Well I'm fine about the donations, I think that's a great idea. I'd just waste it on shoes, you know I would. But I would have liked to have been reminded about the savings plan. How much do I have?"

She says it quickly. "Over $100k."

I just about fall on the floor.

"Til?"

"That's enough for a deposit on a flat. Why didn't Jaimee tell me? I could have entered the property market years ago; all it does is keep going up an up."

"Well, not recently. It's been going down, so Jaimee didn't remind you. I told her not to in case you got scared when you found out you were pregnant and wanted to do something silly like buy your flat from me."

I decide the Sydney real-estate über-God has lost it. Why wouldn't she want me to buy real estate?

"Because you'd be tied down. To Sydney, to fashion. When you can do absolutely anything."

My brain is now humming as loudly as the noise in the background. "Why would I want to do anything else but fashion?"

"Maybe one day, after you've had a look around, you might want to," she suggests.

Which is too much for me to think about right now. "Well, at least I'm solvent. Adam will be pleased, that is, after I tell him I've lost my job."

"You've done what?!"

The phone falls from my ear and I turn around to see a white-faced Adam standing in front of me.

"I've got to go. I'll call you later," I mutter to Jorja as the screams of eight hundred girls, aged six to twelve, hurtle down the phone. I slam it shut before I'm permanently deafened by tweenage screaming.

"That was Jorja. Apparently her school raises more money in a year than the Australian Labor Party," I tell him but he still continues to stare at me.

"That's because the school's full of Liberals."

"You're such an anti-snob."

"No, I'm wondering that if you just lost your job why are you smiling at me like a Cheshire cat?"

"Because we're rich," I tell him excitedly.

"You've won lotto and quit your job. Please tell me that Til, because we have all four big bills coming in this month and the shop's not doing very well. Retail's a real bitch at the moment." He loosens his *High School Musical*-style skinny tie and takes off his shoes which he slides under the couch.

"No, I haven't won lotto, which is probably for the best. We'd just waste it on shoes and champagne."

"There's nothing wrong with that."

"There is, you know there is," I tell him obstinately. "That's not what I want Nina growing up thinking: that being rich means you're successful or you can just consume endlessly."

"You have one hundred pairs of shoes in your closet."

"But only one pair of *Jimmy Choos*," I argue. "Not counting the slingbacks."

"And *YSL* and *Donna Karan* and *Kate Spade* and *Vivienne Westwood*."

"True. But I couldn't live without my *Vivienne Westwoods*, they really are *delish*."

He waves his hands violently in the air begging for the prattle to stop. "Please, Til, just tell me what's happened."

"But you just asked me to stop talking, I can't tell you what's happened if…"

Which makes him emit a strange, crazy man squeal.

"Please open your eyes, Adam."

"Not until you start acting like an adult."

So I tell him, quickly and as painlessly as possible what's happened. Then I express, with great verbosity, how stupid I feel for dedicating myself to something with no real purpose; how I fell for the spiel about the importance of a career; that I have left myself and Nina vulnerable to the evils of the world.

He waves his hand indicating that I should shut up again. That

I'm being overly dramatic and annoying. "But you have savings?"

"Apparently."

"What are you going to do with it?"

"I don't know. One minute I'm telling Mum…"

He interrupts me. "You've already spoken to your Mum about this, before me?"

"I know — weird, right?" and roll my eyes for effect. "You weren't here."

He sits down rubbing his skinny jeans as a way of calming himself. He always does this, right before he pulls them up by the waist, sucks in his stomach and tucks his ass under, a habit he picked up from Pilates. He has the core strength of a gorilla and usually he looks like a pussy cat. Right now, he just looks scared.

"I have about $100k in a savings account somewhere," I tell him proudly.

He stops rubbing his hands frantically through his hair. "Sweetheart, you've got enough money for a deposit on a flat. And not even a West Sydney flat. I'm sure Jorja would sell you this one."

A flat in the eastern suburbs, just five minutes from the beach! It's pretty much every civilised woman's dream. One that, right now, I'm going to have to pass on.

"I don't have a job to secure a mortgage, Adam, and you've forgotten one tiny little detail."

We both look at Nina.

"We won't all fit in here for much longer," I tell him.

"We'll find something bigger," he suggests, desperately trying to sway my mind. "I'm ready to buy a place, we'll go halves. You'll get another job, Til, you're a great marketer, a little on the lazy side but when you do put your mind to it, you do great things. And you don't even have to stay in fashion, you could get a job in an industry that pays a lot more."

"That's what people keep telling me."

"Maybe you should listen. It's not just you now." He sucks in his stomach again, he's probably worried that we're going to starve, maybe not tomorrow, but certainly, soon. "Well, a hundred places would kill to have you," he finally says. "Do you know where you'll start looking?"

"Haven't a clue. But Jorja suggested I look around, see what else is out there. Maybe I can help her raise money for all of these co-ops in Uzbekistan and Afghanistan and Malawi. It sounds pretty cool."

"And take Nina with you?"

I shrug. "Sure. Why not?"

"Only creative people say *why not*, Til, please stop. I am not a creative person, I run a shop that sells over-priced clothing to over-stimulated teenagers, but these days they're acting more mature than me. They want organic *Twilight* t-shirts and bug me about what I'm doing to reduce my carbon imprint while I'm doing the accounts. It's so annoying."

I ignore him. He is a 12 year old trapped in a 35 year old's body.

"Maybe I'll take Nina on a holiday to Paris and then start looking when I get back. Someone's bound to need a fashion marketer who's got a French stamp in her passport," I say with obviously too much enthusiasm for him.

He gives me a funny look which I think is about my myopia.

I sigh and sit down next to him on the couch. "Look, Adam, I don't know what I'm going to do but finding out that I've got savings behind me is a God-send. Maybe I should consider my new-found unemployment status as an opportunity. If I hadn't lost my job, I would have gone back to working for *Enegi* and might not have had to face this decision for years. But now, I can really think about what I want for my career, and for Nina, what opportunities and experiences I want to give her."

For the first time since I found out I was pregnant, Adam looks at me like I'm an adult.

"My life isn't a continuum. I don't have to live my life in the same way as I've been living it. Or parent Nina the same way as my Mum raised me. Jorja's right, I don't even have to keep working in fashion. I can turn my whole life around."

"You're living in a new reality," he says seriously.

Which I think is new age bullshit. "No, I'm not," I say and shake my curls defiantly.

217

"Yes, you are," he says defensively tugging at his jeans in response.

"It's a mindset shift, that's all. I don't know about a new reality."

"It is," he pushes, jamming his face forward, his bottom lip poking out at me.

I stop. Adam gets irritated when anyone challenges him. No wonder he's gay, he'd never get a second's peace from a girlfriend. We remain quiet until I offer an olive branch, after all there's no point arguing. I pat down his hair, "You look like the rough end of a *Killers* act."

He thinks for a while. "We're creatures of habit, aren't we?"

This I agree with. "We're educated to feel fear at every step of our lives. If something goes wrong, we're programmed to panic."

"So we're not going to panic."

"No, we're not," I reassure him.

"What are we going to do then?"

"We'll sit here and not think about it for a bit, watch some mind-numbing TV."

"You know that *not thinking about it* is another creative-thinking technique," he says relishing his role as the drama queen in the unending saga of my life. "How about you don't think about it and I'll sit here and obsess about it?"

I snuggle into him, putting my arms around him to anchor his turbulent ship.

Far from the madding crowd

The sound of seagulls hovering overhead, cruising for chips, is music to my ears. Bondi Beach is at its best today; the sky, empty of clouds is reflecting an azure blue sea back at bathers who lull, carefree and satisfied on waves gently pulling and pushing them around on a bed of blissful tranquillity. Now that March is here, the sun has lost its blinding intensity, has stopped searing every square centimetre of skin left bare; has stopped burning up the pavement and all the little soles that dare to run, skip and jump barefoot across it.

Serenity is not something I usually relate with Bondi; usually, the ocean roars at the crowds clambering for their attention but today it floats off the side of the world next to me, happy in its own space and I stay happily in mine.

I'm sitting under an umbrella with the other parent group Mums, babies sucking at our breasts, the occasional café worker manoeuvring into view delivering decaf macchiatos and chai teas to us, smiling and pleasant with no Bondi attitude in sight.

I'm sitting next to the latest new parent group member: Sarah and her little baby Jarryd. Sam is busy chatting to another new-comer, Kim, mum to the group's only other twins, Zara and Felix. Sam and Kim are talking about the difficulties of timing feeds. The other mums are contentedly nursing.

"Are you planning on doing any baby classes with Jarryd?" I ask Sarah.

"Probably music classes," Sarah tells me. "What about you?"

"I don't know," I say. "I just found out that I've lost my job, so I don't know anything now."

The crowd of Mums return encouraging noises, and I notice

none of them feel sorry for me. In fact, they make it sound like a dream come true.

"I do *not* want to have to go back to work," Loni says, emphatically. "If I could stay home with Rylah everyday until she goes to school, I would."

"You might change your mind when she's two," Sam says wickedly.

"Probably," she agrees, which makes everybody laugh.

"Yeah, let's just enjoy them while they're young," I offer.

"Is Nina crawling yet?"

"She's trying to push herself up now," I tell Nathalie. "And Jeremy, what's he up to?"

"He's sleeping better now, which is a relief. I'm starting to feel more normal again."

The Mums share a compassionate head nod. We slip back into breastfeeding silence. Nina is happy to bob off the boob, have a look around and then go back for second and third course; she has her own timetable to feeding and it usually involves more wriggling and giggling and burping than feeding.

"So what will you do?" Sarah asks me.

"I'm not sure; it's all come as a bit of a shock."

We usually don't talk about our personal issues, unless they relate to our babies, but since this does affect Nina, I open up about it.

"I've only ever had one job, at the same company, as a fashion marketer. My sister thinks I should look wider."

The Mums nod their heads and begin to share their own return-to-work plans.

Four out of six are going back to work part-time when their babies are six months old, citing the usual mortgage pressures.

Three are going back full-time and only one is not returning to work.

Donna explains her situation. "My husband's work has a parental leave policy which they're not honouring. When we found out I was pregnant, I quit my job because I've always wanted to start my own business. My husband planned to work part-time when Elli was born, but his work wouldn't let him go part-time even though there's heaps of women there who do it. His boss said parental leave was for women not men."

I feel a familiar sense of dread return. So, I'm not the only one to be screwed over while on parental leave. Maybe Jaimee's new parental leave policy was the main reason the investors pulled out of the business? But without a practical, government-funded paid parental-leave scheme, firms have no choice but to write their own costly policies, hoping this will help them retain valuable employees. But that's not the way the *Enegi* Board probably saw it. They could only see the costs of running a majority female staff escalating.

"Then why do they have a parental leave policy that they don't intend to honour?" Emily asks.

"Because it takes time for culture to change," Sam adds. "For managers to understand the policy and to be able to implement it. Don't forget that managers are usually male and older, they haven't looked after kids full-time, they didn't have to squeeze a baby out of their genitals, they don't understand the toll of carrying a baby or respect the post-partum recovery process."

Kylie agrees. "They don't understand that a lot of grandmothers are still working so we don't have the same support network that women used to have. We rely on our husbands more now."

"But his work must understand that it's good for business to offer these policies?" I ask Donna.

"Sure, it looks good on paper when you're recruiting staff, but getting them to honour it is another thing. There are two things you should always ask before you start a new job: where's your published redundancy policy and what's the success rate of employees accessing your generous leave policies?"

Sam throws her head back and laughs. "Yeah, like they'd hire you if you did that. I can just see HR now, 'Geez, we won't be hiring an informed employee, that's asking for trouble'."

But Donna looks glum. "I can't look after Elli full-time and work. I'm an accountant and wanted to set up a business providing virtual business management services so I need some time off to meet with clients and do the work. And I can't get a nursery place for her now, there's a two year wait at all the day care centres near us. So, it looks like I'll be parenting full-time and my husband will be working full-time, which is a shame because we both wanted to play an active role in raising Elli. Now we'll end up paying more tax because we won't benefit from two tax-free thresholds and I won't be contributing to my superannuation. So we end up poorer, and in particular, I pay the most for being the one who cares for the baby. Which makes me sound ungrateful. But I feel like we're living in the stone ages."

The other Mums nod their heads.

Kylie adds her own parental leave woes. "My husband's work gave him a formal discipline for attendance. When Koby was only a few weeks old, he got sick and went to hospital and my husband had four days off work. When he went back to work, he was told to work unpaid overtime to catch up. And I was exhausted already because I hadn't had much sleep and all of a sudden my husband's working twelve hour days. I'm doing everything at home."

"But he's allowed sick leave?"

"Officially, it's carer leave. And yes, he's allowed ten days annually of combined sick leave or carer leave, but it turns out his boss didn't understand that. His boss said they're OK about time he took off while Koby was in hospital but I think they're lying. Because the only other time he took off is an hour here or there when I was pregnant and needed someone to watch our other kids when I had doctor's appointments or when I had really bad morning sickness. But when he's away for work and has to leave before dawn and is away for days at a time, his work don't consider that overtime. But what really pissed me off was that my husband bent over backwards for them; he went back to work when he was supposed to be on leave after Koby was born. His leave had been approved for seven months, but they didn't organise for anyone to cover for him. It just makes me so angry. Babies are small for such a short time, if you blink you'll miss it. They're stealing that time from us. Sometimes I can't breathe because I get so worked up about it."

Donna continues, "We're not dying of starvation and we have access to health care, so I feel bad complaining about it, but when the government craps on about how good we've got it, and how fabulous the family tax benefit is and the baby bonus, you just want to smack them in the mouth. The day-to-day difficulties, the exhaustion, the stress of raising a family — they can't compensate us for that."

Nathalie jiggles her son up and down to settle him. "Does your husband work for a small company?" she asks Donna.

"Nope. They're massive. They're an ASX 100 company."

My jaw drops. "And they're giving you a hard time? God, there's no hope for anyone then."

Emily leans forward over her daughter's head, speaking softly so as not to wake her. "I've always called myself a feminist, and I really thought society had made some advances, but now I think, maybe I'm wrong? Women are still contributing more, non financially, to raising our children; we're raising our future society, our future workers, our future customers, and business are not contributing to that. They only contribute a very short-term revenue stream to government. The long-term cost of raising a generation of people and managing our world —business doesn't contribute to that. We do."

I think back to my conversation with Lola.

"We can't return to a society where women work solely in the home and the corporate world is allowed to operate ignorant of its impact on society and the environment," Donna comments. "That would be going backward."

"It's very easy for a society's advancements to be repealed. One day we're living in Australia, the next we wake up and find we're living in Afghanistan. That the conservatives have taken over and all those hard-won freedoms have been taken from us. That's what I'm worried about," Sam says.

The Mums nod and the babies coo, oblivious to their mother's worries.

Sarah detaches Jarryd from her breast and starts to burp him. "I know my grandmother had eight kids and no washing machine or car, no private school fees to pay. But somehow I think I envy her. The kids played in the backyard and she didn't have to worry

223

about paedophiles stealing them while she put the dinner on; the kids could walk to their friend's house without being running over by a car driving 100km an hour down her street; she didn't have to work outside the home; she didn't have to battle a full day at work and then do the kindy and school drop-offs and pick-ups. She fed the kids at five pm instead of at seven pm, which is when I'll be getting home, and she didn't have to compete endlessly with her neighbours or worry about the size of her ass."

A peel of laughter erupts from the group.

"We need to keep going forward. We need to keep challenging our society's expectations of the roles of Mums and Dads and keep fighting for better living standards for our kids. I want to work, don't get me wrong, but I want to do it because it makes the world a better place, not because it makes money for my boss," Emily says.

Loni agrees. "The company I work for is a waste of time. They just import shit from China and sell it, and it all breaks within a few weeks so most of it just ends up in landfill. And it's not stuff people need; I think it's just advertising that creates a need and because it's cheap we buy it. And I work there! It pays my bills. Some days I just want to rip my hair out, I'm so frustrated by it."

Which is something that's been troubling me too lately. "My sister's really opened my eyes to the problems the fashion industry causes," I add. "The insecticides the farmers use to grow the cotton, the deforestation, the over-tilling which degrades the soil's fertility, the chemicals used to clean the cotton, bleach it and dye it, and the endless tankers shipping product all around the world — and for what? I always thought my sister was an airhead for selling real estate, that she was in some way a part of the problem, because prestige property fuels the desire to make more money, but now I can see that I was wrong. I'm the one with the problem. At least she's doing something about it."

They ask me what I mean so I tell them about Jorja's work in funding women's collectives in some of the poorest countries in the world.

"You know, I read about her in *SMH*," Sam says. "She sounds like a real modern day Mother Therese."

I try not to kill myself on the spot. If Jorja is Mother Therese, then I'm the pathetic, ignorant, capitalist stealing food from orphans' mouths. And I'm so depressed and angry with myself that I can't sit here pretending to be a credible part of the sisterhood anymore. I don't deserve it. I'd give anything to really belong, but frankly, the highlight of my life so far has been getting a bias-cut skirt in pin-stripes into *Vogue* and that just doesn't count. Not when my sister is digging wells and restructuring economies.

I make my apologies to the group, feigning tiredness, and head for home. The path back to Tamarama passes by the Bondi Icebergs Swimming Club, the scene of Nina's conception and the sea pool where Fred cajoled my body into labour.

I start to hurtle across the Bondi promenade not caring that I'm pushing the pram over the toes of a few well-heeled celebrities who are stalling outside waiting for the paparazzi to arrive.

I ignore their ugly comments. I turn away from their obsession with outer beauty and toward the ocean. And even though I've been here a million times, I see something I've never seen before. The water contained within the sea pool's concrete walls is not calm and protected at all. With every slap the water tells me how desperate it is to burst its walls, to leave the shelter of the swimming pool behind, to feel the liberty of the great big sea.

When I get home, Louise is waiting at my apartment.

She is unusually animated, smiling from ear to ear, and holding tightly onto her step-daughter Gretel's arm.

As we traipse upstairs she gushes about a fabulous idea she's had. Since Gretel, whom I peed on at my baby shower, seems so enamoured with me (which only makes Gretel roll her eyes and gag uncomfortably behind us) could she possibly conduct her Grade 11 work experience with me at *Enegi*. "When you're back on deck, of course," Louise adds, grinning.

I turn the key in the lock and push my apartment door open. The noise of it squeaking open covers my muttered, "Fuck".

Louise proceeds to gush about how great it is that Gretel seems to be showing more interest in her career options rather than fighting with her friends over which guys they're taking to their end-of-year school dance. I raise my eyebrow and Louise nods. Yes, 'guys', is correct. Each of these 16 and 17-year-old girls is taking at least two guys as dates and some of them will be changing their outfits halfway through the night too. A part of me vehemently wants to be these girls whilst my parenting brain is repulsed. It would kill me if Nina turned out like that, I know it would.

"So? What do you think?"

I abandon my thoughts of Nina as a teenager and return to Louise.

And because Louise has been such a great friend to me, what else can I do but say yes? I try to sound enthusiastic. "Sure, you'll get to see me in action, Gretel."

She replies, deadpan, "I already have. You peed on me, remember?"

I choke back laughter. "I meant, in marketing action, Gretel — market analysis, planning, writing, creating, sponging, all the good stuff."

Louise is grinning widely. She obviously thinks fashionista is a step up from fairytale bitch.

"But first, you have to prove to me that you really want this," I tell her.

Gretel eyes me strangely and I have to give her credit, she has none of the naivety I had. When the Board said Paris, I just believed them. What I should have done was had it written into my contract and called it research rather than a reward, then I would have gone to Paris four years ago and not let the Board wave those five little letters in front of me at performance reviews like a stockbroker waving a coke-smeared financial report at his clients.

I get the feeling Gretel is reading my mind.

"Maybe I should think about it some more…my friend's Mum works for *Dinnigan*," she says hesitating.

"And you can prove to me that you're really interested in fashion, and have the guts for it, by helping out Louise in the shop."

"But…"

"For free, every Thursday night and Saturday until close, doing whatever she wants — filling orders, serving customers, cleaning."

Gretel starts to complain but I don't care. It's not much, but giving Louise some help in the shop is the least I can do to repay the kindness she's shown me and Nina. "And if you don't, I won't let you come to my office." I don't mention that I don't know where my office will be just yet. "Plus, I want a 2000 word essay on the experiences you have with customers and what you think of them."

Louise looks at me, alarmed.

Gretel says, "Cool…you should have seen this deadshit in there the other day…"

But I interrupt her. "And a further 2000 words explaining what they bought, where they were from, what other products they buy, and how you can get them to buy more merchandise from Louise's shop," I tell her.

Gretel shuts up.

"Do we have a deal?"

"Yes."

"Excellent, I'll be checking on you."

While I make us tea, I pull Louise aside and admit the truth about *Enegi*.

She looks shocked, so I reassure her quickly that I'll stand by my promise to Gretel. Somehow.

She nods, cautiously. "What are you going to do?"

I turn around and look at Gretel who is playing with Nina on the floor. "I'm not sure, yet."

Louise follows my gaze. "Gretel's good with kids, that's for sure. She's done more parenting than most parents; she's always looked after her little sister and my kids too," Louise whispers.

Watching her, I have to agree. Nina loves her already.

"To be honest, when I've been working in the shop and her Dad was away with work, Gretel's taken care of all my kids and never complained about it. I really am grateful to her."

I raise my eyebrows in surprise. "That's not something you hear everyday," I tell Louise and she catches my hand and squeezes it.

The real sisterhood

At first, I feel strange stalking my sister on the internet, but I learn more about her in the next week than I have the entire time we've shared genetic links. At first it just seemed like a good distraction to looking for a job, but what I've found has been enlightening!

Because I've found proof that there's hope for everyone. You really can make something of yourself, despite a history of shagging yourself senseless in the backs of cars when you're 16.

A quick internet search revealed 1,499, 398 instant results for "Jorja Kythira Bondi real estate agent benefactor Malawi Uzbekistan women's collectives". Of those, about 1,209,890 actually seem to relate to Jorja and not penile implants. I'm amazed.

As I was graduating from my second degree, my sister was winning a Young Businesswoman of the Year award for her boutique real estate agency. Since then, she's amassed a large real estate portfolio, a mix of commercial, farming and residential properties valuing into the tens of millions of dollars both in Australia and overseas.

I click on the next few pages of search results and the article headings are all breathtakingly impressive. Jorja's success has spilled over from the commercial world into a vast number of humanitarian projects based all over the world:

"Sydney Real Estate tycoon helps enslaved prostitutes in Cambodia."

"Malawi women given new hope by Jorja Kythira."

"Jorja Kythira visits AIDS orphans in the Congo."

"Jorja Kythira wins International Development Economics 'Woman of the year' award."

"Jorja Kythira hits Top Female Australian earners list for third year in a row."

"Jorja Kythira meets the Dalai Lama."

Sam was wrong. Jorja isn't Mother Therese, she's the UN, WHO, World Bank and Angelina Jolie all rolled into one.

She's set up drug rehabilitation centres for girls and women in Cambodia who were trafficked into prostitution and given amphetamines and other drugs to ensure compliance in a routine of daily beatings and rapes. After they've escaped or been rescued (which happens less rarely) these women often can't return to their families because they would be ostracised from their communities.

Some women even return to the brothels because they have no skills and heavy drug dependencies. Jorja's rehabilitation centre deals with their drug addictions, trains them and sets them up financially with a market stall or a sewing machine.

Similarly, in Malawi and other parts of Africa, Jorja has provided money for hospitals to perform fistula repairs on women who have been ostracised from their families for months or even years due to constantly leaking urine and faeces caused by obstructed and long labours. The women then need to be rehabilitated (one woman's legs were permanently bent after lying on the floor and not being able to move for a few years after giving birth) and re-skilled. Most of these women have little or no education and need to learn skills to be able to support themselves after their operations.

Jorja has financed a range of microfinance initiatives from Kabul to Santa Cruz de la Sierra to Mozambique. She has helped thousands of women into businesses ranging from market stalls, crop growing, and sewing. She has even set up a scholarship to send women to university to learn midwifery.

Clicking on the links to maternal health statistics in these countries, I am horrified by what I read. Because families in the developing world are so poor, they don't take labouring women to hospital; they can't afford the bus ticket (or there is no bus and the women have to walk for days) or they can't afford to pay the doctors or the medicines. So women give birth at home without any assistance or with poorly-trained attendants who do things like jump on the labouring woman's stomach to help push the baby out, rupturing the amniotic sac, killing the baby, and causing an infection that then kills the mother.

The leading cause of death is obstetric haemorrhaging which can be reduced through active medical care in the third stage of labour; something that is difficult to provide if women give birth outside of hospital. Haemorrhaging can be caused by obstructed labour (which can then lead to sepsis, ketosis and exhaustion) and by uterine shape or the size of the woman's pelvis (often small due to the mum's age — girls in some countries are still married very early — or because of inadequate nutrition when growing up). And even if the baby does survive the labour, she often dies soon afterwards because there is no one to care for her. Similarly, the older children's lives are threatened without a mother to look after them.

When I found out I was pregnant, it was Adam who was worried, but his concern was misplaced. The statistics don't lie. Maternal deaths in the West are very low; in fact they dropped considerably in the US after women won the right to vote. But for many women around the world it is still a death sentence, particularly those in sub-Saharan Africa, some parts of the Middle East, China and South Asia. But, the problems don't end there.

In one article, Jorja explains her focus on the women's collectives:

"People ask me why I don't just build more hospitals in Africa, wouldn't that solve the problem? But you can't take the 'build it and they'll come approach' to health care in developing countries. Firstly, who's going to work in them? Who's going to take the women to hospital, and in numerous cases, even if you can get them there, the husband may not allow his wife to be treated by a male doctor.

Power and income are intrinsically linked to quality of life. When women are making money, domestic violence drops considerably. They're treated with more respect by their husbands and they're allowed out of the house. They can afford and are allowed access to health care. When women earn money, they spend it on education not beer. When women are educated, birth rates drop, and women access more maternal and child health services.

By enabling women to manage their own businesses; to give them training and equipment, by easing their access to market and giving them group support through the collective structure we give vital help. The women's collectives affect all parts of their lives and their communities. But it's not easy. There's no point in setting these women up in business if they have no customers. It means considering every point of the production, distribution and marketing process: from local cultural law, to dealing with suppliers, manufacturing, developing skilled workforces, childcare, bank accounts, wharves, trucks and roads, and access to the retail sectors both domestically and internationally."

It sounds like one colossal headache.

And my last job.

As divergent as I thought Jorja's and my lives were, we are in fact very similar. She's trying to keep women alive in Africa, Afghanistan and Cambodia; I'm trying to keep women alive in Sydney and China. Our goals aren't disparate at all!

The relief is immense. I am not a total waste of space after all. I fall back against the lounge and breathe an audible sigh of relief. OK, Jorja is a saint and I'm just a capitalist schmuck, but from the articles I've read about her in the past week, she seems to be proffering that a market economy can be a part of these women's solutions. That and involvement in a stable government. Oh and fair trade. Jorja's not just handing out food stamps or dropping bombs on innocent people's heads, she's building the grass-roots of successful communities and marketplaces.

Which is all great, but what does it mean for me?

I stumble into bed, exhausted and drained.

Around midnight, I jump out of bed as the sound of a text message whirs across Sydney and hits my mobile phone.

"It's a girl. Three point seven kilos. Very large head. Mum and baby doing very well. Visitors welcome."

"It's from Lola and John," I whisper into the night.

Nina stirs in her cot at the sound of my voice.

I try to lie as still as I possibly can, my heart thumping and tears streaming down my face.

L'espoir est le rêve d'une âme en réveil

Because I've been through labour, I try to make myself wait a day before we visit Lola. But it's no use. Besides John, Lola has no other family in Australia. So that afternoon, excited and dressed in our cleanest clothes, we race to the hospital: me, Nina, Adam and Dean.

Lola is sitting in bed cooing at her newborn baby and muttering to her in French when we arrive.

John has crammed his entire six-foot long body onto the chair next to her bed and is resting his head on a pillow against the window.

"He's exhausted," Lola whispers to us, giggling. "*Le bébé a vu le jour à quatre heures.*" She switches back to English when Dean and Adam swap confused looks. "The baby was born at four o'clock this morning so John didn't get to sleep until six. *Moi*, I have had nothing for two days. But you'd think he'd run a marathon, he kept complaining of a sore back from bending over and rubbing me during labour. And *moi, moi avec* the very sore hoo-haa, you know there's *deuze* stitches down there, she didn't come out like a baby, she came out like a bomb."

Adam and Dean, who both turn darkening shades of grey, hover at the door. Nina tries to touch the baby's head but I pull her away.

"*Non*, it's OK."

Nina bends forward again, her eyes focused on her prize, which she tries to slap across the head but I catch her hand in time.

"Ah, no," I tell her. "Baby. Gentle," and then I take her hand carefully and show her how to pat the baby's head gently.

"She's beautiful, Lola."

"Isn't she? She's going to grow up to be naughty, yes?"

"Just like her mother," John adds, stirring on the chair, unfurling and stretching nearly all the way to the ceiling.

"Wow — she has your nose and eyes, John," Adam remarks.

"And my hands and feet," Lola adds. "And hair, thick black hair."

"What's her name?"

"Jola," Lola says grinning.

"Of course it is," I reply. "It's perfect. Nina this is Jola. You're going to be great friends." And because I burst into tears, John offers to take the boys with him and make us a cup of tea, leaving us four girls alone.

Lola immediately tries to change the subject so I stop crying. "So, have you seen anything more of your French man?" Lola asks cheekily when the boys are gone.

I haven't got a clue what she's talking about.

"Fred. Your masseur," she persists.

"Fred's French?" I ask her amazed.

"Of course, he is. *Frederick*. Born in France but raised here. Kind of like me, but I was raised in jail. I had no idea my parents hated me."

"Your parents don't hate you."

"*Non*, we're going back to Paris in a month or two, to take Jola to see them, to treat her like the accessory that everybody thinks she is. Show her off, pedal her feet, polish her tiny ears."

I cuddle Nina on my lap. "Your parents won't come here?"

"Don't be absurd, my mother wouldn't last a week without a real brie. She would try to bring it with her — she knows nothing of the cheese police." She brushes her finger along her sleeping baby's cheek and I am overcome by the urge to sit here for a week and watch her with Jola.

"It's hard to think she'll ever grow up and not be this tiny, dependent human being," I say finally, but I know I'm referring to Nina. I feel a stab in my stomach at the thought of Nina growing up, going to school, leaving home, going somewhere exotic and never coming back.

"I find myself sitting here, looking at her, Til, thinking, 'What I hope for my daughter is different to what I wanted myself'," Lola says. "Isn't it funny? I've never wanted to be happy. Maybe when I was a teenager I thought all of that self-obsessed nihilistic behaviour was important: drinking, having lots of friends, being busy all the time, but now I just want to be a good person. And of course, what is 'good' is subjective. There is no escaping it, I am cultured, just like a cheese. Society has a place for me; it categorises me and makes me sit with the other like-minded cheeses. I have spent my whole life battling that and now my daughter will have it even tougher; a half yellow, half white cheese. Will she be happy? She is just a day old and yet already I am conscious of what will define her life. What have I done?"

When Mums talk like this, they're simply expressing awareness of the world they've brought their child into. And it's always the other Mum's duty to try to cheer them up. I fulfil my obligation by talking about what a bad mother I am. I tell Lola about losing my job and feeling like an utter failure because I can't provide for my daughter: not a job, security, or even a Dad.

"What are you going to do?"

"I don't know."

"Well, take some time out, go have sex with that wonderful Frederick, and think about work later."

I laugh at her. Not because I haven't had thoughts about Fred, but because I've managed to push them away. Normally, I'm too tired even to imagine that I have a fantasy life waiting for me just one delusional daydream away. "You know you surprise me, Lola. You're just not a traditional feminist."

"Why would I be? It's pointless to present an alternate view by just joining somebody else's mindset. I must always challenge."

"But you don't encourage me to pursue my career when a million other feminists would, you keep talking about Fred. This man whom I barely know."

"You can't just work, work, work, Til. It's unhealthy. You see a relationship as some kind of threat or conspiracy, and work as your path to freedom and equality. You hide from having an intimate relationship with anybody except your market. How are you going to progress as a human being if you never unveil yourself to anybody?"

"I did unveil myself, Lola. Fred went with me in the ambulance to the hospital, remember? I'm pretty sure he saw everything I have to offer."

"You're being sarcastic," she chastises.

I laugh at her. "Of course I am. Fred's not interested in me."

"Call him," she prompts.

"Don't get me wrong, Lola, he's a gorgeous human being and I'd love nothing better than to have the time and energy for a relationship. But it doesn't work that way."

She contradicts me immediately. "You can have it all, Til — you just have to believe in yourself."

I'm quiet for a minute. "I'm still not sure if you're right. Because what I'm hearing is the opposite, that people don't want you to have it all. That when you get even infinitely close to it, they take it away again."

"We live in a vastly competitive world but you don't have to play their games. You do have to take risks. And from what I hear, you're pretty good at taking risks in public," she says naughtily, referring to the night of Nina's conception. "Miss *Jimmy Choo*."

"Oh no," I tell her laughing. "In that case, I'm definitely never taking another risk again."

When we hear the guys returning I shush her, whispering to her to not talk about risk-taking in front of Adam, "He'll get nauseous and wear a hole in his jeans from worrying."

But Adam looks at Lola anxiously anyway. Then Lola winks at him and he immediately looks relieved. Which I think is kind of funny but with no other non-verbals to work on, I try to drink my tea until Nina does a big poo and stinks out the tiny hospital room, signalling the end of our visit.

It's Lola's fault that my dreams of Paris return.

And my *joie de vivre*.

She has that effect on me; that and a temporary ability to drink tequila and dash naked through the foyer of the Sydney Opera House after a great Fashion Week opening.

So I'm not surprised that our visit to Lola has encouraged my return to form.

After returning from the hospital and feeling satiated with happy new-baby endorphins, I put a very tired Nina down for a late sleep. When she wakes up around four, I make a spontaneous decision to not waste one more minute of the beautiful afternoon. I race Nina out to our favourite seaside playground and we join the throng of mothers and kids all enjoying the last of the day's light.

Now that summer is quickly turning into autumn, the afternoon breeze blowing off the sea soon turns brisk, sending the mothers into a flap. With our feathers ruffled, we try to pin our children into another layer of clothes.

More from habit than anything else, I start analysing the number of mothers dressing their children in Jorja's *trajic* pink or blue, functional mini-cargos and vests, or layers of princess fluff, and develop psychographic profiles based on all the information emanating from their behaviour and their consumer paraphernalia: the motherhood junk (wooden rattles, plastic toys); the type of pram they're pushing their motherhood junk around in; the ever-growing number of mothers using slings; and the type of car that's driven the mother and brood to the park.

Then I make assumptions about the type of house they live in and values they assert. If I had a few thousand dollars I could run a focus group to really find out what these women are thinking, but going to that extreme may be pointless without something concrete to grill them about.

The mothers step back from their knights and princesses now jammed into every warm fibre known to woman-kind, and appreciate their work. I recognise the contented look on their faces: dressing an infant can give a parent a real sense of achievement, probably because it is the hardest task on earth.

My eyes meet the other mothers' and we smile at each other. A gust of wind has threatened to turn our blissful afternoon into a nightmare of snotty noses, but the forethought and preparedness of each mother who has packed for a mild deterioration of the weather right through to a mini-cyclone, has alleviated the pressures of the physical reality of climate.

We are a success. Not just individually but collectively. Because it takes a team of well-organised parents to keep a park full of children tantrum free.

But I want more. More than a communal smile from a collection of mothers on a random afternoon. To find out more about these women and their intense love for their children: their hopes, their fears, their dreams, the books they read to their kids at night, what brands they like and can Nina possibly be the recipient of their children's hand-me-downs so I don't have to borrow everything from my sister?

As the sun dips behind the city's highrises on the horizon, a realisation dawns on me: I don't want to be stuck in a one-way conversation with my own marketing plan anymore. I want to hear more from my audience than which pieces they loved from *Prada's* Spring/Summer range.

I watch the women around me more closely. They follow their children all over the park, pushing some and cajoling others up and down multi-coloured plastic devices.

As the sun lowers even further and the temperature drops, the group of mothers abandon their foothold on the day, fracturing into tiny units. Children are heaved and clicked into carseats before zooming off into the sunset.

With my nose running from the cold and my curls whipping me in the face, I pack up our things and fold Nina into the pram before starting our solitary walk back to our apartment;

I'm exhausted now and highly aware that I'm developing a collection of fine lines around my eyes that were definitely not there pre-Nina. But I'm happy. In fact, I couldn't be happier.

The wind blowing off the sea gathers at my back and gratefully I let it push us back up the Tamarama hill, all the way home.

After feeding Nina, bathing her, and putting her to bed, I collapse myself.

And for the first time in over a week, I fall into a deep REM sleep. I dream that I'm happy. And so is Nina.

In my dream, she is about 12 or 13 and has a great wardrobe, even better than mine. I can tell I still work in fashion by the small office space I work out of but at least I have a job! And it looks like a great job. There are pictures of beautiful babies and mothers pinned to the walls and they're all wearing beautiful clothes; organic garments made from materials grown in pristine environments, wool that has been woven on ancient looms, fabrics that have been dyed and hand-stitched by collectives in Afghanistan and Zimbabwe, Malawi and Uzbekistan. On the other wall are photos of the women who have made the garments and photos of children wearing the clothes. On our HR chart are scientists, environmentalists, sociologists, designers and project managers.

And then it dawns on me: one of those great ideas that you can wait a lifetime for.

In my sleep, I watch the idea unfold as a giant map of Paris spreads at my feet. In the veins of the map I can hear laughter and the gentle threading of life weaving its way into the alleys and cobblestones of history. The future is taken care of by the billowing folds of a garment that is silken and embellished with the knowledge of all human kind. The garment falls into the river and is washed clean.

At *le Palais de Justice*, sit a pew of old women watching me, and by *le Jardin de Luxembourg* wait horse-driven carts. By *le Marais* I sit in quiet contemplation, in the presence of my contemporaries, and we finger each garment as it is delivered to us fresh from carousels. Each work is perfect. The trees in *le Bois de Boulogne* sigh delicately, their fir branches intermingling with an innocence of air I can barely heed; by *Le Republique* I plan an august revolution; by *le Notre Dame*, my gargoyles salute a new day.

Metro signs point to wrought iron gates that squeak and squeal as children pass from inside to out as they play hide-and-seek. They whisper to me, "Hope is the dream" and I answer, "Of the soul awake."

With their games underway, I start to take notes.

240

"Til, tell me again, now that it's two in the afternoon, what you were jibbering about on the phone at three o'clock this morning. It was hard to understand you, considering I was asleep!"

She's kidding. Jaimee wasn't asleep, she was still out. And has been for the past week. Since *Enegi* closed its doors, Jaimee has had nowhere to go. After all, *home* is a foreign concept to her. *Out* is much more comfortable.

But after speaking to me, Jaimee immediately called Didi and Cairine, who were in charge of design and production at *Enegi*, and told them she had a job for them.

She didn't say a proposition, a daydream or even a stupid waste of time. She said a job.

Cairine would have immediately cancelled her plans for a day at the beach and agreed to meet Jaimee at my apartment. I can imagine her relief. With her alabaster skin and bright red curls, she would be sick of the beach by now and dying to get her hands dirty again with some raw fabrics. Didi on the other hand, would have been dragged here by Cairine, kicking and screaming. There is only one thing Didi loves more than fashion and that's the ocean. Every spare second she has she spends scuba diving off the coast of somewhere. Cairine follows, large sun hat and enormous tube of sunscreen in hand.

And now, here they are. Jaimee, hungover. Cairine enthusiastic and peachy. Didi, scowling.

I've been going through my notes all morning, in between trying to feed Nina baby cereal and have her blow it all over my face, give her booby, wash her again, dress her, play with her, and get her to sleep. When I add it up, I've spent about five minutes on the idea.

So now I'm feeling nervous. I started the day confidently, assured the idea was brilliant but now that three people are sitting on my couch waiting for me to speak, I suddenly feel stupid.

So I do what I always do when I'm nervous. I prattle.

I explain my idea to them, ranting about the business model, raving on about its target markets and market entry strategy, the value proposition, core capacities, revenue model, and how we'll build a sustainable competitive advantage. Their eyes glaze over. But they come back to life when they hear the esteemed words French *Vogue*. Jaimee gasps audibly when I say New York Fashion Week.

"Let me get this straight. You want us to design a label of high-end *enfant couture*, a diffusion range, and a ready-to-wear maternity range, *and* find an investor who will back an elite concept store in Paris and ten page of advertising in the French, UK and US editions of *Vogue*?" Didi asks incredulously.

"That's about it," I nod. "It sounds simple when you put it that way, but I'm hoping it will mean more than that. This isn't a fashion label, it's a well-managed and innovative value chain. We won't design, manufacture and sell for the mere purpose of reaping profit, we will involve, champion, improve and invest: we will invest our profits in our manufacturers, our customers will design our clothes, our end-consumers will appear in our ads, and we will ensure that the entire process is a culturally sensitive and environmentally friendly."

"But will it really make any difference?" Cairine frowns at Didi.

But I'm too hyped to take offence. "Let me explain again."

I take a deep breath. "We'll go to Paris and set up a concept store; there we will target our lead buyers; the people with money who will try something new. Let's call them our sponsors. We'll help them design an outfit which will be named after their child. Their child will take her place in the history of couture; their child will be the only child in the world to own that garment; their child will appear in our advertising campaign. We will sell a version of the garment through our diffusion range and money raised from those sales goes to supporting an environmental or socially responsible campaign selected by the sponsor."

"Two major benefits," Jaimee nods at me. "Social recognition and a place in history."

"Exactly."

"Who's going to pay 25,000 euro for that?"

Didi and Cairine aren't as overjoyed at my value proposition as I thought they'd be.

"A lot of people," Jaimee says backing me up. "In Europe there's millions of people with a lot of money. They'd kill for something like this."

"So how do you know our sponsors won't just use us as a PR ride?" Didi asks. "I don't want to be building somebody else's coodies just so they can go and anonymously pollute somewhere else. It's like famous people flying all over the world to get their hair tinted before they go and do some jaunt with the UN."

Cairine raises her crimson eyebrows at Didi. "Kudos. Kudos, not coodies."

I nod. "It's a valid point." And I pause, trying to think of something to say.

But Cairine has already invented a solution. "We could make the sponsors conduct a personal audit, to make sure they're legitimately reducing their impact on the environment as well: reducing their air travel, downsizing from a palace to a mansion, selling their holiday house or at least letting illegal immigrants stay there while their refugee status is investigated."

"People live longer in societies where there is less of a gap between rich and poor" Didi adds, her head nodding in agreement with Cairine's idea.

"But why do only rich people get to sponsor a garment? What if a poor person wants to?" Cairine asks.

"We have to target rich people in our market entry strategy, because we desperately need to raise money in year one. But we could market it to others in years two or three. They'd have to raise money or suggest and manage a campaign to earn the title of sponsor," I suggest.

Cairine frowns. "So, is this fashion anymore or environmental management?"

"Well, like I said before, it's more about managing the value chain. Fashion has been destroying the environment for ages and it's been taking advantage of other people's vulnerability. It's been a tool of the capitalist system, rather than assisting true economic development."

They look at me with confused expressions on their faces, so I explain my idea of using Jorja's women's collectives as our source for manufacturing.

"You want the poorest women in the world who have no skills, no equipment, no access to materials or distribution, to be responsible for making our garments?" Jaimee asks, looking exasperated.

I admit I hadn't raised this point with her on the phone. "It's a high risk strategy," I concede. "We wouldn't have to rely on them at first, we'll look for a responsible manufacturer to manage most of our production, while investing in the collectives, and slowly as their skills and the infrastructure around them improves, we'll involve them more in our manufacturing process. As the infrastructure around them improves, we'll depend on them more heavily. Over time, we truly can support their community's development."

"Well, I like it," Cairine says, emphatically and Didi agrees although I can see she is more hesitant.

I love these girls. Even in the face of madness, they see hope.

Jaimee, however, continues to act mad. "What's your timeline?" she barks.

I'm not upset by Jaimee's attitude, she's not very good at change. She's great at managing but not so good at conceptualising or even implementing change. "If we can get an investor on board then we'll go to Paris asap. We'll set up the concept store in Paris, put some initial designs together, and then go on to show our maternity range at New York Fashion Week," I tell them.

"That gives us six months to get a line together for New York?" Didi's disbelief punctuates the air.

"That's the same timeframe we would be working with if we were still at *Enegi*: Autumn/Winter in October, Spring/Summer in May," I respond.

"Except we'll be showing in New York! And you want a skeleton line for Paris as well to show the sponsors!" Didi, I think, is sounding increasingly despondent. "It can't be done. Especially if you're talking about using production resources we've never used before."

"We'll figure it out."

Didi keeps frowning. "This morning, Jaimee told us you wanted some ideas for designs for a collection in Paris. Now you're telling us you want the world's fashion elite looking at us through a microscope and we've only got six months? You're both insane."

"It's just another show," I tell her trying to placate her. "Its geographical location is irrelevant. I want to go overseas because businesses do better if they go overseas early. New York is where the buyers will be. Maternity-wear is big in the US, not so big in Europe — the Dutch just wear their usual clothes and a big elastic band around their stomachs if they start showing."

"I've never worked with sponsors on garment design though. The whole process could blow up in our face," Didi adds.

"Well, of course they won't be doing all of it. We'll present an idea and let them tweak a hem-length or add a bow, and then tone it all down for the ready-to-wear ranges." I turn to Cairine next. "As production manager, it will be your responsibility to ensure the collectives develop the skills to produce a whole garment. I don't want a half-finished piece being shipped around the planet from collective to collective earning enough carbon debits to sink us all."

"It sounds like I'm going to Malawi for a while," Cairine adds, her enthusiasm waning.

And I understand why. The idea of being separated both from Didi, whom she has worked with every day for the past five years, sometimes for sixty hour weeks, must be scary for her. It's hard enough that her production team, who she hand-picked and developed, has now been strewn all over Sydney. But to have to start all over again, with up to ten teams of women located anywhere in the world, that sounds like a big job. No wonder she's scared.

"Well, you tell us what they need, equipment and skills-wise, and we'll make it happen," I tell her. "It's no different to how we worked before. We swapped factories last year when the manufacturer couldn't offer us chemical-free dying processes."

"I guess so."

"Is Jorja on-board with all this?" Jaimee asks me.

"She will be," I tell them confidently, which of course is a tiny white lie. "I have a pretty strong hunch she's going to like it."

"So — who's in?" Jaimee says clapping her hands together suddenly.

"What are we called?" Cairine demands before committing to a response.

"Giséle. G I S E acute, L, E."

"But Giselle has two L's," Didi interrupts.

"She means Gisele as in the supermodel," Jaimee explains quickly ignoring me when I shake my head.

But Didi's not convinced. "The name is French and if we're going to have a store in Paris it must have two L's," she insists.

Now it's Jaimee's turn to be annoyed. "If Til dreamt it was Giséle with one L then that's how it must be."

"You dreamt it?"

I nod.

Cairine and Didi both say, "Wow", together in awe, as goosebumps spread across their arms.

Despite my years at uni, I can't help but wonder if their synchronized goosebumps are any real indication that the label will be a success. If you looked at the business model right now you'd say we had an imminent disaster on our hands.

"Do you really think we can do it, Jaimee?" Cairine asks, her curls quivering.

"Pass our label off as authentic French couture, with tailoring secrets handed down over generations, based on a collection put together in months instead of years, with materials stolen from *Enegi*'s last ten collections…sure, why not?"

Didi whispers to Cairine that that's where all last year's silk went.

"Not bloody wrong, Didi," Jaimee responds. "I never trusted that Board, they were as dodgy as they come. So I've been stocking up, waiting for one of you girls to get your act together and come up with the idea of the century." She turns to me and smiles. "And it was you, *ma cherie*, my little Til from marketing, and not design at all. How contemporary."

"Thanks, Jaimee," I mutter under my breath.

"Not at all, I knew when I hired you that you'd turn out to be great. And I like this idea because it's so niche-driven and there are just babies, babies everywhere at the moment. The timeline's tight, but you always were a crazy bitch."

Jaimee uncorks a bottle of champagne and the noise of it popping wakes Nina who is sleeping in my room.

"Jaimee," I chastise her, but she doesn't notice, she's too busy digging for champagne flutes in her *Prada* handbag.

I fetch Nina, who already has tears cascading down her face, from her cot. I sit her down on the floor of our tiny lounge room, my legs supporting her back, while I accept a glass of champagne from Jaimee.

"So who's in?" she asks again, holding up her glass.

An eternity passes but slowly Cairine and then Didi raise their bubbling glasses.

"To us, and our petite label, whatever Til said it was called and however she spelled it," Jaimee says and we chink our glasses together as a sign of solidarity.

Before we can even finish our champagne Jaimee starts giving us orders. "Til, you work on the business plan. Didi you draw something and Cairine, you go back to the office and steal every last bolt of fabric and all the sewing implements you can get your hands on. I've given staff until Friday to get their belongings, aka, remove everything that is not capital equipment and listed in the asset register, before the directors lock the doors."

Cairine gathers up her handbag as instructed.

"Oh and, Til, you don't happen to have…."

"A copy of our media list, VIP guest list, agents, media, distributors and buyers? Sure," I tell Jaimee. "Wouldn't leave the office for a long weekend without it."

Six months

Ahem.

I've called this meeting because there's something very important we babies need to discuss. Hold up your rattle if your Mummy has started whispering something called S.T.T.N.?

Just like I thought. Be warned, cherished, cherubic bubs, because this sweet, innocent-sounding acronym is Mummy shorthand for something nasty: *Sleep Through The Night*.

What the hell is that about?

For the first six months our Mums were great. They picked us up when we cried, they jumped out of bed any time of the day or night to feed us and now they're walking around like zombies and complaining about being exhausted.

Now, I know personally that my Mum can go 72 hours easily without a nap, so what's wrong with her now? Suddenly after six months of having me around, she needs a rest?

I'm the baby! I'm the one who needs my beauty sleep so I can cry and gurgle and coo and grin on demand. Do they think being a baby is easy?

So here's the deal. Any time you hear your Mum mention any of the following words, I want you to scream: *sleep, desperate, exhausted, sleep clinic, doctor, lie down, nap, break, shopping, hairdresser, manicure, bath, shower, wash my hair, brush my teeth, get dressed, eat something.*

Except when someone comes over. Then you have to be the best baby in the world so that everyone thinks she's nuts when she complains about how demanding you are.

I know you don't like to upset your Mum, but what she's got planned for you is much worse than childbirth. And believe me, this is the worst kind of torture she could think of. She'll dress you until you get heat exhaustion, she'll put a cold blowing fan on you, she'll turn off the lights (leaving only enough light to cast horrible, hideously scary shadows of monsters), kiss you good night, tell you she loves you, and then — she'll leave you! All on your own!

Mums even give it a name. It's called *Controlled Crying* which means your Mum is training herself to ignore your hysterical screaming, even when you're scared-to-the-core-of-your-immature being.

The books say that a baby isn't capable of feeling fear.

Vomit on them. And this is why.

At first, your Mum will leave you to cry for five minutes. Then she'll come in again, tuck you in and make you feel all nice and cosy again, and just when you think life is grand and you're so sleepy...she'll leave you again!

And no matter how much you cry, she'll leave you for ten minutes next time.

And then fifteen. And so it goes on.

She just doesn't love you anymore.

So get your little lungs ready, babies. And start screaming.

The day of the weendigo is over

I get to work on the business plan. A business plan is a roadmap which will outline the main areas of our business and how we intend to manage them. It covers all sorts of things, like our core business idea, who our customers will be, how we'll market to them, who our competitors are (so we know how to differentiate ourselves from them), how we'll manage our internal resources, what risks we'll face, and how much money we intend to make — and spend.

What's different about this business plan to the ones I used to have to write for *Enegi* is its intent. For *Enegi*, it was all about increasing market share, cutting costs, and returning more money to the owners — me and Jaimee called them the *weendigoes*.

A *weendigo* is an imaginary beast foretold by the North American Indians to warn against the fiercest threat to the survival of their communities: greed. The *weendigo* grew fat on the summer harvest while the rest of the community starved during the long North American winter. It emerged in real form in the modern market. Instead of restricting the *weendigo*, the modern market encouraged its behaviour amongst those who would not necessarily stoop so low. A Darwinist mentality took hold of these new *weendigoes* and honest competitive spirit became blood thirsty. No market was too far, no people too poor, underprivileged, or undereducated to be safe. Unfortunately, not all *weendigoes* are very smart, which leads to poor financial forecasting and the failure of huge economies. But in the end, everybody suffers.

The time of the *weendigo* is over!

Hopefully they won't eat me alive before I can get the message out.

I must be prepared for their gnashing jaws.

I do a quick Porter analysis to help me analyse the external environment and give me a clue as to where to build our strengths and how to negate our weaknesses. I start by identifying what level of influence exists in my industry:

1. The competitive rivalry of the fashion industry: High — *Chloé*, and any other high-end competitor will happily squash me with their marketing might as soon as they hear about me;

2. The threat of new entrants: High — idiots like me are always deciding they want to start a fashion label and most ultimately fail;

3. The power of customers: High — customers are spoiled for choice in the modern market. There are clothing stores at every imaginable pricing point offering varying value propositions. They simply have to walk another five metres and they can spend their money elsewhere — or they can shop online in the comfort of their own home;

4. The purchasing power of suppliers, being the textile producers and garment manufacturers, is sadly: Low. Although I'm growing more committed to the idea of supporting Jorja's collectives, there is a good reason a few hundred thousand other companies all moved their production contracts to China;

5. The threat of substitute products: Low to High — not only are designs imitated and reproduced by the lesser fashion Gods, but are sold at ridiculously less cost. Why can brands charge so much when some so little? Why do some companies invest so much money into advertising and their brand? Lower priced goods are usually more easily substitutable. The brand is less recognisable so less valued. But at the high-end, companies hope their brand is less substitutable. That is always the aim.

The Porter analysis is telling me to stay as far away from this idea as possible: it's a financial deathtrap for a new entrant like me.

Which brings me to market entry. My favourite bit. Usually.

At first, my idea glowed with innovation and guts, but now that Jaimee's reading every word I produce (which is the first time a company director has ever read anything I've written), I'm starting to think we look like an expensive, badly thought out disaster. How the hell are we going to inform our target market and guide them through a purchasing process when their brand loyalty is tied up in some of the world's best brands: *D&G, Bonpoint*, and *Chloé*.

The only option I have is to take it back to what I know. The usual management practices that I was taught at university aren't going to help me now. I throw my Porter analysis in the bin then I take off the scary pants and the dazzling accessories of my competitors and pretend that they're all nude. And then I dress them again.

I give a voile skirt to *Chloé* and a pink sequined jacket and ballet pumps. Which is gorgeous but too traditional even for our market. I make *Chloé* practice her ballet positions in the corner. To *Bonpoint*, I give — well, *Bonpoint*: A red, white and blue cable knit romper covered in balloons. To *D&G*, I whip up a satin tunic that's been over-printed with arabesques, and accompany it with lace tights and a leather corset. Which is nice, actually I wouldn't mind one myself, it's perfect in its fashion sense and would stand out in a magazine. But that's the problem. That type of outfit is just fashion, and the one thing I'm beginning to sense since I became a parent, is that fashion just isn't enough anymore. Showing off at the park is not part of the solution to building a sustainable planet for my child to inhabit.

I look over at Nina who is asleep in her cot. She looks like a tiny angel, her hands curled into little fists next to her head, her little chest rising slowly in and out. There's no way I would ever let my daughter's future be extinguished by a greedy *weendigo*. And I will not let her future blend into the pages of a discarded gossip magazine. But how do I communicate my hope for a better world to the market in just an image? Why am I expecting so much from a few pieces of fabric? Can an outfit change the world? Does it even have to? In the same way *Band-Aid* educated us about famine in Africa and *Wham* started another whole sexual revolution and liberated a few million gay men from pretending to like beer and football, can fashion really achieve something important?

Nina sighs in her sleep and I lean over her cot, putting my hand lightly on her chest so I can feel her breathe.

And I give her something incredible to wear: a black, stretch pant covered in pom-poms (which she will play with for hours — it's got to be better than a plastic, flashing toy and much more age appropriate), an embroidered wrap which doubles as Mum's *hajib* or breastfeeding cloak, and the softest romper ever made, a combination of ethically-sourced bamboo and hand-woven silk. The women's collectives grow and source the raw product, they process and weave the threads, and they sew the clothes. The garments are shipped directly to the consumer, and a high percentage of the profits are used to buy goats and yaks for a mountain community in Afghanistan that lost all of its animals when some idiot blew up half the village. We call the outfit *The Nina* and sell it to thousands of women who upload photos of their babies wearing the outfit on our website.

In some way, the outfit represents everything I want for the label: it's multicultural, political, practical, beautiful, ethical and responsive. In a way, it borrows from some of my favourite designers: the tastefulness of *Burberry*, the panache of *Easton Pearson*, the fearlessness of *Vivienne Westwood*, and the commitment to frivolousness of *Romance Was Born*. And it doesn't talk at the market. It stimulates a discussion and it doesn't dictate to it.

All I have to do, as a marketer, is start this discussion and provide various ways for my audience to respond.

With that covered, I move onto our next area of vulnerability: our financials.

Because of Jaimee's enforced savings plan while we were at *Enegi*, the management team — Jaimee, Didi, Cairine and myself — can all support ourselves financially for the next year and fund the skeleton line of *enfant couture* to present to our sponsors in Paris. But we're going to need an investor to support the all important market entry advertising campaign, the store fit-out and the maternity range for New York Fashion Week. In total, we need a cool $4 million.

It's not everyday you find an investor with that sort of money willing to invest to such a high-risk business. It's pointless going to the bank, they'll just laugh at me. I need someone who's already familiar with development economics.

Jorja.

Jaimee and I spend the next week tweaking the business plan so Jorja will be so impressed she couldn't possibly say no. Some nights the business plan glows, depending on the number of champagnes we've had.

"What if she calls us 'fashion disguised as a do-gooder scheme'?" Jaimee questions.

"I think we're the perfect fit. We're providing her collectives with a real business opportunity. They can grow faster and we can help set up more collectives. You were reticent to use the collectives and you know Jorja. Imagine how hard it is to convince a new potential client of the value of the collectives…this is a god-send for her."

"If she's investing into our business though, she's going to want a return on her money," Jaimee semi-articulates one night. "Otherwise, how else can she fund her collectives?"

"Investment, not money," I correct her.

"Yeah, whatever."

"Jaimee, how is it that you know nothing about business management and yet you were CEO of *Enegi*?"

"I was the only applicant who wasn't drug-addicted," she admits, sucking on the last drops in her glass.

"So why weren't you on the Board?"

"Because I wasn't drug-addicted. I didn't need the money. And I know more people than God. In fact, when God wants to get in touch with somebody, she calls me."

Which has kept me laughing throughout the last week. Even Adam notices I'm happier but I haven't yet told him what I'm working on. If it turns out to be a catastrophic failure and Jorja tells me "no way", then I don't want to have to go through the embarrassing conversation of telling Adam and him raising his eyebrows at me.

At least our bills are paid. The calendar which was sporting four, big, red X's signalling bills to be paid, now carries four gold stars — and we are solvent, for now.

One night Jaimee asks me a question she's never asked me before, "Yes, but is it sustainable?"

She's not talking about the environment. She's asking if our business strategy will enable us to survive in the long-term. She's worried that if we're investing so much money back into the women's collectives and the environmental campaigns that we won't make enough profit to sustain the business.

I tell her that our SCA (I try to use as many acronyms as possible with Jaimee, it makes me sound smart and keeps our conversations short) — our *Sustainable Competitive Advantage* — is our *Emotional Selling Point*. Usually, companies talk about an *Unique Selling Point* but since I'm pursuing an affective-dominant marketing campaign, I'm focusing on manipulating the hormones of our female customers at every step of the purchasing process. "Basically, they won't stand a chance," I tell her. "Our customer base will grow at 1000% a year. We'll be fine."

I keep working through the next week, until I feel ready to face Jorja and Jaimee declares she is bored senseless.

On the morning of our meeting, Jorja walks in dressed head-to-toe in *Chanel* and Jaimee emits a low whistling sound in appreciation. Because I'm too nervous to speak, even though this is my sister and not a Czechoslovakian princess standing in front of us, Jaimee gives the pitch.

She starts with a brief explanation of the business model and although it differs a little from the description I gave her a few weeks ago, I listen to it with a fresh perspective. I analyse every word Jaimee utters and I feel embarrassed by how lacking in real business strategy it is. A week ago it sounded complete, formidable, and foolproof. Now, it sounds wanton, hopeful, and desperate!

I could panic. I could run screaming from the apartment, dive into the sea and let the billions of gallons of sea water waiting off Bondi wash my worries away. But that would be pointless. So I breathe in. Then I remind myself that business planning can be complex and slow and if you wait until the business plan is perfect then you might just miss finding your golden egg. I breathe out.

Jaimee continues, "We need a store in Paris for credibility, to create a relationship with the history of couture. I've spoken to Stephanie at NYFW and she said she'd love to see what us Aussies do to traditional Parisian fashions. I think she's expecting that we'll fall flat on our face and then she can expose us for the frauds that we are, but heck, it's worth a shot. So are you in?"

Jorja gives Jaimee a funny look before turning her attention on me.

"Til, do you honestly think you'll be ready for New York in September? Don't you think you're rushing it? And what about Nina, can you care for her and do all of the work that's required to organise an international penetration in such a short timeframe? And you're not even limiting yourself to one market here, you're suggesting we go after Europe and the North Americas at once."

I shift on the couch. "I know it's a lot to consider, but you have to remember that Jaimee, Didi, Cairine and I have been working together for eight years. We don't have to go through the usual team building processes, we're just moving offices…" I start.

"And markets. Til, I don't mean to be sceptical — and this is what I or any investor would probably say — but you don't have any experience in those."

"Yes. That's true. But Australia is more like an extension of the European and American markets anyway. And we're not presenting ourselves as an Australian label, but a French one. I've found a factory in France who'll sew our first line. That gives us time to bring some of the collectives on board. Just think how thrilled the women will feel to know they're working with a real, fashion label, that they're an instrumental part of our business," I say because I know talking about the collectives as much as possible is my best strategy of winning Jorja over.

But she remains unmoved by my appeal to her sense of humanity. Ever the practical business woman, she asks, "How are you positioned to meet your goals over the next year?"

"We design new clothes twice a year and present them at Sydney Fashion Week. Our production process will change, but we were already using more organic fabrics at *Enegi*, so we're used to that too. By targeting sponsors, we only have to produce a skeleton line for the Paris store. With a ten per cent hit rate we'll raise another half million euros by the end of the year."

"But New York as well? Are you confusing the market by sending it mixed messages?"

"Our print marketing will promote our sponsors, which will have the effect of pulling more sponsors to us. Our online marketing will appeal to the early adopters. Sponsors buy the right to design and name a garment, the early adopters buy from the diffusion range."

"Are we rushing the adoption curve?"

"We need the early adopters or the sponsors won't have an audience."

She keeps drilling me and jotting down notes. "What's your market entry timeline?"

"We'll be in Paris in three months, opening the store in five. Then we'll be in New York for September where we'll present the maternity range. By Christmas, the first advertising campaign will be ready to go, featuring the sponsors' garments. By then, the early adopters will be gagging for us. You can't underestimate the speed the fashion industry works at Jorja. As soon as it hits the catwalk or is worn by a celebrity, the adopters want it. It may take two more seasons for the laggards to adopt it. Eventually they will, which is why the trends will do a complete turnaround again."

"Exactly. No-one wants to look like…" Jaimee adds but Jorja interrupts her.

"Old news," Jorja offers.

Jorja thinks for a second. "I don't mean to sound rude, but I just don't think you understand the women's collectives, Til. You've never been to any of these countries so you don't truly understand the challenges — the complete and total lack of any infrastructure in these communities — and how difficult it will be to bring these women on board as a manufacturing resource, let alone as suppliers of any of our materials."

My heart drops.

"*Coca Cola* do it."

Jorja and I turn to Jaimee wondering what the hell she's talking about.

"If Coke can get their soft drinks into these communities, then why can't we get our product out? We have to try."

And it's times like this when I could absolutely commit my soul to this woman.

Jorja remains tight-lipped.

If she just said yes or no straight away I'd be happy, but the silence is eating at my heart.

"This is a fashion business but all you've shown me is the business plan and some financials. Where are the clothes?" she asks finally.

"Well, it's a business," I reply.

"It's a fashion business. I want to see how you differentiate yourselves visually."

"Didi is sketching now, she should have something in a week," Jaimee pitches.

"Well, tell her to send something over as soon as she can. Since you want $4 million dollars for the marketing campaign, I'd like to know where my money's going and what it's going to look like."

And she stands up. "I'm not saying no, and if I do end up saying no, I do know other people who may be interested. You may have to go slower though, set up the company structure and go further into some organisational and production planning before anyone comes on board financially."

My heart may as well be sunk on the bottom of the ocean floor.

"Don't put all your eggs in one basket," she says before closing the cover of her notebook and seconds later, the door to my apartment (and my dreams) with a thud.

It's only when she's gone that I realise she didn't even say goodbye to Nina.

Adam is sitting on the couch surrounded by my notes for the label.

The business plan has consumed me so much lately that I'd forgotten that I hadn't spoken to him about it. He's been at work, and at Dean's, and when he's been at home I've been so happy that we've really only talked about Nina.

But now he's very unhappy. I stand in the doorway cautiously, Nina sitting on my hip, the huge nappy bag slung over my shoulder. She's hungry again but she must be able to sense that Adam is upset because she stays absolutely quiet too.

"We've been out at the park. We had a meeting with Jorja this morning, and I was hoping to give you good news, that's why I didn't say anything before now," I manage.

"Til, what the hell…?" he begins but trails off, as if he's disgusted in me.

I didn't think he'd react this badly. I'm always coming up with crazy schemes and he usually humours me. But the look on his face says it all.

"You want to start your own label? Are you mad? You're talking about disrupting Nina's life and working an eighty hour week instead of fifty. And on top of that, you'll have no security. And I should know, I have my own business."

"Oh God, Adam," I say. "I didn't mean for you to find out like this, I got so caught up with the idea and putting a business plan together for Jorja, but I don't think she's interested, so you can stop worrying."

But he isn't convinced. Sensing a fight, Nina cooes at us. She's an expert at timing. Instead of looking demanding and expensive, she looks at us like she doesn't have a care in the world — that as long as we're around, that's all that matters.

"One minute you're saying you're going to see what's out there, maybe even take Nina on a holiday, and the next you're planning your financial ruin."

I am certain steam is coming out of his ears.

"Why the hell didn't you tell me?"

I tell him to calm down, that he's scaring Nina. "We can discuss this later, after Nina's gone to bed."

"No. She has to learn to deal with conflict."

"Shouting about it won't teach her anything," I retaliate.

He agrees. He sits down and takes a few breaths. "So you're not committed to this?"

"Without an investor, no. But we're looking into the possibility, yes."

"And when will you make a decision?"

"I don't know." Which is true. "Do you want me to tell you more about it?"

He shakes his head. "No. I've heard it all before. There are so many fashion labels out there, Til. God, I work in fashion and I'm beginning to hate it. Hem here, collar there, it's all so boring. Bored, fucking rich kids who all act like they're so entitled."

"Exactly."

"So what makes your label so special, Til?"

I ignore him.

"Til?"

The thing about differentiation is that it does matter. It's not one of those airy-fairy business concepts that you can sweep under the carpet — like financials. There are really only two main strategies that businesses can follow: cost leadership or differentiation. Companies that pursue cost leadership are brands like *Kmart*, *Target*, *Supré* and (once upon a time) *Sportsgirl*. *Sportsgirl* used to be where I shopped when I was a teenager, it was cool and affordable. Now it pursues more of a *total look* store which is a differentiation strategy. At *Supré,* you can get really cheap outfits, at *Sportsgirl*, you can craft a whole look.

Jorja's girls don't shop at either. Most of Jorja's girls' clothes are handmade and the girls are even allowed to design some of them. That's how Jorja makes them feel special. The other way Jorja makes them feel special is by taking them to *David Jones* and asking the Customer Service desk to call out their names over the store's in-house announcements. Imagine, the girls are wandering through the store's glossy boutique lay out, putting sticky fingers all over *Jimmy Choo* bags and trying on tweenage makeup, when all of a sudden their names are called out from the heavens by the shopping Gods.

Rumour has it that a leading retailer spent a whole year trying to woo Jorja to shop there but she wouldn't have anything to do with it. Their differentiation strategy is to hire a sunny model who looks great in Spring/Summer colours and is all sun-blessed happiness and sex (which I love but unfortunately my pale skin doesn't). Jorja, who is olive-skinned and could pass for a Taihitian princess would look fabulous in any of their catalogues. But she doesn't like Summer. Jorja is a Winter type, elegance not sex, holidays in the Dolomites, her most favourite place in the world: the *Ponte dei Sospiri* in Venice. As a result, she doesn't shop at the summery store. It makes her feel young and sweaty; I guess it reminds her of her foolish youth spent in the backs of cars. And there's no way she wants to go there again, especially now she has young daughters.

So differentiation does matter. Put together the wrong strategy and your market won't buy. It's as simple and as financially life-threatening as that.

"Til?" Adam's voice interrupts my brain noise.

"It's not just a label, it's my future, it's Nina's future," I try to explain.

"That's nice, but I don't think that will sell clothes. Who's your competition?"

I don't dare tell him *Baby Dior*. Instead, I tell him we're creating a new product offering, we can't be compared to anything else out there so it's pointless comparing us with existing brands.

He doesn't buy it. "Your customer will compare your offering to a hundred others. Who are they?"

So I tell him, "*Louis Vuitton, Gap, Bonpoint,* the usual *enfant couture*…."

"Oh my God, Til, you can't be serious. You can't compete against those guys. Where the hell will you manufacture? How will you raise the millions in advertising you're going to need just to get your name out there, let alone create brand value? You may as well have said that you want to give God a run for his money."

To the fashion conscious, *Dior* is God.

I pace around the apartment while Nina watches my shoes, riveted by my anxious steps.

Then I catch sight of our faces in the lounge room mirror. Adam looks downcast, I look desperate. Which I am.

"I know it's going to be hard work, but isn't this the example I should be setting for Nina?" I implore his deeply hidden good side.

He tries one more time to make me see sense. He even waves the business plan in the air like it's a waste of good recyclable paper. "This is something that *Chloé* can afford to do, Til, but not you. You have enough money to put down a deposit on a flat. Now you're talking about moving to Paris and doing something that is — I'm sorry to say this — a lot harder than your skills set is ready for." And he slams the business plan down on our tiny dining room table.

I know he doesn't mean it, he's just worried about Nina. This is exactly the same conversation that I'll be having with my mother when I tell her what I'm up to. Except that she'll just say I'm mad and should be looking for a husband, not an investor.

"You know it's all smoke and mirrors, Adam. All we need is a collection, a space, and a vision. The rest will fall into place. Paris is just a start, to give us some credibility while we build the brand value. Just think about how great this will be, to help women build their own viable cooperatives, to have the power to manage their own businesses and incomes. To play an integral role in improving the quality of their lands. If you're telling me that it's impossible for me to do this, then Jorja may as well stop financing the cooperatives as well. She may as well tell these women to go back to prostitution and starvation, to let their children die from AIDS, and to give up any hope that they have that life will get better. Because if I can't do it, with every advantage that I've got at my disposal, then neither can they."

He stops.

Then he sits on the couch and puts his head in his hands. And he apologises. Then after a very long time while I stand with my back to him and make him suffer in silence, he tells me I should go for it.

"You think so?"

"You are a lot smarter than I am, Til. It's not something I could do, but you'll find a way to make it work. I know you will."

"I don't think I have to succeed. I just have to try."

He takes my hand as I sit next to him on the couch. "I'll miss you, you and Nina."

"We won't be gone for long."

"This isn't a five week fad, Til. It could take you the rest of your life to achieve this."

I sigh heavily. "You were right, you know. This is a new reality for me," I admit.

And then he throws me a curve ball. One that I would never have seen coming. "And what about Fred? If you go to Paris, you'll be giving up on Fred."

Even the mention of Fred's name is enough to make me feel calm and assured. Just that one syllable brings back wonderful memories of being pregnant with Nina. He was the best gift a pregnant woman could ever be given. He knew just the right way to massage swollen feet to increase endorphins which is exactly what you need when you're facing the responsibility of bringing a new life into this crazy world.

"I can repay you financially for Fred, but I can't ever *really* repay you for Fred. You know, that don't you? He made me feel less alone."

Which only makes Adam look really guilty. "Look, I know I should have said something earlier, Til, but you don't owe me for Fred. He never charged me for your massages. He said he couldn't, that you were too nice and not like his other clients who are just selfish cows and care too much about how they look, and that you only care about how other people feel. He said it was refreshing, in a city obsessed with cellulite and image, that you appreciate the female form and only see positives. And those are his words, not mine. You should be proud of yourself for making such a big impression on him."

"Why?"

"Are you nuts? He's gorgeous," Adam says.

"Well, maybe he's only gorgeous on the outside."

Which is a complete lie. A vision of Fred floats in front of both of us: his tanned physique and 100 stomach muscles developed over a life time committed to head stands and organic, vegan food. And then there's the twenty hours a week he spends feeding the homeless. The man would give the shirt off his own back and the food meant for his own belly.

As much as I could spend years fantasising about us being made for each other, it's never going to happen.

But that's not what Adam's face is telling me. In fact, his guilty expression is telling me a whole different story.

I didn't want to admit it to myself but I know what he's talking about. He's talking about Fred's eyes, which are rich and brown like the earth, and the way they constantly swept over me, watching and monitoring, willing danger out of my way, while cocooning me and Nina in all the love Mother Nature could muster in a man.

Suddenly I feel divided. Although I've missed Fred, I've been so consumed with being a new mother that I hadn't consciously thought of his absence. There've been times when I've caught myself talking to him out loud, especially when Nina's been really difficult and I've lost faith not only in myself, but in the entire female species. That's when I've willed him into being, when I'm stripped of my so-called inherent maternal abilities, and he talks me through the process of helping Nina.

But I know I don't have the time or enough emotional intelligence to risk being in a relationship with someone right now. All I can do is help other women feel how I did when Fred extended his charitable energy toward me. I'd give anything to feel cocooned in his presence once more — and I'm sure a million of other women would too. There is no question that he could make a million pregnant women around the world spend an amount of money equivalent to Third World Debt on clothes for themselves and their off-spring. Maybe they could even help us wipe out Third World Debt.

"There's no way Fred would do it."

When Adam asks me what I'm talking about, I realise I've spoken out loud.

I tell him it's nothing. I resort to telling myself that I'm a horrible person. In ten seconds flat, I've managed to turn a whole human being into an objectified marketing strategy. Adam thinks he's talking to me about losing the partner of my dreams, while I'm trying to figure out if Fred would model for our advertising campaign. I know he wouldn't. Which is such a shame. He would look gorgeous in black and white.

"Well, if you change your mind and decide to give Fred a chance, he's going to an ashram in India for six months so you'd better hurry up about it, before he gets swallowed up by some half-nice girl doing her best to impersonate a yogi."

"He's going to India? But he'll be back, right?"

"And so will you, won't you?"

"Of course," I tell him resolutely. But we both know, despite the onerous week I've had writing a business plan, that I can't possibly know what the future will bring.

Seven months

My mother is officially nuts.

She is in a permanent state of peekaboo.

She's pretty funny, though. She likes hiding under blankets so I pretend it's really fun to find her under there. She thinks that when she's under the blanket I don't know she's there. But I do. It's something calling object permanence. Once I used to think that when I couldn't see her she was gone for good, and I'd cry my little heart out, but now I'm beginning to understand that when she disappears from the room for a half hour, she hasn't gone anywhere, she's just forgotten me.

I remind her about my object permanence by grabbing at her hair when she picks me up — only to show her how appreciative I am that she has rescued me from my cold, dark, lonely, unbearable cot — and then she screams at me and tears her hair away. It must be a really fun game for her, because when I grab it again, she goes absolutely wild. Then she gives up and just gives me booby.

After another feed and a burp, I start feeling human again and let Mum go to sleep. Sometimes I like to stay up and just watch her pretending to sleep. Then I show her my appreciation by slapping her in the face. She gets really mad about that, holds me tighter so my little arms can't play, which is really annoying because the only other thing to do then is to sleep.

Or feed. It's nice being able to just attach myself to booby now rather than wait for her to stop her oh-so-busy life to shove it in my mouth.

She's my human dummy, basically. I'd slurp away all

night if she let me, but she finds lying there letting me feed strangely exhausting, and at some time in the night, screams at me when I accidentally bite her with my one monstrously sharp tooth.

I make it up to her the next day by playing with her in the mirror. She points at me and says "Baby, baby Nina," then points to herself, and says, "Mummy". I try to mimic her: when she says, "Baby Nina," I say, "Ba," and when she says, "Mummy", I say "Ga".

She claps and I try to clap too, but sometimes my hands don't meet in the middle.

It's so much easier to just show her my appreciation by slapping her in the face.

Jekyll and Hyde become parents

Going back to work after having a baby makes me feel more like Jekyll and Hyde than ever before.

At *Enegi*, my usual reckless bursts of energy were famously interspersed with small amounts of market research and minor moments of marketing planning. Mostly, I spent a whole lot of time gossiping with Didi and Cairine, preparing for Fashion Week, and organising for sample stock to be altered for my favourite magazine editors.

And it worked. *Enegi* got a lot of space in magazine editorial and I was invited to a lot of great parties. The only angst I ever felt during my old life was regret about the number of martinis I'd consumed before pontificating about the humiliation of falling over the giant feet of another super-waif.

Now, instead of being riddled with vodka, I'm riddled with guilt. I'm neglecting Nina.

Which leads to self-doubt, self-deprecation and self-loathing. Which must all be acknowledged and then breathed out of the body.

I tell myself 20 times a day that it's natural to feel like this. I may not be spending every waking minute of the day watching her (or doing mind-numbing chores), but I am trying to involve her in my work as much as possible.

I read Nina my marketing plan and show her sketches of catalogues, swing tags, and logo designs but like the 21st century baby that she is, she is more interested in my ideas for viral marketing, website design and formaldehyde testing protocols. These pages, she scrunches in her little fists and tries to eat. The rest she covers in baby slobber.

During my meetings with Jaimee, who keeps telling me to pretend that it's not my money I'm risking but somebody else's, we go over the marketing plan in detail. But her assurances don't make it any easier. Because we have an investor on board. Somebody whose money I care about more than my own: Jorja.

Jorja took two days to decide to back our market entry.

She said she obsessed over the decision until she realised, in the middle of a speech to the Canberra Press gallery, that this was a dream come true. "Sometimes you're so used to managing substandard behaviour that when someone exceeds your expectations, you don't know what to do," she told me on the phone.

She said she realised her myopia when a journalist at the Press Club luncheon asked her what her ideal business venture would look like. The journalist explained, "Because today, most of your collectives make cute little ethnic looking toys and knick-knacks but they lack lustre and ambition, they don't fit into a serious value chain. And surely, if the collectives are to succeed, don't they need to do just that?"

(Of course Jaimee later denied it, but I bet it cost her at least $20k to *advise* the journalist to present that question to Jorja in a public arena.)

Jorja didn't elaborate further. She finished our call by simply telling me that she would send her lawyers over the next day. And she hung up. Leaving me holding the phone and my heart beating at a million miles an hour.

The contracts are in front of me now.

For her $4 million investment, Jorja received a 69% share of the business. Figuring out the ownership structure took Jaimee, myself, Jorja's two lawyers and a spreadsheet five minutes.

The first thing we did was input our fantastical future sales figures — in year one, we estimated our sales to be $3 million, $6 million in year two, then $12 million and $18 million — and applied a financial calculation called Net Present Value. The spreadsheet then automatically discounted the incomes across the cash flows (the years we will be earning revenue) and deducted Jorja's capital investment.

The only variable we had to enter into the equation was the cost of capital which the most boring of the two lawyers entered at 30%. Jaimee didn't blink an eye but I just about fell off my chair.

The cost of capital is the rate of return that capital could be expected to earn in an alternative investment of equivalent risk. Which means, Jorja considers this project to be high risk (which I already knew) but also, that she could earn up to 30% return on her investment elsewhere.

Meanwhile my superannuation just went backwards by 12%. I wish I had her stockbroker.

When the lawyer coughed, my attention returned. The Net Present Value calculation gave us an outcome higher than zero which gave Jorja the green light to invest in the business.

Of course, it's all make believe. I don't have a clue what our future sales are going to be, but that didn't stop us, or millions of other businesses, using *projected* figures to value their business and calculate shares.

Wedged between Tweedle-dum and Tweedle-more dum, I realised there was no difference between the stockmarket and the local fortune-teller who works out of the Bondi markets each Saturday. Of course, the financial industry puts on expensive suits and tells you it's all based on hard analysis, but really, it's all a show to get you to spend money (via investments) in their industry. And now we're a part of the show.

To celebrate the deal, I took Nina to the park and put her on a blanket. I wanted to put her on the grass but it looked so dry and crackly that I was scared it might scratch her delicate skin. We sat there and looked for worms and ants but found nothing so ended up playing peekaboo under the blanket instead.

On the way home, we met with our virtual business accountant — Donna, from the Bondi Beach new parents' group. Having successfully convinced her husband's company to honour its parental leave policy (after an elongated hearing at the Fair Work Ombudsman), Donna has returned to work two days a week.

While Jorja's lawyers are responsible for setting up the company structure and guiding us through our responsibilities as company directors, Donna has been hired as an external, objective accountant to keep track of my spending. It's not that Jorja doesn't trust me, but this is business: checks (and cheques) and balances are important.

The fact that we're Donna's first client resonates powerfully with me — and Nina — who spends the entire meeting fast asleep in her cherished, second-hand pram.

"Til, are you trying to milk your own breast?" Nadia asks, staring at me in disbelief.

"So what?" I tell her. "You've seen me feed Nina a million times, why does this shock you?"

"I don't know, it's kind of wrong," Adam agrees shuffling uncomfortably. "Like you're masturbating in public."

I cannot believe them. "Adam, you told me to stop using the breastfeeding wrap and now you're accusing me of pleasuring myself while all I'm trying to do is feed my child."

"Well, what the hell were you pulling at your boob for?"

I put my boob back in Nina's mouth and she sucks for a few seconds before screaming again. "I was checking to see if I have milk."

"Why?"

"Because I think my supply has dropped. Nina's still hungry and I'm out of milk."

"Can't you give her more vegetables?" Nadia asks, looking anxious.

I gather she's witnessing her parenting days as a flashback. Poor Nadia. She must still have nightmares about endlessly pureeing pumpkin.

"She still needs milk, the midwife said between 500 and 600ml a day."

"How much is she getting?"

"It's a bit hard to tell, I can't measure my breast milk. And I can't pump, it doesn't work for me, so I've got no way of telling."

"Except that she's screaming again," Adam offers rubbing his forehead like he's in pain.

"You should have called her Freddy Kruger," Nadia suggests.

"I think you should shut up and go and call Louise for me."

Adam sits awkwardly on the couch watching me squeeze my breast while Nadia calls Louise. She returns carrying a page full of notes.

She starts speaking but we can't hear her over Nina's screaming. Nadia yells, "Louise says that the problem is obvious!"

"What the hell is that supposed to mean?" I spit at her while I jiggle Nina up and down.

"Louise said that Nina's probably going through a growth spurt. She'll feed more because she's hungrier than usual. And that your breasts will make more milk. That or she's teething and just wants to feed; breastmilk can contain an anaesthetic, plus she probably finds it comforting. "

"But she keeps coming off the boob and screaming. I think my supply's dropped."

"She mentioned that could be a possibility. As soon as you turn your work brain back on, it does something to your milk. She also said that you probably wouldn't find a midwife in the country to agree with her, especially when the government keeps printing posters saying that it is possible for women to breast pump at work — that is, if your boobs can stand up to being pumped for a half hour eight times a day without splitting in two, and the nightmare of finding a hygienic, private space to pump and store the milk, carry it home again, sterilize the bottles and pump bits…blah blah blah. She said this happens to just about every woman she knows. Your milk drops either because the baby's not around all the time or just because you're busy and not feeding enough to keep up your supply, or because you're stressed and not sleeping enough because you're working and juggling the demands of a baby." She looks up from her notes. "It might be time to start giving her chicken bones to gnaw on, that's what my grandma did."

"You wouldn't have a clue what your grandmother did to her children, please shut up and tell me what else Louise said," I bark at her, my head spinning.

"That's it. She said to feed more regularly, drink plenty of fluids, eat lots of protein and get lots of rest. It'll come back up in a few days."

"In a few days? Nina's screaming at me now."

"Well, there's something else."

She looks sheepish.

"What?"

"You could try acupuncture," she says, dropping the notes she's holding to her sides defeated.

Adam rubs his hands down the fronts of his pants, Nadia nods her head again and Adam's jaw clicks.

He says, sympathetically, "I'll come with, I know you hate needles."

But I take a deep breath. "Will it work immediately?"

"How the hell am I supposed to know? But it's worth a try."

That's why Adam is Nina's best Dad, I think. "You ring. I'll get ready," I say to him but he's already heading out the door.

A half hour later, I'm laying on an examination table in Bondi Junction, sucking in the smell of lavender, while a very serene woman, Jayne, *listens* to my pulse.

In all my years at the Byron Bay health spa, I've never tried acupuncture. But Jayne assures me she'll tell me when to breathe and it will be totally painless and wonderfully peaceful.

And even though I don't believe a word of it, I'm willing to try anything if it means it might help my breastmilk.

"Your Yin pulse is down. Are you very tired at the moment?" she asks me.

I nod while she swaps to my left arm and listens to that pulse.

"I can put some needles in to help your flow, but I'd like to work on your lung point in your wrist, it works on a thousand points in the body and is very nourishing. In Chinese Medicine, the blood is seen as nourishing food, as is breastmilk; when you're pregnant, your spleen, which produces blood, can get overworked, so if we build up the spleen and the Yin pulse, your breast milk should improve. OK?"

Again, I nod. I'm so busy hating myself for letting my breastmilk drop that I don't even notice Jayne putting the needles in.

"There, all done," she says and then listens to my pulse again.

"Really, is that it?" I ask, lifting my head off the table and catching sight of long thin needles sticking out of my wrists, breast bone, abdomen and legs.

"Sure, now you just lie here for twenty minutes." And she touches my arm in a gentle way that reminds me instantly of Fred. I block him out.

Soon, I begin to feel it: a gentle tugging at my wrist which is strangely reassuring and energizing. It feels like a small fish tugging on a line.

Then a warm sensation starts flooding over my breasts, tingling and buzzing, which must mean that it's working. Already I feel a million times better. I can't wait to tell Adam about.

Jayne appears a few seconds after a buzzer sounds and retrieves the needles.

"So what did you think?"

"It was amazingly peaceful. How on earth did they figure all this stuff out?"

"Years of trial and error, I guess," Jayne laughs. "There are other things you can do to increase your supply at home. There are herbs you can take, Blessed Thistle is one, and there are breastmilk teas. But that's up to you, any herb can work its way into the breastmilk. I've heard the occasional story of some babies reacting to herbs and medicines."

"What else?"

"Feeding and plenty of protein, fluids and rest."

"That's what my friend said."

"Do you sleep with the baby?"

"Most of the time."

"The more skin on skin contact you can have the better. And less stress. Whatever it is, reduce the contact time you have with stress. It can't be that important, can it?"

"In the grand scheme of things, no, it's probably not," I admit.

Jayne nods and leaves me to dress and I take in a few last breaths of lavender before emerging to confront the challenges ahead of me.

"Yes," I tell Adam, when we leave, "that was just what I needed."

"The acupuncture?"

"That and the organic towels and candles, the wholesome attitude, the holistic approach to health. It was all fantastic. It was what I needed to remind myself that I should be taking care of myself and the people around me, and spending as much time as possible with Nina. Work is work, it's not life."

Adam and I walk home together. Over the next few weeks we spend as much time together as we can before Nina and I fly — finally — to Paris.

Nine Months

Mamaaaa.

Maaamaaa.

Have you seen my Mama? Oh, you don't know who that is? My Mama's the one who picks me up all the time and cuddles me, she feeds me from her booby and now she's trying to get me to eat vegetables. So if milk comes from booby where do vegetables come from?

Oh, there you are again, I thought you'd gone. So, what's your name? Everybody has a name around here. It's something to do with the human brain's need to categorise everything because that's how we learn — through association and identification. It means we understand everything in duality: it's either black or not black, and if it's not black, then it's red or not red. See, how the game is played? Here is my big toe which is not my heel and not my little toe. That's the one that goes *weee weee weee all the way home*.

The famous French philosopher Jacques Derrida says everything is about language; that we wouldn't exist without words. I heard all about him on a documentary on the plane. Mum says I wouldn't be here if it hadn't been for *Jimmy Choo*. She really loves him a lot. One day I thought I saw Mum talking to him and I craned my neck to see but then I fell over and cried. And it wasn't Jimmy at all, it was just a shoe.

So are you human? No. OK, so this is a game. I get it. I keep asking questions until you go insane. Are you an animal? No. Vegetable? Yes. Cool. Carrot? Potato? Let me

276

guess, pumpkin again?

"Zoom, here comes the aeroplane."

That was Mum. She's always talking to the spoon. Somebody should tell this woman that if she tries to amuse me when I eat then I'll learn to associate eating with fun and eventually I'll start to eat when I'm bored.

But being bored is the least of my worries.

I'm starting to get scared when she leaves the room. Plus, I've got something in my pants so if she leaves me with it my nervous system just won't cope. Can't she stop playing with the spoon and give me some booby? I used to think she was just a boob, but now that I can see her properly I can tell she's much more a wavering blob in front of me.

When I'm a teenager she'll revert to being a nagging, finger-waving blob in front of me again. Hopefully, for her sake, I will have learned some empathy skills by then so occasionally I'll listen to her and clean my room. Want to know how to help me build empathy skills? Well, when I fall over or get disappointed and scream, don't tell me to toughen up but tell me you understand my disappointment and then explain to me what's going on in my body, for example, "Oh dear, you're feeling frustrated because you want to walk but you keep falling over, that's understandable, but walking's not easy. It takes months to learn how to do it. Let's try again. I'll help you."

I know Mum's too tired to go to all that effort all the time, but one day she'll benefit from her own displays of compassion. I see how tired she is and I know she was up most of the night because I was teething.

I don't know how our society got so far if raising a human is so difficult. I've heard Grandma say how easy Mum's got it, with washing machines and cars these days. Of course, my Grandma had a car and a washing machine too but Mum didn't say anything about that. Instead she said, "I imagine it was easy for you, with all that valium and vodka."

Moya Kate

See, she's hilarious isn't she? Well, I think so. In fact, I'm going to sit here and blow this pumpkin shit back at her face because this little girl just wants to have some fun.

Paris, France

"Can I take it off yet?" I ask the girls, referring to the *Hermes* scarf Jaimee has tied way too tightly over my eyes.

"No, Til. Wait."

I've waited this long to see Paris another few minutes won't kill me, I tell myself. But it doesn't work, the suspense is killing me. Jaimee is insistent my first view of Paris should be breathtaking.

"Your first view of Paris cannot be *McDonalds* at *Gare du Nord*," Didi agrees. "It won't be long now."

I try to believe her. After all, Didi has lived in Paris. I never knew this about her but over the last few months, while we slogged away doing a year's work in three months, Didi kept us motivated by telling us about her adventures in Paris after she graduated from her fashion course and worked here as an *au pair*. Stories about snogging total strangers in the queue at the *Louvre*, sneaking into fashion events by pretending to be a buyer, and participating in an age-old Parisian tradition: of walking the streets of Paris for hours and hours on end.

Her stories sounded amazing, fantastical and surreal.

Now, instead of the sounds of seagulls and buzzing mosquitoes, I'm listening to Didi and Jaimee discuss routes with the cab driver in French. He is having trouble understanding their accent.

I hold onto Nina's hand. As we get closer to the city, the traffic slows and the car horns grow increasingly inpatient. When a moped screams past us the limousine diver cusses him in French.

I grin. I want to tear the blindfold off my face and just soak in Paris, whatever the view is, even if it's of the back of old Fiat.

But Jaimee says it's much worse. We are still 20 minutes from the city and stuck on the ring-road that marks the old city walls. And it's early July which means the Parisians, who are exiting in droves in preparation for their long summer *vacances* at the seaside, are being replaced with tourists: people like us, people who all have a dream of Paris and those visions include the *Arc de Triomphe* and the *Centre Pompidou*, not the ugly sky-high housing estates that you would associate with Detroit or Madrid, but never Paris.

I push the button on my window and it slides down effortlessly. For two seconds Paris is blasted into the car: beeping horns, drivers' yelling, and the sound of ladies' heels click-clicking along the pavement.

I lean my head out the window and am suddenly whacked in the head by what I assume is a baguette.

Didi pulls me back into the car. "Never do that Til, the French are unforgiving."

"I can't bear it, let me see."

After a brief discussion in French, the limo driver huffs and stalls the car in the middle of the street, ignoring the torrent of abuse from his fellow Parisians as he idles around to open my door.

My first view of Paris is a five-foot-tall, chain-smoking Tunisian who smells like a decadent *Junya Watanabe* eau de toilette and who just blocks out the view of the Eiffel Tower, which, for two seconds is illuminated by the sun like a shining beacon of hope.

Breathless, I jump back into the limo to grab Nina and, after stepping around the Tunisian, point us in the direction of the *le Tour* — and our future.

The rest of our first day in Paris is spent looking for Gretel. Gretel, Louise's step-daughter, who as promised is conducting her work experience with me, has joined us as our *runner* — and in keeping with her job title has done just that.

The last time we saw her was at the Charles de Gaulle airport luggage carousel where, thanks to her excessively extroverted personality, she was swapping phone numbers with some local youths.

Gretel, who seemed exceedingly sullen and spoilt when I first met her, has complimented her newly found *joie de vivre* with an equally excessive short skirt.

Jaimee had decided that the best way for Gretel to start learning the layout of the city was for her to hit the ground running — after a gruelling 24 hour, sleepless flight. The logic was sound. Gretel would get a fright at finding herself lost in a big European city, become shell-shocked by the language barrier and come running back to the apartment scared out of her wits. Jaimee was quite confident: Gretel would then spend the next two months doing everything we said without a hint of teenage rebellion.

But six hours later, she was still missing.

I tell myself, there are two options: she is either dead or — and this is more likely — too busy showing the Parisians how big-city living should be done to fathom any tourist awkwardness or guilt about her accent.

My first few hours in Paris are spent unpacking while making frequent dashes to the balcony to look longingly at the view from our apartment — and for any sight of Gretel.

When Jaimee starts talking about calling the Embassy, Gretel turns up. Her arrival is announced by a flurry of doorbells and shouting by neighbours whose lives have been rudely interrupted by the foolish Americans who have invaded their building. Having said we were *Australian* to the all-in-black octogenarian widow neighbour, who delivered us the key to the apartment and a lung full of cigarette smoke, she spat at us, "Ah Americans, I had an American boyfriend in the war, he stole my gin and married by best friend — I heard she gave him gonorrhoea."

I knew better than to react. After years of dealing with my own grandmother's shocking acts for attention, I simply turned on my *Yves Saint Laurent* tribute sandal and clambered up three flights of stairs to my bedroom while acknowledging a strange sense of loss. To have travelled this far to find that human nature has not improved — although the architecture of *Le Marais* is decidedly better than the three-floors-up 1960s brick-shitter where I reside in Sydney — is somehow disappointing.

Which reminds me of something written by Alain de Botton in *The Architecture of Happiness*, which I read on the Sydney-Paris flight while Nina napped: *"Not only do beautiful houses falter as guarantors of happiness, they can also be accused of failing to improve the characters of those who live in them."*

Which is why we need fashion, I tell myself. If architecture fails to be the instrument that can deliver the world and its people to a better place, than fashion must do it for us.

Cairine, Didi, Jaimee, Nina and I squeeze onto a wrought iron balcony and watch Gretel emerge triumphantly from a limousine while a chauffeur retrieves a number of packages bearing the fashion industry's most iconic logos from the boot.

Gretel is beaming. And more importantly, she has won over the Parisians for us.

Our neighbour cries out, "These Americans, they sound like crows but at least they have taste — and money."

"Oh Lord, I hope that's her mother's credit card she's using," I tell Jaimee who is also overtly relieved.

The grace and style Gretel exhibits as she enters the apartment should be reserved for an accomplished woman in her 40's, not a teenage girl visiting her first European city. There are only two people under the age of 30 who can pull off this type of angelic, sexy confidence: Gretel and Abbey Lee, the Melbourne model who became the face of *Gucci Flora* and featured as a pierced mermaid — ah, my second girl crush ever — in *Vogue*'s 50th anniversary edition in a fashion story with my all-time fave model, Catherine McNeil — my first girl crush ever.

"I stopped at *Avenue Montaigne* after getting into *Gard du Nord* — it was only a few stops out of the way," she struts around the apartment, "and picked us up some new clothes. You can't go around Paris dressed like *that*."

In particular, she is looking at me. OK, since having Nina I may not have paid much attention to my wardrobe, and am happy to lounge around in tights and oversized breastfeeding shirts that say things like "give peas a chance" in neon pink, but she's right. My standard apparel is not *de rigueur* for Paris and a far cry from the likes of *Chanel* where Gretel has just been shopping.

"Then I had a quick look at *Rue du Faubourg* and picked up some *Chloé* and *Lacroix* too.

"You have impeccable taste," Didi tells Gretel who nods in agreement.

"Of course, I like *Nicolas Andreas Taralis* and *Valentino* but when I'm a top-shot international lawyer I'm going to wear *Atsuro Tayama* and *Wunderkind* everyday," she says.

"I gather you don't mean humanitarian law," Jaimee smirks.

"Of course not, I'm going to do international business," Gretel concludes.

"You don't want to work in fashion?" I ask. I can hear the disappointment in my voice, thinking about the waste of her talent. The quality of the essay she wrote for me was very good. Even without a degree in marketing she'd managed to analyse Louise's customers into 20 different niche markets and developed extensive profiles (some less complimentary than others) and complex market reach strategies.

"Which is why this placement has been fantastic," she says. "When I asked to do work experience with you I was hoping to meet some hottie to take to my formal, but picking up a trip to Paris and conning Mum into giving me a semester off school is just fantastic. You girls rock."

"And the purchasers were made with …?" Jaimee asks before trailing off, waiting for the inevitable.

"Mum's credit card. I figured she'd find out I'd taken it soon enough so I should get in quick. She can't call the cops and dob in her daughter but she will cancel it."

"What if she reports it stolen? You could be in a lot of trouble," I say to her. "I should tell you to take them back and call your mother, but since you're going to be an international lawyer I'll let you handle this one. Mind you, it might be quite hard to practice if you have a criminal conviction for fraud."

"Oh I won't practise, I'll work for a company like *Gucci*. And besides they can't convict me, I'm underage. I'll just tell Mum I bought some stuff for me, cry about not understanding the exchange rates, and how she only got rich in the first place because she got pregnant with me and then ripped off Dad. I don't feel guilty about it all. After all, I know about the trust fund she emptied."

Didi and Cairine aren't listening to a word Gretel is saying but are carefully inspecting every garment now emerging from the numerous bags. They murmur and nod, point and stroke, immersed in their own utopia.

I try to not look at the garments but the quality of the fabrics and the tailoring keeps catching my eye. I find myself longing to try them on.

"Have you got any idea how much you spent?" I ask still feeling responsible for Gretel's behaviour since she is, essentially, under my wing.

"With the exchange rate, something like $30,000. Mum will hit the roof. Louise will think I'm fabulous. We'd better keep something for her."

And with that I let the whole episode slide. I'll tackle Gretel's rampant consumerism another day, I tell myself, and picking out a one-shouldered, spray-painted *Versace* dress, decide right there and then that I am required to try it on. "It's just my size too," I tell the girls and whisk it way into our quaint French bathroom, in our historical French apartment in the middle of Paris. Then I twirl about in front of an original Renaissance-era mirror for a whole five minutes.

We are staying in *Le Marais*, on Paris' right bank (or *Rive Gauche*, if you must know). Despite some very fashionable labels opening across the river, Jaimee says (repeatedly since arriving, she's driving me nuts), "The writers can have the Left Bank, I'm staying with the prostitutes and aristocrats."

Le Marais, named after its swampy marshlands, is one of the oldest neighbourhoods in Paris and was the centre of aristocracy before it slid into disarray after something called *Le Revolution*. Of course, before I came to Paris and bought a guide book, I thought *Le Revolution* was the name of my favourite bar in Paddington. Live and learn.

It's also one of the trendiest fashion districts in Paris, the world's biggest brands abide here (with no tasteless neon signs in sight) next to restaurants and bars which don't just appear sparingly, they alternate in the landscape. This is what you do in Paris: you shop (at your favourite local market), you drink, and then you eat, and when you're bored with that, you start all over again. There are no gyms, no branded supermarkets taking up valuable retail space on your local *rue*, no tasteless office space proclaiming that any work ethic exists here at all. *Non*, in Paris work is unnecessary. Life is too short, but maybe your skirt should be a little shorter? *Oui?*

Le Marais has stolen my heart, emptied it of salt crystals and sunshine and replaced them with champagne and *La Places des Vosges*.

La Place des Vosges, a square built by, ironically, the English King Henry IV to celebrate the wedding of Louis XIII and Anne of Austria, is in fact, one of the most beautiful in all of Europe. Nina and I have happily been exploring its formal gardens all morning, watched over by the red brick residences, with their steeply pitched grey slate roofs, rooted firmly to the ground by stone pillars. As I push her pram under the glorious vaulted arcades and wonder at the square's superb architecture, my breath catches in my chest. How is it that I have never heard of *La Place des Vosges* before?

I've never been one to believe in fairytales, but perhaps in Paris dreams really do come true? In Paris, you can go to bed a pauper, and wake up to find yourself cocooned in silk duvets and sleeping in a mahogany four-poster bed.

Our apartment has been lent to us by a very generous friend of Jaimee's, whom, when she heard about our impossible task, offered us her Parisian base with the strictest instructions: that we should treat it like our own.

Not only is the apartment filled with antiques and the best French textiles on the market, but the apartment has been lovingly and painstakingly restored and its interior designed by one of Paris' best.

With two croissants firmly tucked into my stomach, all I want to do is laze in the sun in the middle of the square and fantasise that I truly am Marie Antoinette (pre-*Le Revolution,* of course). But if we are going to be here for a few months, to have the audacity to open yet another fashion label in the city of couture, to squeeze even a fingernail's width into the retail landscape, then I feel a duty to explore Paris at once; and even if she doesn't care about us, I know I am ready to fall head over heels in love with her.

We turn our back on our palatial home and head toward the bustling afternoon traffic of *Le Rue de Rivoli* before turning short of the *Hôtel de Ville* and the *Centre Pompidou* toward *le Pont Marie.*

As we venture closer to *Île de la Cîté,* I keep the guide book open over the pram handles and chat to Nina about the sights we are seeing.

"Look, Nina, a real French person, you can tell because of the beautiful way she ties her scarf, it's an organic Gallic trait, along with high cheekbones and delicate feet."

She makes a grunting sound as if she's concentrating on doing a poo but I can tell she's as excited as me to be in Paris.

We turn a corner and for the first time in both of our lives are confronted with the beauty of the twisting, seen it all, *La Seine.*

And we both gasp.

Everybody who has been to Paris has a favourite view of the city. Being a marketer, my first instinct is to compile a list of the top ten opinions and separate those into psychographic profiles:

1.   The view of the bridges crossing *la Seine* — romantic, over 40 female, loves her husband but twice a year goes to a hotel and has a rendezvous with a man whose name she never asks, likes to buy expensive underwear, homewares, fashion magazines, and European cars;

2.   *Les Champs Éllysée* illuminated at night with *l'Arc de*

Triomphe in the background — classic provider, over 30 male, likely to buy insurances and 4WD cars even though he lives in the city, will happily take the kids to the football, never cleans so don't market household cleaning products to him no matter how desperate you are to expand your niches;

3. *La Madeleine* — left banker, over 30 male or female, swinging voters who have up-skilled from an administrative capacity or trade to a degree, also members of the creative class, will buy an investment property this year and hope to hell they aren't pregnant again, will capitalise interest repayments, buy luxury cars and send their children to private school, and yet still consider themselves a part of the avant-garde;

4. *Le Bois de Boulogne* — greenies, used to be referred to as conservationists, now *the energy police*, over 20 under 40, male or female, do not offer them anything that is not wrapped/contained in brown paper or an expensive-looking bottle with fancy type on the label, can also be early adopters especially of technology, will calculate their annual carbon footprint and buy goods made from local materials;

5. The Paris skyline taken from *Montmatre*, except instead of looking toward the centre of Paris, the viewer has turned her attention to the north, to *réalité*, the vast expanse of high-rise and people cramped into the modern Paris — the new artist, male or female, thinks nationalism is oppressive, reads Derrida, listens to rap music, smokes a lot of dope, rejects brand loyalty, only wears second-hand clothing, is committed to a better future and is considered a loser/trouble-maker/bludger by most other segments of the population;

6. The famous Metro signs that introduced Art Noveau to Paris and were initially as hated as *La Tour Eiffel* once was — the new industrialists, over 40 under 80 male, decision-makers, international travellers, independently wealthy,

would like to be photographed naked in the middle of the night in front of *Notre Dame* with 3000 other people;

7.   Long legs on a Parisian woman — man-boy, over 30, under 80kg, owns a *Gameboy* to keep him amused on suburban train trips, usually management or other useless occupation, think of tween advertising then add beer;

8.   Crinkly old men leaning up against the *Tabac* bar drinking coffee and stubbing out hand-rolled cigarettes on a tiled floor — Didi, over 20, female, visually oriented, massive wardrobe, prefers to use online shopping sites, will not commit to real estate purchases unless it is green space for an endangered species of elephant;

9.   *Le Jardin de Luxenbourg* — Nina, under ten, gender irrelevant, loves Paris' parks, especially the pond where children can sail boats, likes wooden toys, all she wants is for her mother to let her out of the pram so she can try out stumbling over these cool cobblestones *sans* shoes;

And, me:

10.   Paris' first Royal Palace, *la Conciergerie,* rising grandiosely above the banks of *Île de la Cité*, and stretching as far as the eye can possibly see is *La Seine,* and it's deliciously brown not black like in the photographs which could be disappointing for some but which I find captivating — mother, age irrelevant, has just spent way too much money on childcare or nappies so don't bother marketing any luxuries to her unless they are for her child, reads labels, realises that wanting everything for her child is a mistake.

But there's something else the usual marketer would miss. In the foreground are my hands pushing a pram containing two little feet, one wearing a shoe and the other bare, as if she has sacrificed her shoe to the streets of Paris, and unbeknownst to its wearer, has merged her story with that of Paris'.

To realise a dream, after all, is something that money can't buy.

Jaimee has given everybody the day off — on account of Didi, Cairine and I nursing wicked hangovers after our first night out in Paris.

Dressed in my *Lacroix* and the reddest *Yves Saint Laurent Rive Gauche* platform shoes (a surprise from Jaimee — they are off the planet!), I looked just as elegant as some of the Parisians dining with us.

Even Alexander, Jaimee's friend (and one-time lover I suspect), made a bee-line for me, and after kissing me three times as is accustomed in Paris, proceeded to ignore me for the rest of the evening lavishing all his attention on Nina instead.

After dinner, Gretel retreated to the apartment to put Nina to bed so I could enjoy myself. After all, it had been nearly a year since I'd been out at night, and longer since I've been out drinking champagne.

Without Nina, I felt more dismally alone than I'd ever felt before in my life.

After trying to listen to a conversation about Soupault and Breton, even the threatened death of *Le Bistro*, I tried to order more champagne but was waved down by Alexander, who insisted on taking us somewhere none of us had gone before — to seventh heaven — to Pernod!

It was hideous. This morning, I can still taste it.

Luckily I had stripped off my silk *Lacroix* number before falling into my four-poster French bed sometime early this morning.

My first view of Paris on our third day is a pile of couture strewn across the floor and an empty cot.

I sit up, panicked, and tear out of bed.

"Where is Nina?" I scream as I fling open the door to the apartment's lounge.

"Here," Gretel says, surprised, picking her up off the floor.

"Of course she is, where else would she be," I manage to say feebly, feeling stupid at my ridiculous, hangover-induced panic.

Nina, who doesn't care if I look a fright with my fake eyelashes falling off me, starts giggling hilariously. She crawls expertly over to me.

"It's funny," I tell Gretel, picking Nina up to cuddle her and smell her (sniffing her is something I always do now and I can't help myself), "but the last few months have been so hectic, I feel like I've missed three whole months of Nina's life. She doesn't look like a baby anymore, does she? Her nose has changed, she's not red and alien-looking and look at her feet, they're huge! Even the stork mark on her forehead has faded. And her hair, she's got curls, where did they come from?"

"Probably from you," Gretel says playing with Nina's hair. "She is gorgeous, Til. Look at those blue eyes and her smile. Her lips are just like yours."

"Do you think?" I ask cocking my head to one side and enjoying the compliment. After all, to be like Nina, who is perfection herself, is all I really want these days.

Of course, I wouldn't mind being Gretel too, but she is too glamorous for me.

Gretel, who has slicked her blunt fringe into an elegant gamine style this morning and now looks like she could be Parisian herself, offers the perfect morning activity, "Let's dress her up like a little French girl," she says and taking Nina from me starts to undress her out of her sleep suit.

We throw open the enormous suitcase containing all of the label's samples.

"This one, it has to be this one," Gretel says pulling out a beautiful layered ice blue silk tunic which has been edged not with lace as would have been done 100 years ago, but with a crinkly metallic piping that Nina thinks is so fantastic she giggles and cooes again and forces it into her mouth.

"See, she likes it."

"Yes, and get it off her now," Jaimee says walking in, saving the *Giséle* samples from more Nina slobber. "They're going to Tours this morning for the *Vogue* shoot if you haven't forgotten. Til, I don't want to see baby goo all over my beautiful range when I open the

September edition of fashion's holy book. This is the first time *Vogue* has ever run a children's fashion feature, I can't believe Alexander managed to get Didi's designs before the editor! It is, as he would say, *"incroyable!"*

"Right, right," I say, carefully lifting the tunic over Nina's arms and head. And Jaimee is right. Our advertising campaign won't feature in *Vogue* for another few months, until the sponsors are on board, so this fashion feature is going to really help introduce the brand to the market. Although the feature will include other brands, to have this sort of endorsement from *Vogue* is — unbelievable. The samples must be perfect if they're to have a chance at being included by the editor in the shoot.

She grabs at a fistful of fabric and starts screaming when Gretel tries to dress her in a stripy cotton playsuit.

"She even pouts like you," Jaimee adds, hoping to alleviate our disappointment, but when the mood doesn't lift she relents. "Oh for Christ's sake, you two are like a pair of spoilt children. OK, she can have it back but not until after the shoot."

Gretel and I smile at each other like evil collaborators. Then Gretel jumps up and asks Jaimee if she can take the clothes over to *Vogue*.

"Good God no!" Jaimee exclaims, abhorred. "Alexander's coming to get them so they can be delivered by a *real* French person. Til will be at the shoot tomorrow but undercover as an Australian buyer, remember? You can go too since it's all the way out in Tours which is in the 16th *Arrondissement* near *Blois* I think, or maybe Alexander said the *Bois de Boulogne*? Why the hell they're doing the shoot there I don't know, these Parisians are crazy."

"The editor suggested it apparently," Gretel says. "Her secretary told Til to meet the team there for the shoot because all the gardens in Paris are too well-known. I looked it up on the internet and she's right, it's perfect. Plus Tours has the most exquisite Tudor buildings, they will contrast perfectly with the modernity in the range. But the editor was talking about going out to *La Maison de la France*, it's this crazily wicked chateau, built across a lake; the French Resistance used to sneak soldiers through one wing of the chateau, from Occupied France to Free France."

Jaimee ignores Gretel's history lesson. "Whatever. So long as it's beautiful."

I turn to Gretel. "The shoot's early in the morning and I've organised to meet the *Vogue* team at their hotel tonight so we'd better be on an afternoon train." And although I'm not ready to leave Paris yet, I'm so excited about going to a real French *Vogue* shoot that I can feel my hangover lifting.

"Well, go and get ready," Jaimee orders. "I'll show you the store when you get back. Didi and Cairine are going to see the manufacturers in Lyon so don't rush back. I don't want you both getting worn out from all the excitement. And buy some more clothes, Til, you can't wear that *Lacroix* scarf twisted into knobs on your head all day and night, you look like something from outer-space."

Again, panic sweeps over me. My *Lacroix* dress, which has been hand embroidered with tiny metallic hooks, is laying on the floor attracting every piece of lint within a five mile radius. But when I look over at Gretel, she's started crying.

"What the hell is wrong with you now?" Jaimee sighs defeated.

But Gretel can't speak. She starts waving air toward her face.

But I get it.

"Shopping in Paris three days in a row, it's just too much," she sobs and runs from the room.

"The scandalous thing," Jaimee whispers to me, "is that she's only 16. Her life can only get better from here."

I nod, thinking that Nina is only a baby and how lucky she is to be visiting Paris, and that I must have done the right thing in coming here — and I start crying too.

"I could try Mum's card again?" Gretel suggests, walking back into the room holding a bunch of tissues up to her face, to protect her *Chanel* cuff.

"Probably best not to," Jaimee directs. "Use mine please. But I have a limit of ten thousand Australian dollars per day, Gretel," she says being very careful to enunciate the numbers and its limit. "Go over that and I will have you thrown into *la Bastille*."

"We'll stop on our way to the train — we'll go to *Printemps*," I say referring to one of Paris's department stores, surprising myself by how casual it feels to say it.

Gretel mouths, "*Lafayette* too" with wide-eyed innocence.

As I head back to my room to dress, I catch Jaimee's face in the mirror. And she's trying so hard to contain her laughter that her eyes are clammed shut and only her ears are wiggling.

Vogue, Vogue, Vogue, Vogue

While we wait for the team from *Vogue* to arrive at the hotel in Tours, I keep myself from hyperventilating by daydreaming about their entrance. Will they be wearing rollerblades like so many Parisians do these days? Will they be impeccably dressed and looking bored and out-of-place as Sydneysiders do when they're visiting small, provincial cities? Or will they smile and act polite and distant, while remarking on the authentic furnishings and décor?

Or maybe they'll walk in and spot our charade straight away: the flash of photographic bulbs will terrify Nina and tomorrow Jaimee will read in *Le Metro* about an Australian fashion scam posing as a high-end French label with ethical roots uncovered in Tours — accompanied by unflattering photo of me squeezed into *prêt-a-porter*.

To abate my fears, I absorb Gretel in some chatter. "What do you think French paparazzi look like?"

"*Vogue* aren't paparazzi. Paparazzi are those swarms of photographers who continually follow Britney to try and achieve candid and uncompromising photos. These *Vogue* stars will be similar to Nadia's team most probably — they'll prepare the shot and direct the model and think they're top shit but at least they produce art, as opposed to paparazzi."

"University will be wasted on you, Gretel," I tell her as we sit in a charming, elegant foyer surrounded by tapestries and glass cabinets holding expensive-looking bottles of champagne.

"Not at all — imagine how scary I'll be when I can write binding contracts across three major economies," she says without blinking an eye.

I sit for a minute wondering how long her excessive confidence will last — probably until she gets to university and, faced with the immense knowledge surrounding her, realise she will never again feel intellectually superior. Her first heartbreak won't rattle her though, and even if she gets impounded with some criminal conviction, people like Gretel always seem to always bounce back. They don't try to change the world — they just scare people into submission.

"You know, I'm really glad I peed on you at my baby shower, Gretel," I tell her, feeling suddenly sentimental.

"I know, you crazy bitch, I won't ever forget that."

And out of the corner of my eye, I see a group of the most elegantly dressed people I have ever seen walk into the foyer.

They are led by two young women dressed in black and wearing sunglasses so big you can barely see their faces: the stylist and assistant. Then two young men carrying boxes of photographic equipment, swaggering as if they're starring in an advertisement for the masochistic history of the media and proof that sexism is still rampant in France: the photographic assistants. Then wardrobe, a woman who pushes a trolley of tiny clothes that hang, unseen within miniature suit bags as if promised to a royal family of midgets; followed by the fashion director, who is dressed like a New Yorker in famously deconstructed *Chalayan*, thigh-high boots and who boasts an ass the size of a postage stamp. Then the photographer, God himself, smoking a cigarette; followed at a safe distance by the agent, parents of models, and three gorgeous petite models — as in ages two to six, not the sizes. And three more trolley boys carting the team's luggage.

"And they're all here for us," Gretel whispers. "And they're from *Vogue*." She half-stands up and then sits down again.

I can't stand because I have Nina on my lap playing with blocks on the table.

"Ah, the American buyers," says the fashion director, beckoning for us to join them.

"Australian," I mutter.

"How did they know it's us?" Gretel asks. "It's not like we look foreign, we're dressed head to toe in French labels."

"That's probably why," I tell her.

Magritte, the fashion director looks us up and down and asks, bluntly, "How much did you spend?"

"Our first day, 30, and that was just clothes. Yesterday, five, and today, ten, but we've had no time to accessorise," Gretel explains her head suddenly droops with shame.

Magritte tuts. "When we go back to Paris, I'll take you shopping properly. That is simply not good enough, I have a country to maintain," she says, as if she is responsible for the whole country's GDP.

Which in a way, she is.

She turns to introduce us.

"*Vogue*," she gestures. "The Americans."

And that's it.

The photographic assistant, who is staring at Gretel, kindly says "*Bonjour*". The others ignore us.

"And why are you here?" he asks. "Buyers?"

Gretel says, "*Oui*" and the photographer shudders. I am saddened that up close he doesn't look like Clive Owen (as so many French seem to) and relieved that he doesn't look like Gerard Depardieu. Instead, he looks like Charlie Chaplin with a shaved head.

"That story," he says with his little moustache quivering, "how the French like the non-French to speak French so we don't have to speak English? It is all lies." He holds his finger up to his moustache and I can feel Gretel holding back vomit. "Shhh. Do not speak — French, English, nothing." And he snatches his key from the receptionist, and is followed to the lifts by the photographic assistants and the two trolley boys.

"Don't mind him, he's Italian," Magritte explains. "But it is unusual for buyers to come on shoots. Do you know why it is that you're here? Could you not get tickets to Fashion Week?" Her mouth wiggles, and again, she looks at our feet.

"That's what happens when you take out thirty pages of advertising in the UK, US and French editions," Gretel shoots back at her. "Even *Vogue* start grovelling at your feet. They begged us to come."

Which puts Magritte in her place.

"Excellent", she purrs. "We'll see you at dinner. Nine pm. Unless you would prefer to eat with the mothers? Talk to them." And she is gone, consumed up by an expensive carpet and an effortless lift.

The mothers are kinder and introduce us to their children: Christabelle, the youngest at two, surly after missing her sleep, looks at us from behind a black, blunt fringe, a *prêt-a-porter* version of Joan of Arc; Lydia, four, with her golden brown curls looks like she could be Nina's elder sister; and Sienna, six, blonde and mischievous, with her waist-length angelic hair, can only be a distant relation of Marianne, the French heroine.

We walk to our rooms, but as the mothers are ordering room service and getting the kids to bed early, they wish us *bon rêves*. Which leaves Gretel, Nina and me with nothing better to do than hunt down the *Vogue* team.

We find the assistants talking in the hotel bar chatting about Paris fashion gossip.

I watch Gretel's eyes light up. Gretel, who at 16 knows more French than I do, is teetering on the edge of shock and excitement.

She translates for me. "The editor of a rival magazine has been charged with indecent activities with an animal — no, wait — a minor! But he's quite hairy down below, that's why they call him the monkey. And six assistants have gone to rehab already this year but that's less than last year — and oh, now they're moaning about being stuck in godforsaken fucking Tours."

I watch Magritte throw back another cocktail.

"Why the hell couldn't the shoot be in Amsterdam or Tokyo?" Gretel mouths next.

"Because they're all supposed to be French labels…" I start to reply before Gretel elbows me in the ribs.

Although I've left the *Lacroix* scarf back in Paris, Magritte keeps looking at me like I'm an alien being. She beckons the waiter and points to herself and the assistants. The waiter brings another round of vodkas and drearily waits for our order.

Gretel orders champagne for me which Magritte approves of. "Even for the little one, yes," she says pointing at Nina. "You can never start them too young."

"Actually, the younger children are introduced to alcohol the more likely they are to become addicted," I tell her and even in English I sound like a prude.

They pout and turn their backs to us.

We escape with a bottle of vintage Moet and head back to our hotel room.

"They really take the title of fashionista to heart don't they?" I complain, popping open the bottle, relishing the idea of not having to share it with anyone.

Gretel pours herself a lemonade and while I breastfeed Nina (before the champagne hits my boobs), we toast the view of the sun setting over *le Jardin Picasso*.

"I think I'll just settle in here for the night, order some pizza, and finish this bottle."

"Are you sure?" Gretel asks, "Don't you want to see Tours?"

"No, you go ahead. I have to put Nina to bed, we've got a big day tomorrow," I say, not feeling at all suspicious until Gretel changes into an even shorter skirt.

She shrugs. "I'll have fun for all three of us," she says and disappears out the door.

Three hours and 400 cable channel flicks later, Gretel still hasn't returned.

"It's happening again," I tell Nina, but Nina doesn't answer me, she's fast asleep in the porta-cot.

The great thing about being alone in a hotel room is:

1. No one knows how much champagne you've really drunk;
2. No one knows how many chocolate croissants you've eaten from the mini-bar;
3. No one knows that you have filled the croissant bag with toilet paper to make it look like you haven't eaten any of the croissants.

I take a sip of champagne and nibble on the last croissant, then taste the champagne again, then the croissant. And that way, I finish the bottle and the croissant.

When Nina wakes, I give her a bottle of formula (because *I* know how much champagne I've drunk) and try to put her back to sleep.

But she wants to watch French cartoons and play the hand-clapping game.

When she starts to show tired signs I realise I have to go looking for Gretel now. If Nina falls asleep again, I'll be stuck here all night waiting for Gretel, or her tiny skirt, to show up.

In the bar is a scene I know all too well: cocktail glasses are strewn everywhere. It looks like a fashionista tornado has just blown through town.

Only the waiters remain. I ask one of them if they've seen Gretel, and he says, "The one in the fabulous short skirt?" and when I grimace, he shifts uncomfortably, scared that I may be her mother.

"She left, a half hour ago."

"You don't know where?"

"Where? Where, I don't know. You'd better ask him."

I take a deep breath.

"Well, let's hope he's underage too," I say and even though I want to run for the lift, the waiter has started playing with Nina's fingers and is counting on them in French. Since it would be rude to just walk away, and I don't want Nina to miss out on any cross-cultural experiences, I wait. And I wait.

At *neuf*, I say, "Oh to hell with this shit," and bolt from the bar as fast as my tight, metallic *Giles* skirt and *Jean Paul Gaultier* bodysuit will allow.

I knock on Magritte's door and she yells an expletive in French.

So I knock again and she flings the door open, one of her bare shoulders almost hitting me in the face. Clutching only a sheet around her, I'm amazed at how anorexic she looks. Behind her, in the bed, is the photographer smoking a cigarette.

"I thought this was a non-smoking floor…" I begin. She slams

299

the door shut but not before I hear the photographer talking about how narcissistic the bloody Americans are.

I find Gretel next door.

And she's still dressed.

But the photographer's assistant is bare-chested and holding a deck of cards.

"We're just playing poker. Guillaume said I didn't have to take anything off since I'm barely wearing anything to start with," Gretel tells me, her eyes sparkling with mischief.

My eyes raise skyward. "Right. We've got an early start tomorrow, so you'd better come now."

She pouts but kisses Guillaume on the cheek and dutifully follows me, which I wasn't expecting.

And she has that twinkle in her eye again!

As soon as we get back into the hotel room, I pounce on her.

"C'mon Gretel, you have to tell me what is going on here.

"Alright," she says nonplussed. "But you can't get angry with me. It was Jaimee's idea."

I raise my eyebrows. This should be good.

"I did it for Nina."

I hiss, "What the hell have you done?"

Her eyes downcast, she mumbles: "I compressed the war tode."

"You what?"

"I compromised the wardrobe," she mumbles again.

And then it sinks in. And I step back and gasp.

"Oh my God, you did *what*?"

"Don't worry, Til, I didn't destroy all the clothes, that would look too obvious. I just tampered with some of them."

But before I can drill her on how bad the damage is, she spills the whole story onto the blood red carpet at our feet.

"Magritte was drinking cranberry vodkas, right? So I accidentally bumped into her when I went down to the bar and it went all over her shirt and me — but by that time she was too drunk to care and said it didn't matter. She even said I was funny and kept calling me Carrie. But I said I had to go change since I'm wearing a new *Sonia Krinkel*, so I stole Magritte's key and snuck into her room.

The samples are all in there! I took a bottle of cranberry juice from her bar fridge and threw it all over the other labels and anything that looked like *Chloé*." Her eyes widen. "And then I heard them…"

I smack my hands up to my cheeks. I don't know if I want to hear the rest of this.

"Them. Magritte and that horrible photographer coming back to the room."

"They didn't catch you, did they?"

"No. I hid in the bathroom. If they'd gone in there, I would have been done for, but they were bumping all over the room, which was hideous to listen to but perfect because tomorrow she'll wake up and think that somehow *she* stained all the clothes. She's going to die."

"Especially if she doesn't eat some thing soon."

"It was kind of fun really, my first corporate tampering incident. Can I text my friends about it?"

"No, you're not to tell anybody about this."

She takes Nina from me and rocks her back and forth. Soon Nina's eyes are closing.

I sit down in shock. "But how the hell did you get out of there?"

"It was a two-way bathroom and on the other side was Guillaume, the photographic assistant. He was kind of surprised to see me but I just said something about being drunk for the first time and that I must be in the wrong room and he said, "Oh *non*, you are in the right room now." I really should have shagged him — it'd be brilliant to tell my friends that."

"Just tell them you did, they'll believe you. Make sure you get a photo of him on your phone tomorrow though."

She nods. "Good idea, Til," and heads off to the bathroom to get ready for bed.

"I've been 16 before, Gretel, we just didn't have that kind of technology then," I shout to her.

And through a mouthful of teeth cleaning, I hear her mumble and then spit.

The next morning Magritte looks like a fallen *Vogue* angel as she walks into the restaurant for breakfast.

She's dressed all in black and wearing round bug-eyed sunglasses.

I hear the stylist next to me snicker. She piles more food on a plate and places it in front of Magritte before sitting next to her with nothing but *un café*.

"Where is Leonardo?" the assistant asks referring to the photographer.

"I guess he is still asleep," Magritte says. "Somebody had better go wake him so we can leave here in ten."

The assistant nods and asks Magritte in which room she would find Leo.

Magritte stiffens. The assistant walks away knowing she has pushed her boss too far and will pay for it dearly.

Gretel nudges me when Magritte turns to Isabelle, the stylist. Isabelle's eye's widen with horror as she listens to Magritte, and as ordered, runs from the room only to return a few minutes later obviously in shock. She sits down and tries to pick up her *café* but her hands are shaking.

They both look at us.

"Is there a problem?" Gretel asks them.

"Are you on work experience?" Magritte asks Gretel suspiciously.

"Yes, as a matter of fact I am," she replies. "Lucky me, hey? That's what you get when your Dad's screwing the head of Austrade."

Magritte chokes and runs for the bathroom.

I can tell it's going to be a long day.

With Magritte out of the room, Isabelle confides in us. "The clothes are ruined! Magritte and Leo got a little too amorous last night and she spoiled her *Chalayan*, amongst other things, but it will be OK, we have a new label we can show, and the rest, well, if we turn the children the right way, the cranberry won't show."

Gretel, who doesn't care that the photographer has finally shown up and can hear her, confidently announces, "*Oui.*"

He walks behind us without saying a word.

"Look at him, strutting around like some peacock," Isabelle mutters. "Poor Magritte, she feels like some silly model for sleeping with the photographer, but in this case, the only reason he slept with her was because the models on this shoot are under six."

"But he's so horrid," Gretel says with horror. "How could she?"

Isabelle and I look at each other, knowingly.

"Long hours at work, no food and a cocktail or ten, that's how," Isabelle tells her. "You too will be vulnerable to the dangers of reptiles like Leo if you're not careful."

"I'll *never* do that," Gretel says shuddering again.

I look at Nina sitting in the high chair blowing raspberries at her morning *pain*. I rise from my seat. "Perhaps you will find meaning in all your relationships, Gretel," I tell her while collecting the numerous bags I'm going to need if Nina is going to sleep and eat while we're out on the shoot. "But life isn't like that. Most of the time our lives are made up of repetition and doing things we think we have to do so we can pay the rent. We live, lusting for the glorious moments of our lives, and sometimes our desire for rare beauty drives us to act truly ugly."

Eleven months

Shh, I have a secret.

Do you want to know what it is? But you must promise not to tell my mother.

I'm getting married! That's right. Yes, I know I'm a little young, but who cares about numbers when I feel so gloriously happy?

It must be the romance of Paris having this effect on me. Because before we left Australia, I didn't really care for my yellow teddy at all, but in Paris, he seems so different. He's so soft and articulate, he tells me stories when I can't sleep at night, and he has the cutest brown button eyes I've ever seen.

And he's real. He was a gift from Lola, and appropriately, has only one ear.

But we have become very fond of each other and I take him everywhere.

My mother thinks we are just friends, that she is still the light of my life, and although I love her, I really do, the person I carry with me all day – is Pierre.

He sits on my knee as we walk around Paris, exploring the streets and parks, dodging tourists and the ever-growing queue at *le Louvre*. And I carry him in my free hand as Mum teaches me to step carefully over cobblestone *rues*. The women of Paris always stop and give me a kiss on all of my three cheeks, for Pierre has introduced me to the artisans of Paris — *les monsieurs* and les *madames aux boulangeries, aux charcuteries, aux pâtisseries, aux marchés*, et *aux confiseries*.

We see them everyday. Even though Mum is busy preparing to open the store she takes me and Pierre to the park everyday. In the mornings we play in the square and then go home for our lunch and nap, presided over by Gretel, and in the afternoon Mum takes us to do the shopping. And we always finish our walk with *un bébé-cino* at a café next to *la Seine*.

Sometimes Mum looks a little sad, especially when she's reading from the books she stashes under my pram: *Half the World*, *Stones into Schools*, *The Bookseller of Kabul*, and *What is the What*. Sometimes her melancholy rises up and pours onto the table and beads down into paths between the cobblestones and over the edge of the embankment and into *La Seine*. Over time these trickles become torrents. I'm beginning to realise that we won't be staying here much longer; Paris is beautiful, but it doesn't make my Mum as happy as she thought it would. Which is funny, because even though I love my Mum, I'm beginning to realise that the world is a lot bigger than her too.

The girls keep talking about what a great experience it is for me to come to Paris — to be immersed in another culture and language at my age. That I must be soaking up the Gallic life like the rays of the sun on my lily white skin. And perhaps it is helping to lay pathways in my brain, but I probably won't remember any of it. I'll look back at photos of my life in Paris, when I was nearly one, and I'll see a tattered, one-eared bear staring back at me. And I will feel regret. For I won't remember him. My first love. And I presume, he won't remember me either.

Prêt-à-pied

Nina's stumbling first steps occur on the floor of our first Parisian store.

I only see this because a four metre long mirror is resting against a wall and is low enough to reflect her first wonky and wavering steps before she crashes against it. And I only see her steps because my body has become attuned to altering itself so my line of vision can include the person I'm talking to and Nina. Even if it is just a reflection of one of them.

"She walked, she walked!" I yell running across the floor and scooping her up. It takes the others another few seconds to break their conversation and understand the importance of what just happened. Soon, four pairs of high heels and Lola's plumbing galoshes are running across the floor toward Nina and me.

People walking past the store are amused, not by the sight of another new fashion store opening in Paris, but by five well-dressed Parisians and an American dyke jumping up and down and scaring a poor baby to tears.

"*Encore, encore,*" Lola says putting Nina back on the floor and steadying her by holding onto her fingers.

We all stand back to watch but Nina has decided she has attracted too much attention and must raise her crying to frantic, fearful sobs.

The girls disperse, leaving me and Nina to cuddle and reflect on the momentous occasion of her first steps.

Which reduces me to tears too.

"But I love her crawling around, exploring and playing with toys, or pulling at my shoes. What will I do if she's walking?" I sob.

Lola consoles me. She is after all, the only other person present who is a parent. "I know, I know. I can put Jola over my shoulder *maintenant* and she just stays there. But they grow up Til, so that they can have a life too, so be happy for her achievement. Let her try, *encore!*" Lola orders me a few steps away so Nina can walk toward me, but this time she won't let go of Lola's fingers.

"She'll still crawl around until she's more confident walking."

But I can't help finding Nina's lack of interest in doing any more walking that day reassuring.

I return to the meeting with Nina snuggled into my shoulder. We still have a lot to talk about.

Over the last two months, Cairine and Didi have been travelling around visiting the 300 year old factory in Lyon that's producing our first line and four of the more established collectives Jorja has organised for us to work with. Since they returned, we have done little work; Cairine and Didi have been recounting the women's stories and while most of what they've had to say has been horrific, I've found solace in the happiness our work has brought the women; apparently they are so ecstatic to be working on clothes for a real fashion label that they are buoyant, and their happiness and prosperity has overflowed into the villages they live in.

A part of me is as jealous as hell that Cairine and Didi have been to visit the collectives. Another part of me knows that my job has been here in Paris, sending out media releases, working on the website and viral marketing campaign, and building a reservoir of knowledge about the communities we're working with and the environmental campaigns we can support. But the more I read, the more depressed I feel. The ocean of need in too many communities around the world is something that one business can never meet. The only thing I am certain of is that we cannot focus on design any longer; our *raison d'être* must be informing our customers of what those communities' needs are. The modern customer must be involved in becoming part of the solution, not the problem. Our whole value chain must be built around this.

Which means I go back to my marketing work with a lot more conviction than I've ever felt before.

"We were just talking about the merchandise arriving tomorrow from Lyon, Til. Do you have any special instructions for where you want styles hung or what will be on the mannequins?" Jaimee says, interrupting my introversion.

"No, I'll leave that up to Marianne," I say, motioning my head toward our new French store manager. Since the store's success will depend largely on the local Parisians accepting the *Giséle* label, I know the best person to organise the store is a Parisian. And Marianne says "*oui*" with such crispness and clarity that I doubt she has ever been beyond *Les Champs Elysee*. She is the perfect choice.

Marianne nods at me acknowledging the compliment. If she does her job as well as I think she will, she will have the Parisians thinking that buying from *Bon Point* is unpatriotic. Just looking at the quality of her fingernails and ankles makes me think our scenario three revenue figures were too conservative.

She is so perfect, her stiff coiffure replaces my anxiety with anticipation, finally, after six months of constant work, I feel resolute that the label is bound to succeed.

"These mannequins are great, Lola. Where did you find them?" Cairine asks referring to the life-size wooden dolls stacked up at the back of the store.

"An antique store in Cannes, would you believe it? I saw them and knew they would be perfect. Even their hair is real. But what I love is this carousel. Jaimee, it's beautiful, the horses are so feminine, it's every little girl's dream to have beautiful ponies and here they are. Even I want to buy something and you know that disturbs me to the inherent core of my anti-establishment being. I shall have to go and throw a brick through a *Prada* window on the way home to make myself feel better."

Jaimee rolls her eyes.

"I like what you all do, don't think I'm being an artistic snob. I am as much a part of the product-making process as you are. We both sell art, but I sell not to the end-consumer, but to governments and their very short arms-length galleries and festivals who show my work to the public. Who then leave my exhibitions feeling somewhat scared and walk into a store like this one, and spend excessive amounts of money to feel a part of something beautiful again, as opposed to a rat in a system of sewerage. So I may as well buy something too, except that you have not paid me so I have no money, and I do not want to be paid so I am back to square one."

"You don't have to buy anything Lola, we have plenty of samples," I tell her and even though it isn't true I feel like I have to offer something. And samples are all I have along with a tonne of clothes that are too small for Nina. "When we go back to Sydney I'll send over Nina's clothes and toys too. We can be mother-rats manoeuvring successfully through the sewers together."

"You know," interjects Didi. "I kind of knew what you were talking about until you got to the rats, but now I think you two are on some serious breastfeeding chemicals. So, if you can leave and take your daughters to the park, we non-rats have cleaning to do."

Lola and I close the shop's wooden doors, which stand an impressive three metres high, and as they thud together I feel a sense of trepidation return.

We head across the river to *Le Jardin de Lux*. But first we stop by *Le Musée D'Orsay* so Lola can ingest her daily quota of art.

She says she's taking me to see the first very example of Modern Art, but instead of leading me up to Manet's *Le déjeuner sur l'herbe*, she leads me into a quiet corner and stands enraptured in front of four small photographs.

"This is it?" I ask her surprised since we seem to be the only two people in the whole museum interested in these photos. "This is the start of Modern Art?"

She nods, sighs, then stands aside so I can see the work.

Suddenly, I put my hand over Nina's eyes. And turn to Lola aghast. "But Lola, he's pooing!" I complain. Although I've changed Nina's nappies a million times before, I find the act of an adult pooing grotesque. Plus, these photos seem to be taken at the beach. What the hell does it mean?

"And he made this nearly 20 years before Duchamp exhibited the urinal in a gallery," she sighs in wonder.

"Who is it?" I ask her, embarrassed by my ignorance.

"It's Toulouse Lautrec, of course, the *enfant terrible* of the art world, the shortest of all artists — although he reputably had a rather large penis."

"But why is he shitting on a beach?"

"Do you want me to answer that from your perspective — or his? Because there are a few billion answers to that question, really."

I stand feeling perturbed, hoping answers will emerge from the monochrome print but I know Lola's right, the only thing that matters is what I think. And I think the man is probably insane, but I don't dare tell Lola that, she thinks that insanity is a virtue.

"They conducted a survey and Duchamp's urinal, *Fountain*, was voted the most important modern art work of the 20th century. And yet, the masses don't know about Lautrec, this genius, who was so intuitive of the woes facing the human race that he took photos of himself defecating on a beach. He thought he was hilarious. I think this work is prophetic."

I'm speechless. "Is this where your idea came from? For the defecating series?"

"In one way, I think, yes...I am trying to raise knowledge of Lautrec's work, but I also came up with the idea myself; I want to stop the shit — our mindless pursuit of material possession, the three million items for sale in the $2 shops, the wasted materials clogging up our refuse stations, people's lives wasted while they stand in factories all day long, forced to make the shit, then to ship it, store it, and sell it. I hate the shit. And the irony is, to draw attention to it, I have become absorbed in the shit too."

I feel a sense of guilt return. "You're telling me that what I'm doing is wrong? I'm making more shit?"

She clutches my arm and squeezes it emphatically, "No, Til, you're not. You're part of the solution. You're removing the shit and replacing it with non-shit."

"But I'm still selling something. It's still an exchange. I still care about what the market thinks."

"Even if the market is stupid?"

"I can't help it. I still want verification from the market, even if the market is manipulated, ignorant and susceptible to group-think."

She shakes her head. "I think you're balancing your needs well,

Til. You're developing a business that's focused on targets that are about reducing toxicity and providing work to people who need it, and you're using your philosophy to attract customers to your business. The idea to open a store in Paris, not to sell clothes, but to attract customers as sponsors of a garment's production process is truly innovative. Your end-consumer will then purchase garments from your various stockists, making their selection because they like the design, or because they like the person sponsoring the garment, or because of the social or environmental activity that the garment represents. You're creating the popularity contest that you need to attract the sponsors and creating a lasting relationship between the sponsor, the garment and the consumer."

"Is it too celebrity-oriented? Our end-consumers will buy the *Alexander* pant or the *Esther* dress, but in this context, it will relate to a real person. It's a little egotistical."

"Didn't you have role models when you were growing up?"

Which takes me back…right back to the start of who I am, when my *Vogue* magazines were my bible and my favourite models were pinned up on my wall. I finally respond to Lola's question by doing the one thing that comes naturally to me…I take a deep breath, and exhale slowly.

Lola continues, "Every design you create will be attached to a person. And every garment to a cause. There is no focus on producing two lines a year, no adherence to seasonal trends, just a collection of initiatives your growing consumer base can join, and an expanding number of collectives who will benefit from the transaction."

And the way Lola says it, she makes it sound like this whole dream is achievable, that all I have to do now is walk the walk.

With Nina stumbling at my side.

I take Nina's hand and she wobbles along next to me as we take in the beauty of Degas' ballerina paintings.

"It feels good, doesn't it?" Lola asks me, her face reflecting the blues and greens of Degas' visions.

But I know she's not talking about the art, she's talking about the smile on my face. I squeeze Nina's hand. "To have found my way?"

I ask Lola and she nods a firm and resilient, "Yes."

"You know, Lola, you always support me and stretch me," I tell her appreciatively. "Sometimes I think you're too good to be true."

She walks ahead of me, away from Degas and toward an exhibition of Freud's life in Paris.

"Perhaps I am just a figment of your imagination, an imaginary signifier created by the part of your brain that challenges your conservative expectations and allows you to create your own ideas."

I run with her line of thinking. "Which is why you're an artist, you're my creative subconscious. And then I made you have a baby, so I wouldn't feel so alone."

"You're not stupid, Til."

"Sleep-deprived and maybe a little stressed about the store's opening, that would explain why I'm having delusional fantasies."

"Which is to be expected," she says matter-of-factly.

"But you painted the store. So you must be real."

"Did you see me paint it?"

I shake my head. Even though Lola is an artist, I've never seen her with a paint brush in hand. A video camera, a camera, a notebook, yes but I own all of this equipment too. I rub my temples. This conversation was fun for a minute, but now I'm starting to worry myself.

Lola laughs at me and little Jola, who is strapped to her chest, sighs deeply. "Don't look so worried, Til. Maybe it's you who's invented? Maybe you're my commercial genius, like when Damien Hirst made his formaldehyde sheep."

I lead us away from the Freud exhibition. "Let's get out of here before we both go nuts," I tell her. "All this Modern Art is doing my head in. Let's take my very real baby, and your very real baby to a deliciously sunny, very real park and then we'll go and eat too many croissants. Because if I see cellulite on your thighs, then I'll know that you're definitely real."

When the store is just four days old, she arrives.

But when she walks through the door, the moment I have been imagining for the last few months feels different.

Most Parisians have returned from their *vacances* in the country and simply shuffled past the store, glancing at the signage and the interior, then mumbled, "We have never heard of this *Giséle*," and kept walking.

But on day four, our first customer walks past the store and hesitates.

After all, she is unfamiliar with the brand. Will her friends snicker if her little girl wears a *Giséle* dress to a play-date? To wear the wrong *enfant couture* is a fate worse than death. It's even worse than the parent getting her own clothing wrong. It can mean eternal shame, endless shunning from the miniature-glitterati circle, having to change schools and take different vacations.

But when the customer rings the bell at the front of the store, she is turned away.

"I'm sorry but you will have to make an appointment," Marianne says to her the intercom. And there on the street, the customer gives her details and arranges to come back in a week.

This is, after all, how it should be done.

This also gives Marianne time to research the customer and find out her daughter's size and which school she attends. So when the customer returns, only styles and sizes complementary to her little girl are presented. Of course, the child will not be present. Children cannot be trusted to try on clothes this exceptionally constructed before the garment has been purchased, not with sticky fingers and inpatient limbs that are likely to bust out of seams even if they have been triple stitched.

The customer will spend most of her time in the store, not looking at the clothes but instead reading all the signs emanating around her — as if the store were a literary text — and compare these to her expectations; not only to the rules of couture but to the rules of commercial and social engagement. Merchandise design and stitching only become important if the store's location and décor, customer service, brand positioning, product offering, and beta data — what is used to calculate the label's risk to financial investors — warrant her spending any money in the store at all. This is after all the 21st century, the clothes may be the best in the world, but if her husband or lover comes home after a long day at the office and moans because he has lost a fortune investing in this foolish *Giséle* label, then owning those clothes will be worse than social death, because the purchase can never be erased from her consumer history nor her social status; she is tainted forever.

It's a difficult relationship: to succeed, the market must accept us, and to purchase, the consumer must be confident we will succeed in the market.

It is one thing to ask a customer to buy our product but to attach her child's name to a design — to do that, the customer has to love everything about us. Starting with Marianne.

Marianne is not a retail vulture; she is the icon of French couture, its protector and its advocate. She knows we have in fact saved a 300 year old factory in Lyon from closing down after another high-end label moved their manufacturing to China. And she recognises the beauty of each garment's design. All she has to do is communicate her earnest wish for the customer to be a part of us.

She approaches this woman and in a delicate, provocative voice, whispers, "Although I cannot give details precisely, I have heard the label is backed by a conglomerate of leading designers and the Office of Culture in an effort to combat the Americanisation of international couture. Only French material and French hands have made these gowns."

Which is true.

"The customer can rest assured," Marianne continues, "we have the biggest advertising budget ever seen and will be featured in the French, UK and US editions of *Vogue*. After we have uncovered our sponsors, all our little girls will appear in our advertising campaign. Your child will take her true place in the history of couture."

The customer hurriedly signs a commitment to sponsor her favourite design and an appointment is made for her daughter to attend a fitting in two weeks.

And with that knowledge, the customer leaves to walk two blocks to another high-end store, where again she says her name through an intercom and is told they cannot possibly see her today and can she come back in a week.

Marianne permits only five customers per day into the store and by the end of the week has two months of appointments.

But by this stage, I have left Paris.

I only have a week to prepare for New York Fashion Week. Because if we are going to have any hope at building a sustainable business, then we need buyers! And lots of them. People who will buy our ready-to-wear pieces, who will give our sponsors an audience, and a reason to invest 25,000 euro on just one hand-stitched garment.

The truth of the matter is simple: to even have a chance at success, we must have Paris, but without New York, we will surely die.

In New York, the *Giséle* marketing must be completely different because in New York we're marketing to the end-consumer, the fashion junkie. In NYC, we must be less refined, more urban and definitely a whole lot louder.

But my budget is empty, which in the world of advertising means I am voiceless. Even with Jorja backing our advertising campaign, I have no money left for New York Fashion Week. And considering it can cost $100,000 to just put on a show in New York, I am up to my ears in stress. But I have to put on a show because there is no other way of getting our designs onto the computer screens of a million early adopter fashion junkies without it. New York Fashion Week is the quickest road to reaching the women whom we hope will become life-long addicts of our brand. Without them, our women of Afghanistan may as well pack up and go homeless for another few hundred years.

Ugh.

On the plane to New York I tell Jaimee to update the Net Present Value of the business based on our most outrageous revenue scenarios and she braces herself. She knows what I'm thinking. We're just about to run out of money and need to raise some more cash by raising the estimated value of the business. By resizing the size of the business, we can sell off a further chunk without reducing any existing owner's investment which could cause them to panic. After all, Jaimee met with some very interested investors in Paris; investors who were comfortable with the fashion business and recognised our innovative business model.

But no investor likes it when you say the well is empty. Better to just build a bigger dam.

But any money from new investors won't be in our piggy banks for a few days at least, and I have a New York Fashion Week show to organise. It's impossible, I tell myself as we hover over JFK airport for what seems like a week.

The city emerges suddenly like an enormous, grey monster, its teeth gnashing as we descend through the clouds. Even as the plane flies over Queens, I can see that the city stretches for an eternity, with skyscrapers that lean into the heavens where boards of mass market brands sit majestically, coercing our little lives with their future trends. But unlike the majesty of Paris' architecture, these skyscrapers do not give me hope. Because they are a brash advertisement of the luminosity of our rivals. They are not beautiful in the slightest: they are enormous!

And they tell me one thing: this is the city of Mr Big.

And I am not Carrie.

New York, New York

Even before we leave the airport my headache begins.

"Have you ever heard such noise?" I complain to Gretel as we queue with 5000 other people for a cab.

"It's kind of what I imagine being on the inside of a locomotion engine would be like," she yells as one long jet engine continually takes off over our heads.

New York State has ten airports and this is only one of them.

"I'm exhausted. I can't believe it took us five hours to get through immigration. They're fucking nuts," Cairine says, her curls flattened by the mist and pollution.

I can barely stand to look at her. Cairine, who prides herself on her alabaster complexion, has mascara ruining her cheeks. Even her eyes, usually a clear, sparkling blue Pacific lagoon, look bloodshot.

It's not the city's fault. Immigration had separated us and asked us individually why we were coming from Europe if we were Australian.

"I think they thought we were high-class prostitutes," Jaimee decides. "We all look a little weird in all this French designer stuff. Especially you, Til, how many times have I told you to take off that damn *Lacroix*. You look like you're going to a convention of alien hookers at the *Ritz*. Every second person here looks like they're going to the gym."

"True," Didi agrees looking pear-shaped and glum in comparison to the New Yorkers swirling around us. "As much as it pains me to say it girls, it's time to look like New Yorkers."

Jaimee utters directions. "*Sass and Bide* leggings, just make sure you don't all wear the same styles, boots up to your ass or sneakers you can barely see, and anything on top, *Donna Karan*, the *Gap*,

317

even an I Heart NY t-shirt, I don't care."

We shuffle along in the cab queue.

"We could take the train into the city," I suggest.

"Are you nuts? And get mugged trying to heave our luggage up from the subway? Get real, Til!" Gretel moans, and for the first time since we've left home, I feel her confidence slip.

Two hours later we reach the front of the queue just as it starts to rain. Nina grunts as she does a poo.

"No way are you changing that baby in my cab, lady, are you nuts?" the driver yells at me.

"I can't leave her sitting in it," I yell back at him.

"Then get another cab," he snarls.

I am about to tell him he is driving on the wrong side of the road when two people push past us and jump into the cab and it takes off at breakneck speed before skidding to a halt when it hits the traffic jam 20 metres from us.

I quickly change Nina on a bench in front of the airport while Jaimee takes on a role of quarterback, threatening to tackle anyone who dares take our place in the queue.

When I'm finished we huddle together and she gives us direction. "Gretel, Til and Nina, you go in the first cab, we'll go in the second."

Nina grunts again and we break away, Jaimee shoving our luggage into the boot of the first yellow cab and waving us off as drive out into the abyss.

I stare sadly out the back of the cab's rear window watching their three figures grow smaller and smaller.

The only thing that separates us from New York City is two million cabs all honking their horns.

I try to be excited. After all, New York is grinding past my window.

But it doesn't feel right. This city is supposed to be full of life and energy; everyone here lives in a time vacuum, every second sucked up into the frenetic pace of a New York minute.

I've never moved so slowly in my life!

Gretel tries to cheer me up. "Look, Til, it's stone-the-crows New York. Can you believe it?"

I smirk in response.

"Look, Central Park, shit, it's bloody beautiful too. We'll be able to take Nina to the giant fountain that was in *Home Alone 2*. Maybe we'll even see the bird lady?"

Which reminds me that Gretel is still just a kid.

But her accent is killing me. As we crawl closer and closer to Manhattan, she sounds more and more Australian. Two hours later, when our cab arrives at our hotel, I jump out and slam the door behind me. I just can't take it anymore.

The hotel is in Midtown, not far from Times Square and a few more blocks from Bryant Park where Fashion Week is held.

The doorman arrives to help Gretel with the bags, allowing me to sink into the peace and quiet of the Hotel MT lobby.

I tell the concierge, "We're here for Fashion Week, we've got a show."

But nothing impresses this woman. She's seen it all, heard it all, and met it all before. She smirks, hands me a super-slim card the size of a matchbox and points to the lifts.

I walk past the mezzanine bar and pool and even in the midst of my leaving-Paris depression, I wait for Gretel and the doorman to squeeze into the lift before jamming my finger on the button for the eighth floor.

The floors slide by effortlessly. I can't wait to get to our room and sink into my huge American bed and sleep for a week.

But Nina needs feeding and is irritable after another international flight, the hideous wait at customs and never-ending cab ride. Jaimee wants us to go to Bryant Park and meet with the coordinators but my priority is to get Nina settled in her cot and then put my feet up.

I push open the door to my room.

Or more accurately, to my closet.

"You can't be serious," I tell the doorman, but he ignores me and pushes the luggage off the trolley and onto the floor — the luggage takes up all the spare room.

The cot, which has already been assembled as requested, blocks the door to the bathroom. To get to the toilet I'm going to have to leap-frog over Nina.

"Geez, didn't you get lucky," Jaimee announces behind us. "You three got the big room."

"What do you mean, you three?" I ask her suspiciously, resting my head on the door frame, defeated.

"You, Nina and Gretel."

But she can't be serious. I whine at her, "I can't even walk around the single bed, Jaimee, where is Gretel supposed to sleep — on the ceiling?"

"It's called a loft, Til. Pull down the ladder and climb up, Gretel. I think you'll find a futon up there for you."

That's why I'm going to have to bend over when I take shower. The architect stole two foot of extra space for a loft by dropping the height of the bathroom to the head height of hobbits.

"It's so cool," Gretel says flying up the ladder.

I fall onto the bed exhausted, and scream out when I'm jolted by a sharp pain in my back. Reaching around, I find two small packages and an envelope underneath me.

"Who the hell sends mail these days?" Gretel scoffs. Now that we're in Manhattan proper, her confidence has returned with full force.

The name on the envelope says Caroline Banks and I snort about how appropriate that is, considering we are in New York and broke. I don't bother to open the envelope, turning my attention to the packages instead.

"Perhaps they're for Nina," Didi says, remembering it's Nina's birthday soon.

The first package is from Nadia. Which is accompanied by a note for Gretel saying her mother is onto her and a map of the *Sex and the City* tours for Didi and Cairine. For me, she has sent a picture of a gun plus a blank Last Will & Testament with instructions that I am to fill it out and leave the label to her in the likely even that I am mugged during our visit. And a book of Australian animals for Nina.

"Nadia's hilarious," Cairine says.

The next package is from Adam, who having heard the hotel has a pool, has sent Nina the cutest pink and green bathing suit. And for me, eight *Aussie bum* togs which are meant to be worn by the male models I can't afford to hire for the show.

"Oh my God, he's a ripper," Gretel grates as I pass them around.

The way the girls finger them you can tell they have a lot of experience working with fabric.

"These are great, they really support the testes, they're going to look hot on our models," Didi enthuses.

"But can they wear them in the show, I mean, they're not ours?" Cairine worries.

"Oh, who cares," I bite back, firing one of the togs at her like a slingshot. "The men are just eye candy anyway. The focus for the show is the maternity wear. And we all know where pregnant women are, virile, gorgeous blokes are hanging around perving at their breasts," I say acerbically.

"I love this, she's totally lost her nerve," Jaimee almost snarls at me.

The other girls look scared.

"What are we doing here, Til?" Jaimee snarls again.

"We're putting on a show, the same as we do every Spring/Summer, Autumn/Winter," I retort. "We need thousands of hits. We need people talking about us on the street. It will happen, so just ignore me, I need some rest. I'm probably coming down with something, and I'm bitchy after the flight."

Jaimee says, "Exactly. And whilst I'd love to sit here feeling useless, I'm going to go Byrant Park. I need to delay our meeting with the stage manager and Til is going to organise a go-see. In fact, we don't even have a list of models for a go-see, do we? What the fuck are we doing here?"

"Like I said, we're putting on a show. So please don't bite my head off, I'll find some models tomorrow. The other thing I have to tell you is that I want to do the show off-site."

"You want to do a Fashion Week event off Bryant Park?"

"That's right, I want to do it here."

"Here? In this shoebox? You won't even fit a pregnant woman in this room," Jaimee yells, and her voice rebounds off the stark, white walls.

"Don't be silly, Jaimee, I want to do it downstairs, in the pool mezzanine. The hotel was written up as the 'coolest, budget-chic place in New York'. The pool is hot. They're going to go nuts for it."

"Budget-chic?"

"Sure," I say resolutely. "We can do this, Jaimee," I tell her, but I can feel the nerves of everybody around me are on edge. "I know this is a little disappointing after Paris, we're squeezed in like sardines, but this is New York. We can't compare apples with champagne."

Five pairs of eyes look at me for salvation. For the first time in the whole three months we've been away, I feel homesick and scared.

"Well, I don't know about you no-hopers, but I want to go shopping so badly it hurts. This city is so hot I could die right now."

We all turn to Gretel and break out in laughter. At least we can rely on Gretel to see the bright side — even if total failure is just a few days away.

"Then go and get me some organic baby food for Nina, be a darl," I ask her.

She nods happily, quickly changing into my *Sass & Bide* pants as per Jaimee's airport instructions and after straightening her hair and putting on my *Gucci* sunglasses, she runs out the door again.

Jaimee and the girls leave with her and two minutes later, both Nina and I are cuddled up together on our single bed, fast asleep.

During the night I wake up sweltering and fumble around on the wall for the air conditioning switch. But even though I push the buttons continuously, the temperature doesn't move, the cheap-skates at this hotel must have permanently set it!

In the bathroom, I push open a tiny window and stick my head out into the night air. Cool air wafts past me into the bathroom and after splashing my face and neck with water I start to feel a little better.

Sitting on the floor, it hits me that my attitude stinks.

My favourite *Louboutins* sitting at home in my cupboard would be ashamed of me. So what if we're cramped into shoebox-sized hotel rooms? The best things come in small packages, don't they? And when I was pregnant, Nina fitted into my stomach, shoved up between my ribs and small intestine. So what if my cervix didn't move when it was time for her to come out? We still got her out, the doctors found a way.

And so will I. Even with no money, I'm going to put on a show and it's going to be fabulous. After all, that's what New York Fashion Week is about.

All eyes turn to Bryant Park every February and September. In fact, Stan Herman once said, "American fashion made this Park the heart of the city."

Central Park is the lungs of New York, circulating and cleansing the city's overly polluted air, but Bryant Park is the city's cultural centre, the heart and soul of this big-brand metropolis. On one side of Bryant Park is the New York City Library which during the Depression set up outdoor displays and let the many unemployed read their magazines, books and newspapers for free and often without a library card. It gave the unemployed and impoverished NY intelligentsia something to do but when World War Two erupted, the displays closed down, because, ironically, work had reappeared.

The displays are back again as a tribute to the days of earlier generosity. And for one week in late September, the tents of Fashion Week start appearing on the landscape as well. The world's fashionistas descend on Bryant Park, after being waxed, preened and detoxed into a size zero outfit — preferably by *Calvin Klein* or *Diane Von Furstenburg, Carolina Herrera, Herve Leger*, or *Ralph Lauren*. Personally, I have my eye on some RL gold sequined, wide-leg pants and am hoping to swipe some while backstage as a NYC souvenir. I want to be able to wear them and feel ecstatically happy while strutting down Fifth Avenue. I am definitely not going to stuff them down the back of my suitcase, morose and ashamed that I let one of the world's biggest cities beat me.

Maybe Jaimee's right. Maybe I should be showing at Bryant Park. But there's only one thing I want more than showing at New York Fashion Week, and that's the opportunity to be pregnant again, to slip into the Bondi sea pool and feel the cool water drip deliciously over my magnificent belly. And since I'm not pregnant, the next best thing is to hire women who are and project my desires onto them — whilst sitting in the audience exquisitely adorned with draping, organic fabrics that make me feel like a Greek goddess.

After all, this is New York, the one place where you can have it all.

I splash some more water over my face until I start feeling cool, sleepy and determined again. I go back to bed, the weight of the world drifting away.

Six hours later I'm woken by very loud knocking at the door. Alarmed, I throw open the door hoping to see a smoke-filled hallway and a gorgeous fireman waiting to carry me from the burning building. But it's just Jaimee, who seems to have ingested way too much *Starbucks* already.

I don't even get the chance to ask her if she's chewing gum. She starts spitting words at me, a million miles a minute.

"Didi and Cairine slept in I heart NY g-strings," she complains. "I don't know how the designers managed to get so many words on something so small, but they did." She looks me up and down and seems quite relieved that I have answered the door dressed in floor-length pyjamas. "I think we should change dorm partners."

Which is her way of saying she still hates the place.

Then she asks me where Gretel is.

We both look at Gretel's empty loft bed.

I panic. "Oh my God, I sent her out to get Nina some food, she hasn't come back yet? Oh my God, she's dead, Jaimee. It's been twelve hours."

"Gees, calm down Til, I'm pulling your leg, she slept in our room as she didn't want to disturb you. Look, she even managed to slip the baby food into your room in case Nina woke up."

Jaimee leans into the room and picks Nina up off the bed. "Hello, angel, welcome to New York city, the place that will make us, but most probably, break us."

"No news on more investors?" I ask her, but my hope fades when she doesn't smile — not even at Nina.

"Nope."

"I don't suppose Jorja...?"

"Nope."

"Even with the updated business plan?"

"Even with." Jaimee jiggles Nina but hands her back when she starts paddling to be put on the floor. "So, I'm off to Bryant Park to talk lies, lies, lies and you're due at the agency to pick out some models we can't afford."

I take a deep breath. "Jaimee, I don't want to use models for the show."

Which makes Jaimee sigh again, her eyebrows criss-crossing with fury. "You know this is a fashion show, Til, and the people who walk at fashion shows are people called models. Tall, lanky creatures with funny little names, who carry fluffy white dogs who have even funnier, little names?" Her hands gesticulate madly and her voice rises until she sounds like she's been sucking on a helium balloon.

"Which is exactly why I want to use real women and not models."

She doesn't even bat an eye. "Do we have to pay them?"

"Hopefully not. Who wouldn't want to walk at Fashion Week?"

"Whilst weighing a tonne and looking puffy? Gee, I don't know, Til — absolutely no-one in their right mind," she yells.

I ignore her tone and say brightly, "Well, lucky we're in New York. It's renowned for its crazies."

Her long fingernails tap against the door frame. "What's your inspiration?" she demands.

She's fishing for a visual brief, anything she can give to the organisers at Fashion Week.

Finally I tell her my concept for the show. I've been scared up until now, because it's definitely something we haven't tried before. "My theme is *Harem*. Which may sound ironic since we'll be working with women in the third world who've been enslaved prostitutes, but I'm using the traditional context of the word when it was introduced to English from Arabic: Harem meant women's quarters. And if you've read Virginia Woolf's *A Room of One's Own*, you'll know that women's space is intrinsically related to the concept of women's rights and is universal. I want the show to question how women's rights became subverted by men; how a woman's space became sexualised and turned into a prison. In much the same way as we need to ask ourselves why we still allow women in developing countries to live in poverty and repression."

Jaimee keeps her eyes narrowed.

"The women in the show will assert their universal rights. The male models, who'll be wearing the Aussie Bum togs, won't be concubines, the togs will prove that for us, nor will they appear as their masters, but in solidarity with the women.

"And you want to do all of that in a fashion show?"

"It ties in with our business proposition. This is our first show, it's really important that we communicate our message to the market." Because she still looks unconvinced, I try again. "Visually, you need to think of the beauty of the neoclassical painters, like Ingres' *Grande Odalisque*, or even the Spanish painter Quintana Olleras or the Italian painting *Harem* by Gianantonio Guardi.

But all she says is, "You want to put a skinny, naked woman on show in Bryant Park? You are mad."

"Pregnant women, Jaimee. And not skinny, pregnant women, but normal ones, ones who eat ice cream and can't see their feet for months."

"Nobody's eaten dairy here for years. That's worse than carbs. So where are you going to find these non-waif mothers-to-be?"

"At a maternity hospital. I'll take Didi and Cairine for the day and sort out the talent. You and Gretel can take Nina for the day, go and see the Fashion Week people and do the walk back from Bryant

Park to the hotel. Ask Gretel to take notes."

"People aren't going to walk from Bryant Park to the hotel, Til," Jaimee says while I busy myself packing Nina's bag for the day.

"I'm not asking them too. Can we rent some bikes for them to use?"

She ignores me. In all our years of watching *Sex and the City*, we never once saw a person (who wasn't a courier or criminally insane) ride a bike in New York.

I pick up Nina and give her to Jaimee. "If we do it here, we just need some chairs and a DJ."

"What about lights?"

"No, I'm going to let New York light us."

She gives me a look that says it all. "*DKNY* are spending hundreds of thousands of dollars to put on the schmickest show at Fashion Week, full of marching models and music timed to the split-second; and you want to use a wedding singer and a cacophony of different lighting sources that will probably make our models look green to accent their nasty fluid retention. Once I thought you were a genius, now I think you have lost your mind."

But she doesn't say it out loud. She lets me sling the nappy bag over her shoulder while she holds Nina in her skinny left arm and I shut the door in her face, leaving me alone while a fluorescent light hums noisily from the bathroom.

Didi slips the doorman ten bucks to hail a cab for us.

I'm just about to tell her she's nuts when the lobby doors slide open.

And New York hits us in the face with the force of a bomb explosion. The noise pummels us and we dive close to the sidewalk, falling into a waiting cab, relieved to be out of the angry waves of New Yorkers who yell, "Hey fuck-face, watch it," if we step in their way.

"Ten bucks? I'll give him $100 if he lets the cab drive into the foyer to drop us off again," I tell Didi.

But I don't have $100. Feeling small and scared, I tell the cab driver to take us to the biggest yoga centre in the city.

As long as it's in the Midtown.

He shoots the cab out into the traffic and we hold our breaths and squeal as he does a u-turn just in front of the oncoming traffic — all while telling us about his sister's break-up and a great yoga place just 20 blocks away.

Didi takes her fingernails out of my arm as the cab finds its place in an ever-present New York traffic jam. I have a feeling I'm going to be doing most of my work from the inside of a cab while we're here.

"Why are we going to do yoga, Til? We have no models and from where I'm sitting, not even a show. Shouldn't we be doing some work?" Didi asks, without any subtly.

"And when you sit around playing with fabric and drawing with a beautiful pencil does it look like work to the rest of us poor, mere mortals?"

"I guess not," she says ashamed of herself for second-guessing me.

"Then let the marketing guru try and figure out what the hell we're going to do," I snap at her.

She agrees, but doesn't look happy about it.

In the midst of Jaimee's, and now Didi and Cairine's doubts, I try to return to my vision.

I focus on the beautiful sight of Fred's body bending and twisting, resting and meditating, leading and encouraging and even though I look at him from all angles, his frame is totally absent of any brash neon hue.

All I need to do now is to find eight men just like him.

"You want us to do what?"

The incredulous look on his face as he hooks an *Aussie Bum* swimsuit on one of his fingers tells me that my idea is not coming across well.

"I want you to help us," I tell the yogi.

"By wearing this?"

"Precisely."

"And nothing else."

"It's not about the clothing, it's about the body. We're presenting a line of maternity clothing and I haven't even decided if the women will actually wear the clothes. On one hand it's a fashion show so the audience will be expecting clothes, but I'm trying to present the beauty and physicality of the expectant body, so perhaps the clothes should be hidden, left hanging in some of the hotel rooms. I just don't know yet."

"So why do you want us to wear these then?"

"Well, the pregnant woman didn't do it all on her own did she? So I need a male presence. One that's nurturing and supportive. I also need to get three hundred people to walk eight blocks from Bryant Park to the hotel, so I'd like you and seven other yogis to mark the way. You'll be the beacon of light, guiding the way. And the backdrop of the frenetic New York City streets will make the experience of wandering upon you even more incredible. Don't you think?"

"It's starting to sound like an Annie Liebovitz photo."

"Good, so you're starting to understand my vision. I'm so relieved, because your first reaction wasn't positive at all."

"I still think you're nuts," he says emphatically.

I hear Didi mutter under her breath behind me.

The yogi looks at her sharply. "I'll ask around," he says. "But I can't promise anything. How much are you offering?"

"Two hundred a piece. It should only take about an hour of your time. Once the crowd's gone, you can stop."

"In New York, the crowd never stops, honey."

"Alright, my boss will tell you when to stop," I say hurriedly trying to ignore the growing urge to punch him in the face. "If you want to do it, just show up at the MT hotel on Thursday at 2pm with or without your mates."

"Can we keep the...*togs*...is that what you called them?" He fingers the material and I can tell he appreciates the support they give.

"Yes and yes."

"How about $100 now and $100 on the day, and I'll take the togs now?"

"No and no." I take the togs from him and push them right down into the bottom of my oversized, fake *Gucci* bag. A tassel catches around my finger as I try to zipper it shut and I yell, "Fuck", a little too loudly.

He frowns at me, tells me, "*Namaste*," and walks off.

As soon as we step out onto the street we all let out a sigh of relief.

"God, I thought he was going to jump us for the togs," Didi exhales.

"And he's a yogi, imagine what the rest of them are like," Cairine says, flicking her curls with frustration.

"That's not what I want to hear right now," I tell them. "He'll be there. Didn't you see him react when I said it was for Fashion Week?"

"Yeah, he just about did a salute to the sun out of joy," Did says sarcastically.

"I betcha he shows up with 4000 fliers," Cairine adds, nudging Didi in the ribs.

I ignore them. "Life is one marketing opportunity after another, even for inner-city yogis. He'd be stupid not to show up. If somebody just landed that sort of publicity on my door I'd be kissing their ass to help."

Didi and Cairine take bets about the yogis while we crawl further downtown to the nearest maternity hospital. I can tell the cab driver is wondering which one of us is knocked up because he keeps looking at our breasts.

"Man, there's heaps of hospitals in New York. Why don't you tell me which one you want to go to?" he asks.

"The nearest."

"Are you Jewish?"

"Does it matter?"

"There's the Beth Israel that's why. Supposed to be good."

"Well we're not. Just the nearest maternity hospital will do."

Which the cab driver tells me is in Chelsea.

"Oh, we must be near Carrie's house," Didi says excitedly as we head further downtown.

The cab driver rolls his eyes. More bloody *Sex in the City* freaks.

When he stops the cab, I tip him generously and he gives me a lecherous smile that makes my skin crawl. But I smile back. I need all the good karma this city can summon for me.

Three sets of high heels step out of the cab onto the sidewalk and stare up at a four storey brownstone building.

"I don't see any pregnant woman," Cairine says disappointed.

"That's because it's the Chelsea STD clinic," Didi says, taking off her sunglasses.

"Pregnant women get STDs?"

"The bastard."

Cairine and Didi turn to me. "He took us to an STD clinic. And I fucking tipped him. Damn."

I turn on my heel and hail a non-existent cab.

"I feel dirty," Cairine says and a passer-by stops and smiles at her.

I glare at him. "I can't believe I'm running around looking for models in an STD clinic when I should be trying to get some celebrities to our event." I bash my hands on my forehead. "God, why am I even bothering? We are so out of our game here."

Didi and Cairine stay silent.

I know I should shut up. The last thing I should be showing my team is my ugly, open fear.

"And we haven't even been to Bryant Park yet," Didi mutters quietly to Cairine. "Wait til *Roberta Cavalli* treats us like sewer rats, that's when our confidence will really hit rock bottom."

Cairine shushes her. But Didi takes my arm.

"Til, I hate to say this but I don't think we can do this," she says to me. "I think we need serious help."

"What is this, an intervention?" I ask their serious faces.

Which makes them both laugh.

"No. But we can't go back to the hotel without models. Jaimee will kill us," Cairine says.

"What about an agency, Til?" Didi suggests.

"I tried," I admit. "When I asked for eight pregnant models they laughed. So then I said what about just fat models and they hung up on me."

"They must have plus-sized models here," Cairine comments.

I sigh. "I really need to be getting some press releases out, not traipsing around town looking for models. Not that anyone will come — which is preferable considering I won't even have a show for them to see."

"What about that agency Nadia told you about? Maybe they can help with the media too."

"Maybe they can get Paris Hilton to come to the show," Didi suggests.

"Or bigger," Cairine adds.

"Bigger than Paris doesn't exist, Cairine."

"It has to. Because we need her," I whisper to New York.

After a quick call to Nadia's contact at a modelling agency, who tells us she can't help us with pregnant women, Paris Hilton, or even Elton John, we resume our search for a maternity hospital.

The next cab driver drops us at an Ear, Throat and Nose hospital.

And the next at a veterinarian clinic.

We all admit it's a lost cause. At four o'clock we hit the subway instead of trying our luck in another hour-long traffic jam.

We drag our weary bodies to our rooms.

Jaimee wants a report but I glare at her and all she says is, "OK, later then."

And when I open the door to my room I see Nina curled up next to Gretel and they're both fast asleep.

And a new envelope lying on the floor at my feet.

But I ignore it. Sleep beckons. I crawl up into the loft and toss and turn before falling into a restless sleep.

I dream of yogi cab-drivers swearing at me, their beautiful bodies covered in chemically infested clothes and pollution. And in the boot of our car is Nina who is now giant-sized and desperately trying to escape.

Her cries wake me an hour later.

I jump out of the loft and pick her up and she clambers all over me muttering, "Mama" and my heart soars.

"Oh baby girl, I missed you," I cry into her hair. "This place is horrible, I can't believe I brought you here. And tomorrow's your birthday. Let's do something nice, just you and me."

"We did something nice today," Gretel says stirring. "We went to Central Park and played on some beautiful lush grass and Nina met some New York city kids. Some kid's Mum bought us ice creams. She said she worked for a media company and could help you with some PR if you wanted.

"She what?" I ask Gretel incredulously.

"She said to drop in and see her tomorrow. I told her we were dirt poor but she didn't care, she said she loves Fashion Week, that she'd love to get into that scene."

"What did you tell her exactly?"

"That we'd called the label *Giséle* and were from Australia and had spent most of our money manufacturing in France and opening a store in Paris. She seemed to like that, especially the name bit. I told her we were going to run all these environmental campaigns and return our profits to the planet. Anyway, here's her card."

"I don't know what I'd do without you, Gretel," I reply. I thumb the heavy stock of the card and its gold embossing. *Jacobs Lane PR. 112th and 46th street.*

"We've got an appointment to see her at eight am tomorrow."

"Gretel, I could kiss you," I tell her my heart soaring. "How do you do this?"

"I don't know, there's people out there who can help us. We just have to ask."

I bounce Nina up and down and we both squeal with delight. "Let's celebrate, Gretel. Tell the girls to get ready, we're going out for an hour."

"Alright, I'll be back in a New York minute," she says running out the door, happy to see me hopeful again.

That night, Jaimee takes us to *Eleanor's*, a famous Midtown eatery where we play spot the celebrity and Nina tries to feed herself organic falafel and couscous. I try to eat an enormous salad but find the cocktails easier to swallow.

"An organic cocktail bar, now that's a good idea. Why didn't we just do that instead of burning ourselves into the ground with this 'must be a global brand and reinvent clothing for pregnant women and over-nourished rich kids'," Didi teases.

"Didi, you're getting too glum for words, please try my blackberry martini," I bubble at her. The music, the hum of the restaurant and the squillions of berries slushing around in my tummy is making me feel fantastic.

By eight pm, Nina is showing signs I have pushed her too far so I pack her up and take her home, leaving the other four to wander down Broadway and take in some sights.

A wave of tiredness overcomes me as soon as we walk into our hotel room. Nina is asleep in my arms, so I put her to bed with the light off. I don't even see the envelope that has been slid under the door — this one bearing thick, red, scary lettering.

One year

What the hell's happened to me?

First, I was having a whale of a time, humming along in this whooshing, warm, red space then bam! Somebody's hand pushed me back up into my mother's uterus and they cut her open and pulled me out into this freezing cold place. Then some guy cut my lifeline to my mother, who made me suck on her booby and that gave me wind worse than they get in Chicago.

It's getting better though. I can fart by myself, which is quite a relief.

Mum's gone a bit nuts. Even more than usual. She's here, she's there, she's everywhere, then she's gone. I'm not handling the *gone* bit too well. Every time I cry my Mum announces to everybody, "It's separation anxiety," but sometimes it's not. Sometimes I cry because the great big world I have been born into just seems so void of compassion and tolerance that I feel a tidal wave of depression sweep me off my feet and I crash onto the ground.

Who knew walking would hurt so much? All I'm trying to do is see the world and then something that I didn't see coming trips me up and I land on my face.

And you adults are just so competitive. You're all pushing your babies out into the world in fabulous outfits and trying to pretend that we are extensions of your own identity and will do better in the world than you ever did.

Of course, I like that I'm an extension of you. Otherwise, I'd just be me, and that would make me feel really scared and alone. Especially when the world, which is full of dark, ominous skyscrapers, keeps growing bigger and bigger every day.

At first I thought the shadows were just people; they stand so solidly and block out the sun, but now I know they're not. These giants are made out of concrete and glass and if I get a step wrong in this city, they're going to crush my skull with their pavement feet. I'm constantly getting trampled on in this town: "Get the pram out of the way, get off the sidewalk, what the fuck is that, a *Bugaroo*?" The torment is endless.

It's enough to make my head hurt.

I just want my Mum.

I want a cuddle, I want to sleep in my own bed. I want her to read me a night-time story and stroke my feverish head. I want her to scare the monsters away and shadows that creep along the walls in the early afternoon.

Meeting God

Jaimee's face says it all.

I can tell something bad, very, very bad has happened. The knocking on the door is even louder than it was yesterday and she has a support team: Gretel, Cairine and Didi are all standing behind her.

"Why didn't you tell me about the fax, Til?"

"What fax?" I ask Jaimee while trying to rub the sleep out of my eye.

She flinches.

"Oh, that," I concede. I can see the envelope out of the corner of my eye, still sitting on the tiny bed-stand. "I didn't read it yet, I didn't get around to it. Why?"

"It's from a Caroline Banks. She's sent several apparently, and when you didn't respond she even dropped in here last night to tell you the news. So now I'm going to have to tell you. But first, you'd better sit down."

"God Jaimee, you're scaring me. Is everything OK? Is it about home? Is everyone OK?

She nods and my heart, which had stopped beating for a few seconds, starts up again.

"It's the label. They're going to put an injunction on us."

"A what?" I scream at her. "We're just about to go see some fabulous PR company Gretel stumbled across. This can't happen."

"It can. And it is."

I take the paper from her. Both our hands are shaking.

"Even Gretel's read it and she said it looks bad."

Gretel nods seriously.

"Gretel's 16," I scoff. "No offence, Gretel."

"It's the end of the line, Til," Jaimee tells me. "They're going to let us keep our store in Paris but we have to change the label's name. She's really mad apparently."

'Who is?"

"Gisele Meichen."

"I named the label *Giséle* not Gisele Meichen. And I have an international trademark. They can't stop us."

"She's an international supermodel with millions of dollars to throw at lawyers. We can't even afford to pay our models for the show. The organisers are on my back too, they want to see a walk-through today or we're off the program."

"I can't believe this," Didi whines. "All the work we've put in and we're going to be nothing but a sandwich board out the front of an empty tent in Bryant Park which says, 'Due to catwalk incident, this show has been cancelled'."

"She doesn't own the name Giséle," I say steadfastly. "If she did, they wouldn't have given us the trademark."

"Trademark, schmademark," Jaimee retorts. "She wants to meet with us. ASAP."

"Who does?"

"Caroline Banks."

"Well, let's go then. Gretel, call your friend and tell her we can't make it this morning. See if you can reschedule for this afternoon."

Gretel nods and starts punching numbers into her tiny phone.

I turn to Nina who is sitting on the bed looking sad. "Happy Birthday my little girl," I tell her picking her up. "I'm sorry, it's not going to be the day I'd hoped for." Then I kiss her cheek and because I am flushed with anger, I decide that it's me who is a little warm and not Nina.

"That's right, it's Nina's birthday," everyone gushes and squeezes into the room to shower her with kisses.

Nina, of course, doesn't understand a thing, except that she is now the centre of attention and her world has been righted.

Our two cabs crawl across town toward the Upper East Side and eventually arrive at the super skyscraper of Caroline Banks. We take the elevator to the 45th floor. I sway toward the receptionist who ushers us into Caroline's office lobby, which is bigger than the whole Hotel MT, and brings us green tea.

But my blood is boiling. I have to calm down. So I take the tea and even bow my head to the receptionist who tries not to raise an overarched, heavily waxed eyebrow at my sarcastic reaction.

And I try to breathe. I imagine that I am floating in a pool and every time I take a breath, my body fills with air and my body pops to the surface of the water and holds the universe in place.

Until a buzzer sounds. And I crash to the bottom of the pool.

Caroline sits behind a glass desk and in front of a glass window while New York City spreads out behind her. I stop dead, knowing if I take one more step I will fall a thousand metres onto the street below. The only reason Caroline doesn't fall is because she is God.

The God who runs New York is a woman. I should have known.

We all sit down on glass chairs.

"Now, we seem to have a problem," God begins. "You should not have avoided my faxes."

"I didn't read them, I didn't have time," I admit to her.

Out of the corner of my eye I see Nina rubbing her eyes and looking vacantly at God.

"You seem to have left your New York Fashion Week production very late. I've spoken to the organisers. They've told me you haven't even started the go-sees."

"So?"

She ignores my sarcasm. "Fashion Week events are spectaculars. They do not come together at the last minute."

This is what I hadn't counted on. Launching onto the international marketplace via the NYFW seemed like a great idea, except for one tiny detail: the fashion industry knows everything weeks before it even happens. My stealth strategy has just imploded on my face.

"I told Gisele about your little label and she was furious. She feels that you have stolen her name and have no intention of paying her any royalties," Caroline announces.

I suck in my breath. "Caroline," I'm so glad I didn't call her God by mistake, "we make children's clothes and maternity wear. We have a flagship store in Paris with wooden dolls staging a tribute to the Renaissance. You represent a German model who looks like a *Barbie* doll and has no interest in merchandising beyond some over-priced bikinis. We are worlds apart."

"Still, you have used *Giséle* with one L just like Gisele Meichen. And wouldn't you know it, but she's an icon of the fashion industry, a brand unto her own, and now that she is pregnant everyone will think…"

But she doesn't get the chance to finish her sentence.

Because we are all erupting with amazement, "Gisele's pregnant?"

"How come we didn't know?" we all voice.

"How long … when's she due" I ask feeling a flutter of excitement.

Caroline silences us with a long fingernail and I feel scared that she might rip me apart with it. Nadia was wrong, you don't need a gun in this town just four inch nails, five per cent body fat and a walk-in wardrobe full of *Jimmy Choos*.

Even Nina doesn't like her, I can tell, and Nina likes everybody. Didi tries to shush her, but she squirms and wriggles.

Looking at Nina, I remember why I started this adventure in the first place. And it wasn't so I could sit here in glass chairs. "Well, we wish her luck, and maybe your Gisele *Meichen*," I emphasise her surname, "could try trademarking her brand next time she wants to try and intimidate some hard working, start-up with a combined experience of about 40 years and substantial financial backing from property developers in Australia — all who abhor American intimidation techniques," I fume and stand up. "We will be putting on our show at Fashion Week in five days and as we have a lot to do, could you kindly discuss your client's embarrassing, self-obsessed, anally retentive behaviour with our patent attorney."

"I've spoken to Fashion Week. You're not going on."

Jaimee nods her head. "I had a call this morning, Til. If we don't have the models by the end of today we're off the program."

"So what the hell are we doing here then? This is just a smokescreen, can't everybody see that?" I shout at my team.

"You will never get your models in time," Caroline tells me deadpan, "so you may as well pack your bags and head home because you will not be showing in New York and you will not be selling in New York."

"What you're proposing," Gretel says, jumping in before I rip the woman's nails from her hands one by one, "is that any model can claim intellectual property to her name. And considering the number of models out there, you're proposing that all fashion labels must now be numbered, to avoid any difficulty?"

"It's not my problem what other people do with their labels. I'm only interested in protecting Gisele's potential fortune."

"You mean she's not rich enough?" Didi asks shocked.

"The investors, who would help finance her next venture into a maternal, merchandising line wouldn't think so. Gisele is such a strong brand, investors can predict an additional 20% return on their investment."

"And we're promised our investors a return greater than 30% and our NPV has already trebled," Jaimee quips, finally getting on board my outrage and confidence. "Our investors won't like us bowing out just because your client has a twist in her readily expanding thong."

Caroline doesn't respond.

"Our trademark was approved. You'll have a very hard time stopping us," Jaimee tells her.

"That's irrelevant. This is the United States of America. International trademarking laws barely matter as the Chinese have been proving for years. All I have to do is make a call to Stephanie at NYFW and you will be off the program before I even put the phone down. You will be hard-pressed securing any orders on either side of the Atlantic when Gisele Meichen opens a competing label backed by a conglomerate with $20 million."

I walk towards the door. "And by the time you finish your designs, Gisele will have given birth and you won't be able to capitalise on her pregnancy. Let's go girls, I want to call our Board and tell them we've had some good news, we should go ahead with our furnishings line a little earlier than expected."

Caroline's face turns stormy. The New York clouds behind her gather with such dark force that I am scared the second I step outside the building I will be struck dead by lightning.

We walk the wrong way up Park Avenue, pushing against a pack of New Yorkers steadfastly walking toward us with force.

"Shove over!" one bites at us.

"Don't you know how to walk?" another screams and we cower on the edge of the sidewalk until Cairine is elbowed onto the street and into the path of an oncoming cab.

Jaimee shrieks and pulls her out of the way. "They're like wild animals, I've never seen anything like it," she wallows.

"Where are they all going?" Didi asks.

"Wall Street?" I suggest sarcastically.

"Too far downtown," Gretel comments. "There's probably a sale on...."

"And you're not going," Jaimee tells her.

We teeter on the edge of the sidewalk not knowing what to do.

Until Didi grabs my arm. And before the words are even out of her mouth, I know that something is wrong.

"Til, I know this isn't the time but I don't think Nina's well. She's got a temperature."

My hand shoots up to Nina's head. And then my lips to her forehead. "She's really hot, but her hands are cold," I say and start tearing her little clothes off her. "Damn, she's got a rash, right across her chest."

Nina cries and struggles against me.

I want to yell but I can't freak Nina out. Instead I look up to see four scared pairs of eyes looking at me. "She was fussing on the plane but I didn't think anything of it, and she was hot last night but I thought it was just the room temperature was too high. And in Caroline's office, she was being difficult but I thought she was just bored."

"What do you think it is?" Didi asks.

"It could be anything, there are thousands of viruses that present with a rash, and most of them don't even have names."

"Is it serious?"

"I don't know. But we have to find a doctor."

"We need a hospital," Jaimee says and I thank her for panicking. Of course that's what I want for Nina, but parents always feel guilty about overreacting.

"We'll get a cab," she says.

"No!" Cairine, Didi and I all shout in unison.

"We did that yesterday. By the time a cab driver finds a real hospital Nina will be…" Didi starts.

"Better." Jaimee interjects, seeing my panic escalate to full blown terror.

"Thinking positive is fine for you yogi gurus, but I'm going to start freaking out right about now," Gretel replies.

I look up toward the ominous, dark sky and a skyscraper that disappears into the heavens.

One minute ago, Caroline Banks' office was the last place in the world I would want to be, but now it's precisely where we have to be. Because what I need is a native New Yorker — even if she is an overly aggressive twat.

We head back into the elevators, my heart pounding as we fly past every floor. The receptionist, seeing the look of sheer panic on our faces doesn't stop us from storming into Caroline's office. I'm so absorbed in Nina's illness that I don't notice a six-foot supermodel sitting opposite her.

"Nina's sick, really sick. We need a doctor," I start crying as Nina struggles in my arms, whining at me.

Caroline and Gisele Meichen both jump up and grab their mobile phones.

"I'll call my obstetrician," Gisele says to me. "He'll know where to take her."

"I'll call the paramedics," Caroline says.

And we all hold our breaths.

"Hi, Tony, it's Gisele. I have a friend whose baby's ill." She walks over to me and Nina and even though I'm totally obsessed with my panic, I take two seconds to acknowledge how beautiful she is.

"He wants to know her symptoms," she says and touches a long hand to Nina's head.

"She's really hot," we both say together.

"And she has a rash," I tell her and expose Nina's chest to her. "I think it's meningococcal. Her hands are cool, she's breathing rapidly and won't let me hold her."

Gisele looks at me, her brown eyes wide open as she repeats my words into the phone. "I'm at Caroline Banks, on Park Avenue," she tells the phone before hanging up.

"He's coming here," she tells us. "He'll be ten minutes. Caroline, how are you doing?"

"I'm through, they're sending a team."

I break down again and Jaimee and Cairine hold me up off the floor.

"The sofa. Put her on the sofa," Caroline tells them and they shuffle me over.

I hold onto Nina for dear life.

Gisele disappears to fetch a wet towel which she drapes over Nina's chest.

Nina starts screaming and tries to pull it off.

"If it's too cold you can make the temperature worse," I tell her taking the towel from her. "The body thinks it has a chill and raises the temperature even more. Can you wet it again please, just make sure the water is tepid not cold."

She races off to do as she's told. And it's then that I notice her bump. Not quite a bump, more like a pimple.

"When are you due?" I ask her when she returns and lays the towel over Nina's chest.

"Early January, some New Year I'll be having!" she says and dabs the towel over Nina's horrible, red-purple rash.

"In three months?" I yell flabbergasted. "You're barely showing." Which instantly reminds me it's Nina's birthday today and I start crying again. Nina jerks uncomfortably as if she hates me holding her. Caroline paces at the door. Gisele wipes the towel over Nina's head and starts to shush me, trying to calm me down.

Caroline turns to us. "Gisele, should you be doing that? I mean, is it a risk to the baby?"

Gisele looks up at her, shocked. "Caroline, the baby will be fine. But I think the mother here will have your balls on a platter if you keep trying to scare her."

"Oh God, I'm not trying to do that, I'm sorry, I'm just thinking about the baby," Caroline says.

Despite my panic, it's not lost on me that Caroline means Gisele's baby, not mine.

"My baby will be fine," Gisele says again. "We just have to concentrate on this little one now."

And she means Nina. My little baby. My universe.

"Nina," I tell her. "Her name's Nina."

"Nina," Gisele smiles. "And she's gorgeous too."

"And I'm Til. I can't believe we were in here ten minutes ago fighting with each other, via Caroline, and now you're helping us."

"I only found out about your label five minutes ago," Gisele whispers to me. "I've been away for a few weeks, I thought a holiday would be nice, our last before the baby you know. I thought I was coming in here today to make sure my tax has been paid, everyone's a little jittery after Wesley Snipes got sent to jail."

I nod. After all, Gisele's personal worth was calculated at about $20 million (when I was breastfeeding Nina I used to watch *Entertainment Weekly* every day). She doesn't need to micromanage her business, she has scary people like Caroline Banks do it for her.

Gisele keeps talking using a low voice. "If you ask me, taking you out of Fashion Week is a bit drastic. I know you have trademarked the name successfully. I was disappointed when I found out about you girls, but I've just decided to pursue a maternity and children's line whereas you've been working on it a while. So good for you." She points her head in God's direction. "And as I explained to Caroline, I am not the only Gisele in the world, am I? Caroline's a little aggressive and she has to be, so many people have a vested interest in me. I know I'm just a model but the brand Gisele sells — and not just clothes. Pretty much anything I put my face onto sells."

"Nina's breathing is a little rapid, don't you think?" I ask her butting in. "Don't get me wrong, I am listening to you, but I'm scared as hell. What if she *dies?*"

"She'll be fine," Gisele says. "Her breathing is a little fast but she's sick, you have to expect that."

Gisele keeps talking, her hand resting on my arm, passing her supermodel strength to me via the osmosis of touch. I admit to myself how reassuring her elegant, mashed up accent is.

"My obstetrician will be here soon, he's the best in the city, he'll take really good care of Nina."

Which makes me cry again. I could kiss her for being this kind. Just being in New York scares me, but Nina being ill has raised my terror to an all time high.

I tell Gisele, "Whatever it is we're here to fight for, I just don't give a damn about anymore. I just want Nina to get better. And I've been totally ignoring her lately, since this stupid idea for a label came into my head."

Gisele rubs my back reassuringly.

"God, what if something happens to her? I'll never forgive myself for not spending every second with her," I say and my whole body starts convulsing with sobs.

"And Caroline's given you such a hard time. I'm so sorry, Til."

"It doesn't matter now, we won't be showing in New York."

"Yes you will, Til. Little Nina will be fine. I'll get my team onto your show, you'll have your models by the end of the day, OK?"

"I don't care anymore, I just want to get Nina to the hospital and make sure she's OK."

"Of course. And she will be. But I'll do everything I can to help you." She smiles at me. "Us mothers have to stick together, hey?"

At that second, Gisele's obstetrician bursts into the room and the immediate effect is audible.

All of the women sigh with relief as the storm erupts overhead, lightning mixing with thunder as tonnes of water break free from the clouds' protective banks and bash against the glass windows.

Nina screams as he lays her on the carpet to examine her and all seven women stand around her, tears streaming down their faces at her pain and anguish.

In the distance, I hear a siren racing toward us, and the New York traffic slowing and parting, just like the Red Sea, so help can get to us sooner.

By lunchtime on Nina's first birthday, she had been admitted to hospital.

By three pm she was worse.

And by six pm she was stable.

Every hour of the day had passed slowly, a procession of doctors and nurses checking her vitals while the girls hovered around the hospital. Now, only Jaimee keeps me company.

"One year ago today, you were the one in the hospital bed, Til," Jaimee tells me, patting my back as I sit and stare at Nina who's now sleeping, with little tubes in her nose. "And Nadia and I sat with Adam, just like this and held his hand until you were safe. Nina will be OK, just like you were."

"Oh God, Jaimee," I complain to her. "I'm exhausted and I just want to concentrate on Nina. Please don't hate me but I'm not capable of anything more than this."

"That's fine," she says. "Gretel will be here in the morning with fresh clothes for you. Maybe they'll let Nina come home tomorrow."

Home. At the mention of the word, I feel the hot, Bondi wind fly off the water and hit me on the cheek. Sydney. "God, I'd like to take her home," I tell Jaimee. "As soon as possible."

That night is the longest in history. At three am, Nina's temperature drops and one of the all-American, drawling doctors tells me she's out of danger, I throw my arms around him and with the energy of the city behind me, hold onto him tightly.

When Nina wakes up, on her second day in hospital, I kiss her and play with a curl of her hair.

"Mama," she smiles a quivering, gentle smile at me and reaches for my face. I kiss her little fingers and tell her for the thousandth time how much I love her.

"This is a pretty good way to get Mum's attention, little girl."

"And mine too," a voice behind me says.

I spin around to see Gretel grinning at me like she's spent another $50,000 in less than four hours, and behind her, a very serious-looking Adam.

"He flew out straight away."

"As soon as I heard," Adam says making a beeline for Nina's bedside.

We spend a half hour recounting the horrors of the previous day before Nina starts to protest with tiredness.

"I'll stay, you go for a walk. Central Park's not too far from here," Adam says. "Get some fresh air or at least a break from these damned humming lights," he says looking up at them and frowning.

And I break out laughing. Because before he said anything, I thought I was going mad. I thought I was the only one in the whole city who knew how annoying they were.

Having deposited Adam safely, Gretel slips away again disappearing into the throng of the hospital traffic.

"I don't know if Gretel's coming home with us," I tell Adam. "She kind of belongs here." And when I start sobbing he hushes me. He knows I'm not talking about Gretel at all.

"Nina's going home with us, Til. There's nothing to worry about. There are lots of people here to help you and right now, you just have to be there for Nina. And to do that you'll have to let go of *Giséle*."

I cry and it's a mixture of enormous sadness, relief, anguish and happiness — and it's a feeling that deserves its own word, its own place in the dictionary but has been neglected of the honour — because it is a depth of the emotion cannot be described in words but can be witnessed when mothers blink and softly nod.

Five days after Nina's birthday, she is discharged from hospital.

Despite Adam's pestering, I haven't left Nina's side since she got sick. Since I'm as white as the hospital walls, exhausted and a whole lot skinnier than when we arrived, Adam comes to the hospital to help me bring Nina back to the hotel.

And as we step outside the hospital doors, it's a different New York that greets us.

As the cab cruises toward Broadway I wind my window down and take a fresh look at a glittering New York. Instead of an angry and aggressive city ready to defend its market share at all costs from the advances of some antipodean upstarts, today the city has forgiven me for my fanciful fashion onslaught and turned on the charm.

And I am falling for it.

Summer has relinquished its wilting salad days hold on the city, its obsession with painting the city green, garlanded with steel grey high-rises, yellow cabs and lurid flashing advertising, and been supplanted with a sophisticated, autumnal hum. A crisp chill has cleansed the air and painted the city's backdrop a clear, postcard blue. Even the children of New York have appeared, thrust out of the air conditioned shoeboxes and into the city's parks. Instead of the sound of a million horns all blasting at once, the sonorous echoes of children and adults laughing together prevails. The traffic seems to be flows freely.

Until we reach Broadway.

And the traffic comes to a snarling halt.

"What the hell?" the Albanian cab driver (who has the strongest Brooklyn accent I've heard yet) yells, slamming his hand on the steering wheel. "Now I've seen it all, some bloody crazy person is doing a head stand in the middle of Broadway."

"What did you say?" I ask him leaning over the front seat to get a better look.

"Some dude is standing in nothing but his jocks…on his head in the middle of Broadway. Some cop's trying to move him but he won't budge."

"Speaking of budgies, those are some nice ones," Adam says

admiringly and leans out the window to get a better look at the yogi who, judging from the tightness and lift in his groin area, is wearing the *Aussie bum* togs I had picked out for the show.

"What's going on?" I ask him suspiciously but Adam stays unusually tight-lipped.

A block later we pass another yogi in mid-Garudasana pose, as Adam tells me, the Eagle pose, and at the next block he catches his breath.

"That's Pincha Mayurasana, that's pretty impressive."

We all look at an upside-down bony man who is doing an arm-stand, his whole body weight taken by his forearms. Even Nina is looking curiously at him from her car seat.

I yell at him. "You'd better tell me what's going on — now!"

Which is met with silence.

So I do the only thing I know will work: I dig my nails into Adam's leg and he lets out a blood curdling squeal.

"Alright," he screams. "Jaimee wanted to tell you, the show's still on, Til. Ouch, now let go of my gorgeous leg before you do me a serious injury."

I release him. "The show? But how …?"

"It's amazing what you can accomplish when one of the world's biggest supermodels comes on-board as a new investor," Adam beams at me and my mouth drops.

"Gisele?"

"Who else?"

"She bought out most of Jorja's shares! Jorja's ecstatic by the way, she's made a fortune. She's talking about starting up ten more collectives this year, way ahead of schedule."

But I don't look pleased; in fact, I look absolutely despondent.

Adam reads my mind. "She gave you the cash injection you desperately needed. But Gisele can give you more money and bring you a lot more publicity. Gisele wants proprietary ownership though, if she's going to help. So Jorja's stepping aside. She'll still helping you set up the collectives, but this way she can invest her money into the collectives instead of *Giséle*." He pauses and brandishes a hand somewhere out toward the meat packing district. "I think she's out there somewhere in New York buying an apartment for you and Nina to stay in when you come to town for Board meetings."

"Jorja's here?"

"Yes. You'll see her at the show," Adam beams giving my arm a squeeze.

"Is this really happening?" I ask him bewildered.

"Yes," Adam says purposefully. "You've got Gisele on board and in thirty minutes your label will be showing at New York Fashion Week. It's surreal, but it's happening. I really can't say anything else but congratulations, Til." He pats my leg and his face shows concern when I turn green.

"Thirty minutes? But I'm not ready," I panic. "I haven't organised anything."

"Don't worry about it," Adam says. "Caroline's hired a consultancy to manage the buyers' orders after the show. And before you get stressed about this all happening quickly, Jaimee's staying on for a while until all the contracts are signed with Gisele."

"Gisele Meichen," I mutter feeling all of a sudden, star-struck.

I think back to our meeting in Caroline Banks' office. God, was it really five days ago? Being with Nina in hospital, watching her fade, then slowly recover and regain her strength, felt like years not days.

"Soon, your little label is going to be the talk of this gigantic town," Adam whoops. "By the way, the girls wanted me to give you this," he says and hands me a package.

I don't know if my heart can take anymore but I reach into the bag — and take out a copy of the latest edition of French *Vogue*.

"It came out on Nina's birthday," he says, and puts his arm around me to hold me up.

Tears stream from my eyes and onto its historic cover: this is the first edition ever to run a children's fashion story and they chose one of our designs for the cover!

"I can't believe we're in the French *Vogue*," I finally whisper turning to the Tours shoot and finding another four of our designs made it past the Editor's highly astute eye.

"You could have worked your whole life and never achieved

this, Til. It is amazing. With French *Vogue* behind you and Gisele on board, you'll be unstoppable. The question is can you manage the growth stage of your business while maintaining the business's core values?"

Trepidation returns with a thunderous clap of reality. "We can't do it. It's impossible to grow this quickly. We haven't tested anything yet. We can't make that many garments."

"You'll work it out. Jorja will bring you the collectives, Caroline's got a team of geeks working on the website as we speak, it'll be ready to take on-line orders within hours of the show. The factory in France is ready."

But I still look dumbstruck.

He looks at me concerned. "Til, this is what you wanted. When you came up with the idea for the label and called it *Giséle*, you had a hunch this would all happen. You talked your sister into investing $4 million and the girls their life savings. You can't walk out now."

"I never said I was walking away." But I know I did, my face said it. "I'm worried about Nina. I want to get her home, I want her to rest, I want to go back to how it was before. To us, and going to the park everyday and spending time together, and not having to think about work."

"But you can't. Even if you go back to Sydney, you'll be going back to work. Now, we can buy a house with an office and you can work from home. Hire some dammed assistants if you need to. You don't even have to work on the management team, you could just sit on the Board if you want to and do everything via teleconferencing. Make sure that the company adheres to your vision and doesn't go off-course."

"That sounds good. What does Jaimee think?"

"That you're God. She wants to stay in New York and work from here."

"Good. Yes, that's probably a good idea. And Didi?"

"She's happy to go with Cairine to Malawi, Uzbetkistan, wherever you need them to go.

"Good. So everyone's happy then?"

"Yes. They've been scared about Nina, but getting on with their job while you've been looking after her."

"Sounds like it. I'm sure they've done a fantastic job putting the show together."

"There's just one thing."

"What?"

"About the maternity line."

"What about it? Is something wrong? It can't be. That's what we're showing today."

"Exactly. Gisele thought it best to differentiate between the kids' range and the maternity line."

"Sure. So what was her idea?"

"You'll see. Please don't scream. That's all I ask," he says. And he smiles, a little too hard.

Before I can drill him for anything our cab pulls up outside the hotel and Adam is pushing me and Nina out of the cab and through the people crowding the entrance. He starts shouting at me, "The show's starting in 25 minutes. You've got enough time to take Nina to your room and get her settled. Then it'll be back downstairs to see your first New York Fashion Week show — which just happens to be your own label."

"Adam, I can't leave Nina," I tell him and stop still in the middle of the traffic.

"I'll watch her," he says reassuringly prodding me to move again. "She'll probably be ready for a sleep."

"Then I want to be there for her."

"Til, you're turning into one of those neurotic mothers," Adam chides.

Words which make me feel like one of those angry mothers.

"What I mean is that it's OK to take time out. You've worked hard for this, Til, and Nina would want you to see it. In years to come, she'll want you to tell her all about it."

Which is true, I know it is.

I don't get a chance to change my mind again. Jaimee has found me.

"Oh my God, *Vogue* are here! Til, go upstairs now and straighten your hair. Hello Nina-beautiful, you look much better than you did yesterday," she says and Nina grabs her finger and pulls it. Jaimee squeals, much to Nina's delight, who laughs and tries it again.

"No, Til, go get ready," Gretel interrupts. "Now! Upstairs!" she orders and we all follow her to the lift. She leans into the lift and shoves her face right up against mine, so I step back onto Adam's toes.

"Damnit, what's wrong, Gretel?"

But all she says is "Hmmn, I'll see what I can do. It's impossible really, but I'll have to try."

The doors slide shut.

Jaimee turns to me. "Now, Til, you know the drill. You've done this a hundred times before, this is just another show. Every show is important to us, no city is better than another."

"Except that this is happening at a million miles an hour."

"It's New York. I was a little uncomfortable with it myself, but this is how they work. So let's go show the world what an impetuous little day-dreamer you are."

It is the world's shortest (and probably the strangest) motivational speech I've ever heard, but I like it.

I let the familiar pre-show nerves erupt somewhere near the surface of my heart.

Standing in front of the tiny pull-out mirror in my bathroom I can see what Gretel was concerned about: magnified 3000X are my clogged pores and the emergence — yes — explosion of 40 new fine lines! Unfortunately, what I can't see is the *L'Wren Scott* green silk dress and the *Maison Martin Margiela* elastic bolero that I'm wearing.

"Brilliant, very classy, what a combination," Adam says playing with a tassel on my jacket.

"I feel like I need plaits," I complain. "Or a goat, or maybe you could yodel and I'll do a little dance around a maypole?"

"You've never pole-danced and you're not about to start now,"

Jaimee orders, her head appearing in the doorway.

I turn to her and feel an immediate pang of jealousy. "Nice. How come you get to wear a *Dolce and Gabbana* straw-blend bodysuit? And no leggings? What happened to the New York style bible you made us swear on at the airport?"

"You have to know when to break the rules," she says facetiously.

"But who chose my outfit?" I ask miserably, noting that Jaimee looks like she's been airbrushed, her skin is totally void of fat and hair. Oh, to be half-Japanese.

"Gisele. What, you don't like it?"

"It's not really me, is it?"

"No…that's why it's so great. Don't forget, Til, you work in marketing not design. And you're very good at *whatever* it is that you do. Now, don't look so glum, get downstairs and sit in the front row at your first New York fashion show."

I kiss Nina goodbye. And even though my heart is breaking in two and Adam has to pry her from my fingertips, she doesn't even cry when I leave her in his capable hands. But I don't have time to think about that.

Because down the hall, strutting toward me is Gretel. And she has the biggest smile on her face that I've ever seen because she is wearing, yes, what I think it is: it's funky, elegant, über-chic to the max. It has to be.

"Gisele bought it for me, can you believe it?" she squeals and starts jumping up and down. "I mean, it's mad. It's *Junya Watanabe*, this is absolutely, the best fucking work experience placement anyone has ever had."

She spins and laughs and I suddenly find myself in the best mood I've been in since arriving in New York.

Behind her is Didi, dressed in true Australian-designer mode in her favourite *Akira Isogawa*, and Cairine in a purple, effortless *Proenza Schouler* and dishevelled *Burberry*-style socks and rope heels. And Jorja! Wearing a black *Louis Vuitton* tuxedo of course.

Holding hands with my real sister and my fashion-sisters, the team who made it all possible, we head downstairs — to make peace with the fashion Gods and await our fate.

I baulk when the lift doors open again and my breath catches in my throat.

Cairine crashes into my back and steps on the hem of my dress, and it's almost pulled down to my waist.

I hitch it up again and silently punish Didi for not realising this supermodel cast-off would be miles too long for me. How embarrassing, the whole of New York is here and I look like a 12 year old dressed up in her mother's clothes.

"It's Elli Shoshana. She's here, at our show!" Jaimee squeals excitedly.

"Model gold," Didi states, touched.

"Model royalty," Cairine corrects her. "Shall we go introduce ourselves?"

"Sure. Let's do it."

But I stay back. There is no way in hell I'm going to meet Elli Shoshana while I look like this.

Only Jorja stays with me. "There's somebody else here you will want to see, Til, but it's a surprise, c'mon."

And with her hands over my eyes, she shepherds me toward our reserved front-row seats.

I hear Jorja ask Kirstie Tolza and Naomi Jones, the Editor-in-Chief and Fashion Director at Australian *Vogue* respectively, to shift up a seat.

Which puts them directly next to Sarah Jane Prouzer and Glynn Stefanos.

And puts me, directly next to…

"Nadia!" I scream, peeking a look between Jorja's fingers.

"You crazy bitch," she screams back, grabbing me in a bear hug, and everyone in the room stops and stares at us.

"When did you get here?"

"Three days ago. And before you go nuts at me for not coming to see Nina, this is why."

And she hands me a catalogue.

"It's beautiful," I almost gulp the words. "It's perfect. Oh, Nadia, well done."

In the picture, the real Gisele stands Garudasana-style, her left leg wrapped around her right, her hands resting gently over her beautiful bump, and wrapped around her is Fred! My Fred. I mean, my masseur. His face is nuzzled into her ear and his strong frame supports her as her feet hover above the earth.

It's exactly how I felt when I was pregnant and he massaged all my pregnancy ills away and made me feel amazing, like my heavily pregnant body was floating on air, giving life, being life, exuding a vibrancy I'd never felt before. Of course, I was pudgy with pregnancy hormones and my skin kept erupting but looking at this photo, this is exactly how I felt.

Except they are shot in black and white and their near-nude skins are flawless.

Visually it's perfect. And then I see the text.

"But it's called *MILF*. That's not right, it's *Giséle*."

"Ah, about that," Nadia starts. "The company is called *Giséle*. The kids' label will continue to carry that name but the maternity wear is now called *MILF*. Gisele suggested it and the girls all liked it. They wanted to ask you but Jorja said not to worry you."

My gasp is audible. "Oh my Lord, she didn't. My beautiful label is an acronym for *Mother I'd Like To Fuck*?"

"You said you wanted the label to be sexy," she responds innocently.

"Oh dear God."

"You'll see that it actually stands for *Mothers In Liberty and Fashion*."

"What a bunch of shit. As soon as anyone sees *MILF* they'll know what it means."

"It's definitely brasher. Very über-now," she suggests.

"And Fred's in the catalogue! How the hell did that happen?"

"Well, you told Adam you wanted Fred in the marketing material right from the start. He didn't think Fred would do it but when he emailed him that Nina was sick, Fred flew out from India straight away. Jaimee had sorted everything out with Gisele and the show was back on. The only thing we needed was a catalogue."

"And you were here too?"

"I was coming to see the show. Jaimee wanted me to shoot the show so you had something for the website. But Jaimee and Gisele decided they needed a catalogue for the show, something to link the real Gisele to the label. Jaimee picked me up at the airport and took me straight to Gisele's apartment."

"You've been to Gisele's apartment?"

"I know. I stole a roll of toilet paper."

I don't even bother to act shocked. "Of course you did."

"Anyway, I heard Fred was here, pacing the hallways trying to pluck up the courage to go see you at the hospital and get so badly rejected all over again, so I made him come to the shoot with Gisele and they just clicked. She had pretty bad indigestion; five minutes later Fred started lifting her into this stretch. It was amazing. She said it totally cured her reflux. It was my idea for him to take his shirt off."

I nod. I'm sure it was. "He did the same thing for me once — while wearing a shirt. And it was totally innocent. But the way you've shot it, her belly hanging over her briefs and him standing behind her, it makes it look like he might be …you know."

"Oh my God," Nadia gasps mockingly, her hand going to her mouth in pretend shock. "Are you saying it looks like he's…?" She smacks me across the arm. "I am a genius, aren't I? At first glance, it looks like a beautiful photo, two people genuinely in love and he's her protector and she's the nurturing force of the universe. But then you read the label and take another look and you see the overtly sexual message. No wonder he's smiling. It is very naughty, I know Lola's going to like it."

I can already feel my curls starting to un-straighten and go frizzy. "And you told Fred I wanted him in the campaign, from the start, just like this?" I ask her nervously.

"Pretty much."

"Thank God that was when I wanted the label called something pretty, not an urban cheer for mother-fucking. And now I've called the show *Harem*. What will people think of me?"

"It works.

My head hangs with shame. I'm never going to be able to look Fred in the face again. Just looking at the catalogue and feeling his gaze on me makes my heart quicken. If he ever knew the thoughts that used to go through my pregnant mind, I'd die of shame.

"Hey, beautiful."

A sound so warm and smooth that my body nearly falls to the floor.

I turn to the voice and see Fred sitting directly behind me. And next to him is Adam who is smiling at me, smug, and holding an awe-struck Nina.

"Fred!" I gasp, as an embarrassed, red flush spreads all over my face. "What are you doing here? I mean, why didn't you come and see us?"

Out of the corner of my eye, I see Adam roll his eyes. Yes, I know I am totally screwing this up but what else am I supposed to say, "Oh Fred, it's you! I heard you flew from India to see us, but then you met Gisele and decided to go for her instead? The fact that she's pregnant isn't a deterrent — she's a supermodel for Christ's sake, any guy would be glad for the chance to hit on her, even in the middle of labour. There is no way you've been waiting for me to make the next move, to invite you into our life. As a friend….or…"

Again, Adam rolls his eyes. I hate that he can read my thoughts.

Fred just continues to smile at me as if I am the light of the world and the whole of New York and this crazy fashion show doesn't exist.

He leans forward and I feel his warm lips against my cheek making my face suddenly feel like Mt Vesuvius .

"Shhh. We'll talk later," he says. "Your show's starting."

My stupid mouth tries to utter another sentence but he puts his finger to his lips as the lights begin to flicker and the room fades to black.

I turn in my seat as a deathly silence falls around us. "Oh my God, I never got round to writing a plan for the music," I whisper to Nadia anxiously.

But she shushes me. "It's OK, Gretel did it."

I sigh another audible sound of relief. Of course she did. Which means it will be perfect. I sit back, looking at an empty catwalk which stretches across the mezzanine pool, and close my eyes as the sound of children's laughter fills the room.

The lights stay down.

And one by one, we hear a splash as six pregnant models slide into the pool. And slowly, the lights come up again until the room looks like a sunrise over the island of Majorca. Six pregnant mermaids slide effortlessly through the water, emerging from the pool dripping wet, wearing only bikini bottoms, to sun themselves on rocks.

Before slowly dressing in the label's clothes, re-arranging what they're wearing by borrowing from one goddess and giving to another.

"It was a disaster," I say, which is what I always say after a show.

"No, Til, we're a hit," Gisele tells me grabbing me by the shoulders and bumping her tiny tummy against me. And when I say tiny, I don't mean miniscule, but tiny in comparison to how huge I was. But then, I'm about a metre shorter than Gisele so her baby's got a stretch limo to kick back in, as opposed to Nina, who spent her nine months living in a clapped-out, two door mini — no wonder she spent the last few months with her feet sticking into my kidney.

Which is what she's trying to do now. She wedges her feet into my stomach and arches her back so she's looking upside down at Gisele. And she giggles hysterically.

The hotel has kicked us out for an hour so they can clean up and deal with the publicity, leaving us to de-stress at an organic restaurant just around the corner. The models are ravenous, whereas I cannot touch a thing.

"Nervous?" Adam asks me.

"No," I blush, for he's forgetting Fred's presence. I can't eat because I can barely breathe.

"Everybody said it was great. Even that dude from Italian *Vogue* was gushing all over Gisele."

"They always gush, it's Gisele."

"No, Til, you're wrong — it was wonderful, they accepted it, they were a little shocked but they got it."

But I don't believe him. And I won't believe anybody until that all important phone call comes from Anna Wintour at US *Vogue*, to say she's wants to do a shoot next week. I sit for the next hour waiting for the phone call to come.

Nadia sits on the other side of the table, ordering margaritas and trying to keep me calm.

She doesn't have to do much. One glance at Fred, who is sitting next to me, his brown eyes never moving off my face for a second, is doing something to my stress hormones. I'm floating on a massive cloud, my body moving about in all directions, swaying and swirling in time with a universal energy.

Until Jaimee's phone rings. And I jump sky high.

She listens intently, and then hangs up.

"Well," she breathes and everybody stops eating, forks half-way to mouths, except Gisele who keeps shoving it in.

Then Jaimee screams, "We're a hit, they bloody loved us! We're in *The Times* tomorrow and *Vogue* are writing us up as 'the naughtiest discovery of the century'."

She screams again and all the models jump up and down, hugging the person next to them, even if they can't get their arms around them because of the enormous protrusions sticking out of their bellies.

The real lady of New York

"She's beautiful, isn't she?"

The girls are oohing and ahhing at the Statue of Liberty as our ferry dashes about on the sea off Ellis Island.

After a month of post-show organising we've finally reached our last day in New York, so have abandoned planning, last-minute pattern adjustments and meetings with the Board to spend it together.

We're all here, except for Jorja who flew out straight after the show to start bribing officials in four different economies so our finished garments would be expedited out of their countries and not sit on rotting wooden wharves for six months. I don't envy her job at all.

Jaimee is staying behind, to head the new New York offices of the *Giséle* business.

Didi and Cairine are flying off to Malawi to oversee the skills development at six new collectives. I'm as jealous as hell but my priority is getting Nina home for a while. And Gretel. Before she can spend anymore money.

The real Gisele and her investors now own a majority share of the business. Which is great news for her, because within a half hour of the show, Nadia had the photos up on our website and we were being hit so hard the site's been crashing at least a hundred times a day.

We're an overnight success story. Collectively, our team has brought about 1000 years of experience to the label and $24 million, but the crazy people of New York are happy to believe the Cinderella version.

At least Adam's stopped glaring at me. Now that we're a success and I've sold half of my shares, I can return to Sydney and buy a modest little house a few blocks away from the beach. Adam is already trawling the internet looking for a three bedroom house close to Tamarama so Nina can still go to her favourite park everyday.

Gretel is the only one who is glum.

While millions of emigrants, many of who narrowly escaped starvation, death and political persecution, have leaned over the bows of their ships, clamouring for their first glance at the grand lady of liberty, Gretel sits head in hands, staring at the mould growing on the boat's deck.

Her behaviour is disrespectful. I'd planned on making her visit the Ellis Island Museum, but now she'll be writing an essay on the influx of millions of desperate emigrants to the US as well.

"You can't send me home, Til," she moans at me every five minutes. "I can't go back to Sydney after this experience, I can't just go back to school. I want to stay here and live with Jaimee and help run the business."

Thankfully, Jaimee is happy to deal with her, telling her resolutely, "No, you're going home, you're going to finish high school, go to university, and you're going to be a much friendlier version of Caroline Banks. We need you to be able to write legally binding contracts in five economies, remember."

"But it's so much work, it'll be years before I'm back in New York."

"Yes. But Til didn't get to Paris when she was 16. She had to wait until she was 34 and look what happened, she blew it and New York off the map."

Gretel mumbles some more about how unfair it is.

Didi and Cairine rise to her defence. "You can come and do work experience here every year, OK? It'll do Jaimee good to have you helping her," they champion.

While Nina was in hospital, Jaimee had taken over looking after Gretel and it's been great to not have to worry about her. Jaimee has made Gretel stick to her like glue. They've been going to meetings with Caroline Banks everyday and Gretel has earned an honourary degree in US commercial law. And with Caroline's team stepping straight in to mastermind the US marketing campaign, I have had little to do except nod my head and sign off on their well-resourced budgets.

But I've been keeping busy too. Or to be more precise, Fred and I have been busy for the past month, taking Nina to Central Park to play with the local kids, or to the Natural History Museum, and hunting down organic falafels which seem to be her favourite food at the moment. And busy getting to know each other.

It's a little strange, getting to know another human being while gigantic posters are going up all over town of him snuggling a pregnant woman from behind.

But I'm getting used to it. Every afternoon we visit our favourite billboard at Times Square. While Nina's been back at the hotel having her lunch sleep, watched by Gretel, we've been ordering a couple of gelatos and hanging out while the rest of New York rushes around us.

As the days have floated past us in a sweet, sugary rush, we've slowly noticed a growing crowd of women gathering to eat gelato with us. At first there were only a few women standing gobsmacked on the corner staring up at a naked Gisele being spooned mid-air by Fred. But the next day they were there again, and they brought friends. Who bought gelato.

Soon, there were thirty women perched on hard, metal chairs staring up at Fred and licking very large serves of gianduja gelato dipped in dark chocolate and rolled in pistachios.

At least he sees the funny side of it.

Which is great because there's no way we could both hang out in my hotel room while Nina sleeps. His legs hang off the bed and even though he's a yogi, he has trouble doing simple things in my hotel room, like bending over to have a shower or brush his teeth. Grooming is just not something a highly evolved man like Fred is meant to do while squatting like a gorilla.

One thing's for certain, I won't miss being cramped in New York. Next time we'll stay at the Plaza and cycle everywhere to off-set my guilt about staying in a luxury establishment.

And I won't miss the constant pestering by the media for interviews. Gisele and I are even appearing in the next US

Vogue, giving a tell-all history of the label's development and our collaboration. Of course, most of the interview focused on Gisele's dream of making the world a better place, and I will come off as nothing more than her assistant, but I can't complain.

It's a dream come true, really. I may not have had my romantic walk under the Eiffel Tower with the love of my life, but I did show my daughter that anything is possible. As Adam would say, sometimes you have to be flexible, because you can't deny an excellent opportunity, even if it is a little crazy.

When a fleet of cabs arrives to take us to the airport, I feel a sudden rush of emotion overwhelm me. And in the middle of Broadway, I start blubbering like a fool.

The girls rush around me but they don't know what to do.

"We're going home — and it's just such a relief to know that we did our best and we did OK," I tell them while Gretel stands bawling next to me.

"OK? We did fabulously, Til, what are you talking about?" Jaimee says. "We've got a billboard on Times Square. When you get home this media circus is going to start up again. You don't have to micro-manage all the marketing now, just hire a few people to handle it; you just do the big stuff."

But Adam knows what to say. "Even though we're going home, Til, there's no going backward from here. You're ready for the next adventure to begin."

And he's right. Of course he is.

Caroline and Gisele arrive at the last minute to wave us off.

"You'll come back and be my doula, won't you?" Gisele asks me anxiously and I try to put a smile on my face.

"You may be gorgeous Gisele, but there's no way I'm staring at your hoo-haa for hours on end, but Fred here might come and massage you if you like?"

Fred jumps into the cab next to me. "Why do you keep throwing me at other women? First you make me do this nude modelling shoot with her and now you want me to massage her?"

"I didn't say a perineal massage, Fred, I just meant her shoulders or something, it's not that big a deal," I tell him, while thinking about the way his brown eyes are resplendent with more stars than all of Broadway.

As our cab crawls toward the airport, I watch people racing past us on the sidewalk.

And I find myself staring at a familiar sight.

Inside an expensively decorated store, a young woman sits surrounded by boxes of designer shoes glittering on the floor around her. And as she stands, she wavers and falls, laughing while a shop attendant does her best to retrieve the shoes.

"Look Nina, *Jimmy Choo*'s brought another New Yorker to their knees," I tell her.

And as I cuddle my daughter on my lap, feeling her little chest rise with each breath, her heart pumping under my hand, and adore the way her little knees poke out under her dress, I realise that this — this is my most favourite view of New York.

L.M.P. (2)

"Hey, that's my arm rest. Get your own airplane."

"Gee, you're an aggressive little ovum, aren't you? If we're going to have to share this space for the next nine months, I think you're going to have to take a chill pill."

"A what? What are you calling me?"

"I just think you should take it easy, that's all I'm saying."

"I will not."

"Look, I'm not getting into an argument with you, I think you'll get used to this, and one day you'll look back on this experience fondly."

"No way. I am not sharing this space with any baby. Go get your own fallopian tube."

"No."

"No?"

"That's right. I'm not going to get upset about anything. Besides, you may not even make it."

"What do you mean?"

"Well, you might not live long enough for the sperm to reach us. You might die before you even get fertilised."

"It's a long flight. The in-flight entertainment isn't that good. I reckon I've got a good shot."

"Maybe you're right. These seats are comfortable. You've got to love first class."

"Ah, here we go. They've turned off the lights."

"The plane hasn't even taken off yet."

"It won't be long. I'll do the count."

"No, I want to do the count."

"It was my idea."

"No it was my idea."

"I am not sharing this uterus with you another second longer."

"Stop hitting me in the head."

"I'm not hitting you in the head."

"Well, what is?"

"Blast off."

And now, a word to my sponsors:

My husband, Gavin. Very big thanks to you for your support and letting me tap away at the computer at night instead of cleaning the house. And for being such a great dad to our babies.

And our beautiful children, Hazard, Djuna and Caruso (and bub) for inspiring me.

Hazy, because of you I started thinking about kids' fashion seriously (and myself). You are my light. And my broccoli. I'm already worrying about where to hide you when it's time for you to start school.

Djuna, I started writing this just after you were born. You are Nina. Beautiful and very, very loud. You deserve all the attention you get. And fairy dresses.

Caruso, your development amazes me every day. You are adorable, blessed with rhythm and an ability to make the world smile. My fierce one.

And to the baby who is currently kicking me while I'm typing this, yes, I do know you are coming out very soon. Hence the rush. We can't wait to meet you and take you with us on the next adventure.

My family and friends. There is no such thing as a start or end to a book. And no limit to the number of people who have helped make this manuscript a reality. Thank you to my parents for taking me to the library and facilitating my education (see, those French lessons did pay off); to my Aunty Moya for letting me live with her and her beautiful family in Melbourne — my own fashionista-cousins Sloane and Ebony, and the very talented and musical Blase of Beddoes (where's my freight train?).

Tip Atkins-Moore (for being especially supportive and motivating); 'Ja' to Esther and Alexander. Clare Murphy (for everything from hand-me-downs to integrity); for giving the world the girls, Evangeline, Orlando and Véve.

Thanks to the cameos:

Kylie Stewart, Adam Lamb (just let me say publicly, no two Adams could be more different) and Koby. Kylie Agustin (for taking me to my first Parent Room — I guess that makes you Nadia) and Annabelle and Carter. The parent group Mums and bubs: Emily Brady, Lilja and Felix (thanks for the Dinosaur fun!), Sam Johnson, Amelia and Isabella, Nathalie Stephan and Jeremy. And more mums: Celona Bishop and Rylah, Donna Prescott and Elli (and Baxter), Sarah Head and Jarryd, Kim Harrison, Zara and Felix.

And everybody else. There are too many of you to mention individually, and I apologise for that, but I remember you and I acknowledge you.

And now, for the professional acknowledgments:

Thank you.

Ellie O'Gorman (for the editing).

Raoul Teague (for the wonderful cover).

Catharine Retter at the Australian Book Group who has been very generous with her experience.

Steve Hodges at Griffin Press.

Helenka King and Robin Sheahan-Bright and all the great Queensland writers I met while working at the Queensland Writers' Centre. And to Linda Carroli for always encouraging writers to experiment with digital environments. I have never met a nicer group of people anywhere.

Thanks also to the Brisbane City Council, Arts Queensland and the Australia Council for your support of my early creative development.

Funding from these bodies is vitally important to the development of Australia's Creative Industries. Just one little grant can nurture a life-time's work.

About the author:

Moya Kate (Baldry) is a mum to three children (all under 5) with a fourth on the way. She has been awarded grants from the Australia Council, Arts Queensland and Brisbane City Council for her *Grafgirl* interactive environment which provides creative, cross-curricular and cross-border learning experiences. She has worked at the Queensland Writers' Centre, NVC Arts (London), Channel 4 International (London) and the National Gallery of Victoria.

She uses her daily experiences to inform her blog, *The World's Best Raising Kids blog (by the world's worst mum)* which pretty much sums it up. This blog deals with the reality of suburban parenting: being abused by another mum at the park, managing multiple little personalities, and the storage wars. She does all of this on a computer with multiple keys missing and using toothpicks to keep her eyes open. Something all mums can relate to. Moya holds a Bachelor of Business (Journalism) and MBA, both from QUT in Brisbane.

Visit her website at www.moyakate.wordpress.com.

Forthcoming titles by Moya Kate:

Mama Couture 2

Til Fisher's adventures continue. Just weeks after leaving New York, Til and Nina are boarding flights for Cambodia, Kenya and Bangladesh to meet with the women working in the Giséle collectives. Til soon starts wondering if she's bitten off more than she can chew. She finds herself swapping her designer shoes for hiking boots and juggling the demands of guiding her growing international business through the global financial crisis, while losing her malaria tablets and vomiting all over the Indian Ocean.

The Cinderella Syndrome

When three children go missing from a Melbourne school ground, the Police immediately begin interviewing all the paedophiles in town and searching for the father who has just as mysteriously disappeared. When one of the kids is found dead, riddled with bullet holes, the news captures Australia's attention. Days later, riots break out and the Government issues a terrorist alert. As the nation descends into chaos, one woman, a refugee haunted by her past, emerges as the only person willing and able to help the children.

The Cinderella Syndrome confronts our contemporary hysteria and asks whether we are ready for constitutional change, and what skills and structural change do we need to become worthy of calling ourselves citizens.